This book is a work of fiction. Although some characters were created by Mister Charles Dickens, any similarity to any other characters, events, organisations or locations is purely coincidental. All other content is a product of the author's imagination.

British Library Cataloguing-in-Publication Data

A catalogue record for this book is available from the British Library.

This edition first published in Great Britain 2019

John D. Payne is an author and cartoonist living in Skelmersdale, Lancashire. When not writing or drawing he does whatever his cat tells him to.

This story is told in twenty-five chapters, so if you like you could read a chapter a day starting from 1st December and finishing on Christmas day. I understand if you can't though. You've got that last-minute Christmas shopping to do, and chapter nine's pretty long. However you choose to read it, I hope you enjoy it, and have a merry Christmas.

Also by John D. Payne

Richmond's Rarity: A Short Story

Richmond's Christmas Rarity: A Short Story

Richmond's Rarities: A Collection

Bright Future: A Short Story

JOHN D. PAYNE

For Denise and Badger. Christmases past, present, and future with you are always merry.

"Faith is the daring of the soul to go farther than it can see."

William Newton Clarke

PROLOGUE

The snow was falling in that elegant, graceful manner which so perfectly distinguished itself from its cold, dank and miserable brother the rain. Like a dream it was; the whole world trapped willingly in a winter wonderland. There was no place and no one the snow couldn't touch, and the perfect way of reminding everyone, young and old alike, that it was Christmas time.

As he jaunted through the streets whistling a tune to himself, of which he had no idea how had popped into his head that very morning, the old man saw all the good people dashing around, their arms weighed down with presents. Young men chased young women with mistletoe. Children threw snowballs and – but what was this? Suddenly, he felt a cold, icy heaviness on the back of his neck. It made him freeze in his tracks and he turned around slowly to see which young scoundrel had dared to strike Mister Ebenezer Scrooge with a snowball.

'Tiny Tim,' Scrooge bellowed 'did that snowball belong to you, perchance?' It had taken him what seemed like an age to get used to that look; the look that Tiny Tim had shining all over his face. The lad was actually pleased to see him. He wasn't recoiling in terror and running for the hills after realising he'd just made the biggest mistake of his short life.

'Yes, it did, Mister Scrooge,' Tim said.

'What have I told you?' Scrooge struggled to screw his face up the way he used to. He loved to jest with people – especially Tim – by making them think, momentarily at least, that he had gone back to his miserly ways. 'What have I told you, Tiny Tim?'

'That I should call you… "Ebenezer", Mister Scrooge.'

'Precisely right, my good fellow. No need for formalities between friends, eh?'

'But,' said Tiny Tim, 'as I've tried to tell you many times before, Mother and Father say that it is disrespectful to refer to our elders that way. That—'

'Well,' Scrooge interrupted 'I say, that most people who refer to themselves as elders are more likely than not to be or to have been in their past – as I have – discourteous to many other people and do not necessarily deserve respect themselves. Oh, I'm not suggesting that you go around calling every Tom, Tom and every Mary, Mary, but I know that I am no better than you, my dear chap. Therefore, I absolutely insist that you call me that which I requested.'

Tiny Tim looked reluctant Scrooge thought, but then he spoke.

'I shall. I shall call you Ebenezer. Although, I know I shall get rather peculiar looks from others when I do so. I do have one condition of my own though.'

'Name it,' Scrooge said, beaming.

'You must take away the "tiny" from "Tiny Tim". Father says I am a full foot taller than I was this time last year and a full two feet taller than this night two years ago.'

Scrooge stood back, as if in awe of a tall building or tree that had suddenly sprouted up from the ground. 'By golly you're right, my dear boy,' he said. 'You have grown, and a growing lad deserves a grown-up name. From this day forward, I shall call you "Timothy", if you will consent to calling me "Ebenezer".'

'Agreed,' said Tim and they sealed their pact with a firm, gentlemanly handshake.

'Well, good day to you, Timothy.'

'And a good day to you, Ebenezer.' Tim spoke nervously, looking around to see if anyone other than Scrooge had heard him.

Scrooge turned around and giggled to himself as an idea popped into his head. He checked to see if Tim was watching and then leant down and started to gather up some snow in his gloved hands.

'Mister – um – Ebenezer?' Scrooge quickly whipped the snowball behind his back as he turned to face his friend again.

'Yes, Mister Timothy?' Scrooge said, laughing to himself.

'You *are* still coming for Christmas dinner tomorrow, aren't you?'

Scrooge almost came out with his answer straight away, but he suddenly saw an opportunity. 'Of course I am. As sure as Father Christmas himself is standing behind you.'

As planned, the boy turned to look and Scrooge took his shot and hit him with the snowball, right in the back of the head. A fit of laughter erupted from him. It was the kind of laughter that's so powerful, it takes on a will of its own and cannot be stopped for anything or anyone and it spreads to everyone around like a pleasant version of the plague.

Scrooge finally got a grip on himself. 'I'm sorry, Tim – Timothy,' he righted himself 'but you can hardly expect me to resist an opportunity like that.' Another, shorter burst of laughter escaped from him without warning.

'No, I don't suppose I can,' the boy said, brushing the snow from off his coat, which, Scrooge noticed was the very coat he had gifted him last Christmas. The memory of it, made Scrooge smile; the very smile that everyone always said they thought of when they thought of him. 'Well, we shall see you tomorrow,' Tim said, 'Father told me to ask you to arrive around one.'

'Then in that case, Timothy, I shall arrive at twelve precisely and help your fine mother peel the potatoes.'

'She would like that very much. We shall see you tomorrow, Mister_ I mean, Ebenezer.'

'See you tomorrow, Mister I mean Timothy,' Scrooge joked as he waved and headed towards home.

1

It was a pleasant walk home, full of people wishing Scrooge a merry Christmas and him wishing them the same back, tenfold, but just as he was approaching the final street he noticed something out of the corner of his eye: Something that should have been a rare, if not impossible sight in that part of London; in *his* part of London. In the light of a window down the alley there was an old tramp with a long tatty beard, shivering and crying with cold. Scrooge was appalled to see that he had his eye on a rat that was skittering about, probably in search of sustenance itself.

Without hesitation, he quietly and carefully crept down and moved slowly down the alley, not wanting to scare the old man. How strange, Scrooge thought, that he would think of the poor fellow as old, at least compared to himself. Underneath all the rough skin and ragged hair he could well have been several years younger than him. All the man's attention was fixed on the rat, and he was like a coiled spring, ready to pounce the second his prey made a wrong move. Scrooge was about to say something, when suddenly the man turned to him with shocking speed, his eyes piercing his heart. Scrooge froze with fear.

'What d'you want?!' the man demanded with a gruff, parched growl. His eyes were blood shot and pulsing with anger, and for the first time in a long time Scrooge felt afraid for his own life.

'I – I – I just—' But before he could finish, the tramp leapt forward with the energy he'd been saving for the capture of the rat, and before Scrooge could move, his hands were wrapped around his neck.

'I said what d'you want?' The man whispered now, either in an attempt to scare him further or to ensure that no one else would hear their struggle.

Scrooge couldn't speak; he could barely breath, so he tried to appeal to the man's better judgement with the only thing he could use: His eyes. He looked the man straight in the eye, and to his surprise, he saw something. Beyond the rage; the hell-bent fury of a man angry at the whole world, Scrooge caught a glimpse of a smidgen of gentleness. Maybe it was all that remained of the man's hope; a memory of his life before the streets swept him into their cold, dank embrace, but it was something. There was less anger there now, and slowly, ever so slowly, he loosened his grip on Scrooge's throat, as if he was reluctantly admitting that he never really intended on doing him harm.

'I'm sorry,' he said, looking away from Scrooge. 'I'm a good man. I *was* a good man. Bad things have happened to me and, well, here I am.'

Scrooge was still gasping for breath, but he didn't want to seem disinterested in the poor soul's plight, so he struggled to get a question out. 'How did you end up here, if you don't mind me enquiring, sir?'

The anger seemed to momentarily spark up in him again, but it was just a brief flash across his well weathered face. The man screwed up his eyes, as if trying to contain the rage – or maybe tears – it was hard to tell. There was something else there, maybe suspicion. There was a wealth of emotion in every subtle movement and contortion of his face and Scrooge could see now that this was certainly no old man. Everything he'd been through had aged him beyond his years, but the skin between the wrinkles couldn't have been much older than forty years. He was looking into nothingness now; recalling his former life.

'I… I had my own business. A toyshop. Small, but quite enough for me to handle.' He smiled, as his words took him back there.

Scrooge could almost see his face glowing amongst all the colourful playthings.

'Some of them I made myself. I was particularly proud of a model of the Tower of London. I remember how reluctant I was to sell it, but needs must.'

'That sounds delightful,' Scrooge said, softly, his voice returning now.

The man suddenly whipped his head around to face him again, angry at having been distracted from his reminiscences. 'Oh, it was,' he said 'until one Christmas, I was struggling a bit – everyone was. My wife was ill: Dying. And I was neglecting the bills and taxes. No, not neglecting. I just… got behind and… I had to borrow some money.'

Scrooge knew where this story was going. He'd suspected from the start, but his hope had covered over it. The urge to run was natural and strong, but his need to stay and face his demons – to help the man – was somehow stronger than the fear that was making his heart shake in his chest.

'Jacob Marley and his partner. I forget his name.'

The man whose name used to represent everything wrong with the world took a breath, and he knew that what he was about to do had nothing to do with bravery; it was just the right thing to do. 'Scrooge,' he said. 'His name is Ebenezer Scrooge.'

'Yes. Yes! That was it. How could I forget? I pleaded. I begged with them to give me more time to pay up and they just stood there, revelling in it. They were like a pair of devils, lauding their power over me.' Tears were coming to the man's eyes again. 'I'm sure I wasn't the first, or even the last of their victims, but I heard that at least one of them has left this life and all his riches behind now. I hope he's rotting away in his own personal corner of hell, his soul burning for eternity.'

The man took great comfort from this notion, Scrooge could see, as his eyes lit up and sparked with life, as if the flames intended for his dead partner were reflecting in them.

'It's Jacob. Jacob is the one that died.' Despite his conviction, Scrooge could hear his voice cracking, the truth of reluctance exposed in every word.

The man's manner suddenly changed. It became slower and more considered. He turned to Scrooge and looked him square in the eye, his gaze almost as powerful as the grip he'd had on his throat. 'On first name terms with him then, were you?'

'Yes… Yes, I was, sir.' Scrooge's voice trembled as the man's gaze chiselled away at his conviction, but he would not let that stop him from doing the right thing.

'So, tell me, stranger: whatever happened to his partner? Scrooge, you said his name was.' The man moved forward with a gracefulness that belied his ragged appearance, forcing Scrooge to back up until he could feel the ice-cold alley wall on the back of his balding head.

'He changed,' Scrooge said with renewed confidence. If this was to be his end, he needed it to be true to the man he now was. 'He changed, and perhaps the fact that you failed to recognise me is proof positive of that. I am Ebenezer Scrooge, and I can help —'

The man let out an animalistic growl and wrapped his hands around his throat again, and this time he lifted Scrooge up so he couldn't move or even think about getting away.

2

'Everything! I lost everything because of you and your partner. My wife! My son! I don't even know where he is. He could be dead too for all I know. He went away to find work; to help us. He doesn't even know she's…' That thought suddenly changed him. His anger was replaced by a cloak of sadness and his grip on Scrooge's neck weakened a little.

He still couldn't breathe or escape, but he managed to get out a single word: 'Please.'

The broken man turned back to him, quickly and viciously. '"Please?" Now you're begging for *your* life? Who says there ain't no justice in this world, eh?' There was something that could almost be described as joy in his eyes. 'And now, I find myself in the perfect position to dispense some justice of my own. Not just for myself, but for everyone else you've forced out onto these wild, rotten streets. I'll be hanged for it, but at least I'll die a hero. There'll be rejoicing in the streets. They'll divide up y'clothes and possessions, as if y'was just another nobody, like me.'

'I… know. I've seen it,' Scrooge managed to get out.

'What?'

'It doesn't… matter.' He was of course talking about what the ghost of Christmas yet to be had shown him on that fateful night, but he saw little reason in wasting his final breaths on explaining it to his would-be murderer. 'Everyone deserves a… second chance.' The words echoed around his head as the outside world started to fade away.

'A second chance?!' The man scoffed. 'You think *you* deserve a second chance? You got quite a sense of humour for a dead man, don't you.'

Despite his words, Scrooge could feel the grip around his neck loosen just a little bit; just enough for him to get more words out. 'Me? Honestly, sir, I'm not certain that I do. All the wrong I've done with my life, all the lives I've destroyed. All I could do was try and make up for it, but honestly, I'm not sure I ever can. Good men – better men than me – deserve second chances. No, sir, I was talking about you.'

The man loosened his grip a little more and – probably more as a sign that his arm was tiring than anything else – he eased Scrooge down to the ground but stopped short of releasing him completely.

'What d'you mean?' he said.

'You need – you *deserve* a second chance.' A wheezy cough escaped from Scrooge's throat, and mercifully he felt the man's grip give a little. 'I can give you that chance. I owe you more than that, I know, but I can start by giving you a roof over your head and new clothes.'

The man looked away for a moment and seemed to be considering Scrooge's proposal. Then, something brought him back to the way he'd been thus far. Most likely, his pride. 'Listen, if y'think y'can buy my forgiveness by —'

'No,' Scrooge said, plainly, 'that's certainly not what I'm trying to do. I just want to help. No, I'm not doing this for forgiveness, sir. What I do from day to day, now at least, is try to put some good into the world. Good for goodness' sake, not for any reward. Just to try and make the world a better place in which to live. If you can forgive me one day, then I'm not going to lie, that would be nice, but only as a happy consequence of knowing that I've made your life more… well, more than it is presently.'

The man had almost completely released his grasp on his neck now, and his hand was more or less just resting on Scrooge's shoulder. He could see that he was getting through, gradually. He just had to keep pushing. 'Please, just let me help you. Let *them* help you. I have a shelter with a marvellous staff. Some of the best and kindest people I've ever known.' Scrooge could see that the man was at a tipping point, and he wasn't sure how he'd react to what he was about to say. It could push him either way, but he had to risk it. 'You're a good man, I can see that. And from that, I can see that you're a good father.'

At that, he looked sharply at Scrooge. He looked like he was torn, unable to decide what to do. Then suddenly his expression softened, and tears were trickling from the corners of his eyes.

'The last… the last thing I said to him was – it wasn't true. I —'

'It doesn't matter,' Scrooge interrupted. 'You know why? Because what's more important is what you're going to say to him next.'

The man looked at Scrooge, his mouth gaping. He was speechless.

'I'm going to find him. If it takes the rest of my miserable, wasted life, I'm going to find your boy and return him to you, where he belongs.'

The man still couldn't speak; it was as if Scrooge was the one now doing the strangling.

'How?' he managed to get out at last, 'How will you find him?'

'Never you mind about that, young man. Just know that I will. Let your heart be lighter in that knowledge, and please, let me take you to a place where they'll look after you. You'll get your own room, some new clothes, and there's a huge fire for you to warm yourself by.'

The man – Charles his name was, he told Scrooge – needed no more convincing. Over the duration of the short walk to the shelter he told Scrooge everything he could about George, his missing son. He even gave him one of the only pictures he had of him. It was crinkled, torn and soiled from the years it had kept him company on the cold, lonely streets, and at first Scrooge refused to take it.

'Please,' Charles insisted, 'take it, so you can find him quicker. I have my memories. They're enough for now, and if you find him – when you find him, I'll have new memories to look back on.' So, Scrooge took the picture with a promise to return it, along with Charles' son.

The Jacob Marley Home for the Homeless was everything Scrooge had promised it would be and more. At first, he hadn't been sure what to call the place. He didn't want to name it after himself because he didn't want to seem conceited, and he didn't want to name it 'The Scrooge and Marley Home for the Homeless' because of the associations people would draw from their two names side by side. So, in the end he settled on what the place was now called. Scrooge thought it wholly appropriate and just that the man who ultimately saved him should be given credit for saving others, as well.

As soon as they opened the green doors the heat from inside swept over them like a wave. The fine staff welcomed Charles with open arms, and because Mister Ebenezer Scrooge himself had brought him, he was treated more like a king than a fallen toyshop owner. Scrooge made sure he got one of the best rooms in the house, and that he got the first cut of the glorious goose that Mrs McGuiness had just liberated from the oven.

Once Charles had settled in and joined the others sat in a semicircle around the raging fireplace, Scrooge took a look around. He couldn't help but feel proud of what had been achieved there. When he first came across the old place again it had been in a sad state of disrepair, just another forgotten warehouse taking up space on the street. It was only when the ghost of Christmas past had forced him to revisit, that he remembered where it was and how much joy had emanated from the very walls and people who worked there. Yes, old Fezziwig – had he still been alive – would be pleased to see the place back to its former glory. The only thing that was missing this Christmas Eve was the dancing, but the spirit of hope and joy that Fezziwig's parties always brought to people's hearts was there none the less.

Scrooge went from room to room, checking on the poor souls who had found themselves back there once again. He listened to their woes, did his best to comfort them, and invited them to join him and the others by the fire. It brought Scrooge some relief to see that Charles was now regarding him with more warmth than before. Perhaps he'd seen from his actions that he truly had changed and wanted to help, to make up for the sadness he had brought upon him. Several mince pies and glasses of wine later, Scrooge decided it was time to head home.

As he walked up the old, familiar street, admiring the lovingly decorated fir trees in the windows, his happy, joyous thoughts were snatched away and replaced by fearsome ones. Regrets of a life half lived; love lost, and many enemies made. Incidents like the one in the alley were rare these days, but they still occurred and still affected him, deeply.

He found himself at his door now, and as he fumbled in his pocket for the key, the door knocker caught his eye. Sometimes he could stand to look upon it, yet other times he saw Jacob's fraught face again and he had to turn away. The pain of regret was like a knife in his side which only got deeper the more he resisted.

Therefore, this time he looked up at it and tried to remember all the good that had come of that Christmas Eve five years past. How his fate and the fates of Tiny Tim and many others like Charles had hopefully been altered. He liked to think that life was better now for everyone, but even as these happy thoughts flooded his mind, he couldn't help but feel some darkness slip back into his heart. Oh, not the kind of darkness that would alter his mind set and change him back into the Ebenezer Scrooge of old, but the kind that brought deep remorse and regret.

He could never truly return the favour – not a grand enough word, but the only one that came close – that poor old Jacob had done for him. Yes, he was now leading a better life, but he had no way of knowing if what Jacob had done for him had had any great effect on Jacob's own circumstances. Sometimes this knowledge – or the lack of it – ate away at his now fair heart, but this in turn only spurred him on to do even greater deeds, which would make Jacob proud.

Scrooge swallowed and turned the key, and a blast of warmth greeted him, as well as Wilkins.

'Good evening, Wilkins and a happy Christmas Eve to you,' said Scrooge as he brushed the snow off his coat. 'I know I probably said that to you this morning, but I find that one can never say it enough, especially since it comes but once a year.'

'Agreed, Mister Scrooge,' replied Wilkins with a warm glow in his smile, 'so a happy Christmas eve to you too, sir.'

'I see you've kept the house nice and toasty.'

'Yes, sir. And the fire in your bed chambers is roaring heartily,' Wilkins said enthusiastically.

'Very good,' Scrooge said as he took off his jacket and handed it to his manservant. Then, he suddenly remembered something. 'Are we still on for cards tonight? I'm due a win, I think.'

Wilkins suddenly looked very apologetic.

'Um, it's Christmas eve, Mister Scrooge.'

'Yes, yes and a happy Christmas eve to you again, Mister Wilkins.'

'Thank you, Mister Scrooge, but I just meant that I usually meet up with Joe and some of the other servants this night, traditionally I mean, to make merry and all that.'

Scrooge could feel his face go blank for a moment and then he remembered for himself.

'Oh yes, of course. Forgive an old man's memory, won't you. Have one on me,' he said, as he reached into his pocket for a few shillings.

'No, no, no, Mister Scrooge, I couldn't possibly take any more of your generosity. You've been kind enough this season, and as I've told you many a time, Mary and I are so grateful for my duties here.

'Why don't you come along with us, Mister Scrooge? You'd be more than welcome, sir.' It seemed to Wilkins that his master was considering the proposal with some seriousness, as his eyes seemed to be looking off into the distance.

'No, no. I think I'll stay in tonight, Wilkins. I've had rather an eventful evening, which has wearied my old bones, but I promise to take you up on your offer another time. I have certain traditions of my own that need seeing to tonight.' He looked up to the top of the stairs, grimly, as he said this, then snapped back to Wilkins. He pulled his hand out of his pocket and opened it to reveal three shiny shillings. 'I think you dropped these, Wilkins,' Scrooge said with a grin that couldn't be contained.

'Mister Scrooge, you're terrible,' Wilkins said matter-of-factly, as he took them from his palm. He knew full well that if he didn't take them now, his master would find some way of getting them on his person.

'Have a good night, Mister Wilkins,' Scrooge bellowed, as his manservant retreated to his chambers.

'And the same to you, Mister Scrooge,' Wilkins said, leaving Scrooge alone in the hall.

About six months ago he had converted the downstairs lounge – which he rarely made any use of anyway – into living quarters for Bertie Wilkins and his lovely wife Mary. He'd overheard Wilkins describing his woes to the landlord of the Fox and Goose and had decided to offer him a job on the spot, something he never would've done in the bad old days. It was good to have a young family around, and their laughter, which filled the empty halls, always brought a smile to his face.

Scrooge slowly made his way up the stairs. Of all the things that had changed about the old place, the creaky stairs were not one of them. Every time Scrooge climbed those stairs, the night that Jacob and the three other spirits came to visit was at the forefront of his mind. The events of that night always imposed their influence on him, making him strive to better himself every day. However, certain aspects – particularly seeing his own grave – he would try not to dwell upon, as it turned him cold with the fear of death that naturally grips us all.

As he got to the top of the stairs, the sudden burst of warm air from under the door retrieved Scrooge's temporarily dampened spirit back to the reality of the present. He'd been out for most of the day, and Wilkins always made sure to keep the door closed once he'd set the fire going. It wasn't something that Scrooge insisted upon – in fact, it wasn't even his idea – it was just one of the many ways Wilkins had of showing his master how grateful he was for what he'd done for him.

He stopped for a moment to take in the glorious fire. If it hadn't been for the guard, it would have been in serious danger of engulfing the room in its luxurious flames. All the decorations were in place. You may find it odd that someone would have Christmas decorations in their bedchambers, but Scrooge's name was now synonymous with Christmas, goodwill and festivity, so it should come as no surprise that he had organised and helped to decorate his entire home with decorations. Wilkins and his wife took care of the downstairs whilst Scrooge had revelled in decorating the entirety of the upstairs rooms. Every picture was adorned with garlands and paper chains hanging down either side, and almost every wall had handmade letters hung up on string spelling out 'Merry Christmas'. The tree was quite a sight to behold. Amongst the candles were various decorations – tin toys, dried fruit and gingerbread – sparkling in the firelight. There were several trees of varying heights scattered throughout the house, but the one which kept Scrooge's reading chair company was his favourite, as it was always his first sight in the morning at this time of year.

Scrooge sat down in his chair between the fireplace and the tree. The whisky and glass were sat there on the small table as usual, along with the book he'd been reading: a series of Christmas stories by a local author. But before he could start reading and settle down for the night, there was a tradition to uphold. So, he filled his glass right to the top, stood up and raised it high into the air.

'A merry Christmas to you, Jacob Marley, my old friend. Wherever you are, I hope that you are at peace.'

Scrooge came to with a start, as the old grandfather clock struck twelve. His book had dropped to the floor, and although the whisky glass was still in his hand, most of the contents had spilled out. It took him a moment to realise what had happened and as he did, he chuckled to himself.

'Every year, without fail,' he said, pulling himself up out of the old chair. He noticed that the fire – which had been a virtual inferno – had now dwindled down to something far more subtle and comfortable, and he watched the flames dancing around each other, vying for his attention. He removed the guard and immediately felt the sharp heat, once more.

That lad can surely make a fire, Scrooge thought. What did I ever do without him? He momentarily toyed with the notion of going downstairs and wishing the Wilkins a very early merry Christmas – he knew that they'd be back from the pub by now – but then decided against it: he always liked to keep this night to himself, to ponder on what he used to be and how far he had come.

All his nightclothes were laid out on the four-poster bed, and the bumps at the end of it told him that Wilkins had placed two bedpans of hot water in there to keep his master company.

'God bless you, Bertie Wilkins,' Scrooge said, as he got changed into his night clothes.

He was about to ease himself into the warm comfort of the bed, when he suddenly felt a cold chill on the back of his neck. Strange, Scrooge thought, as all the windows were closed and the fire was still dancing away.

He looked around carefully to see if there was any other explanation – maybe one of the windows was open a crack – but there was nothing. He almost left it there and dismissed the cold chill as some random draught from an unseen crack in the floorboards or wall, but then he saw something move: A shadow, on the edge of the darkness that the light from the fire couldn't reach.

Instinctively, Scrooge reached under the bedsheets and grabbed one of the pans. Some of the water spilled out onto his hands, but luckily it was only lukewarm by now and didn't scold him. He looked again at the place where the shadow had been, half expecting it to have backed off into the darkness to defend itself, but it was still there. In fact, whoever it was that the shadow belonged to was moving towards him in short sharp steps, as if they were just getting used to the act of walking.

Scrooge didn't know what to do. If whoever it was meant to do him harm, there was no way he could get to the door in time. No. He would have to stand his ground and hope that maybe, somehow, he could overpower the man. At least this way, he wouldn't have to turn his back on whoever it was.

As the figure got closer and closer, he realised something: Whoever it was, his footsteps were making no sound on the floorboards. Maybe he didn't have any shoes on. He dismissed this straight out of hand, because surely, he'd still make some kind of sound, as he himself was doing in his bare feet.

Then it dawned on him. It should have been obvious to a man with Ebenezer Scrooge's experience. He squinted, attempting to see if what he hoped in his heart was true. 'Jacob? Jacob Marley, my friend, is it really you?' he bellowed.

The spirit was free from the shadows now and glowing in the hazy moonlight. Scrooge dropped the bedpan, and as he fell to his knees, he could barely feel the lukewarm water soak into his nightgown, because no: it was not Jacob Marley. The joy in his heart was immediately replaced with dark, ominous fear. He could almost feel his heart stopping. He trembled and could see right through it as it slowly but shakily leant down to address its reluctant host.

It opened its mouth, unsurely. Somewhere between his fear and rationality Scrooge could see that the spirit was very unsure of itself, as if everything it was doing, it was doing for the first time as the spirit it now was. It opened its mouth half a dozen times, as if to loosen its jaw up in preparation for speech. Scrooge noticed that as it did this, the spirit's form was solidifying in part. So, whereas before he was shivering and quaking before the form of disembodied lungs, veins and bones, the skin of a young man gradually faded into being before his eyes.

The spirit suddenly made a sound which mimicked the sound of someone gasping for breath. Except, the way it was doing it was as if it were dying all over again, or perhaps, in a fashion, coming back to life. Despite the fear crawling all over him, Scrooge felt himself moving forward, perhaps out of morbid curiosity. Then suddenly, the spirit straightened up and looked to be more in control of its faculties than before. It looked around the room, as if it had only just noticed where it was, and a smile gradually started to grow across its face then stopped, as if it were remembering a joke that was told in poor taste.

Scrooge felt afraid again, but before it could get a proper hold upon him, he wanted to speak, to say something to try and normalise the situation, as much as was possible. 'Spirit, why… why are you here?'

The spirit snapped its head to look at him, only then realising it had company. The eyes pierced through him, like two spikes knowing exactly where to strike. 'Why… am… I… here?' The voice was cold and distant, as if it were coming from everywhere except the spirit, and the room grew colder. 'Why am… I here?' This time it sounded more grounded, but confused, as if it were asking a question of itself. Then, in a mockery of human behaviour, it put its hand to its mouth in shock: it had remembered the answer to the question. Its mouth contorted into a smile, which seemed to a scared Scrooge more unnatural and unnerving than before, as if the face had never hosted such a pleasant thing as a smile.

'I am here…' The voice was quicker and more youthful now than before. 'I am here to save you, Ebenezer Scrooge.' And the room grew colder still.

3

Save him? What did the spirit mean by that? Had Jacob not already saved him? Shown him the error of his ways? Changed his path? Had he been doing something wrong? Helping the wrong people? Or maybe, just maybe it meant it in a more literal sense. Maybe the spirit meant it was here to save him from another would be attacker? Maybe it was here to warn him? He wanted to grab hold of it and demand an answer, but he knew that was impossible.

Since its big revelation, it had been floating around the bedchamber, ignoring Scrooge and poking its head in and out of drawers and wardrobes like a child let loose in its parents' rooms. If he hadn't felt so scared, he would've told the cheeky so and so to stop being so nosey. But he *was* scared; very much so. He had almost forgotten how unsettling it was to have a dead man walking – or in this case, floating – around his bedchambers. He didn't know what to do. There was nothing he *could* do, and that feeling of helplessness and uncertainty was the most unnerving one of all.

He could go on no longer without knowing what the spirit meant. Clenching his fists, which were hot and sweaty despite the cold, he walked determinedly over toward the spirit. It was currently passing its hands through the wall, utterly fascinated and amused by its own actions. Scrooge cleared his throat. 'Oh, Spirit?' he said. It didn't look up, but Scrooge thought he heard it say something like: 'This is so cool.' Funny, he thought. I didn't think ghosts were affected by the atmosphere of the living world. 'Spirit.' He said this a tad more forcefully, as he was getting a bit fed up of being ignored by an intruder in his own home.

The spirit finally looked up, clearly annoyed at the interruption.

'I'm sorry,' Scrooge said defensively, stepping back as he spoke, 'but you said you were here to save me. May I ask from whom or what are you here to save me?'

The spirit suddenly spun to face him and floated slowly, creepily closer.

Why can't spirits make the effort to at least try and act the way they did when they were alive, he found himself thinking. Like walking. They could at least waggle their legs about a bit for some semblance of normality, if only to put me a bit more at ease. I suppose that's the last thing it wants me to be.

As the spirit drifted closer, it appeared to stand up straighter, as though before then it had been slouching. It was growing taller and taller, now, until it stretched right up to the ceiling. If it had been corporeal it would've banged its head, but as it was, its head went right through the ceiling and the rest of it continued to go up through the roof and out into the cold winter London night; and yet, its feet were still touching the floor, or at least pretending to be. Suddenly, just as Scrooge thought that the spirit couldn't grow any bigger, it stopped and began to shrink back down again. The speed at which this happened was dizzying. So much so, that he jumped back in shock when he saw the spirit's giant face looking down on him with the malevolence of a child about to step on an ant.

It appeared to take in a deep breath and then let some words out, as if the words were poison that had to be expunged. 'You know the answer, old man!'

'I… I do?' said Scrooge.

The spirit gasped again, and it felt like it was sucking every last morsel of warmth from the air around them.

Scrooge couldn't tell how cold it was exactly because his nerves were making his body shift and spasm so much, so he took a quick glance at the fire. That told him precisely how cold it was: There were icicles in place of the flames, as if time itself had frozen over and stopped in its tracks. For all he knew, it may well have done.

'If I have to tell you,' the spirit continued, 'then you're even more lost than they say.'

At these words Scrooge felt something break inside him. He didn't know who "they" were, but he could hazard a good guess. He could feel his legs failing him, so he tried to gain some semblance of control over the fear that felt like it was drowning his whole body, pulling him down. 'Spirit!' he shouted, forcing all his strength to the fore. 'Enough of these theatrics, I beg of you. Just tell me who you're here to save me from!'

It looked shocked at Scrooge's sudden courageous outburst, but it didn't give a word in answer. Instead, it slowly, creepily shrunk back down in size until it was no more than one or two feet taller than Scrooge; still a fairly intimidating height, I'm sure you'll agree. As it did this, it appeared to be looking around the room for something.

Scrooge couldn't move to see what it was. He couldn't even speak. Was there someone in the room with them? Had the spirit arrived just in time? He knew deep down that after the last thing it had said, that that couldn't be the case, but fear had been stopping him from facing the truth. Still without saying a word, the spirit lifted up its arm and pointed at something behind Scrooge. This reminded him with a shudder of the last ghost that visited him and he turned to look.

No. That couldn't be right. He was facing the window, very much frozen over now. He couldn't see through it, but Scrooge knew that was not the spirit's intention. All he could see was a reflection of himself.

'Me?' Scrooge felt a sudden surprising surge of anger come over him, even as the fear of moments ago was swept aside. He flung himself around to face the spirit, who looked slightly flawed by the anger in his demeanour. 'Me? You're here to save me from myself? How can this be?' he ranted, hardly pausing for breath. 'I've done everything I can to be a better man, a better person. And now you're saying that all of that was for nought? I've set up shelters for the homeless. I've given my profits to charity. I am a good man!' Scrooge wasn't given to fits of vanity, but he felt he could say that, because of the man he used to be. 'Go, Spirit! Leave this house!' Scrooge shouted. 'And check your records, because my soul was saved this very night five years ago, by a man named Jacob Marley.'

The spirit looked stunned. It hadn't been prepared for that. For a moment he saw a flicker of doubt on its face, and with the pretence of authority lifted, its youth shone through. How young had it been when it was released from the mortal coil? Seventeen? Eighteen?

The spirit's face changed again. It was more intense, and Scrooge instinctually backed off.

Then it said, in a barely audible whisper: 'I'm sorry. But do you think that five years is all it takes to make up for a lifetime – a wasted lifetime – of cruelty and wrongdoing?' It rose up into the air, its arms spread out and its fingers seemed to be curving around an invisible sphere – or perhaps Scrooge just couldn't see it – which might have represented its reluctant host's wasted life.

He tried hard to stand his ground, but he could feel his resolve breaking like a single crack in a window, branching out. 'I - I'm sorry, Spirit, I didn't mean to raise my voice,' he said, shaking. 'It's just that you've seen – I mean, you *must* have seen all the good I have done with my life.'

The spirit withdrew a little, and looked intensely at him, as if considering Scrooge's argument.

'Surely my future has changed. My legacy? Surely these past few years count for *something.*'

'Your future?' the spirit said, raising an eyebrow.

'Yes. I mean, I know I can't change the past, but I've been trying so hard to forge a better future for everyone I know and for those I —'

'All I see in your future, Ebenezer Scrooge' the spirit interrupted, 'is sorrow and pain and suffering.'

On hearing these words, Scrooge fell to his knees, utterly defeated. Everything was moving in slow motion, and the thud of his knees on the floor was like a rumble of thunder in the distant night. Scrooge felt the despair of a man who had reached the top of a very tall mountain, only to discover that he hadn't reached the top at all. Maybe the top had never even existed and had only ever been there in his mind; in his hope.

He froze with his arms hanging limply at his sides, not supporting him, and yet somehow, he didn't fall. Pure undiluted despair seeped inside him. He was lost. Regrets and questions swirled around in his numb head. Why? Why had he been shown all those things: his past, present and future, if there was no hope for redemption? What was the point in it all? Was it all a sick joke by the inhabitants of the afterlife? Why had he been helping his fellow man if he couldn't even help himself?

An unnatural darkness washed over his eyes, as if the despair that was consuming him from the inside out was so strong that it had managed to take on physical form. And then, through the flurry of questions and doubts, an argument emerged. An argument voiced by a shrill and sinister voice which caused him further despair, as he recognised it as his own.

'What is the purpose in being good if all that will greet you in the end is death and despair? An eternity of misery.' Then a different, warmer voice, which was somehow also his own, spoke up.

'Being a better man; a good man, brings its own rewards. What does it matter what happens to me, as long as I try my best to make this world a better place?'

'"*What does it matter what happens to me?*"' the first voice mocked. 'Of course it matters, you fool. It's *all* that matters. We come into this life on our own and we leave on our own, so what purpose can there be other than self-interest?'

'No, you're wrong.' The second, supposedly weaker voice, was stronger now. It could win the argument, Scrooge found himself thinking with an odd detachment. 'If it takes me my whole existence, before and after death, I will prove you wrong. Goodness will shine from me, the way evil spewed out of you the whole time I let you —'

Suddenly, both Scrooges were interrupted by a deafening, booming, low cry. Under normal circumstances he would have taken the sound for the wind from a sudden storm, but as Scrooge snapped his eyes open, he could see that it was coming from the spirit. It had grown large again, but this wasn't the worst part: The spirit's mouth had now grown to a size frighteningly out of proportion with the rest of it. It was as if it had to be bigger to utter the word which was now echoing around every corner of Scrooge's rooms. He couldn't tell what the word was until the last syllable of his name started to fade. As it did, the spirit shrunk down to a much more agreeable size. Still, Scrooge cowered; every bone and organ shaking. Then, the spirit said the most unusual and unexpected thing:

'I'm sorry.' His face did not convey the same feeling. 'I hope that wasn't too OTT, but I had to snap you out of whatever that was you were doing.'

'Oh tee tee?' Scrooge stammered.

The spirit looked flawed for a moment, as if it hadn't meant to say that. 'It means, um, "Over the top".'

Still, Scrooge didn't follow.

'Oh, for crying out loud. You know… Too much… Too dramatic. Ah! Too theatrical.'

'Ah, I think I see what you mean,' Scrooge said softly, not wishing to enrage the spirit further. 'Please tell me, spirit: Why am I still doomed to misery? As I told you, I do all I can for —'

'Ah! But tell me this, Scrooge: Have you ever actually saved someone's life? Directly, I mean. Have you ever jumped in front of a moving car – I mean "carriage" – Horse and carriage, and pushed them out of the way?'

Scrooge had to think about that, but before he could, the spirit started talking again in that odd "too theatrical" manner of his.

'Well, today, Mister Ebenezer Scrooge is your lucky day, because I'm offering you a once in a lifetime opportunity.' He seemed to realise that maybe he was being "too OTT" again, because he quietened down and drew closer to Scrooge. He spoke softly now. 'I'm giving you a chance to make up for all the wrongdoing, all the evil acts that you've ever committed in your miserable life.'

Scrooge felt his despair lighten a little.

'Do you want to know how you can do that?'

'Y – Yes, of course, Spirit. What would you have me do?'

The spirit turned away, as if he'd had a sudden change of heart. 'I'm not sure you're up to the challenge. *They* are not sure you're up to it.'

'I am! I am up to it,' Scrooge pleaded, half to the spirit and half to the unseen ones.

The spirit looked more serious now, staring through him, thinking. 'I think you are, Scrooge, and since they sent me here, I think that really they think you are, too. Otherwise, why send me in the first place?'

'What do I have to do, Spirit? Please tell me and I will —'

'Well,' the spirit said, 'if it were up to me, I would just say what they want of you, but unfortunately it's not.' He looked genuinely sad about this. 'What they're asking of you, before your mission is revealed to you and should you choose to accept it…' The spirit stopped and smiled to himself as if he was in on a private joke.

'Of course I'll accept it. What do they need of me?'

'They need a leap of faith, Scrooge.'

'A leap of —'

'Exactly! A leap of faith,' the spirit shouted, pointing into the air.

'What do you mean?'

The spirit looked exasperated, as if he were speaking a perfectly understandable language and Scrooge was a foreigner from the middle of nowhere who'd just stumbled into the country.

'I mean – I mean, "*they* mean" – This is all them, Scrooge, not me,' he insisted. 'They mean that you need to do whatever I say, no matter how crazy it sounds. Does that sound like a good deal, Scrooge old boy? A fair enough price for redemption?'

Scrooge turned away from the spirit. Despite his fear, he felt that something was a little peculiar. The way the spirit spoke, his manner; very odd indeed, but that wasn't what was really bothering him. If his soul was so scarred with evil – so lost – then why not simply leave him to his fate? Why not could give someone else a chance? Someone who'd not done quite so much damage. Of course he wanted to be saved, but as they say nowadays, something didn't quite add up.

'Well?' The spirit snapped. 'What's it to be? I can't do this all in one night, and there are others I could recruit.'

Scrooge didn't know whether to believe that or not. He was torn between confronting the spirit with his doubts and following his instructions, just in case. He decided that it was probably best to do what the spirit wanted, and that ultimately he probably didn't have much choice in the matter anyway. 'Yes, I shall do it,' he said 'Whatever it is they need me to do, I'll do it.'

'Brilliant,' the spirit exclaimed, rubbing his hands together, briskly, as if even *he* were feeling the cold. 'Now, I want you to get your most modern looking suit and your most valuable possession. Bear in mind that your most valuable possession might not seem that valuable now, but where we're headed, it could well be the most valuable thing in all of England.'

'Why?' Scrooge said. 'Where are we going?'

At this, the spirit slanted his head and looked him square in the eye. The way he was moving his arms, as if he was holding a globe that was getting bigger and bigger, he thought he was going to make *himself* bigger and out of proportion again, but the spirit merely put on his most dramatic tone of voice and said:

'The future.'

4

He stared at her from around the bedroom door, making sure not to let too much light in from the landing; it was still early, after all. The one thing Carl Phillips had done right in his entire life was lying there, sleeping, as peaceful as a lazy Sunday afternoon; his perfect little slice of Heaven: his daughter. If nothing else he did from now on worked out, he knew that he'd always have Sara to be proud of. He couldn't help but feel sentimental. It was Christmas time, so why not?

A slight beam of light from the waking sun was creeping across her face through a gap in the curtains, threatening to disturb her. He thought about going in there to adjust them, but he didn't want to wake her. She looked so happy and peaceful, like an angel. How could he tell her? How could he tell Kate? How could he tell the two most important people in his life that with just days to go before Christmas he'd been made redundant?

He was having a hard time processing the news himself, and the managing director's speech was still playing over and over in his head, like a song stuck on repeat, infecting every moment. Sometimes he thought that it had finally stopped, but then the very act of realising that made him remember it all over again.

'We're very sorry to have to announce this, particularly at this time of year... We considered leaving it until the new year, but we can't put it off any longer, and there's never a good time for bad news, is there...'

One by one his colleagues were called into the manager's office, and one by one they came out, their feelings written all over their faces. He had hoped against hope that he wouldn't get called in there; that fate had saved him, somehow, from the axe; that all his years of thankless, loyal service had been for something. This very thought made him feel guilty: Why should he be saved? He wasn't the only one with a family to support.

'We want to take this opportunity to thank all of you, whether you're relatively new to the company or you've been with us for years…'

Carl couldn't face that miserable canteen with its watered-down coffee, and stale, past-their-sell-by-date cakes, and since it had happened he'd taken to making his own sandwiches and having his lunch in the park with the ducks. They always cheered him up. Ducks didn't judge, they just took your bread and quacked their gratitude. Some evenings after work he would go back there and consult with them. It had been quite a mild winter so far, so he would park himself on one of the least bird muck covered benches and rehearse how he was going to tell 'his girls'. The moonlight reflecting on the water almost took him out of himself, to a different, less complex time; away from his worries. Cold, hard reality always managed to reel him back in though, and, when he remembered to switch his phone back on, there would always be several worried voicemails and texts from Kate asking where he'd got to.

'Well,' he'd said to the duck that had been pecking away decisively at his reduced loaf, 'if she's worried now, what's she going to be like when I tell her?' He remembered looking at the duck, hoping for an answer, but of course, it never came.

He suddenly realised that Sara had opened her eyes and was looking straight at him.

'Hey, Dad, what's wrong?'

Carl put his hand to his cheek and realised that he'd been crying. He came up with a quick lie. He'd become too good at that. 'Oh, it's these cold mornings, Poppet, they always make my sinuses leak,' he laughed. Then he realised something and went over to the bed. 'What's all this "Dad" business? When did you stop calling me "Daddy"?'

Sara's face lit up, as if she'd been awake for hours. 'When I was six and three quarters,' she said.

'Ha ha, very funny,' he said, dryly. 'When did you become so sarcastic?'

'Oh, that didn't happen 'til I turned seven and a half.'

'But you still believe in Santa, right? Because if not, I can give him a call and_'

'Of course I do, Dad. Depending on what he brings me.'

An ice cloud suddenly stopped Carl in his tracks. Had he bought all her presents? She was a good girl and never asked for much. This had the opposite effect on him of wanting to spoil her a little bit more, especially at Christmas. His face went blank as he tried to picture the presents in his mind.

'Dad, are you alright?' Sara asked. This snapped him out of his trance.

'Yeah, yeah, of course, Honey, I'm fine,' he said, stroking her curly ginger locks. 'Just trying to straighten everything out in my mind. You shouldn't worry so much. You're just like Mummy, I mean "Mum".'

Sara suddenly put on a mock serious expression and deepened her voice. 'Well, someone has to worry.'

'Woah, where did Sara go?'

'Ha ha, very funny, Dad,' she said, lying back down. 'You should be getting to work, anyway. Look at the time.'

'Yeah, you're right. What would I do without my very own human alarm clock, eh?' he said, getting up.

'They'd sack you and you could stay at home with Mum all day and you'd drive her crazy.'

He thought about saying something then, or at least giving a preview of the bad news to come, but he couldn't do it, so he just said:

‘Well, it’s a good job we’ve got you then.’

5

White. That was all Scrooge could see. He had a vague sense of movement, but only from the way his body felt, and his clothes were moving. There were no buildings or people to mark his strange journey, and at different points he felt like he was looking at himself from a great distance, from out of himself, I suppose what you and I would call an out of body experience.

He could barely make out his new spiritual companion; there was only a vague impression of him – like creases in a bed sheet – but he could feel his presence everywhere. He was sure that he'd never forget this experience, and yet at the same time, he knew that if he was ever asked to describe it, he would never be able to find the words. Maybe he was dying. Maybe he had died peacefully in his sleep and the whole encounter with the odd spirit was a result of his brain shutting down; closing in on itself. That would perhaps explain the strange behaviour and language he'd been spouting. It could all be a way of him coping with the trauma of the eternal sleep, he thought.

Then, just as he was getting used to the idea, accepting it, and perhaps even growing fond of it, more creases appeared in the "bed sheet". Scrooge couldn't tell what they were at first, and then, almost as suddenly, he heard voices. There were just two or three at first, but this was enough to make him realise that, up until now, there had been no sound at all. He'd been moving in the silent void, growing accustomed to its comfort, and now it was all changing. He was instantly filled with sadness at the loss, and, almost as instantly, the folds in the white gained shape and texture, and the voices he could hear became louder and more aggressive. Other unfamiliar sounds came hurtling toward him, trying to deafen him. He tried covering his ears, but it wasn't enough to block them all out. Buildings were in front of him now – dark buildings – and, as he moved toward them at impossible speed, he braced himself for the impact, covering his eyes now, instead of his ears.

Nothing happened. He was scared to move his hands because he knew he was still moving from the way the sounds passed his ears. And then, a voice which was louder and clearer than the others, and yet came across as a kindly whisper, said:

'Don't worry, Scrooge, we're not there yet. You can open your eyes.'

After a moment's hesitation, Scrooge did just that and was astounded by what he saw. He had stopped moving, but the world around him was shifting and changing. In a matter of moments, walls were erected in front of him. It was all happening so fast that, at first, his mind couldn't register the phenomena. It was like nothing Scrooge had ever witnessed before, and he could feel his heart pumping away, as if it would explode at any given moment.

'Calm down,' the spirit said, his voice coming from everywhere, yet still in a whisper. 'I didn't go to all this trouble just for you to die on me. It's no biggie, just time passing at a faster rate than you're used to, like a DVD on - No, like a movie projector - No, they haven't been invented yet either, have they. Maybe you *should* just close your eyes after all.'

But the more Scrooge saw, the more he wanted to see; it was hypnotic. The only experience he had in his memory which even came close to what he felt was when he saw the sea for the first time at Brighton. The way the waves slunk up and down had been awe inspiring to his young eyes, and he remembered feeling like the world was so much bigger and stranger than the city he'd lived in for most of his life. He used to think of the world as nothing but a bunch of buildings clumped together – almost like a machine – but that week at Brighton, which was spent mostly on the beach at his mother's insistence, opened his eyes to the idea that the Earth was a living, breathing thing that didn't exist purely to have buildings set upon it. Scrooge felt a sudden pang of regret, knowing how that innocent, pure view was lost to him later on in life. Seemingly this view was lost to everyone in the future, as well, because all he could see now were buildings.

He was just noticing how the styles of the brickwork were changing when a blinding flash of light exploded all around him. When the dust settled at a faster rate than it normally would, most of the buildings were gone.

'Oh yeah, you've got two world wars ahead of you,' the spirit said solemnly. 'But on the bright side, you'll be long gone before any of it kicks off.' Scrooge was starting to grow weary of the way the spirit spoke to him – those strange phrases like "kicked off" and "deeveedee" – but he suspected that if he did ask what he meant by those things, he'd just be met with even more oddness.

Now that the buildings were gone, he noticed the most astounding thing of all: The sun. It was going up and down faster than his old eyes could follow. It was so fast that the light which surrounded him had an odd twilight quality; just as hypnotic as the building walls, moving and shifting.

Then, as if the world around him knew exactly what he was thinking, walls started appearing around him, blocking his view. The style of everything had changed drastically, and the pervading tone of all the décor was much lighter. Gone were the dark hues of purple and rose painted walls with which he'd been so familiar. People of the future preferred lighter colours it seemed. Perhaps it was because there were so many more buildings blocking out the light from the sun. Maybe people felt trapped and wanted to recreate the light inside. He'd often thought that his living rooms could stand to be a tad lighter. Suddenly Scrooge let out an uncontrollable burst of laughter; the odd mix of witnessing the future unfurl around him and his private thoughts of redecorating his home well warranted such a reaction, he thought.

'What's so funny?' The spirit's voice boomed all around him again.

'Oh nothing, Spirit. Just a funny thought.' Then, before the spirit could say anything else, the world seemed to settle down around them. The building stayed constant: its style and height, and then suddenly a curtain and three walls appeared around him. He felt more enclosed than he had done since the buildings came back after the two wars. It reminded him of that night years ago, when the curtains of his four-poster bed had been drawn, and Jacob had visited him; helped him. Then suddenly, it came upon Scrooge that time was once more moving at its usual, more comfortable rate. All the sounds, which had become one big noise around him, separated and suddenly made a bit more sense, and what he could see – which wasn't much – became sharper and the movement of the curtains was less dreamlike.

Had he really arrived at his destination? Was he really in the future? The journey had seemed to take several hours, and at the time of it he'd gradually accepted that it was real; that he was really travelling through future ages. Now though, he felt like a man who'd been asleep for a very long time: well rested, with a dream fading from his mind. He remembered snippets of it, but even they were disappearing as he took in the reality of his surroundings.

It was such a small space. Was this how people lived in the future? In tiny rooms with barely any room to swing one's arms? There was definitely no room for him to sleep or lie down, and there was a panel jutting out of the wall which could best be described as a shelf with a mirror just above it. Perhaps people of the future had evolved in such a way that they could sleep standing up. Just as he mused over all the possibilities in his mind, the curtain swung open. He wasn't at all prepared for the explosion of colour which greeted him on the other side. He thought she was a woman, but she was like no woman he had ever seen before. Her hair was so bright it strained his eyes. Her lips were bright blood red and her bright pink top and dress – at least, he assumed it was a dress – were so tight, so revealing, that he didn't know where to look. He was so distracted by her clothes that he was barely prepared for the scream which was now uttering from her mouth, as if someone was murdering her where she stood. Scrooge's hands automatically snapped to his ears to protect them. He was already feeling like they were getting too old for the rest of him and the screaming wasn't helping matters. The relaxed feeling he'd got from floating through time and space was all but gone now; replaced by the sudden explosion of harsh sight and sound in front of him, blocking his way out of the tiny room.

A smartly dressed young woman and a black man, who was even more smartly dressed, suddenly appeared beside the screaming woman, attempting to calm her down. Scrooge tried to open his mouth to ask what was going on, but the smartly dressed black man put his hand firmly on his shoulder and said in a very deep, intimidating voice:

'Sir, you need to back off now, before you get yourself into more trouble.'

Scrooge didn't understand. What was it that he was in trouble for? The woman was the one who opened the curtain. She was the one who disturbed *him*, surely. Dazed and more than a little confused, Scrooge toyed for a moment with the idea that maybe he was in trouble for his time travelling. No, that couldn't be it, he thought, immediately dismissing the notion. How would they know that he'd done that? He needed to clear his mind. The sudden shock of the scream had left him feeling dizzy and he felt like the whole world was spinning around him. It had to be something to do with where he was. He wasn't supposed to be there, that had to be it. The brightly dressed woman seemed to have calmed down a bit now – in as much as she'd stopped screaming and had moved away from the curtain – but she was using some words that Scrooge had never heard before. I suppose that's to be expected, Scrooge thought. It was hard to tell whether the smartly dressed woman had heard any of the words that were coming out of the other woman's mouth because she had a look of complete indifference on her face. The black man –

who was clearly a figure of some authority – was standing with his arms folded, looking alternately at Scrooge and the brightly coloured woman.

'I want to know what he was doing in there,' she said, pointing at Scrooge. 'And if something isn't done, I'll sue. I'll sue anyway, whatever happens.'

This seemed to rile up the black man, who, up until now, had been relatively calm. His face flared up and his already substantial upper body seemed to bulge up beneath his white shirt and tie. 'Now listen, madam,' he said. 'There's no need for threats. If you just calm down, I'm sure there's a way we can sort this out, without resorting to_'

'I want to see the manager, right now,' she demanded. The smartly dressed woman – who, Scrooge now realised, was younger than he'd first assumed – let out a sigh and rolled her eyes. 'And I don't appreciate this one's attitude,' she said, pointing at the black man. 'I'm a paying customer and I deserve more respect.' Scrooge heard a low rumble come from the direction of the black man, but before the woman could say anything else, he turned to his colleague.

'Claire, you heard what she said. You'd better take Mrs —?'

'It's "Miss", actually. Miss Sharp.'

'Okay. You take Miss Sharp to see the manager and I'll take Mister Smith to the office.'

Mister Smith? Scrooge thought. Was he being mistaken for someone else? Was that what all the trouble was about? He was still a bit dazed from the trip through time, but he certainly knew what his name was. 'Um, no, I'm not Mister —'

The man interrupted him before he could finish. 'That's alright, Mister Smith. I'm sure you just got confused again, didn't you. We'll sort you out and phone your family.'

Scrooge was about to protest again, but there was something in the man's tone and intense eyes that told him that he should just play along for now. 'Yes, yes of course. I'll do whatever you say.'

'Is that satisfactory to you, Miss Sharp?' the man asked her with a tone of derision in his voice which told Scrooge that he didn't really care.

The woman looked away, as if considering the matter deeply, maybe even planning something. 'Yes, I think so,' she said finally. 'But I still want to see the manager, and I don't see why I should have to pay full price for these, not after the trauma I've been through today.'

Her comment was met with silence from both the black man and the young woman, so she held up the clothes, which, to Scrooge, didn't look any more like clothes than the ones she was just about wearing.

With a grimace the man turned to his colleague. 'You heard the lady. Take her to the manager.'

Claire mumbled something which Scrooge couldn't quite make out, and then she said quite clearly and with a forced smile on her face: 'If you'd like to come with me, madam, I'll contact the manager and we'll see if we can sort something out.'

Miss Sharp followed her without so much as a "thank you" down the short, brightly lit corridor which had the same curtains running down it on the left. Scrooge couldn't figure out how or where the light was coming from. It was much too bright and constant for candles or gas lamps, but then, what other source of light could there be?

'Right,' the man said, as soon as the other two had gone around the corner. 'I don't get paid enough for this.' Then he turned to Scrooge. 'If you'd like to come with me, sir. The manager will probably want a quick word, just to mollify Miss Sharp.'

'Um, yes yes, of course. I would like to go with you.' Scrooge wasn't sure what else to say, so he followed the man down the corridor of curtains. As they got nearer the end, he suddenly realised that there had been an odd sound coming from somewhere and it was getting louder. It sounded like bells, somehow, but there was another sound mixed with it which he didn't recognise.

It was accompanied by singing, but even that sounded odd to him. Then, as he followed the man around the corner, it suddenly all made sense, because immediately adjoining the corridor of curtains was a giant hall. There were countless people moving around, pushing and shoving. None of them seemed particularly happy to be there, and despite the grand scale of the hall there didn't seem to be anywhere near enough room for all of them, even with the other floor above. In fact, Scrooge could see several floors above, all crammed to bursting with people who looked miserable as sin, weighed down with colourful bags. He was in a shop – he could tell *that* much – and then he noticed something else: Banners stretching from the far corners of the impossibly bright hall, and giant baubles hanging precariously from the ceiling. There was even a ginormous fir tree which stretched right up; and then it dawned on him: It was Christmas time! And that odd sound with bells and singing? Carols! Despite his current predicament, Scrooge felt a warmth move through his body and the hairs on the back of his neck stand to attention. It was Christmas! He knew where he was with Christmas. Everything would be alright.

'Are you okay, sir?'

'What?' Scrooge said.

'You seem a bit… distracted? If you could just stick with me, the office is just over there,' The man pointed to a door which Scrooge could barely see for people dashing past it.

'Oh, yes of course, my good fellow,' Scrooge said. He'd not realised that he'd stopped to take everything in. He had a million questions about the shop – about the future – including the staircase he'd only just noticed which appeared to be moving on its own. People were stepping on it and it was transporting them to the top without them having to move their legs. Very handy.

When they got to the door, the man opened a small box just to the side of it which he proceeded to poke and prod at. A loud buzzing sound came from somewhere as he pushed it open, and he gestured for Scrooge to go ahead. Stretched out before him was a long corridor with doors on either side, but before he had time to take a better look, the man was unlocking a door on the right of them, this time with a key. Again, he gestured for Scrooge to go first. The room was infinitely smaller and duller than the hall of marvels they had just marched through. The walls were white but looked like they could do with a lick of paint, and there was a table in the corner with an odd-looking chair next to it; at least, he assumed it was a chair.

'I'm sorry about this, sir,' the man said as he walked over to the table. 'But we have to take any complaints – or at least be seen to take any complaints – seriously. I mean, I know you probably just got lost or something, but people tend to overreact these days, don't they. Any opportunity for a bit of compo, eh? Well, um, Mister —?'

'Oh yes, I haven't introduced myself yet, have I? How very rude of me,' Scrooge said, deliberately jovial in an attempt to lighten the mood. 'I'm Scrooge. Ebenezer Scrooge.'

The man looked baffled at this. 'That's an odd name.' He backed off and made himself seem larger by folding his gigantic arms. 'Are you screwing with me? Because —'

'Screwing with you?'

'Yeah. Screwing. As in joking?'

'Oh, no no no, my good man,' Scrooge said quickly. 'Although I suppose it *is* the season for jokes and japes.'

'Tis the season to be jolly,' the man said, dryly.

'Exactly. But that is my real name; an old family name. I was named after my grandfather and he was named after —'

'That's fascinating,' the man said. 'I'm Dave.'

'Well, a great pleasure to make your acquaintance it is, I'm sure, Dave. What an unusual name you have too, if you don't mind me saying.'

Dave started to look a little worried.

'And a merry Christmas to you thrice over, in case I don't get the opportunity later, my good man.'

Now Dave looked very worried indeed. 'Right,' he said. 'Well, if you'll just wait here for me, sir.'

'Ebenezer.'

'Yeah, Ebenezer. If you'll just wait here, I'll go and see what's happening with the, er, the —'

'The manager?' Scrooge suggested.

'Yeah, the manager. Thanks.'

Dave backed out of the door, looking far more frightened than was needed, Scrooge thought. A moment later he shut the door behind him, and a small click indicated that Dave had locked him in. Despite this, Scrooge was still feeling very good indeed. Yes, he had no idea how far into the future the spirit had brought him, and, yes, he had no friends or family here, but on the other hand it was Christmas.

'Why are you looking so happy with yourself?' The familiar voice came out of nowhere. A second later, the familiar face which went with it appeared through the door, although the door was still locked.

'Spirit!' Scrooge bellowed. 'I can't believe how pleased I am to see you.'

'Thanks a lot,' the spirit said, looking thoroughly dejected.

'I have so many questions for you.'

'Yes, yes, I thought you might, old man,' the spirit said. He seemed preoccupied. 'But we haven't got time for that right now.'

'Time?' Scrooge laughed. 'Time? It seems to me, Spirit, that we have all the time in the world. A few hours ago I was in the nineteenth century enjoying a quiet Christmas eve drink, and now we're in the – actually, which century are we in, Spirit?'

'It's the twenty first century.'

'The twenty first century? The *twenty first* century?' Scrooge uttered. 'Oh my. Oh… my… Forgive me, Spirit, but I can't quite believe it. Then again, you spirits are capable of so much, aren't you. You showed me my past, present *and* future, so it only stands to reason that you could take me into the far-flung future as well. Tell me, Spirit: are all of you capable of travelling through time, or is it merely a chosen few? Is Jacob? Have you seen Jacob?'

'Enough, Scrooge, enough.' The spirit became slightly big and scary again, as if to remind him of what he was truly dealing with. 'Do not forget why you are here, old man: to redeem yourself.'

Scrooge tried to calm himself and backed away. 'Please forgive me, Spirit. It's just that I'm so overwhelmed by what I have seen and the gift you have given me, I'm —'

'It's okay, Scrooge,' said the spirit. 'I forgive you, but we still don't have much time. Now, you're not going to understand a lot of what I have to say, but you're going to have to take my word for it that I know what we have to do. Right now, the manager of the store is in a small office with the security guard that you just met.'

'Oh, Dave you mean.'

'Yeah, yeah, whatever,' the spirit said, waving his hand dismissively. 'They're watching security footage – you won't know what that is and I don't have time to explain – but basically, right now they're wondering how an old man like you managed to get into the women's changing rooms without being stopped by a single member of staff. There's no sign of you on any of their cameras up until when you were discovered by that loud woman. In a few minutes, the security guard and the manager and probably some of the other guards will come back here to make sure you don't get away before the police arrive.'

Scrooge could feel the blood draining from his cheeks. 'The police?'

'Well, that's a worst-case scenario, but considering the circumstances we can't really afford to consider anything less than that,' the spirit said, matter-of-factly.

'So, what should we do?' Scrooge asked.

'We have to get you out of here.'

'I definitely agree with that, Spirit, but how? The door's locked.'

'Yeah, I assumed it would be. Why did they have to have the women's changing rooms where your bedroom used to be?' His face seemed to brighten as an idea came to him. 'Scrooge, how do you feel about small spaces?'

'Wh-What do you mean, Spirit?'

'Well, I was thinking you could remove one of the panels up there,' he said, pointing to the ceiling, 'and make your way through the ventilation shafts.'

'Um, I'm not sure I could —'

'No, you're right. It's too risky,' the spirit said. 'You could fall through the ceiling and break your neck or something.'

'Oh, okay, let's not do that then.' Scrooge felt himself turn pale at the thought. 'Spirit, why don't we just —'

'Quiet, Scrooge. I'm trying to think. I've got it.' A huge smile stretched across the spirit's face. 'You could set off the —' but before he could finish that thought, the door burst open. Dave had returned, along with a stern looking plump man, whose hair looked older than the rest of him and – as the spirit had predicted – two more of what he had called 'security guards'.

'Right, Mister Scrooge,' the plump man said. 'I'm John Staunton, the manager of this store, and you've got some explaining to do.'

Scrooge looked at the spirit, a silent question in his eyes, but he wasn't picking up on it. 'Can they —'

'Well?' the manager persisted.

'Well,' said Scrooge, moving back to where the spirit was. 'You don't seem as frightened as I thought you would be.'

The manager's stern expression didn't seem to change, even though one of his eyebrows moved slowly upwards, as if it had a life of its own to be getting to. The two other guards, who didn't look quite as tough as Dave, backed away a little bit.

'Should we be frightened?' the manager said, not seeming the tiniest bit frightened at all.

'Well, it's not every day one sees a spirit from the afterlife, is it?'

'Scrooge,' the spirit said, 'stop talking right now.'

'Unless, maybe it is an ordinary occurrence here. Spirits wandering around with everyday folk. Who knows what this future world has to offer, with its moving stairs and lights.'

'Mister Scrooge, I think you need to sit down.' Dave tried to smile as he spoke, but Scrooge could see the doubt in his eyes.

'Great. Perfect. Now they think you're mad,' the spirit said, putting his head in his hands. 'Wait. Maybe this could work to our advantage.'

'What?' Scrooge said, turning to the spirit.

'They can't see or hear me, Scrooge. As far as they're concerned, you're talking to thin air.'

'Mister Scrooge,' the plump manager said. 'Do you have a next of kin; a family member we could call, to come and pick you up?'

'A family?' he said. Scrooge's demeanour shifted, and he could feel the reality of his situation hit him like a carriage at speed. 'No, no, I never had time for a family. I only realised until it was too late. I have a nephew, and the Cratchits are like family to me, but they're centuries gone.'

'Okay,' the manager said slowly, before turning sharply to Dave.

'They're going to call the police, Scrooge. Couldn't you have just made someone up?'

'I - I'm sorry.'

'It's okay,' the manager said. 'We're going to get someone who can help. Just try and stay calm.'

'You're going to have to expose yourself, Scrooge,' said the spirit.

'Expose myself? What do you mean?'

'Hold on,' the manager said, facing Scrooge like a shot. 'What did you just say?'

'Scrooge, this is your only way out of this,' said the spirit. 'You have to do it quickly, before they get the chance to call the police.'

The spirit looked serious, but he couldn't possibly mean what he just said, could he?

'You need to tell them that unless they let you walk out of here, you'll strip off right in the middle of the shop floor where everyone can see. Believe me, it will work; they think you're crazy enough to do it. Remember,' the spirit said gravely, 'you said you'd do whatever I say.'

Scrooge turned away from the spirit and attempted to look convincing as he issued the threat.

'I'm sorry.' He cleared his throat: the words were reluctant to come out. 'But if you do not let me walk out of here, I will expose myself in the middle of the shop floor.'

The manager, Dave, and the other two security guards were staring hard at him now, as if he were a ticking time bomb about to go off.

'Good,' the spirit said, a bit too jovially for Scrooge's liking. 'That got their attention. Now, remind them that there's no point in contacting the police, because by the time they get here you could have already exposed yourself, and all the Christmas shoppers will have run off and gone to another, more family friendly store which doesn't let old men expose themselves.'

'Is that really necessary?' Scrooge pleaded with him.

'Yes, it is.'

'Mister Scrooge, you're forgetting something quite important,' the manager said, moving forward with a somewhat evil glint in his eye (no one threatened to send his customers elsewhere, no matter how crazy they were). 'There's four of us and only one – no, sorry – two of you, if I include your invisible friend in the equation. We could quite easily keep you locked in this room until the police arrive.' Scrooge turned to the spirit in the hope that he'd contradict what he'd just heard, but the spirit just sighed.

'He's got us there. There's only one thing left for us to do.'

'What's that, Spirit?'

'Look, Mister Scrooge, if you're going to continue —'

'Run,' the spirit shouted. 'I hope this works.'

'You hope what works?' Scrooge said.

'This.' The spirit suddenly transformed into a pure rush of energy and surged forward, knocking the four men off their feet. 'What are you waiting for?' he shouted. 'Run, Scrooge, run!'

Scrooge got himself together and lunged at the door. Luckily, it was pulled to and not actually locked. He didn't suppose that they wanted to be locked in a room with someone they thought to be a madman. He ran down the corridor and opened the door, which, to his relief, wasn't locked either. The giant hall seemed even busier than before. It was a sea of people, and somehow, he had to find a safe course through, before the manager and his guards caught up with him. The whole situation was making him dizzy and overwhelmed, and he could feel his old legs buckling under the pressure. And then, just as he was wondering where the spirit had disappeared to, he appeared again, a few feet above him.

'Follow me.' The spirit moved forward, and Scrooge took a breath before diving into the crowd.

'Excuse me. Sorry. Pardon me, madam. So sorry.' This was all Scrooge could hear himself saying as he moved in and out, bashing his elbows and knees on people's shopping bags. He didn't dare look back to see how well his pursuers were doing, but he thought he could see what must surely be the exit to the colossal shop, up ahead. The mass of people was thinning out now, so he allowed himself a glance back and immediately regretted it; because there they were, about eight heads back from where he was.

'Don't worry,' the spirit shouted above the noise. 'As soon as you get out of the shop, they'll stop chasing you. You'll probably get barred for life if they remember your face, but what does that matter?'

No, Scrooge thought. Even if he did plan on staying in this future time – which he certainly did not, thank you very much – he'd make certain never to darken their doors ever again. Speaking of which, there was a clear path now between him and the doors, which were opening and closing, all by themselves. They had a mind of their own, just like the stairs. Were all the doors and stairs alive in the future? What about windows? Surely not. He allowed himself to slow down a bit, just as he was approaching the doors; who knew what bold new world awaited him outside? He wanted to prepare himself, but just as he was approaching them, another surge of shoppers burst through, making him stop in his tracks. And the next second, he felt a heavy hand drop down on his shoulder.

'Mister Scrooge. You're pretty spry for an old white guy. You still going to 'expose' yourself? You're welcome to try.'

Dave had a smugness about him now which left Scrooge with a bitter taste in his mouth.

'No?' he said, before he could respond. 'I didn't think so. Now, shall we go back to the office? And I think maybe we'll be searching your pockets this time; in case you got any smart ideas on your little excursion to the door.'

'But I didn't do anything,' Scrooge started.

'Punch him, Scrooge. Punch him,' the spirit shouted. 'We're so close.'

'Grandad?'

Scrooge heard this third voice from behind him, closer to the door.

'Grandad, is that you?'

He turned around to see who the delightfully soft voice belonged to, and he was faced with a very attractive young lady with really bright ginger hair, and a sparkle in her eye.

'It *is* you. Thank God.'

The girl is surely mistaken, Scrooge thought, but he didn't feel as sure as he should have. The trip through time and all the running had left his brain and body in a state of bewilderment. Why shouldn't this beautiful young woman be his granddaughter?

At that moment, Dave chimed in. 'Are you saying that this man is your grandfather?'

'Well,' she said, 'I think that much was implied by the way I called him 'Grandad', don't you?'

Scrooge liked this girl, whoever she was. She'd taken complete control of the situation within seconds, running rings around the security guard.

'Well, Miss,' said Dave, trying and failing to gain the higher ground 'You should be aware that your grandad here threatened to expose himself in front of all our customers.'

The girl looked at Scrooge with amusement and bewilderment, and yet, with a look of familiarity, as if she'd known him for years.

'Oh, Grandad, not again. Did you forget your medication?'

She was very convincing. Maybe he *had* forgotten his medication. Maybe it was a bit of bad cheese. The girl seemed to be convinced that he was her grandfather, so who was he to argue with her? Maybe he *did* belong there, in the twenty first century.

'Are you sure this man is your grandad, Miss?' The girl, whose short ginger hair bobbed up and down with every movement of her head looked even more taken aback now; maybe even offended.

'Excuse *me*. I think I know my own grandad when I see him. Particularly when I arranged to meet him here.'

Dave didn't look too convinced. Scrooge felt like he was caught between two rivals, each one waiting to see who would blink first.

'I think we'd better be leaving now, don't you, Grandad?'

Scrooge decided that he liked this girl, whether she was his granddaughter or not, and she was so convincing he still couldn't be sure which it was. Dave looked as though he was about to try and grab him again, then his "granddaughter" spoke up, this time in a slightly more threatening tone.

'Unless you want me to tell all these nice people how you've threatened my poor, sick, dear old grandad? And at Christmas of all times.'

Dave looked stumped.

'The customer is always right, remember?'

This really seemed to rile the security guard, and Scrooge could see his giant chest moving up and down, as if it were about to explode.

'Okay, you win,' he said finally, 'but if I see either of you in here again, I'll be watching.'

At that moment, another mass of people entered through the magic doors, but the girl grabbed Scrooge's hand and led him straight through the middle of them. She seemed just as keen as him to get out of there. As they went outside, they were met by even more crowds of people; more than Scrooge had ever seen in his long life, and snow! Beautiful, pure white snow, dancing around and lighting up the air around him. Of course, he'd seen snow before, but it felt so good to be surrounded by it after being trapped in the superficial atmosphere of the shop. And then he noticed, just up ahead, some odd structures, crawling along what he assumed to be the road. They looked as though they were made from some kind of metal and there were so many of them. He was so distracted by everything that he'd almost forgotten his saviour: the girl. She was looking back into the shop, presumably to see if Dave had stopped watching them.

'Are you okay?' she asked, turning toward him.

'Um, yes. I think so.'

'Good,' she said. 'I know what they can be like in there. Not directly, but a friend of mine has heard things about the security team in there. They pick on old people like you – no offense – but they do.' Scrooge couldn't help but feel overwhelmed. Everything was so different than what he was used to. Nothing made sense, and he felt sick with the weight of it all.

'Are you sure you're okay?' the girl asked. 'You seem a bit weirded out.'

Scrooge snapped out of his stupor.

'So, you're - you're not my granddaughter?'

'Your granddaughter? Um, no. They didn't hit you on the head, did they? Because if they did, you could be in the money.'

Scrooge couldn't see the connection. 'Um, no, I don't think they did.'

'Pity. Oh, sorry! I didn't mean that the way it sounded. I'm Grace by the way. Grace Bright.'

'Oh, very nice to meet you. I'm Scrooge. Ebenezer Scrooge,' he shouted above the noise of the crowds.

'That's a… unique name. Are you Polish? I don't hear an accent.'

'No, it was my grandfather's name, actually.'

Grace suddenly looked as though she'd remembered something very important, and she grabbed a small, black rectangular box out of her trouser pocket. So, women in the future wear trousers. Interesting, Scrooge thought.

'I'm sorry, Mister Scrooge, but I'm meeting some friends for drinks.' She said this as she looked around for something. 'It was really nice meeting you. Take it easy.'

And before Scrooge could ask her what it was he should be taking easy, she was gone into the never ending crowd of people, constantly moving and shifting like tortuously slow swarms of bees.

Now that his saviour was gone, Scrooge looked around at all the amazing lights which hung from every building at every conceivable angle. There was a tree between two of the buildings which made the ones he had at home look really rather pitiful by comparison. The whole city with its unfeasibly tall buildings was like an explosion of joy, but the odd thing was: not a soul seemed to be enjoying it. As he stood there in silent wonder, taking the time to let everything sink in, Scrooge could feel his bewilderment drifting away, as if his old friend Christmas was still helping him. And yet, he felt like he was the only one seeing all of it. Since he'd arrived in the future he'd been screamed at, threatened, chased, and even locked in a room like a prisoner, but all the lights – which he still couldn't explain – and decorations, and the glorious snow filled his heart fit to bursting with unadulterated joy, making him forget his woes. Yet, everyone around him, children and adults alike, were miserable. Despite the fact that they were running around with arms full of what were presumably Christmas presents, they seemed completely unaware of the season; too busy bumping into each other.

Scrooge looked around to see if the spirit was anywhere to be seen. He had a whole new set of questions for him to refuse to answer. And there he was, just a few feet away, and on ground level this time, staring into space, looking even more miserable than everyone else who was walking right through him as if he wasn't there.

'Spirit,' Scrooge said, trying to snap him out of it. 'Is everyone in the future so —'

'That's quite a coincidence, isn't it,' the spirit said.

'What is?'

'That woman. The one who helped you.'

'Yes, she was quite charming wasn't she,' Scrooge enthused.

The spirit looked at him, as if he and Scrooge were the only ones in the overcrowded street. 'Scrooge, you're here to save her.'

'Wow. She's quite charming, isn't she, mate.' Carl was a little preoccupied, but he could see that Warren was trying his best to snap him out of it. Rather than meeting up with the ducks again, he'd decided to take Warren up on his offer of after work drinks. He'd only just started talking to him a couple of weeks ago – around the time the redundancies had been announced – but they'd clicked almost immediately. Nothing like bad news to bring people together. Warren had been with Locomart for a while, and there were always dodgy rumours floating around about his shady past, but Carl liked to think that he was the kind of person not to make brash judgements against people based on other people's judgements of people.

'*Charming*?' he said. 'What are you? Two hundred years old?'

'Hey, what can I say? I'm an old-fashioned kind of guy. Maybe I should take my mistletoe over and see where it goes from there.'

'You and your mistletoe are going to get us kicked out of here if you're not careful,' Carl said.

'I'm sorry, mate, but this thing has a life of its own. Woah, it's moving again. I think it's picking up a scent.' He moved the mistletoe as if it was actually trying to drag him over to the women at the bar, and Carl let out a sniff of a laugh, despite his best efforts to be miserable.

'Do y'wanna go over and try our luck? With this mistletoe, the odds are stacked heavily in our favour.'

It seemed that Warren was trying to be deliberately enthusiastic to try and rescue him from the doldrums, but he was wasting his time. 'Not that I wouldn't be honoured to be your wingman, mate, but I'm kind of married with a kid. I should be getting back to them actually.'

'Oh yeah,' Warren said, 'I forgot about that. Actually, I'm not sure if I knew that about you. It's a smallish shop, isn't it, but it's usually so busy no one ever gets chance to talk. I mean, even in the canteen no one talks to each other. They just stare at their phones like zombies or sheep, or zombie-sheep.'

'Yeah, I suppose they do,' Carl said nonchalantly.

'So, how long have you been married?' Warren asked, as he knocked back his pint.

'Um, it'll be eight years in April.'

'Wow. Y'don't look that old, mate,' Warren said, trying but failing to look genuinely shocked. 'It must be a struggle, I mean, raising a family on our wages. Does your wife work?'

This was starting to feel like an interview. 'Um, yeah. Well, sometimes. She's with a temp agency, but we can't always arrange a childminder in time, so she has to turn a lot of work down.'

'That's rough,' Warren said, staring off into the distance, or at the ever-increasing amount of women at the bar, he couldn't decide which. 'It's hard to do what you want in life, isn't it.'

'Woah, you're getting a bit deep there, mate. We've only had one drink,' Carl said, trying to lighten the mood.

'I'm sorry, but it is, isn't it. There's always someone telling you that y'can't do this and y'can't do that. Stay away from there. I mean, it's hard enough to start with, but when you've made the bad decisions I've made…' He looked straight at Carl now. 'I know you've probably heard stories about me.

Well, they're probably all true. The thing is though, once you've made those choices, they stick with you, no matter how hard you try to shake them. It's like you're a dog and someone's constantly standing on your tail, stopping you from moving forward.'

Carl felt bad for the guy. Here he was, spilling his heart and soul, and even going to the effort of coming up with colourful metaphors, and all he could think about was how he was going to tell Kate and Sara about his impending redundancy.

'You seem like an intelligent guy,' Warren carried on. 'Don't y'wanna do something other than work in a shop for the rest of your life?'

Carl let out another sniff of a laugh. 'What?'

'Oh, nothing,' Carl said. 'It's just that I've not really thought about that for a long time.' It was true, he hadn't. He had had dreams of doing something great with his life, but as the years flew by, that's all that they remained: just dreams. 'Yeah,' he said, 'I used to draw. Cartoons mostly. I thought about branching out and doing more realistic stuff like figurative drawing; maybe get into graphic novels or something. Before I got married and we had Sara I used to use every day off and most evenings to draw my silly little pictures. It was kind of like being a superhero, if that doesn't sound daft. Y'know, mild mannered shop assistant by day, cartoonist by night. Somehow though, nothing came of it.'

He took a large swig of beer and noticed that it was getting warm. It felt good to talk. He'd not told anyone about that stuff for ages, and Warren seemed enthralled with his every word, so he carried on.

'I sent stuff off and I got some nice rejection letters back. They liked my work, but not quite what they were looking for. Gradually my will broke down, and here I am, talking to you about it.'

'Well,' Warren said. 'It's good to talk about stuff, even if it is painful, especially at this time of year.'

'Yeah, I guess so.'

'I suppose you heard how I got the job, didn't you.'

'Actually, no,' Carl said. 'People don't talk about you *all* the time you know.'

'Well, that's something, I suppose.' He stopped and looked at Carl, as if he wanted to tell him, but something was stopping him.

Carl couldn't resist. 'How did you get the job then?'

'I thought you'd never ask. My uncle knows the manager. Back in the day, when I made those bad choices, I couldn't get work anywhere. No one would take me on. And now… now it's gonna be the same story all over again. No one's gonna take me on.'

Despite still feeling sorry for himself, Carl was warming to his new drinking partner. 'Oh, come on, mate. I'm sure that's not true. I mean, it's difficult for everyone at the moment, but something will turn up.'

'Nah, I'll be lucky if they let me shine shoes on the street with my record. This was the one thing I had going for me.'

'Well,' Carl said, downing the last of his warm beer. 'Speaking of shoes, we're all in the same ones at the moment, aren't we.'

Just then, Warren lifted his head up high so Carl could see right up his nostrils, as if he was about to divulge a great secret.

'What if I was to tell you that there's a way out of our current financial woes, my friend.'

Carl didn't like the way he said "my friend"; it just sounded so fake compared to the heart on sleeve stuff he'd been coming out with moments before. Even so, he indulged him. 'What do you mean?'

'Just what I said: A way out.'

The intense way in which Warren was staring at him made Carl feel on edge. Warren seemed to pick up on that as he lowered his head into a more relaxed, nostril-view-free position. 'Is it—'

'Illegal? No no no. Funny how I knew you were going to say that, isn't it,' Warren laughed. 'We must have a real mental connection.'

'Yeah, well I'm sure there's something mental going on,' Carl said under his breath.

'What was that?'

'Nothing.'

'So, what d'you reckon?'

Warren didn't seem to be picking up on his reluctant vibes, so he spelled it out. 'Nah, you're alright, mate. This was good, but I'd best be getting back to Kate and—'

'Your daughter?'

'Yeah, my daughter.' Warren was really starting to annoy him now, finishing his sentences for him.

'Have you told them yet? About… you know.'

Carl turned away.

'I didn't think so,' Warren said, a little too smugly. 'What if I told you that there was another job on the horizon; one that paid quite a lot better than our current, soon to be expired positions?'

'Then I'd ask again, is it illegal?' Carl whispered, remembering where they were. Warren looked hurt, but he couldn't tell whether he was winding him up.

Warren's expression suddenly changed as he looked at his watch. 'Oh, is that the time already? I should be going.'

'So, I take it that's a definite "yes" then,' Carl said dryly.

'If you think you already know the answer, then why are you still asking the question?'

'What?' Carl sputtered. 'What's that supposed to mean? Are you trying to draw me in with your enigmaticness?'

'I don't know,' Warren said, looking a bit bored of the conversation. 'Look, if you're interested, I'll be here again tomorrow night, same time. If you're not, then, well, it's your loss, mate.' And with that, he downed the last of his pint and left.

Carl still had some of his drink left, and he could've just left it and got the next train home, but he was surprised to find that after five minutes he was still there sipping his warm beer and thinking about what Warren had said, or rather not said, about a way out. He cursed himself when he realised that a further five minutes later, he was still sat there thinking that maybe he should give Warren the benefit of the doubt and come back tomorrow night.

'Cheer up, it might never happen.'

He looked up to see who had snapped him out of his deep thoughts with such a blatant platitude. He was all ready to have a go at her; to tell her that it had already happened, or at least that the thing that was happening which she knew nothing about would be happening in a few months' time, and there was nothing anyone could do about it. Then he looked up and saw that it was the girl from the bar, the one that Warren had called 'charming'. Up close, he could see where Warren was coming from. He suddenly realised that his mouth was open, but no words were coming out.

'Are you okay?' the girl asked.

Carl tried to pull himself together. 'Oh, yeah yeah, I'm fine. Sorry.'

'What are you apologising for?' the girl said. 'I'm the one who's encroaching on your space.'

'Yeah, I suppose so,' Carl said.

The girl suddenly changed tac and put her hands on her hips. 'Oh, so I'm encroaching, am I? I'm sorry, I'll leave you alone with your oh-so-important thoughts.'

'No no no,' Carl said quickly. 'I didn't mean to—'

'It's okay, I'm just messing with you. It's one of my least annoying character flaws, unfortunately.'

Carl laughed. 'It's okay, it's not that annoying.'

'I'll go anyway. I should be getting back to my mates.' The girl turned to go and then something stopped her, and she turned back to Carl, as if she'd forgotten something. She said softly: 'Are you going to be okay? You seem… troubled. No one should be troubled this time of year.'

Carl's immediate reaction was to say something cynical – it was the way he was feeling, he couldn't help it – but he stopped himself. There was something about this girl. She was so open and forthright, he felt like he could be the same and tell her what was on his mind. 'That thing that might never happen; it already has. Or, at least it's going to in a few months.' Now I'm the one trying to be enigmatic, he thought.

'Is there anything you can do to stop this thing – whatever it is – from happening?' the girl said, moving forward.

'I'm being made redundant.'

'Oh, I'm sorry. I didn't—'

'It's okay,' Carl said, looking up at her. 'The thing is, a possible opportunity has come up. Maybe it's a way out of having to worry about the whole redundancy thing. I'm not sure what to do.'

The girl seemed to be considering his words deeply. Very sweet of her, considering it wasn't her problem.

'Well, in my experience, when someone asks someone else what they think they should do, ninety-nine percent of the time they've already made up their mind.' She said this slowly, thoughtfully. 'They're only asking someone else because they want them to tell them that they're right. What's your first instinct?'

Carl fell silent and thought hard about what he was going to say next. He didn't really want to tell her that he was thinking of doing something that was more-likely-than-not to be illegal. Then again, she didn't know it might be illegal, any more than he knew it probably was. 'I suppose my first instinct was

– I mean, what I was thinking before you so rudely interrupted me,' he said with a wry smile, 'was, yes: I was going to do it.'

'Then you should,' she said firmly. 'Things happen for a reason, and maybe this opportunity has come along as a way of the universe balancing things out for you.'

'Yeah, the universe has been giving me a bit of a raw deal lately, so maybe it's been feeling guilty.'

'Seriously, I mean, I was late getting here to meet my girlfriends, and who knows, maybe I was supposed to be late so we could have this conversation, and I could convince you to do whatever it is you're going to do.' She stopped and looked at him, as if she was about to tell him something really important, but then one of her friends from the bar shouted over.

'Hey, Gracie! Are you getting a round in tonight or what?' She suddenly looked slightly guilty and shouted back.

'Okay, okay, I'm coming!' Then she turned back to Carl.

'I'd better get back before they lynch me,' she said. 'It was nice meeting you, anyway, and I hope things work out for you, and that you have as good a Christmas as possible.'

'Thanks,' Carl said. 'You too.'

7

It had been quite a day for Scrooge. In fact, it had been quite a one hundred and fifty years, which was approximately how far forward in time the spirit told him they'd travelled. Scrooge was suffering from a sort of time traveller's jetlag: he'd lost all account of time and wasn't sure whether he should be sleeping or not. He certainly felt like he could sleep for quite a fair while, but since getting there, they'd been on the move for hours, and the spirit showed no sign of slowing the pace.

Scrooge bombarded him with questions about the matter of saving Grace, but his companion just kept moving; floating forward above what seemed like millions of people. No one even seemed to notice Scrooge shouting questions up into the air; they were all too busy talking into their little boxes or shouting for the other people to get out of the way. Finally, Scrooge shouted to the spirit that if he didn't want to answer his questions that was fine, but could he please do him the courtesy of at least floating next to him on the ground, so he wouldn't get a crick in his neck. The spirit eventually obliged, and although it seemed odd at first to see the crowds of people pass through him as if he was nothing, he started to feel slightly more comfortable with the situation.

They walked and floated for at least an hour and crossed countless roads filled with metal horseless carriages, which the spirit told Scrooge were called "cars". It seemed that the spirit would reveal some things about the future, but only enough for him to get by. For instance, the countless roads filled with countless cars had a system of organisation – a necessity for sure – called traffic lights. In fact, the people had one, too, for crossing the roads. They were powered by the same extraordinary thing that had made the clothing store so bright: Electricity. This one concept filled Scrooge's head up, and he started to think that maybe the spirit had good reason for not explaining everything about twenty-first century London. Everything he came across was a marvel; even things as simple as the clothes people wore. It was still unmistakably London, just not the London he had grown up with.

After a while, the spirit led Scrooge down a side street, which, whilst still bustling with Christmas shoppers, was nowhere near as crowded as the people-packed streets he'd been drowning in thus far. As they walked down the street, which had shops on either side, the amount of people thinned out and he felt as if he could breathe again, and then, something else took his breath away.

The spirit had stopped outside a shop, which looked completely and deliberately different to all the others Scrooge had seen so far. It was almost as if one little portion of the London he knew and loved had slipped through a crack in time and followed him there. It had the familiar wooden front with square windows within windows, each of which had undisturbed snow resting at the bottom.

'I thought you'd like it,' the spirit said. 'Like a little piece of home, isn't it.'

Just then, something very odd occurred to Scrooge; although – considering how odd his day had been – maybe it wasn't so strange that he reached this conclusion. 'Tell me, Spirit; does this have something to do with you?'

'What do you mean?' The spirit seemed defensive all of a sudden.

'I mean,' Scrooge said, moving closer to him, remembering that to all but himself he was apparently talking to thin air, 'did you bring this shop here from my time?'

The spirit looked baffled, his eyebrows raising to above their natural limits. 'Oh, I see. No, Scrooge, no I didn't. It's just designed to look old fashioned. Or perhaps it's just a building which hasn't changed over the years. It's an antiques shop.'

'Oh… You mean like a curiosity shop?'

'Okay, whatever. Shall we go in then?' Without waiting for Scrooge to respond, the spirit floated through the unopened door.

As Scrooge opened the door – as any normal corporeal person would – he was greeted by the pleasantly familiar sound of a bell, which rang as the door opened. He was home. The sights and musty smells which greeted him made him feel like that door had been a gateway back to his own time.

Everything on the tables was so familiar: a coal shovel; a hand mirror; a clock under glass. Yet in amongst these everyday objects, which had price tags on them that seemed peculiar to Scrooge, there were unfamiliar, alien objects. Amongst them were several odd appliances which looked like guns, yet they had dials with numbers on. And then there was a black box with a long cable running out of the back of it. Scrooge picked it up to examine it – it was heavier than it looked – and found that there was a flap at the front of it. He pushed his fingers inside, and he could feel little bits of metal poking him.

'Hello there.' The voice came from behind, startling him. 'I see you've spotted the odd one out.'

Scrooge turned around, and stood there was a tall man with thinning, grey hair; he was perhaps a few years younger than he was.

'I know it's not strictly an antique, but the wife wants rid of it. Obviously, we have a DVD player, but I keep telling her we should keep hold of it. Technology moves on so quickly these days, doesn't it, and that bulky thing will be worth a fortune to a collector in a few years, maybe. Heck, even her fancy pants Blu-ray player will be soon, with everyone streaming stuff.

Scrooge understood roughly two words of what he'd just heard, but still, he had to agree with the sentiment. Maybe he'd found a kindred spirit; a man out of time.

'I think the remote's there somewhere.'

Scrooge made a show of looking for it on the table, even though he didn't have a clue what a "remote" was.

'Scrooge.' The spirit suddenly appeared in front of him, making him jump and gasp.

'Are you okay, sir?' the antiques dealer said.

'Show him your watch. You do still have it, don't you?' the spirit said.

'Yes, yes I'm fine, thank you,' Scrooge said to the antiques dealer, whilst feeling inside his coat pocket.

'This is why we came here, Scrooge. To get some money,' the spirit said forcefully.

'I'm still not sure about selling it.'

'Oh, you have something you want me to value do you, sir?' The poor man had no idea he was part of a three-way conversation.

'No,' Scrooge said quickly.

'Yes, he does.' The spirit seemed to momentarily forget that the antiques dealer couldn't see or hear him. 'Yes, you do, Scrooge. Unless you want to walk the entire length and breadth of London for the rest of your time here. We need travel money. And do you really want to let Them down?' He said, pointing straight up.

'But it was a gift from my father. You can't expect me to—'

'I don't. I mean, there's no pressure here, sir. You don't have to sell whatever it is to me. I don't even have to value it if you don't want me to,' the antiques dealer said, looking more and more bemused at Scrooge's behaviour.

The spirit pointed upwards again, saying nothing and Scrooge scowled at him. He didn't trust the spirit, but what could he do? Could he really risk his soul for the feeling that something wasn't quite right?

'Um, sir? Are you sure you're okay? You seem a bit stressed. Perhaps you'd like to come back another day?'

'No,' Scrooge said, without turning his gaze from the spirit. 'I'd like to sell you my watch,' Scrooge said through gritted teeth, 'as long as the price is right.'

The spirit said nothing; he just looked rather smug. He'd won for now.

'Well, okay then. Let's take a look at what you've got.'

The man led Scrooge to a glass cabinet at the back of the shop, which seemed to double up as a shop counter. Beneath the glass, there were all manner of trinkets, some of which Scrooge recognised and, of course, some he didn't. He took the watch out of his coat pocket and out of its protective cloth and lay it gently down on the countertop. As he did, he noticed something in the man's eyes. Scrooge saw this simply as curiosity, but the spirit, apparently, saw something else.

'Be careful here, Scrooge. Don't let him rip you off.'

Scrooge ignored him and focussed on the antiques dealer.

For a moment the man looked as though he had no idea what he was looking at. Surely, they still had watches in the future. The antiques dealer craned his head forward and squinted, all the time not touching it; almost as if he were afraid to. Then, he caught his breath.

'Would you excuse me for a second, sir?' Before Scrooge could respond, the man disappeared into a small room behind the counter which looked to be full of books. A moment later, he was back, and he carefully placed an old dusty book on the countertop and started flicking through its pages. Then, he suddenly stopped, and his eyes lit up: He'd found what he was looking for. 'I wasn't sure at first, but if you don't mind?' He gestured to Scrooge for his permission to turn the watch over, and as he did so, his face froze. 'I don't believe it.' He picked up the watch carefully and put it next to the picture on the page. 'It is.'

'It is what?' Scrooge asked.

'Well, sir, what you have here… This timepiece; well, I don't know how well you know your history, but back in seventeen sixty George the Third became king. One of his passions was watches, timepieces, clocks. He had quite a collection.'

'And this was one of them?' Scrooge guessed.

'No. Close, but no. In eighteen ten there were all sorts of celebrations and events organised for the fiftieth anniversary of his royal highness' coronation.'

As the man spoke, Scrooge tried to remember what he was doing back then, but it was fuzzy. Probably busy counting money and making people miserable.

'Two brothers were commissioned to design a watch quite literally fit for a king, that king being George the Third, of course. They were quite old at the time, I'd say around sixty, which was probably deemed ancient for that period.'

Scrooge held his tongue.

'Tragically, one of the brothers died before they finished – there were rumours of foul play, but that's another story entirely. Anyway, the remaining brother who had problems with his hands – probably what we now know as rheumatic arthritis – was left to finish the piece, but because of his debilitating condition he struggled with it. When he presented it to the king, well, he was less than satisfied with the end product, and handed it back, along with a few choice words.

'Now, up until now, no one knew what happened to this watch. If you notice, this picture is only a drawing of the piece, based on the original designs. Did you say that your father gave you this?'

'Yes,' Scrooge said. 'It was for my fiftieth birthday, if I recall rightly.'

'How very interesting. How very very interesting.' The man turned the watch over again. 'I don't know how au faix you are with roman numerals, sir, but that,' he said, as he pointed to a large *L* engraved on the back of the watch, 'is the roman numeral for fifty.'

'Yes, I knew that,' Scrooge said. 'I assumed that my father had had it engraved for my birthday. Are you saying that the watchmaker – what was his name?'

'Dickenson.'

'Are you saying that he engraved it for the king?'

'That's the odd thing,' the antiques dealer said, in a whisper. 'By all accounts, Henry Dickenson would never have been able to keep a steady enough hand to engrave it. So, either your father had it engraved for your fiftieth, or Dickenson had someone else do it for him.'

'Yeah yeah yeah. This is all very fascinating,' barked the spirit impatiently, 'but do you think we could find out how much the thing's worth, sometime this century, Scrooge?'

Scrooge scowled at him for interrupting, even though, technically, it wasn't an interruption, but even *he* had to concede to some curiosity as to how much it was actually worth, considering its colourful history.

'Sir, do you have any idea what it might be worth?' Scrooge said this quietly, as if anyone could be listening in. The shop was in fact empty.

'Worth?' the man laughed. 'How much is it worth?'

Scrooge looked at the spirit, who looked very cautious.

'My dear chap. This piece of secret history is absolutely priceless. To a collector – and I'm a bit of a collector as you can see – it's… well, it's priceless, as I said. I could sell everything in this place and it still wouldn't be anywhere near enough. You should feel very privileged to own such a rare piece of history, Mister?'

'Scrooge. Ebenezer Scrooge. So, what you're saying is that there's no way you could afford to buy this off me?'

'Um, no,' said the man, his words full of regret. 'Not many people could. In fact, the only people that could, probably wouldn't even know what you've got here.'

Scrooge looked at the spirit and shrugged his shoulders, as if to say: *You heard the man; we can't sell it to him.* This, however, did not slow him down.

'Ask him how much he's got in his safe,' he said. 'No! No, don't do that. He'll think you're trying to rob him.'

'Well, what do you want me to do then?' Scrooge burst out, forgetting himself. The spirit gestured toward the antiques dealer, who was starting to look worried.

'Oh, I'm sorry about that, my good fellow,' Scrooge said, turning on the charm. 'I live alone, and have a tendency to thinking aloud and before I realise, I'm conducting entire conversations between myself and I. Nothing to worry about.'

The man didn't look at all convinced.

'Tell him you'll take five hundred pounds – No! Six hundred pounds for it.'

'Six hundred—' Scrooge started and then caught himself doing it again.

'It might seem like a lot to your Victorian mind,' the spirit said, coldly, 'but believe me, he'll have at least that much in his safe, and you do need money, unless you plan on sleeping rough for the next couple of nights.'

Again, Scrooge found himself glaring at the spirit, then turned to the antiques dealer. 'My good chap, I need money for… for Christmas presents, lots of Christmas presents, and coal isn't cheap, is it?' Scrooge could see that the man wasn't sure what to make of what he was saying, but he carried on. 'What I'm trying to say is, would you be willing to take this off my hands for… six hundred pounds?'

'Six hundred pounds?' whispered the antiques dealer.

Scrooge wasn't sure what to make of his reaction. He seemed pleased, surprised, and suspicious, all at the same time. He was looking around at the empty shop for something. Could he sense the spirit?

'Is this some kind of joke? Is this a hidden camera show?' Then, he looked closely at Scrooge, making him feel very uncomfortable. 'Are you Ant or Dec?'

Scrooge looked over to the spirit for some guidance, but he just said:

'It's a long story. Just tell him you're not joking.'

Scrooge turned back to the man and tried to reassure him.

'I'm not sure what an "Antordec" is, but I assure you, dear chap, I am not joking. As I said, I need the money and—'

'But did you not hear me? The story? It's priceless. If I gave you a mere six hundred pounds for it, I'd be practically stealing it from you. No, Mister Scrooge, I can't do that to you, especially at Christmas. You're obviously a bit confused. I don't know, maybe you're a bit worse for wear, but I can't take this watch off you.'

Scrooge looked over at the spirit once more, but as he expected he was shaking his head. 'Look,' said Scrooge, 'just take it, will you? In the spirit of the season.' He thrust it into the man's hands and hoped that his gamble would pay off. Being an honest man himself, he liked to think that he could sense that same quality in others, and he was sure he could see it in this fellow, despite the spirit's cynical view.

Scrooge opened his eyes – he hadn't realised that he'd shut them – and the antiques dealer was still holding the watch, staring at it, as if it were a chunk of gold.

'Okay, okay,' he said, pulling his eyes reluctantly away from it, 'but there's no way I'm giving you six hundred pounds for it.'

Scrooge's heart sank. How had the man tricked him? He seemed so honest and forthright. He forced himself to look at the spirit. He looked more angry than anything, and he was about to say something, but then the shopkeeper spoke again.

'No, if you insist on me having this, it's only the decent thing for me to do to give you as much as I can afford to give you for it.'

Scrooge's heart leapt for joy, not because of the money. No: because he'd been right. The man was honourable.

'Now, as I won't be selling it,' the man continued, 'not here at least – actually, I'm reluctant to sell it at all, it's such a work of art – I'll have to withdraw some money from my private account. I have a couple of grand.'

'No,' the spirit cried. 'Scrooge, that's far too much to be carrying around with you, so he'll probably want to transfer it to your bank account, which you don't have. You have to insist on cash.' He paused to think. 'Tell him you'll take seven hundred, eight hundred at the most, but no more than that.'

Scrooge did as he was told and despite much objection from the shopkeeper, who, Scrooge discovered was called Dennis, he finally agreed and the three of them went to the bank a couple of blocks away to get the money.

'Well,' Dennis said, trying but failing to hide how pleased he was with his recent acquisition, 'it was a pleasure doing business with you, Mister Scrooge.'

'*Ebenezer*, please,' Scrooge insisted.

'Ebenezer, sorry. Please, allow me to pay for your taxi.'

Scrooge felt flawed for a moment and then relieved. 'They still have taxis here? But where are the horses?' he said, looking around the bustling street.

Dennis just laughed. 'Ha! You're not that old. You're not that much older than me, I'll bet.'

'Well, I'm not sure about that,' Scrooge said, smiling to himself.

The taxi ride, as Scrooge had expected, was like no taxi ride he'd ever been on. The spirit had got him to hail one, and as the black metallic beast pulled up next to him, he realised that the fellow in the front seat of the carriage was, in fact, controlling it. The spirit had already explained – however curtly – the concept of cars, and Scrooge could feel his head still swelling with trying to fathom it, but he was grateful for what little light he could shed on, well, *anything*.

As the driver sped them along to their destination: a small bed and breakfast – and talked about more things that Scrooge couldn't fathom – brexit, the EU, the bleedin' X Factor Christmas single – he noticed a slight change in the spirit's attitude toward him: He seemed a bit more relaxed. Maybe it was because he'd done everything he'd asked of him so far. Maybe he'd continue this way, as long as he did so. Not an altogether comforting notion, but what choice did he have until he knew exactly what was going on?

'Alright, old fella. We're here,' the taxi driver said. 'You sure y'want me droppin' you 'ere? This ain't really the best place for a fella, y'know – of your years.'

Scrooge looked at the spirit and he nodded.

'Yes, old chap, this is the place.'

'Well, I 'ope you got friends 'ere.'

Scrooge could hear the genuine concern in the cabbie's voice, so he decided to lie. 'I do, yes. Just around the corner from here.'

'Glad to hear it. That'll be… twenty-two seventy please, fella.'

Scrooge got the money out of his pocket and looked through the unfamiliar notes. The bank had given him the eight hundred pounds in twenty-pound notes as the spirit had instructed.

'Just give him two twenties and tell him to keep the change,' the spirit said. 'It's Christmas, after all.'

Scrooge did exactly as the spirit said and the response from the driver was as grateful as Scrooge had expected.

'See you again, hopefully, old fella,' he shouted, as he left Scrooge in a part of the city which reminded him of some of the places he'd visited in recent times in his London.

He looked around and saw how much of a contrast there was between where he'd been and where he now was. Instead of the thousands of lights which tried to defy the fact that it was night-time, almost blinding him with their power, there were only a few streetlights flickering on and off. As they did, he caught glimpses of homeless people trying to keep warm in doorways and under blankets, which had clearly seen better days. He wanted to help every one of them, and instinctively started walking towards an old woman who was shivering so much that he could barely make out the details of her face.

'Scrooge, what are you doing?!' the spirit barked.

He shrugged. 'I'm going to help her. That's why I'm here, isn't it? To help people. With all this money, surely I can—'

'Keep quiet about the money! You know what'll happen if you start handing out money to random strangers around here?'

'Do enlighten me.'

'More strangers will come, and more, until they're around you like a pack of ravenous wolves, and all of them will be asking you for money until you have none, and the ones left with no money will be quite angry about that. It won't be pretty.'

Scrooge hesitated and then turned away from the woman. He had to admit that the spirit probably had a good point.

'Look, Scrooge, I know you want to help people. That's why you've been chosen for this mission, but you have to understand that you can't help everyone in the world. Some people are more… consequential than others.'

'Like Grace, you mean,' Scrooge said, looking the spirit square in the eye.

The spirit avoided his gaze. 'Yes, like Grace.'

'So, what is my mission exactly, Spirit? I've done everything you've asked of me. I came to the future with you, I nearly got arrested, I sold my watch. What more do I have to do to prove myself?'

The spirit looked as though he was about to tell him at least something, but he started looking around. Small groups of the people that Scrooge had seen moments earlier had gathered together and were shuffling towards him. He shuddered as he heard snippets of their mumblings.

'Nice coat he's got there. That'd suit me, that would.'

'I'll fight y'for it.'

'Did he say he'd sold his watch?'

'Um, Scrooge? I think we should move,' the spirit said nervously. 'The B 'n' B is just around the corner. You should be safe there.'

Without argument, Scrooge followed the spirit. He could feel all their eyes focussed on him.

'Come on, Scrooge, pick up the pace, will you.'

He needed no convincing, and as soon as he reached the corner and there was a bit more space between him and the group of strangers, he broke into a run.

This seemed to put most of them off the chase, but one of them, who seemed much more spry than his friends, broke away from the group and bounded after him with the dogged determination of someone who'd been saving all his energy for just such an occasion. He was exhausted from the day's events, and he could feel his whole body screaming out for him to stop, but he couldn't. He spotted the patch of ice too late and slipped and flipped into the air. He landed with an almighty thud, taking the full impact on his back. He couldn't move anything except his neck, and even that was in agony, and his bones ached as if someone was pulling them in all different directions.

He craned his neck toward the sound of the quickening footsteps, and he could see the man getting nearer. His face was a blur of shadows and movement, but his body language told Scrooge everything he needed to know, and then he caught a glimpse of something shiny in his upside-down hand.

'Get up, Scrooge! Get up! Can't you see he's got a knife? Get up!'

But Scrooge didn't respond. He just lay there. The moment before his death seemed like it was being stretched out to infinity.

So, this is it. This is how I leave this world. Killed by a complete stranger. Probably very apt, after all the people I've hurt whom I've never even met. Nothing I do can ever make up for what I did with my life; and who knows, maybe I'm indirectly responsible for what happened to this man.

And then, there he was, hovering over him like a spectre of death. Despite believing that he deserved to die that way, Scrooge instinctively tried to plead with the man.

'Please! Please don't kill me. I have so much to make up for. So much good to do.'

'Well,' the man grunted, 'you can start by giving me your coat. Then maybe I won't kill you, old man.'

'Yes, yes of course, my coat,' Scrooge said with more than a touch of relief.

The spirit suddenly appeared above him.

'No, Scrooge, you can't give him your coat. You have all your money in there.'

'My money?'

'Your money?' the man with the knife said. 'Well, well yeah. I suppose I should've mentioned that I'd be taking your money, but I thought it went without saying.'

'No – I—'

Before Scrooge could beg anymore, he saw something else shiny move swiftly through the spirit and connect with the man's head. He looked confused, but before he could turn his head to see what had happened, the something shiny had hit him again and he moved even faster than before to escape a third blow.

Scrooge recoiled and closed his eyes, waiting for the spade to hit him, but it never came.

'What are you doing?' a kindly voice said. 'I'm hardly going to hit *you*. I was trying to save you.'

Scrooge opened his eyes and looked up to see a wrinkle-headed bald man wearing a jumper that seemed to have a pattern of a Christmas tree on it. He was an unlikely saviour to say the least.

'You going to lie there all night?' the bald man asked. 'Because I think you'll find it a bit cosier inside. Come on, give me your hand.'

Scrooge's hands were shaking, and his blood was running cold, but as the man drew his hand nearer, he managed to grab it firmly enough, and he helped him to his feet. As he dusted himself off, he saw to his surprise that there was a warm orange glow coming from the open door of the Bed and Breakfast, as if the whole place was on fire within.

'You're the owner of this establishment?' Scrooge asked.

'Well, joint owner, yes. Own it with the missus. This is an odd part of the city for you to be out on your own, if you don't mind me saying. Dangerous, too. It's lucky for you Mrs Ward just now asked me to clear the doorway of snow, in case we get any visitors, and here you are. Come in! Get warm.'

Mister Ward led Scrooge through the door and down a short hallway which barely had room for two pictures hanging on one side of it. They looked like family paintings to Scrooge, but they were painted very realistically. The hall led to a small square room with a desk to the left and stairs leading up on the right of it. There was a woman sat behind the desk of similar age to Mister Ward – she had more hair – and she looked very similar to her husband. Even her jumper was the same.

'You must be Mrs Ward,' Scrooge said softly.

'Yes, and who might you be?'

The similarities with her husband stopped at the jumper, Scrooge thought. She seemed far more suspicious of him.

'Oh, I'm Scrooge, Ebenezer Scrooge.' He held out his hand for her to shake, and although she did so, she didn't seem too happy about it, as if she was expecting him to pull her hand out of its socket. There was the sound of a clearing throat behind him.

'You'll have to forgive my wife, Mister Scrooge. She's a bit wary of, well, everyone who comes in here.'

'If by wary,' she said, addressing her husband with a steely eye, 'you mean not taking in every Tom, Dick and Harry under the sun, then yes, I'm wary. Someone needs to be.' She looked back at Scrooge. 'I take it you're wanting to stay here?' She eyed him from head to toe; she had to stand up to do this, and she was surprisingly tall.

'Wait a minute. Where's your bag? You're just another bum off the street, aren't you. What kind of name is "Ebenezer" anyway? Made up, I bet.'

'Now come on, Margaret,' Mister Ward said, leaping to Scrooge's defence. 'Look at him. Does he look like he lives on the streets? He's pretty well dressed for a homeless person, don't you think?'

'If you had your way, we'd just take everyone in, wouldn't we, Frank. Let's go and get the rest of them in, shall we?'

'No, I'm just saying… Look, he was being chased by that skinny guy with the knife, and he wanted his money. Maybe he's already had his bags stolen.'

'That's it!' This was the spirit, and he made Scrooge jump with his sudden outburst.

'You okay?' Mister Ward asked.

Ignoring the fact that there were two other people in the room trying to talk to Scrooge and fathom him out, the spirit told him what to tell them about his bag. A cover story he called it, and Scrooge relayed it word for word.

'What it was, was I got the coach in to Leicester Square from Bracknell this morning, hoping to do a bit of Christmas shopping and meet up with an old friend, Jacob. But as soon as I got off the coach, I put my suitcase down to rest my old hands and someone grabbed it and just scarpered.'

Mrs Ward was looking intently at Scrooge, as if she were looking for a nervous tick, or a hole in his story. This made him feel very uncomfortable, but he knew he had to carry on.

'Well, luckily I had my bankcard in my pocket, and I withdrew just enough money to get by on, plus the money for Christmas shopping. Unfortunately, my phone was in my suitcase and I can't remember Jacob's number. Somewhere along my journey to here my wallet must've been stolen, but I keep my money separate because my wallet's full of old receipts.'

Mister and Mrs Ward looked at each other, as if they were trying to decide silently between themselves whether Scrooge's story had any credibility.

'Well, I'm convinced,' said Mr Ward, finally.

His wife screwed up her eyes and looked as though she was about to shout him down.

'Oh, come on, Margaret. You know what it's like in Central London. I've had my wallet stolen twice before now.'

She still didn't look convinced, but it seemed like she might be cracking. Her eyes seemed to soften, somehow.

'Come on, love. He's clearly no danger to us. He's an old fella like me. We've got to look out for each other.'

'Okay, okay. I suppose you're probably right.' She turned to Scrooge with what could almost be mistaken for a smile. 'I'm sorry, Mister Scrooge. It's just that you can never be too careful these days.'

'That's quite alright, madam,' Scrooge said, 'I understand completely.'

They went on to discuss the charge for the room. Apparently, it had something called “Freeview” but no “Sky”. This baffled Scrooge in more ways than he could count so the spirit said that he’d explain it later, if there was time.

‘It makes a nice change not to have to carry bags up these creaky old stairs,’ Mister Ward said as they ascended. ‘Oh – I’m so sorry. I didn’t mean to – I just meant—’

‘It’s alright, my friend,’ Scrooge said. ‘Like you said, it happens a lot.’

‘Well, yes. That’s part of the reason we moved away from the centre of London. I mean, yes, it’s still a bit rough round here, but most of the time people leave y’alone as long as you don’t look them in the eye. It also helps being married to a Rottweiler with a shorter than short fuse,’ he laughed. ‘And rents around here are a tad more reasonable, as you can probably imagine. We used to run a hotel on Euston Road, but times are hard and, well, here we are.’

‘Yes, I wish I could help you out, Mister Ward,’ Scrooge said. ‘You seem like a—’

‘No,’ Mister Ward said, ‘here we are. This is your room, and please, call me Frank.’

‘Oh…’ They were still on the stairs and there was no landing, just a door.

‘You be careful on the stairs here, Mister Scrooge. I know it’s probably not the best location for you, but it’s the only single room we have I’m afraid, and you’d be surprised how busy we get this time of year, despite, y’know, the missus. If it makes you feel any better, someone gave us four stars on Trip Advisor, but I don’t suppose you use that, do you.’

‘I’m sure it will be fine,’ Scrooge said, ignoring the fact that he had no clue as to what a ‘Trip Advisor’ was.

‘The good news is, it’s all en-suite, so you won’t have to struggle down the stairs to the toilet in the middle of the night. Can I ask how many nights you’ll be staying with us?’

Scrooge suddenly realised that that was another thing his spiritual companion had neglected to mention.

Frank could see that he wasn't sure. 'It's okay y'know. I mean, we don't charge extra for Christmas day or anything, and it's nice to have a bit of older company. You still seem a bit shaken up. Are you okay?'

Before Scrooge could assure him, the spirit's face suddenly appeared through the door and through Mister Ward's face, so that the face in front of him resembled neither of them, just a grotesque deformity of both.

'Two nights,' the spirit said, before disappearing again.

'Um, two nights,' Scrooge repeated straight away, before Frank could say anything more. So, they were on a tight schedule, but this didn't really give him any more clue as to what the spirit would have him do with his time here.

'Okay, two nights it is then,' Frank said with a smile. 'Breakfast is served between eight and nine. It's quite basic but filling, and you can have either cereal or melon for starters, and we've got the full English for you after that.' As he opened the door and stepped inside the room, Scrooge followed him. 'As you can see, it's got all the essentials. Oh – and the Wi-Fi password is Christmas rocks nineteen fifty-six, all one word and all lower case and numbers.'

Scrooge looked at him, speechless.

'Oh yeah, sorry, I forgot you lost your phone and you're probably not a big social networker anyway, I suppose. Although, some older people have surprised me and I myself like to – I'm sorry,' he said, 'I'm yammering on and you probably just want to get some rest. I'll let you settle in.'

Before Scrooge could thank him for his kindness and hospitality, and most importantly for saving his life, Frank had skittered back down the stairs, presumably to attend to more chores for Mrs Ward. So, he took a proper look around the room. And what a room it was. Although it was quite small, it had everything and more that he needed. Some things he recognised: the bed, the wardrobe and the chest of drawers, although they were radically different in style to what he was accustomed to. There was a lamp – he presumed it was a lamp – by the bed, and the spirit was kind enough to tell him how it worked.

He could feel a million questions forming in his mind about everything around him, but before he could voice any of them, the spirit pointed to a black rectangular panel with two legs on top of the chest of drawers.

'That's a television, or "TV", Scrooge. The best I can describe it to you and your Victorian mind,' the spirit said, 'is that it's like a theatre in a box – several theatres – except you control what you watch. There's a lot of rubbish on it, but I'm sure you'll find it fascinating.'

And that he did. He sat on the end of the bed, flicking through all the channels, each one a new window on the world. At first, he asked the spirit a million questions about it, most of which he didn't know the answers to, but gradually Scrooge became so mesmerised that he almost forgot the spirit was there.

'Right, well, I'll leave you to it,' the spirit said, 'but don't stay up too late, Scrooge, we've got—'

'Just a minute,' Scrooge said, switching off 'the box of miracles' as he called it and standing up to face the spirit. 'As I said before, I think you owe me an explanation.'

'But I've shown you everything, Scrooge,' the spirit protested.

'I appreciate you showing me all the wonders of this time, but you've still not told me the most important thing. I've done everything; everything that you've asked of me so far. So, please just tell me why I'm here.'

The spirit floated back and seemed almost humbled at Scrooge's confrontational approach – maybe even flawed. He closed his eyes as if meditating on the secrets he was about to reveal. 'You're right, Scrooge. You're right.' He said this with a great sigh, as if a massive weight had been lifted from his shoulders. 'I haven't been completely honest with you, and for that I'm sorry. I'll tell you now, why I brought you here. I'll tell you *everything.*'

The spirit sat down on the long side of the bed; well, he put himself in a position to make it look as though he was sat on the bed. Of course, by doing this, he didn't affect the bed in anyway.

'Spirit, is that not a great strain on you?' Scrooge asked.

'What? Sitting like this? No. I'm just an image essentially. No physical form, unfortunately. No muscles to sprain or strain – not anymore, anyway. Just one of the many things I miss about being alive. I just thought it might make you feel more comfortable.'

'Well,' Scrooge said, sitting down next to him, 'the gesture is much appreciated. Now, you were going to tell me why I'm here.'

The spirit looked right through him for a moment, as if Scrooge were the ghost in the room. 'I'm sorry,' he said, 'I'm just trying to think of a way of explaining everything that you'll understand.'

'Well, you explained the tellyvision to me well enough.'

'*Television*,' the spirit corrected him. 'This is far more complicated. I've not been there long, in Heaven, I mean. I don't think so, at least. It's kind of like dreaming. Time passes in an odd way, as if every moment has already happened and you're living in a memory.'

Scrooge didn't follow him. 'What does that have to do with why you brought me here?'

'Well,' the spirit said, looking to Scrooge as if he was buckling under the strain already, 'I can't explain one without you understanding the other. At least, I don't think so.'

He fell silent for a moment. He was a world away from the cocky, oh-so-sure-of-himself spirit that Scrooge had met earlier in the evening of almost two hundred years ago.

'Management!' he suddenly shouted.

'Management?'

'Yes, you're familiar with that word, aren't you, Scrooge.' The spirit looked more sure of himself again. 'You know – like back home, you're the boss and Mister…'

'Cratchit?'

'Yeah, Mister Cratchit is your employee, and he's the boss of his family in a way, providing them with whatever meagre pay you give him.'

'I'll have you know; I pay Bob rather handsomely these days and—'

'Whatever,' the spirit said, glibly, his old self shining through. 'I'm just trying to help you see. Up there, in Heaven – well, it's not really up – but let's not complicate matters. Up there, there's sort of like a three-tier system. I'm at the bottom, with everyone else who's recently ceased to be, if you know what I mean. Although, that's not strictly true. I was talking to someone who's been dead for two hundred years and he's still on the bottom level. It all depends on the sort of life you lived before, well, before you kicked the big bucket.'

'I see.' Scrooge wasn't sure that he necessarily did, but he was happy that the spirit was finally at least attempting to explain the situation.

'Anyway, the next level up – they're in charge of us, I mean me, and the others like me. We never see or hear from them – well, hardly ever. And above them is the big man – or woman – depending on what you believe. Most of us are fine with that arrangement. We're stuck there but stuck there with the hope of moving on one day. There are others who aren't so blessed. They're made to float around the Earth, unable to stop or be seen, or influence anyone or anything.

'There was one. He found a way to be seen. The first time he came across, he saw his old friend making all the same mistakes he had and chiselling himself a path which would lead him to the same dark fate. He couldn't stand to watch this. So, he devised a plan. Knowing that his visiting times were short, he met with three other like-minded spirits who weren't literally being tortured but found the act of looking down on the Earth torturous enough in itself. He arranged with them to haunt his old friend and business partner, and to change his future history for the better.'

Scrooge could feel his face brighten. He knew exactly who the spirit was speaking of. Tears escaped from his eyes as the familiar name uttered from his lips. 'It was Jacob, wasn't it. Jacob Marley.'

'Yes, Scrooge, it was,' the spirit said, smiling.

'Where is he? Can I see him? Was he granted more freedom after what he did for me?'

'I don't know,' the spirit said, sounding irritated by Scrooge's barrage of questions, 'but that brings me to why you're here. Why *we* are here.

'The powers that be – the ones above us – found out about what Jacob had done. 'Meddling' they called it.'

'But—'

'I know, Scrooge,' the spirit said calmly. 'That was what they said at first. Then they had a thought: If more people did what Jacob had done, then the world would be a better place. I personally think that they were coming from a more selfish perspective. If the world became a better place and they were seen to be the ones to approve such a scheme, then the big guy would think it was all their idea.'

'So, what are you saying? That—'

'That this mission has been approved by one of the highest authorities.'

A warm glow filled Scrooge's heart. 'So, I'm not doomed? I'm not beyond redemption?'

'Um, well, no one's saying that, Scrooge,' the spirit said matter-of-factly. 'The fact is that you've done a lot of bad with your life. It's only relatively recently that you've improved, isn't it. All the good things you've done – no one's denying that they're good. However, when weighed against the lifetime of bad, they barely make a dent. This scheme should help tip the scales in your favour,' the spirit reassured him.

Scrooge felt confused again.

'With my guidance you can find the right people to help; the ones who, without your help, would have gone on to do nothing with their lives. With your help, they can change the world for the better. This, and only this, will assure you your redemption.'

'But, Spirit,' Scrooge said, 'surely every life is worth saving.'

'Yes, I know, but as I said before, we can't save every single person individually. But if we save the ones that could go on to save more people themselves…' He gestured for Scrooge to finish his thought.

'Then the world will be a better place to live in?'

'Precisely. So, what do you say? Do you want to help me, Scrooge? Or shall I drop you off back in the nineteenth century so you can continue fighting a losing battle?'

Scrooge thought for a moment. He was glad that the spirit had finally confided in him, but he still couldn't help but be suspicious. There was something niggling at him: Why had he taken so long to tell him about this? Surely, if the scheme had been endorsed by this high authority he spoke of, there would've been no problem in telling him straight away, without all the dramatics. Of course, he could always ask him why he'd delayed telling him, but would it be the truth? No, he decided that he would need to keep following the twisty-turny path that the fellow was leading him down and wait for the truth to show its face.

He turned to the spirit; conviction written all over his face. ‘Who do we help first? Grace?’

‘That’s the spirit, Scrooge old boy,’ the spirit made a show of patting him on the back. ‘No, not Grace. Not yet. We need to change the fate of someone else first. A man called Carl Phillips.’

Carl fumbled around in his pocket for his keys, and as he did, he felt something slip past his hand. The next second, he heard a clackety sound on the pavement. He knew immediately what it was: his phone. He felt a little dizzy from the beer – he couldn’t take it the way he used to – but as he looked down, he could see that it had fallen just millimetres away from a puddle of melted snow. That was where his good luck for the night ended, because as he picked it up and saw that it was undamaged, he noticed that he had five missed calls. They were all from Kate.

Oh no, he thought. I must’ve forgotten to call her to say I’d be late.

He opened the porch door, and it emitted its all-too-familiar creak, it suddenly dawned on him that he hadn’t forgotten to phone her. In fact, it was the first thing he’d done after swiping out of work, because he knew she’d worry. He’d told her that he’d sort his own tea out and not to wait. So why was she—?

And then he had his answer. He opened the living room door to be greeted by a letter, which, at first seemed to be hovering just in front of his face. Then he realised that Kate's hand was attached to it, and behind that was her beautiful face; beautiful, but more angry than usual.

'When were you going to tell me about this?' she demanded.

Carl gently eased the letter – which had the Locomart company logo at the top of it – out of her hand and read it to himself.

Dear Carl,

As you have been informed, the company has had to make some very difficult decisions recently and—

'Well?' Kate said.

She wasn't shouting at least.

Sara must have gone to bed, he deduced. 'How did you find this?'

'I was tidying through some of your clutter and I found it open on one of the shelves on your desk,' she said. 'I assumed it was important because the envelope was marked 'urgent', but maybe losing your job isn't so important. Oh – wait a minute – yes, it is, isn't it.'

Carl hated it when his wife was being sarcastic. It beat the outright rage which came out every so often, but it was just a veil, covering over that rage to protect Sara, so in some ways it was worse.

He thought about having a go at her – Outsarcasticing her, if that was a thing or even a word – but the drink had gone to his head and he knew he wasn't the sharpest when alcohol was involved. Anyway, he felt too guilty about keeping the news from them both for so long to pull her up on the technicality that she shouldn't be rifling through his private mail.

He decided to go for honesty. Yeah, hopefully that would get him the most sympathy and understanding. 'I'm sorry, honey,' he said, lowering his head for maximum effect. 'I was going to tell you… I was going to tell you weeks ago, but I could never find the right_'

'Weeks ago?' Kate was straddling the line between talking and shouting now. 'You've known for *weeks*? How many weeks?'

'Does it really matter?' Carl looked her straight in the eye now. 'You know now. I've wanted to tell you, but y'know, it's Christmas, and I didn't want to ruin it for everyone. I've been so lonely, carrying this on my own, and I just… I just didn't want to let you and Sara down.'

He could feel tears coming now, as he realised that the moment he'd been dreading for such a long time – the moment he'd imagined going off in his head over and over again, like a million bubbles bursting in a loop – had passed, and he felt just about as bad as he thought he would. All that time he had to try and guess and prepare for Kate's reaction. He'd narrowed it down to the two extremes of abject sympathy and shouty shouty panic. Even after all these years he still found it hard to predict what Kate's reactions to crises would be. It was what he reckoned attracted him to her in the first place: she was like a firecracker lodged in a five-foot skinny volcano.

Right now, she wasn't doing anything. She was just stood there in front of the sofa, her face expressionless. Of all the reactions Carl had imagined, this one hadn't come up. Then he noticed tears trickling down her flushed red cheeks. It was as if she was silently melting in front of him. He grabbed her and tried to hug her, but she refused to move her arms, as if she were an alien being who didn't understand the simple concept of the hug.

'Hey, come on. It'll be alright,' he whispered into her ear, trying to pull some kind of reaction from her.

'You don't know that,' she said finally, her voice like cracking glass.

'Well, I don't suppose I do, do I.' He could feel himself faltering now. His body shivered, then he felt Kate's hand move and settle on his back. There was a moment of silence, but not an awkward, pained silence – No, it was a silence of harmony, of mutual understanding. This is what hugs are supposed to be about, Carl thought. It felt warm but still uncertain.

'What are we going to do though, hon? I know you've always been looking to get out of there, but what is there out there? It's scary.'

'It's okay. We'll—' And then, without him really thinking about it, it just slipped out. Maybe he was more into the idea – even though he didn't exactly know what it was – than he thought. He just wanted to make her feel better. Whatever the reason, the words just came out.

'An opportunity's come up.'

Kate pushed herself away and out of the hug and looked at him.

'What kind of opportunity? Why didn't you tell me?'

'Well,' he said, 'you were a bit busy being mad at me.'

She shook her head and Carl could see the anger bubbling up again, so before she could say anything more, he said: 'It's another shop. More shop work, but it's full time, so no more random overtime shifts. Better pay as well.'

She seemed to be buying it, which made him feel much worse. Not telling her the truth about anything was much better than telling her an outright lie.

'Oh. Well, that's good then,' she said, sitting down on the sofa.

Maybe she was right. Maybe it was good. Maybe the work that Warren had for him was perfectly legit. After all, he hadn't said it was illegal. He hadn't said it was legal either, but more to the point, he hadn't said it was illegal, so maybe he should be given the benefit of the doubt.

Maybe I should stop all this maybe business and just take a risk for once in my life, he thought. Because maybe, just maybe, this opportunity could change my life.

Maybe.

9

She was in front of the frosted-up windows, finding amusement in the snow and dancing with the wind in chaotic but short movements, like a young ballerina, gaining confidence through practise. He couldn't believe he'd left it this long.

Suddenly he was there next to her, and as she spoke, her voice was as soft and warm as he remembered.

'You sought me out, my love. You sought me out.'

'Yes, my dear,' he heard his young voice say. 'I have seen the error in which I was conducting my life. Material gains engross me no longer. My aspirations are much simpler now. They are a straight line, which led me back to you. Please tell me that I have not returned in vain.'

'Oh, Ebenezer.'

'Scrooge.' A deeper voice finished his name.

'Oh, Ebenezer.' The softer voice returned.

'Scrooge.' The deep voice was getting louder and more abrupt, and yet, the word was coming from out of his angel's mouth.

'Scrooge. Scrooge. Scrooge!'

He snapped his eyes open and shuddered with shock: The spirit was floating just above him, his face, the very picture of exasperation.

'We really need to get you an alarm clock,' he said. 'Actually, that reminds me, we really need to get you a mobile phone.' The spirit was clearly more agitated than he was. It was as if he was the one who'd just been abruptly awoken from a pleasant dream and not the other way around.

He'd not had that particular dream for a long time, and it had left his head swimming with pure emotion. He'd not seen Belle for even longer; not since the ghost of Christmas past had shown him how happy she was with her family. Scrooge knew that he was happy for her, and he couldn't change what he'd done and how he'd broken her heart, but still, it would be nice to see her again, he thought. Maybe when I go—

'Come on, Scrooge, stop your daydreaming,' the spirit said.

'What's got your goat?' Scrooge asked wearily.

'What? Oh, nothing.' He had a faraway look in his eyes. 'It's just that, y'know, it's our first mission today, and if anything goes wrong, I'll get the blame. Those up above won't be best pleased with me, cos the big guy above them won't be best pleased with *them*. Y'know what I mean?'

Scrooge decided to just nod in apparent agreement. He'd just accepted that he would never fully comprehend all the nonsense that came out of his mysterious companion's mouth.

'Look at the time. It's nearly time for breakfast,' the spirit said, pointing to the thing he called a "digibox" underneath the thing he called a "television". There was no clock on the display, but there were numbers lit up in bright red which read *7:55*.

Scrooge went downstairs to breakfast feeling as fresh as a daisy – the bed had been far more comfortable than he was used to – and when he saw Mister and Mrs Ward, he stopped just short of hugging the two of them. He settled for wishing them a happy Christmas and sat down to eat what looked like the best breakfast he had yet to taste.

'Well, I'm glad you liked it, Mister Scrooge,' Mrs Ward said afterwards, sounding well and truly flattered with his compliments, and considerably less frosty than their first encounter. 'Was the black pudding to your taste?'

'It most certainly was, Mrs Ward, and if I don't have one tomorrow, there will be no consoling me.'

Scrooge wanted to stay a while longer and converse with them. The two of them were most pleasant company and reminded Scrooge very much so of Bertie and Mary Wilkins. Something suddenly occurred to him: back in the nineteenth century, they would be missing him. They would've gone up to his empty bed chambers and, failing to find him anywhere else, they would have surely summoned the police by now. Then it occurred to him that Bertie and Mary Wilkins would be long dead. From his perspective, he only saw them last a couple of nights ago. Or was it just one night? He could feel a pain throbbing in the side of his head, and he knew then and there that he would never get the hang of all this time travel nonsense. It did comfort him slightly that if the spirit could so easily bring him to the future, then surely, he could return him to the present just as easily when their work was done.

Just at that moment, as if he knew what Scrooge was thinking, the spirit appeared; he'd reluctantly agreed to give Scrooge some privacy during breakfast, so he could conduct a normal conversation in which all the participants were aware of each other.

'Come on, Scrooge,' he said. 'We've got work to do.'

After a cautious walk back down to the main street – he shivered as the nightmare of last night's events came back to him – Scrooge hailed a taxi and they were off, back into Central London.

'Where y'headed to, young sir?' the cabbie said cheekily. Scrooge looked to the spirit for guidance.

'Tell him to drop us at Oxford Street,' he said.

'Why? Is that where Carl lives?' Scrooge asked, forgetting once more that they weren't alone.

'Y'what, mate?'

'Oh, nothing. Sorry,' Scrooge said, 'I was just thinking aloud. Could you drop us – I mean me – at Oxford Street, please?'

'No problem, mate. I'm always talking to myself. Don't see what's wrong with it m'self. It beats keeping it all locked up inside, don't it. I mean, it helps me to think, strangely enough.'

As the cabbie carried on, the spirit completely ignored him and told Scrooge what was waiting at Oxford Street: A mobile phone stall. Scrooge understood just two of those words, but that was okay because the spirit explained the rest.

Apparently, mobile phones – or mobiles for short – were what ninety nine percent of the population owned in the twenty first century, and they couldn't live without them. Scrooge found this hard to believe, but that wasn't the point. The point was, that everyone was reachable all the time. If you needed to talk to someone on the other side of the world, then they were just the touch of a button away.

'But who am I going to want to "phone", as you put it, Spirit?' Scrooge whispered. 'Everyone I know is almost two hundred years in the past and long dead.'

'Me,' the spirit said sharply.

'But, Spirit, you're right here.'

'Are you slow, or just old?' Before Scrooge had time to be offended, the spirit continued. 'It's a way of helping you fit in. Not everyone is going to be so accepting of an old man who holds conversations with himself. Basically, whenever we want to talk to one another, you just hold the phone up to your ear like this.' He mimed the movement. 'And then we can talk as if you're not mad and I'm not dead.'

'Right, well, yes,' Scrooge said. 'When you put it like that, it makes perfect sense, Spirit.'

After another confusing conversation – this time, with the young lady at the mobile phone stall – Scrooge was now the proud owner of his first mobile phone, and after yet more confusion and a lot of help from the spirit, he was on the underground train network, or, "the tube". Just as he was getting used to the cramped and claustrophobia inducing conditions, the spirit announced that it was time for them to get off.

'That was quick,' Scrooge said.

'Just try to keep moving and you'll be fine.'

'What do you mean?' Scrooge said, but as the huge crowd of people who were on the cramped carriage suddenly pushed forward, he knew exactly what the spirit meant. It was like a wave that he could get caught up in. When he'd got on the train at Oxford Circus it hadn't been anywhere near as busy as it was now. Of course, he was used to hordes of people living in his London, but Scrooge was used to more organised hordes.

It was an unwritten rule that everyone moving forwards would stick to the left and everyone moving toward the people who were moving forward would stick to the right. This was just pure chaos, and he started to panic.

'It's okay, Scrooge,' the spirit shouted. He'd moved forward to the front of the crowd. 'Just aim toward me and you'll be fine.'

It took some doing, and it seemed to Scrooge, for a while at least, that he wasn't moving at all. He felt like a small and fragile rowing boat in the middle of a vast ocean, with no landmarks to navigate by. He could feel the panic taking over; his heart beating faster; everyone staring at him. They knew! They knew he didn't belong there. He wished that he could just close his eyes and go home, but he couldn't close his eyes; he had to see ahead of him. And then he caught a glimpse of something in another man's eyes, and then a woman's. In fact, everyone around him wore the same expression: a look of quiet desperation. They wanted the same thing, to get home to their families. It was the spark he needed to spur him onward.

Eventually, he got to the barrier and did what everyone else did to get through. The crowd thinned out, and he was relieved to see two escalators just ahead, which forced everyone into two neat rows moving upward and out of the stifling air of the underground.

For once, the spirit seemed sympathetic to his plight.

'I always used to hate travelling by tube,' he said. 'Y'can't breathe down there. Now, I can't breathe at all, of course.'

Scrooge hadn't failed to notice all the little comments the spirit had made about his own death. Obviously, he wasn't happy about it, but all the spirits that visited him on that fateful night – apart from Jacob – had nothing to say about their own experiences with death. They were more concerned with helping him improve his life. According to this spirit, all that had been a waste of time anyway. Scrooge still couldn't accept that. There was something else going on, and little did he know, but he would soon discover what that something was.

A couple of blocks later they reached a building which looked to Scrooge to be very much like every other building in London. The lower half was all modern and shiny and the top half seemed to be an entirely other building, which, despite the efforts of modern-day architects, stubbornly sat there with its statuesque motif, refusing to accept that things had moved on.

'This is the place,' the spirit said grimly. 'This is the supermarket where Carl Phillips works.'

'What the blazes is a "supermarket"?' Scrooge said into the phone whilst looking straight at the spirit. 'What an odd turn of phrase that is.'

The spirit looked at him with exasperation, probably for the thousandth time since they'd met. 'It's not really that odd. It's just a place everyone goes to get their weekly shopping. It's got everything under one roof, so people don't have to walk all around the city for what they want.'

He still didn't quite understand, but that was nothing new, so he just ignored it and moved on. 'So, what do we do now?'

'Now, Scrooge,' the spirit said, with a distant and lost look in his eyes, 'we go shopping.'

Scrooge followed him through the automatic doors and picked up a metal framed basket in which he would place his shopping. According to his ghostly companion, in the twenty first century, and for most of the latter part of the twentieth century, shopping had become more than just a necessity: it was a national pastime. Apparently, a lot of folk went shopping to make themselves feel better. This was called 'retail therapy'.

'What an odd world it has become,' Scrooge mused.

'I won't even get you started on online shopping then,' the spirit said dryly.

Scrooge looked around at some of the strange objects on the shelves. 'What's this?' he asked, picking up a square piece of plastic with a colourful picture of a rather scantily clad young lady on the front.

'What? Oh, that's a CD. A compact disc. People listen to music on them, kind of like a record player or gramophone. Have gramophones been invented in your time yet?'

'Um, no, that doesn't sound familiar,' Scrooge said, hesitantly. 'And what's this?' he said, picking up another, larger plastic case.

'It's a DVD. Look,' the spirit said bluntly, 'are you going to ask me about everything in here? Because that's going to take all day. We need to find Carl Phillips. That's the priority – That's the mission.'

'What about Grace?' Scrooge couldn't help but sound like a spoilt child who'd been chastised for misbehaving. 'I thought she was the priority.'

'Yes, yes, of course. But it's all connected, isn't it. It's all the same mission.'

'Oh,' Scrooge said. 'Well, I didn't know that. You didn't tell me that, Spirit.'

'I didn't? I didn't, did I.' He cursed. 'I wasn't supposed to tell you that 'til later. They're not going to be happy,' he said, looking upward. 'Just forget I told you that, Scrooge, okay?'

'Okay, you got it.' Scrooge's attempt at a modern vernacular – which he'd heard several times on the TV last night – sounded odd coming out of his nineteenth century mouth, so he silently promised himself never to try it again. He also told himself not to forget what the spirit had let slip. So, they were connected: Grace and Carl Phillips.

Interesting, Scrooge thought. The first strand of the mystery has unravelled. Maybe if I keep pushing him and asking pointless questions, he'll let a bit more slip and I'll have more idea of—

'There he is!' the spirit shouted, nearly deafening Scrooge.

Ahead of them, at the end of the aisle was a young man, who Scrooge guessed to be in his late thirties, stacking a shelf.

'That's him? The young man we're here to help?' Scrooge said, forgetting to lift the phone up to his ear.

'Um, yeah. I guess.' He seemed suddenly hesitant.

'Well, is he, or isn't he?'

'It's complicated, Scrooge, but yes. Yes, we're here to help him.'

'Alright,' said Scrooge firmly. 'So, let's go over there and tell him.'

'Tell him what?'

'That we're here to save him, of course,' Scrooge said, a little too loudly. At that point, they both noticed that some of the customers had stopped moving and were staring at them – well, at Scrooge – and were backing away.

'Scrooge. Phone!' the spirit said through gritted teeth.

'What?' Scrooge whispered.

'Put the phone to your ear.'

'Oh, yes. I forgot about that, sorry.' Scrooge did as he said and smiled innocently at the people that looked just a little bit frightened of him. This didn't really help, but luckily, they all continued backing away and silently decided it was best not to get involved with whatever it was that was happening to the crazy old man. 'Shall we go over and talk to him then, Spirit?' Scrooge said, this time into the phone.

'No,' the spirit said, attempting and failing to grab Scrooge's arm.

'What? Why ever not, Spirit? You said—'

'Look, Scrooge. We can't just go up to people and tell them we're here to save them. I mean, what would you do if someone did that_' he stopped, as he realised the flaw in his question. 'Okay, you're a bad example. In this century, people are a bit more… cynical. You go up to Carl Phillips and tell him that you're here to save him, then best case scenario: he'll dismiss you as a religious fruitcake. Worst case scenario? He'll get security on your back, and we both know how well that went for you last time.'

'Yes, I suppose so,' Scrooge conceded. 'So, what do you want me to do? It would help if you told me exactly what was going on.'

He turned and stared at Scrooge. He looked like he wanted to tell him more, but something was stopping him. 'I – I can't. Not yet.' He sounded like a broken man. 'It's been so long since I... since... I'm not sure what to do,' he finally admitted. 'I thought I'd know when we found him, but he just seems so normal. Doesn't look like he could—'

He suddenly stopped and seemed to have convinced himself of something. He'd regained at least some control and his expression seemed more fixed and focused as he said: 'Follow him. Follow him, Scrooge, and see who he talks to.'

So, that's exactly what Scrooge did. Wherever Carl went, he went. For the whole day, his prey didn't really speak to anyone, except to point out where certain products were around the store. In fact, he seemed rather lonely and glum, Scrooge thought. Thankfully, the spirit did elaborate a little bit and told him to narrow down Carl's encounters to anyone "dodgy looking", but still, no one fitting that description or otherwise approached him. It had been several hours, and Scrooge was starting to flag. He wasn't used to walking around quite so much, and it seemed that since he had arrived in the twenty first century, that was all he'd been doing, with several bouts of running thrown in for good measure.

'Spirit, can we have a rest for a—'

'Where did he go?' the spirit shouted. 'You were supposed to be watching him.'

'You were watching him as well,' Scrooge said.

'Yes, but I—'

'Can I help you there?' a new voice chimed in from behind Scrooge, making the co-conspirators jump. They both turned around and saw Carl stood there with his arms crossed.

Scrooge froze and didn't know what to do.

'Look,' Carl said under his breath, 'I'm not being funny, but it feels like you've been shadowing me all morning – always there in the corner of my eye. I thought you were going to follow me into the back when I pretended to go to the toilet.'

'Humbug,' Scrooge said. The word just popped out of his mouth in a panic.

'I'm sorry?' Carl said, looking around to see if his line manager was watching.

'Humbugs,' Scrooge said, trying to compose a look on his face as if Carl was the one not making any sense. 'I'm looking for humbugs. Do you still have them here, young sir?'

Carl stared at Scrooge, trying to figure out what his game was, but he decided to just play along. After all, it wasn't his first encounter with eccentric old customers.

'Humbugs are on aisle two with the rest of the sweets.'

'Thank you,' Scrooge said, and then stopped sharply, because the spirit was suddenly floating right in front of Carl, glaring at him and shifting his gaze, as if he was looking for tiny defects in his skin.'

'What are you looking at?' Carl asked Scrooge, his patience wearing thin.

'Does it feel colder to you? I mean, compared to a moment ago,' Scrooge asked.

'Um, no. Well, maybe. Why do you ask?'

'Oh, nothing. No reason,' Scrooge said, trying not to look at the spirit. 'I'll leave you alone now, I've taken up enough of your time. Have a happy Christmas, young man.

'Um, yeah. You too.'

Carl was still looking at him as if he had something hanging out of his nose, ear, or both, so Scrooge backed away, almost tripping over a mother and her pram.

'Row two for humbugs you say?'

'Yeah, that way,' Carl pointed, and Scrooge made a show of heading in that direction but walked straight past them – he never did like humbugs – and out of the shop.

Carl watched as the old man walked straight past the sweets and out of the shop. Strange guy, he thought, but at least he'd been a distraction from the constant conflict in his head.

It was like the old cartoons. He had an angel on one shoulder, telling him what a good man he was – the voice of this particular angel was comedy *oirish,* for some reason – and telling him he should do the right and moral thing. On the other shoulder was a little red devil telling him the opposite, in a voice not dissimilar to the actor Joe Pesci.

The more he thought about it, the less convinced he was that Warren's 'opportunity' was legal. He still hated himself for telling Kate that it was more shop work. The truth was, he had absolutely no idea what it was, making it virtually impossible to decide what to do one way or the other. To make matters worse, Warren hadn't turned up for his shift and he wasn't answering his phone or responding to any of his texts, so he couldn't ask him what it was until later, at which point he could well imagine that the pressure to say "yes" would be turned right up to eleven.

The imaginary Irish angel on his shoulder was right: he should do the right thing, and the right thing was whatever would help his family, wasn't it? No matter what. No! There are limits, he told himself sternly, as he continued stacking up the tinned cranberries into a neat little tower.

After another agonising five minutes of going around in philosophical circles, he came to a decision. And that was, to not make a decision until he knew exactly what the work was. I'll find out tonight, he told himself, and I'll give Warren a firm 'yes' or a firm 'no'. That's it. As simple as that.

Five minutes after an all-too-brief recess, the debate in his head started up again at full throttle.

'Where did you vanish off to?' Scrooge asked the spirit when he reappeared in the carpark five minutes later, this time remembering to hold the phone to his ear.

'I don't know,' the spirit said flatly, 'I just needed some alone time. Spirits need solitude sometimes as well y'know.'

'Yes, yes, I can well understand that,' Scrooge said. 'It must get rather tiring, being all aloof and keeping secrets all the time.'

'What's that supposed to mean?' The spirit's voice was suddenly several octaves higher.

'I think you know what it means, Spirit.'

'Maybe you should stop calling me that,' he said, looking around to see if anyone was listening to Scrooge's half of the conversation.

'Well, if you could be bothered to tell me your name, Spirit, then maybe I could address you by it, but since we've met, you've not—'

'Jack,' he said, solemnly. 'My name is Jack. Jack Thornhill'

Scrooge fell silent for a moment. He was stunned and couldn't quite believe that the Spirit had finally told him his name. It shouldn't have been that big a revelation, but considering the minimal information Jack had shared with him thus far, Scrooge felt like he'd just been handed the biggest secret in the universe.

'Jack,' Scrooge said, mostly to himself. 'That's a good, strong name.'

'Well, I'm glad you approve of it, old man,' Jack said sharply.

'So, what's our next move, Jack? It felt peculiar to Scrooge to be referring to the spirit by name. None of the other spirits had volunteered their names and he'd been too scared to ask.

'Our next move,' Jack said, 'is to wait here for Carl to finish his shift and then follow him, to see who he meets up with.'

'Alright. I don't suppose it's worth me asking why, is it?'

Jack turned to Scrooge and without saying anything, he smiled.

'Didn't think so,' Scrooge said with a sigh.

For the next few hours they sat there on a bench near a trolley bay, waiting for Carl to finish. They took turns standing up to watch the doors of the shop. Scrooge thought this was rather unfair, as Jack didn't have any muscles or in fact any real legs to strain, so he could have stood there the whole time. Conversation was minimal because, well, Scrooge wasn't sure how to make small talk with a ghost, especially one who from the period of time they were currently abiding in. The only things he could think to say were questions about everything around him and he was getting tired of Jack's blunt and dismissive non-answers, so he ended up saying nothing.

Several hours of silence later, Jack got a familiar focussed look in his eye again. 'There! There he is, Scrooge. Get after him.'

For the last hour or so, Jack had been on spying duty and Scrooge hadn't complained, but now his bones and muscles had something to say on the matter.

'Ooh,' Scrooge moaned, 'my body's seized up. I'll need a minute.'

'You haven't got a minute,' Jack snapped. 'Another few seconds and we'll lose him completely.'

Scrooge looked up, and although the car park wasn't particularly crowded, past the gates there were rows and rows of people, and if Carl managed to get there before him, he'd never find him again.

'Come on, Scrooge! He's nearly at the gate!'

'Okay, okay. I'm doing my best,' Scrooge groaned. But his best wasn't good enough, because although he was moving as fast as he could, the younger and fitter Carl was faster. Scrooge was only halfway across the carpark when his prey got to the gate and disappeared into the crowd. He looked up at Jack, half-hoping that he'd tell him to forget about it.

'Great!' Jack shouted. 'Now we'll never find him again.'

Scrooge sighed his relief, but it was short lived.

'We have to find him, Scrooge. I didn't come this far to fail now. I'll fly ahead and see if I can spot him. Try to keep up, will you?'

Before he could protest, the spirit did just that, and Scrooge was left alone. Looking at the rows and rows of people ahead of him, just outside the gates, an overwhelming feeling of despair came over Scrooge. How was he supposed to find one person, in amongst the seemingly millions of people in London? He was reminded of his promise to find Charles' son. Somehow, that hadn't seemed quite as taxing an idea as finding Carl, but it reminded him of how vital it was that he get back to his own time, and the only way to do that was to do what Jack asked.

He was at the gate now, and he took a deep breath as he stepped out onto the street. Surprisingly, he wasn't immediately swept away by the masses; there was a small gap in which he could breathe, so before going any further, he tried to see if he could see Carl, or at least the back of Carl's head.

'Still looking for humbugs are you?'

The voice came from just behind him, so Scrooge turned around to face him. Carl was stood just behind the brick pillar that the gate was attached to.

'Who are you?' he said. 'And why are you following me?' He shouted to make himself heard above the crowd.

Scrooge hesitated for a moment. He'd not expected to find Carl at all, let alone, so quickly, and he was hoping to have more time to prepare for what he was going to say to him. 'My name is Ebenezer Scrooge,' he said resolutely, 'and I'm here to help you.'

'To help me? You don't even know me.'

'I know your name, Carl Phillips. That's a start, isn't it?'

'You could've asked anyone in the shop that,' Carl said, firmly.

'Yes, but why would I do that?' Just to – Just to—'

'Just to creep me out, I reckon.'

'No, no, no! Creep you out? Listen, young man. Maybe we should go somewhere a bit more private.'

'With you? I don't think so, pal,' Carl said, as he slowly backed away. Scrooge could see that he was trying to get away from him. I can hardly blame him, he thought. If I was in his shoes, I'd jolly well be doing the same thing. If only Jack could have told me what or who it is I'm supposed to be saving him from. Then suddenly, an icy chill passed right through him and Jack was there, next to him.

'Tell him not to do it. Go on, tell him, Scrooge.'

'Not to do what?!' Scrooge yelled. 'I'm sorry, Spirit – Jack, but your constant mystery is driving me to distraction. Once and for all, just tell me why I'm here. How do I save him? What did he do?'

He really is mad, Carl thought. Maybe I should help him. He must have a family. He's probably wandered off, escaped his care home or something.

Jack hesitated and opened his mouth several times before any actual words came out. Scrooge was about to push him for answers again, but then he finally spoke.

'For a start, you're not here to save him. Not really.'

'Then why, Spirit? Why am I here?'

'You're here to stop him.'

No one else here cares, Carl thought. There's an old vulnerable man lost in the middle of the city, talking to an imaginary friend, and they're all just walking past as if it's nothing. The spirit of twenty first century Christmas. Beautiful. He walked back over to where Scrooge was flapping his arms.

'Basically, you're here to stop him from robbing a shop,' Jack said. He was staring coldly at Carl.

'He robs a shop? I'm here to stop him from robbing a shop?' Scrooge said. 'I'm sorry, Jack, but isn't that a job for the police? It seems a bit elaborate for you to whisk me here to—'

'What are you talking about?' Carl said, joining the conversation. Scrooge fell silent, as he thought about how he was going to explain.

'Are you… Are you planning on robbing a shop?' he whispered to Carl.

'What? What are you talking about?' Carl couldn't believe what he was hearing. How could he? But then, it all clicked into place: Warren.

'He's bound to deny it, isn't he,' Jack said, still glaring at Carl. 'Ask him if he's planning on killing anyone while he's at it. Go on.'

'What? He's going to kill someone?'

'Yeah, he's—'

'What are you on about?' Carl said, upset, but still trying to keep his voice down. 'Where are you getting this from? Do you know Warren?' He grabbed Scrooge by the shoulders as he fired questions at him.

'Warren?' Scrooge said.

'Are you psychic or something?'

'Ah! That proves it's him,' Jack said victoriously. 'Why would he ask you that if he wasn't planning on doing it? Tell him you are. Tell him you're psychic.'

'Look, Jack. He doesn't seem like a killer to me,' Scrooge started.

'I'm not! I'm not a killer. Why would I kill anyone?' Carl suddenly remembered where he was and whispered. 'Who are you really? Why are you doing this?'

'I am who I said I am.' Scrooge turned back to Jack. 'I still can't believe what you're saying, but surely now that we've told him, he won't do it.'

'It's not that simple,' Jack said, his face taking on a whole new level of seriousness. 'Don't you remember what I said? You have to do whatever I tell you to. You have to stop him, to make sure he doesn't kill… anyone. Scrooge, you may have to do the unthinkable.'

'If you're saying what I think you're saying, I'm not – I'll talk him out of it. I'll tie him up, but—'

'You'll have to catch him first, Scrooge.'

Scrooge turned around.

Carl was running.

The masses of commuters had turned out quite conveniently for Carl's escape from the mad old man and his invisible friend. All thoughts of helping him were gone now. He just wanted to get to Warren and shake the truth out of him.

It occurred to him that he should've caught the next tube home and forgotten about the whole thing, but something had stopped him. He couldn't believe that Warren would knowingly – willingly involve him in what the old man had claimed he was caught up in. At a push he could imagine him robbing a shop, but murder? No way. Not an ice cube's chance in his old freezer that kept going on the fritz. He must've gotten mixed up with some bad people. The least he could do was warn Warren before he got in too deep.

'That might've been our only chance to stop him, and you've blown it, Scrooge. You blew it!' Jack shouted as he flew alongside him, ignoring all the Londoners he was passing through.

Scrooge didn't bother responding to the spirit's criticism, he was too preoccupied with finding Carl. Not an easy task, but he guessed Carl would be one of the only ones trying to run through the human traffic.

'Couldn't you've just strangled him? Is that too much to ask, after what I'm trying to do for you?' Jack shouted.

'After what you're doing for *me*?' Scrooge said. 'You really think that I still believe that you're doing this for *me*?'

'I am. I am—'

'Why would a spirit – someone who's died – ask me to commit the ultimate sin? Why would They get me to do that? No, my transparent friend, you're in this for one person, and one alone: Yourself. And as soon as I find out what you're after, I'll—'

'You'll *what*, Scrooge?' Jack suddenly looked more controlled and composed again. 'Your life is in my hands, whether you believe what I'm telling you or not. Who was it that brought you here? And who is it that can take you back again? Who is the *only* one that can take you back again?'

'You... you are.'

'That's right: Me.'

He felt utterly defeated. He realised that he had no choice but to follow Jack down whatever dark path he led him, but how could he possibly justify it? If he did make it back to his own time, how could he live with himself, even if he did manage to find George? How could he look Charles and his son in the eyes, knowing what he'd done to get back? He felt like crawling down a hole and never coming out.

'Look, Scrooge... Ebenezer.' The spirit sounded softer for a moment, more friendly and empathetic.

Scrooge thought it was probably just another one of his manipulations, but he listened.

'I don't *want* Carl to die, not really. You probably don't believe me, and I don't blame you, but I don't.'

'I *don't* believe you,' Scrooge said looking away from him, trying to distract himself from his misery by focussing on the passers-by, who apparently were oblivious to the fact that he was talking to himself.

'Good people die every day,' Jack said solemnly, 'but good people sometimes do bad things. They make mistakes – irreparable mistakes. With this new project of ours, we can make the irreparable, repairable, if that makes any sense.'

'No, Spirit, it does not,' Scrooge said matter-of-factly. 'You want to prevent bad things from happening by doing bad things – no – by getting *me* to do bad things. That makes no sense.'

'Maybe not from your skewed perspective, Scrooge, but I've seen all the good and all the bad at once, and believe me, some sacrifices are worth it.'

'That's easy to say when you're not the one making them,' Scrooge said. 'There must be another way. Like you said, Carl is a good person who's about to make a mistake. A terrible mistake. We can stop him. Talk to him. I bet he's already thinking about what I said, and who knows? Maybe just by what happened back there we've already changed things.'

'No. No, we haven't, Scrooge,' Jack said. 'We'd both know it, believe me.'

'There you go with the mystery again.'

'I'm sorry, Scrooge, but it's necessary. Maybe you're right though. Maybe there's another way.'

'So, fly up there and use your "perspective" to find him, and then, who knows what will happen.'

Without another word, the spirit did just that and almost immediately sped back down.

'There must've been a hold up or something,' he said excitedly. 'He's not too far ahead, waiting for the lights to change.'

Carl had been thinking about what he was going to say to Warren. How was he going to convince him that he already knew what he was going to ask him to do? Surely, he couldn't know that what he was getting involved in would lead to someone's death. He didn't know Warren that well, but he didn't seem like someone who'd be okay with that. Did he? Then again, he knew precisely squat about the crazy old man, and yet, here he was acting on the words of warning he'd thrown his way.

There was something about him that made him believe it. Probably because I had my doubts about it in the first place, he thought. I just needed another push to convince me that there was something wrong. Suddenly, the push of the crowd snapped him out of his thoughts as the lights changed.

'He's on the other side now,' Jack shouted down from on high. 'If you run, you should catch him.'

Scrooge was only half listening as he tried to run forward through the crowd. He noticed an odd space where no one was stood. A circle which people seemed to be avoiding. He thought nothing of it, other than that it might help him get ahead, but then, before he knew what was happening, he was flying through the air. His feet and legs framed the buildings above and then a huge impact shocked him to his core and his whole body felt like it was broken.

He was flat on the pavement, lying on a layer of ice. As he slowly realised what he'd done, time seemed to start up again and the crowd moved on around him.

'Scrooge! Scrooge, are you okay?' He could hear Jack, but it sounded like he was impossibly far away.

'Hey! Stop! Wait!' A new but familiar voice struck Scrooge's ears. 'Can't you see that someone's fallen? Animals,' she muttered under her breath. 'Come on, hun',' she said to someone that Scrooge couldn't yet see,' give me a hand.'

Everything looked blurry, but a face came into focus as she leant over him.

'Hey, we've met, haven't we?' she said. 'Ebenezer? Ebenezer Scrooge, isn't it? Don't know how I remembered that. I'm usually rubbish with names.'

'G-Grace?' Scrooge stammered. The cold was seeping through him now. Right through to his bones.

'That's right,' Grace said, 'at least your memory's not damaged, eh? Are you okay?'

His vision was still a little blurred, but he could see her. He was pleased to see her. The first friendly face he'd seen when he'd arrived. Her face seemed to glow amongst all the darkness of the night sky.

'You know this guy?'

That voice. He knew that voice, too.

'Yeah, I helped him last night. Are you okay, Mister Scrooge? You've not broken anything, have you?'

Nothing felt broken anymore. He just had a general shocked feeling throughout his body which had come from being vertical one second, and horizontal on the cold ground the next. 'I-I'm okay, I think.'

His vision was starting to sharpen up. Jack was hovering high above, circling around and stopping to look down every few seconds. He was in a panic about something, but why wouldn't he come down? He was there as well. Same clothes, same face. Exactly the same face.

'Jack? Is that you?'

Grace turned to the young man next to her: the young man that was gawping down at him. 'You know him, too?' she asked. 'Why didn't you—'

'I've never seen him before in my life,' the young man said.

'Jack, how are you doing that?' His vision was back to normal, but the confusion remained. 'How are you down here? How can Grace see you? How can you be down here and up there?'

'What's he on about?' he could hear Grace saying.

Scrooge looked up and pointed at where Jack's spirit was, and just as he did, he broke out of his circular motions and disappeared into the cloudy night sky.

10

Carl looked over his shoulder for the millionth time. He knew it was a pointless exercise; even if the old man was still following him, he had as little chance of spotting him as he did him. The crowds were suffocating and no one – except maybe a small child – could possibly move independently of the human traffic and track him down.

During the course of his slower-than-slow journey on foot, he had thought about heading for the next tube station and going home. I could just tell Kate that the opportunity fell through, he thought. But then she'd be mad at me, and probably accuse me of not trying hard enough. I could explain that an old guy on the street warned me that someone would get killed if I went through with it, but she's not going to believe that.

He felt like he was being pulled towards one destination now, and the constant movement of the shoppers was forcing his hand – or feet, as it were.

I can still say no, he told himself. It's an easy word to say: no. It's shorter than 'yes', so that helps. It takes around the same amount of time to say, but technically it is shorter. Sometimes Carl's internal debates drove him mad. If only, he often thought, he could have these debates out loud with other people, but he just couldn't. Whenever he found himself cornered into an argument and he needed to put his point across, the words in his head left his mouth, but somewhere in between they lost all sense and meaning and he froze up.

This time would be different. This time, someone's life was at stake, probably. Then suddenly, there it was: Hartley's bar, just across the street. The sign flickered. He'd always noticed it and had meant to ask the owners if it was intentional or just dodgy wiring. In that moment it seemed to be deliberately trying to attract his attention.

He moved forward with the flow of the crowd, and just as they got to the other side of the street he broke away and looked into the window to see if his dodgy friend was there. And, lo and behold, there he was, making a pest of himself with his trademark seasonal dating appliance: mistletoe. It looked as though he'd just struck out again: a girl wearing a bright, glittery red top, flashing in the light was backing away from him with a look of disgust on her face. Carl would have almost felt sorry for him, if his anger hadn't been getting in the way. He took a deep breath and went inside.

'Hey, buddy. Where've you been?' Warren said, as if it was just another lads' night out. 'You've been missing all my success with the ladies. I came this close to getting someone's phone number, but she forgot to give me all the digits and—'

'That's fascinating, mate, you'll have to tell me the whole story when we're cell mates and run out of things to say,' he said, impatiently and a little too loudly.

'Whoa, whoa! What are you on about, man?' Warren said in a whisper. This was pointless, it was so noisy in there, even if anyone was interested in what either of them were saying they wouldn't have been able to hear it.

'What exactly are you mixed up in?' Carl demanded.

Warren fell silent and gestured for Carl to follow him to a miraculously empty table. The stools surrounding it were ridiculously high, so they stood either side of it.

'Well?'

'What exactly is it that you've heard, mate?' Warren shouted above the music.

Carl thought for a moment. There was no point in telling him how he thought he might know about what was going down, so he just asked him outright. 'Are you planning on robbing a shop?'

He could see that his friend was shocked and at the same time, trying to think of a way of lying his way out of it. If it had been quieter, he would've been able to hear the cogs grinding away. 'You are, aren't you,' he said. 'What's the matter with you? And why exactly did you think I was going to help you with that?'

'I don't know. Revenge?'

'Revenge?' Carl said. 'What are you on about? Revenge for what?'

'Oh, so you *don't* know anything,' Warren said, a little too smugly for Carl's liking. 'Well, whoever told you our plans obviously missed out a major plot point. It's Locomart we're going to be stealing from.'

Carl couldn't believe what he was hearing. 'Our shop? The place where we work?'

'We'll be wearing masks, mate.'

'The company that pays our wages? Are you_'

'Not for much longer, they won't be, mate. They're making us redundant, remember?'

Carl stared at him, trying to fathom why he would do anything so stupid. Even more so, he wanted to know why Warren had assumed that he wouldn't have a problem helping him with something so stupid.

'What's the matter with you?' he said, still looking his idiotic friend in the eye. 'Yes, they're making us redundant, but that doesn't justify what you're talking about. You've been to the meetings. You know that their backs are against the wall.'

'Are they? Are they really?' Warren said, his face like stone. 'You don't think there's other ways they could deal with it? Throwing us out on the street? That's their big solution?'

'If you've got such great ideas, then why don't you share them with the big bosses?'

'They don't listen to the little people – the cogs in the machine – you know that,' Warren said coldly. 'We're just the ones who do the hard work so they can get rich.'

'Y'know what, mate, I agree with you,' Carl said, 'I really do, but that doesn't justify this. I'll help you find a job. We'll help each other. This – what you've got planned – is not an option.' For a moment, Carl thought some of his words were getting through, but then something else grabbed his friend's attention: His phone.

Warren took the phone out of his pocket and his face dropped as he looked at the screen and the caller ID. He looked gravely at Carl. 'There's no option for me, mate. I ran out of such luxuries a long time ago.' He put the phone to his ear and the tone of his voice changed. He was clearly afraid of whoever it was on the other end of the line.

'Did you hear that?' he said to the person on the other end of the phone. There was silence, as Warren listened to the answer. Then: 'Yes, I thought you were probably listening. Do you want me to put him on?' Warren looked up at Carl and passed the phone over to him. 'He wants to speak to you.'

Carl took it off him and looked at it, as if he'd never seen a phone before and he was disgusted by it. The caller ID read: 'unknown number' and he went to put it to his ear and then stopped himself. This was a turning point; he could feel it. This was where he could get off the road the old man seemed to have laid out for him.

'No,' he said firmly to Warren. 'I'm not speaking to whoever that is.'

A look of panic swept over Warren's face.

'I'm sorry,' Carl said, 'but – no, no – why do I do that? I'm not sorry. Not at all. I'm not going to speak to whoever's behind this dodgy little scheme of yours, because if I don't speak to him then there's no way I'll become involved in this sordid little business, and I can just walk away. And you should too, mate. Maybe it won't be as easy for you, but you can.' He handed the phone back to Warren and he put it back to his ear.

'No, no. I didn't think you would be,' he said to whoever was on the other end. I can find someone else.'

Carl didn't hear the rest of Warren's half of the conversation because he walked away. It was over for him. As he held the door open for a loved-up couple, he found himself already thinking positive thoughts again.

He got out. He'd escaped what fate supposedly had in store for him – although, he still didn't know how the old man had known about it. Maybe he'd been a part of it and he'd gotten out too. Whatever it was, he was grateful for his intervention and he could now get on with his life, conscience clear.

He started to think about what on earth he was going to tell Kate. He didn't really need to tell her all the seedy little details, but he'd have to at least placate her with something. Who knew? Maybe another opportunity would present itself soon, so neither of them would have to worry so much. Whatever happened, they would face it as a couple – as a family.

I should phone her, he thought. Let her know I'm safe and on my way home. At that moment, as he stepped out onto the street, he felt his phone vibrating in his pocket. She must be ringing to see where I am, he thought. I thought I told her I was meeting Warren tonight. Oh well, it'll be nice to hear her voice anyway.

'Hi, hun,' he said into the phone.

'Hi, hun.' Carl jumped, because not only did the voice not belong to Kate, it was coming from behind him and was accompanied by something cold and firm prodding into his back. He instinctively started to turn around.

'Oh, I wouldn't do that if I were you, Mister Phillips,' the voice spat into his ear. 'If I were you, I'd do the wise thing and just keep moving, and yes, that is a gun I'm pointing into your back. Can't remember if I left the safety on, so it's probably best not to try anything heroic slash stupid.'

Carl's mind was racing. A million different thoughts and reactions bounced around in his head and almost instantaneously cancelled each other out as he realised how stupid they were. Turn around and grab the gun. Grab the gun and run. Just run and hope?

He'd heard somewhere on telly that people were capable of superhuman feats once their adrenalin kicked in, but now that it was happening to him, he thought that maybe that was a slight exaggeration, since the best he was doing was walking down a dark alley in the direction that the stranger with the gun in his hand was pointing.

'You're doing great, Mister Phillips.' The voice behind the gun sounded more like a dentist or physical therapist admiring his first tentative steps on the road to recovery than what he really was: a psycho with a gun. 'Nearly there now, Mister Phillips. Just a bit further and we'll be at the perfect distance.'

'The perfect distance for what?' Carl managed to ask. At that moment, they passed some boxes, and as Carl walked forward, he was relieved to feel the gun withdraw from his back. For a split second he thought about running again, but as he looked ahead, he could see that it would be pointless. His would-be-killer could easily pick him off before he was anywhere close to the hustle, bustle and relative safety of the people packed street. And there was his answer.

He turned to face the man who'd brought him down there. Carl didn't know what to make of him. Mostly because he couldn't see much of him. He had a wide rimmed black trilby hat and a dark scarf covering everything except his eyes. The rest of him was donned in a long, black trench coat. He looked like a long shadow, broken free from a wall.

'So, are you going to shoot me then?' That sounded pretty brave, given the circumstances, he thought. Maybe the adrenalin was kicking in.

The stranger rubbed his chin – he had gloves on – as if contemplating what his captive had suggested. 'Now, why would I want to go and do a thing like that, Mister Phillips?'

Carl hated the way he kept calling him that. It was like he was conducting a job interview, which in a strange, twisted way, he was.

'No, Mister Phillips. I never said anything about shooting you. I suppose you could have got that idea from what I was saying to you about the safety and all that, but I don't want to shoot you.'

Carl saw a straw, and he clutched at it, desperately, pointlessly. 'So, you're going to let me go?'

The stranger leant his head back slightly. Carl guessed that this was a show of disapproval.

'You're not making any sense, Mister Phillips. What would be the point in me bringing you all the way down here, just to let you go? That would be the very definition of a waste of time.'

Carl could feel his heart beating ever faster and he felt peculiarly warm for such a cold night. 'So, you're not going to shoot me and you're not going to let me go? That seems like a bit of a contradiction, if you don't mind me saying.' He didn't know where this burst of bravery was coming from, but he was glad of its company. Then, the stranger burst his bubble.

'Mister Phillips, I didn't say I wasn't going to shoot you. In fact, I believe my exact words were "I don't *want* to shoot you." Now, depending on your interpretation of my words, that means that given the wrong set – or right, depending on which side of the matter you're on – of circumstances, I may be forced to shoot you.'

Carl's blood froze in his veins and the best he could do was to nod to show that he understood.

'Now, I know that it's a bit of a cliché, but then, they are generally only clichés because they're true, aren't they? You know too much, Mister Phillips, and although in most situations knowing too much is a distinct advantage, in your case it most certainly is not.'

'Um, yeah. I can – I can see that,' Carl stammered.

'Another cliché – one of my favourites, actually – is "I know where you live." And I think it should go without saying that I know where you live, Mister Phillips. Privacy settings on social media are a responsibility, not an automatic assumption.'

Carl could guess what was coming next, but fear held him back.

'And I think from that, it goes without saying that I know about your wife Kate and your nine-year-old daughter Sara and what they look like. Now, I know I've said a lot there about things that should go without saying, Mister Phillips, but I just prefer things to be clear cut. You can understand that.'

Carl wanted to throttle him for threatening his family. He could picture himself with his hands around the man's neck, but something held him back.

'So, you see now, it would be in everyone's best interests if you help us out with this thing,' the stranger said, seemingly unaware of Carl's anger. 'I mean, I could always find someone else, but I've done all my research on you. It's such a hassle and on such short notice as well. If I shot you here, I'd have to move your body to prevent it from being discovered, and look – both sides of this alley, full to bursting with people. If I don't move it, someone will come across it, and although I do try my best to cover my tracks, I'm always paranoid that I'll forget something, and then I lose sleep and I can't concentrate on the job at hand. Not that that will matter on this little job. Now, the best thing for you would be to ask me what it is I want you to do.'

Carl could feel himself staring blankly. The situation was so unreal to him; he felt like he was watching himself from a distance, like an out of body experience, or a TV show or movie: A close up of his terrified face. Then, an extreme close up of his tears mingling with his sweat, then cut to a medium shot of the dark stranger, patiently waiting for a response.

'Well?'

'Well what?' The sound of his own voice brought Carl back to relative reality.

'Are you going to ask me what it is I want you to do?'

He thought about running again, but even if he thought it was a practical escape plan, his body wouldn't cooperate. It was numb with fear. 'What do you want me to do?'

The stranger moved closer, his gun in his pocket now, clearly confident that he wouldn't need it.

'I want you to tell me exactly how you knew what you knew about the plan. Did one of my men tell you? No. No, that's impossible. They know the rules: No contact with any member of the team they don't need to be in contact with. They gave their word.'

Carl thought for a moment. Was that paranoia he could hear? Was there a seed of mistrust that he could help flourish and ultimately tear the guy's gang apart? But before he could finish that thought, he grabbed his shoulders.

'Well?' There was a gravelly tone of menace in his voice which dislodged any coherent thought that may have gone on to develop into a plan, and Carl just gushed words out in a panic.

'There was a man. An old man in his seventies maybe, tracked me down in the shop. He warned me not to go through with it. I don't know how he knew, but he did.'

The stranger eased his grip on Carl's shoulders and backed off into the shadows again. 'Okay, Mister Phillips. You'll be glad to know, I believe you. You're obviously too scared to lie. It's the alley. I have a lot of success in this alley.' He patted the wall as if it were a pet that had just performed a trick. Carl half expected him to give it a treat.

Just then, the sound of footsteps drew Carl's attention, and as he turned around, he was faced with another shadowy figure. He could tell from the surly gait: It was Warren. As he got nearer, he slowed down and seemed reluctant to join them.

‘Ah, Mister Connelly. It’s good news,’ the stranger said, putting his arm around Warren in a mock hug. ‘I don’t have to shoot your friend.’

‘That’s good.’ Warren’s voice sounded like it was breaking with fear.

‘There’s bad news as well, though. Carl, Warren. I can call you “Carl”, can’t I?’

Carl saw this as the mockery it was. They both knew that if he wanted to call him Carlotta or Carla, or anything else, he would let him. He just nodded.

‘Oh, no, that doesn’t sound right, does it. We’ll stick to surnames. That way, we all know who’s in charge.’

‘So, what do we call you?’ Carl said.

‘In the underworld, I’m known as “The Silent Partner”. Anyway, as I was saying, there’s bad news.’ He took a breath, as if deciding on how to break it to them. ‘Because of Mister Phillips’ encounter with the old man, we’re going to have to move our plans forward.’

Carl didn’t like the sound of that. He needed some time to think; time to plan a way out. If he could just calm down and think straight, he knew he could think of something.

Scrooge tried to calm himself down. He’d been walking for ages now, attempting to find a quieter part of London so he could gather his thoughts, but it seemed like an impossible task. Although he could still feel twinges in his back from the fall, that pain was secondary to the confusion racing through his mind.

Maybe the stress of the journey is finally getting to me, he thought. It would be more than enough for a younger man to cope with I reckon, but I'm really feeling my age today. He hadn't felt so old in a long time. The future, it seemed, was no place for the elderly. In his day, the young made time for the old; respected them. But here and now, he found it hard to distinguish between the two. He was haunted by images of people on the television whose faces looked strange and contorted, like reflections in fairground halls of mirrors. Jack had explained that surgery and something called Botox was to blame for that. Then again, it was hard to believe anything that came out of that particular young man's mouth.

He'd seen double. He had seen two of them, and he knew it wasn't the shock of the fall. He'd known his old eyes long enough to trust what they showed him. No, there was only one possible explanation. He'd known Grace when he was still alive and—

Something suddenly snapped him out of his maze of thoughts: Singing. Beautiful, melodious singing. And, unlike all the songs he'd been hearing in the shops and streets with the artificial bells added on afterwards with lyrics that made no sense to his old mind, they were songs he knew. Songs that warmed his heart and took him back to his own time. They were Christmas carols. People still sung Christmas carols! He suddenly felt a renewed energy come alive inside him. Each melodious note lifted him higher and higher, as if he were one of the angels that were the subject of the song. From feeling desolately alone with no hope of getting home moments before, now, he felt like a part of something grand and limitless; something that took him home to his friends and his warm fireplace.

He turned the corner and ran down the side street from where he could hear the singing. When he got to the end and out the other side, he saw something even more incredible than he could possibly have hoped for. It looked exactly the same as it had in his time: It was his local church. Yes, there were newer buildings surrounding it, and with their straight lines and brighter than bright interiors they probably looked more attractive to the modern eye, but to Scrooge, it was more like the London – the home – he knew than anything else he had encountered in the twenty first century thus far.

He stared up at it now, almost afraid to go inside. Afraid of what he might find. Yes, it was the same on the outside, but what of the interior? He didn't want to be abruptly forced back to the harsh reality of the future.

'Come on, Scrooge. Be brave,' he told himself, and stepped forward. As he entered the grounds through the front gate, he passed lots of tombstones – many more than when he'd last been there. They were fighting each other for space, with barely an inch between them. It made him sad to see so many of them in awful states of disrepair. One had fallen over completely, and then, without warning, he thought of that night, many years ago now, when the most dreaded spirit of all had shown him his own grave. Nothing in his life up to that point had chilled his bones quite so much. Then it occurred to him that maybe his grave was there somewhere.

He was torn. On the one hand he was curious as to what his epitaph might have to say. Would he be remembered for the all-too-few years of goodness, or the many decades of darkness which hung over him; the decades which Jack had claimed he'd still to make up for? On the other hand, he didn't want to know. That night still came back to him in his dreams, and was there really any reason to let reality – however queer that reality was – reflect the nightmares which still found corners to hide behind and jump out from when he least expected. After a moment's reflection, he decided it wasn't worth it, and given the choice, he didn't want to know.

As he got closer to the church, he noticed subtle changes. There were, of course, electric lights scattered in and around the crevices of the structure. He'd come to expect that, with the amount of fairy lights he'd seen around the city. The fir tree by the entrance had at least a thousand of them. Scrooge had to admit they were pretty and one of the few improvements on Christmas that this time had to offer. The door was new, and although it looked similar to the one he was familiar with, as he walked through it, he noticed that it lacked the creaking sound which always got the congregation's attention when some poor soul was running late.

From that point on, *everything* was new. Scrooge couldn't help but be bitterly disappointed at this, but he had half expected it. Like everything else in this time, the church was a shallow representation of what had gone before. Where the stone floor had been, now there was bright red carpet. He found it more comfortable and easier on his old feet, but at the same time it was wrong. Where once there had been stone arches, now there were plain windows, not even stained-glass ones. Although, at a glance, he could see that the original stained-glass windows remained on both sides of the main hall area, so that was at least something familiar.

'You okay there, sir?' A middle-aged man, smartly dressed, suddenly appeared from nowhere. According to the badge on his jacket, he was "Assistant Steward Dave".

Scrooge stared at him for a moment, unsure of what to say. He decided that on this occasion the truth would be the most appropriate recourse.

'I used to come here, many years ago. I was just noticing how much it's changed.'

Dave looked around. 'That must have been a while ago. Me and my wife have been coming here for years, and it's hardly changed a bit in that time.'

'Yes, it was a long time ago,' Scrooge sighed. 'A very long time ago. I just hope I can go back.'

'I'm sorry, what did you say?'

'Oh, nothing.' Scrooge looked forward at the congregation behind the glass. They'd stopped singing and now the vicar's voice – which seemed as loud as the singing had been – was ringing out from the pulpit.

'Would you like to join us, for old time's sake?'

'Yes. Yes, I think I would. As long as the singing starts up again soon.'

'Oh, well you've come on the right night. It's our Christmas candlelight carol service tonight. Lots of singing to be had.' He suddenly seemed to light up, as a smile spread across his face at the thought of all the carols.

'Could I?' Scrooge gestured to the congregation.

'Of course. Here's a song sheet, and I think I can see some space on the pew at the back there.'

Scrooge thanked him, took the sheet and headed in.

As he opened the door, he gasped as the singing suddenly became so much louder. The glass had cut the volume by at least half, but he didn't need to shout to get people to step aside; they saw him coming and moved back, allowing him to squeeze through. He ended up sat next to a young couple and their little daughter. He gave them a smile and cleared his throat, ready to sing his heart out.

As he lifted the song sheet and the words of "*God Rest Ye Merry Gentlemen*" came out of his mouth, he suddenly realised that he didn't need the song sheet. He knew the words; of course he did. Everyone did. Despite everything, all the differences between his time and theirs, he finally had something in common with these people.

There was a woman in the pew in front of him who seemed determined to be heard above everyone else. It was as if she wanted to prove that she meant every word of it. He saw that the little girl had noticed, too, and they looked at each other, both with an expression that silently said: *Who does she think she is?* Then he had a thought. He moved his mouth in an exaggerated impression of what the lady in front was doing. He closed his eyes, put his hand on his chest, and moved his head from side to side, looking like a clown doing an impression of an opera singer. He could see the little girl laughing, and he must have lost track of where the song was up to, because suddenly everyone stopped singing and now, he could hear her, as clearly as if there were no one else in the church. Suddenly he realised that the whole row of people in the pew in front of him were staring accusingly at him. The girl carried on giggling as everyone sat down, despite urging from her parents to stop, and as the echoes of the sound of the congregation faded away, Scrooge tried to hold in a mischievous giggle himself.

As the service continued, Scrooge got lost in the songs and very nearly forgot that he didn't belong there. At some point, past and present collided and merged and the songs took him back to his recent days of Christmases past. Christmas mornings spent at the church with Bob Cratchit and his family. Tiny Tim, who was tiny and Tim no longer. Flashes of these memories came back to him now and the family sat next to him – even though he had barely said a word to them, nor them to him – reminded him of the Cratchits and how much he missed them, his extended and impossibly kind family.

Scrooge was brought back to the present by the vicar's voice booming out from the pulpit. 'I hope you've all enjoyed the service,' he said. 'We've got tea, biscuits; and I believe we also have some mince pies on offer in the Havisham Hall, right now. Everyone is, of course, very welcome.'

With that, everyone got up, headed to the front and went through a set of double doors. The parents of the young girl gave Scrooge a strained look and went past him without saying a word, but the girl let out another giggle in memory of Scrooge's performance and said 'Seeya later,' before obediently following her mother and father to the hall.

The main church emptied in no time – it seemed promises of food and drink were an even bigger draw than the carol service – but Scrooge didn't feel much like joining them. He wanted to sit in the quiet and remember the church as it was, or had been. He looked up at the roof. That hadn't changed much, apart from the obligatory lights of course. Somehow, with everyone gone he felt less alone. It was just him sat there, but as he closed his eyes, he thought of everyone he knew. All long gone now, of course, but being in that place made the memories more vivid, as if he could reach out and touch the people he knew. He'd had enough of this time and its people. He'd had his fill of Jack's lies and deceptions. He just wanted to go home.

He looked up again at the roof and he felt compelled to say something out loud. Perhaps it would have been a prayer, or maybe just a simple question. A request to be sent home. Was that too much to ask? To live out the rest of his days in the right time? Before he could think of the words, he was interrupted.

'Hello again.' It was Assistant Steward Dave. Scrooge tried hard to disguise his annoyance at him for the disturbance, but obviously not hard enough. 'I'm sorry,' he said, 'were you having a moment there?'

'It's alright. I, um, I was just remembering people. People I've lost,' he said solemnly.

'I'm sorry,' Dave said, not knowing where to look. 'It's worse at this time of year, somehow, isn't it. If you'd rather be left alone…'

'No.' Scrooge even surprised himself. 'I've spent far too much of my life alone as it is. Now, what was it you wanted, young man?'

'Well, I was just wondering if you'd like to join me and my wife for a mince pie? They're very good. Well, I have to say that. My wife made them, but they are honestly very good.'

'Yes,' Scrooge said, as if in defiance of some old part of himself and habits. 'I would love to join you. 'Never let it be said that old Ebenezer Scrooge was too miserable to enjoy a mince pie at Christmas time.' He pulled himself up out of the pew and heard a couple of bones click back into place, and then he noticed the look on Dave's face. 'What? What is it, man?' Scrooge said.

Then, almost as suddenly, his joyous expression was replaced with a confused one. 'Scrooge,' he said. 'Ebenezer Scrooge?'

'That's right,' Scrooge said. 'Why?'

'It's the strangest thing. I feel like I've heard that name before. No offense, but it is an unusual name.'

'Yes, that has been mentioned a few times to me.' Scrooge tried not to sound too irate.

'I want to say that I've seen it written in a book or something. An old story? I really don't know, but never mind, I'm sure it'll come to me.'

'That's it!' Dave shouted, his voice echoing around the now empty church. Scrooge noticed that his face had turned an odd pale colour. 'I know where I've seen it; your name. How could I forget? I must be getting old. It's always been a bit of a mystery, and I don't know – maybe you can help us solve it.'

'Where? Where have you seen my name?' Scrooge said, but he had a feeling that he already knew.

Any man would be loath to do it, even once, of course, but for the second time in his life Ebenezer Scrooge found himself looking down at his own gravestone. If anyone were to ask him how it felt, he was certain that he wouldn't know how to put it into words. Seeing his name once more engraved into stone sent an undeniable chill throughout his entire body. It was a solid reminder that, like everyone, death awaited him, a dark stranger judging every selfish action he had taken in his life.

Then, he noticed the epitaph. The last one had had no epitaph. He'd always assumed that the reason for that was that no one cared enough to bother summing up his life in a couple of lines. No one cared enough. Ha! Scrooge laughed at his own understated notion. They were glad to be rid of me, joyful even. Now, however, after the spirits changed his path, there was a sentence which moved him to tears. He could feel them escaping and rushing down his cheeks, and he didn't know how, but they felt different to the other tears he'd shed so far. His life had been summed up with this sentence which he read out loud:

He knew how to keep Christmas well, if any man alive
Possessed the knowledge.

'It's quite an epitaph, isn't it,' Dave said, politely ignoring the fact that Scrooge's face was doing an excellent impression of a waterfall.

'Yes. Yes, it is,' Scrooge managed to say.

Dave gently brushed a bit of snow from the top of the gravestone 'As a young boy I was always fascinated by this grave. The message really stood out to me. It was an inspiration, and I've always wondered what kind of person he really was. Was he that time's equivalent to Santa Claus or something?'

Scrooge laughed at the irony of Dave's question. 'Ha! Maybe in later life, young man, but I'd never—'

'So, you know the story, do you? You know what happened?'

'What do you mean?' Scrooge said, turning back to Dave. 'What story?'

'Oh, it sounded like… Well, I tried to find *this* Ebenezer Scrooge in old newspaper stories of the time, with some degree of success, but there was something that didn't add up. Major contradictions.

'What do you mean?' Scrooge asked.

'Well, in some of the stories he's an absolute swine, to put it mildly. He did whatever he could to basically get as much money out of people as possible, no matter how much they suffered. The corrupt bankers and politicians of today could learn a few tricks off him.'

Scrooge blushed at this.

'But then, some of the other stories I found were the complete opposite. He changed. Not just a little bit. No, it was like he was a completely different person.'

'Really?'

'Yeah,' Dave continued, not noticing the wry smile spread across Scrooge's face. 'So, I investigated further. I mean, a lot of the newspapers were lost over the years for various reasons. The wars must certainly have been a major factor in that, but I did manage to find some articles which were very close, date wise, to the Christmas period.' Dave leaned forward and cocked his head, as if he were about to reveal the answer the mystery.

'One of the articles revealed how he had put yet another business out of, well, business because they'd been a bit behind on paying back a loan.'

Scrooge turned away as his face flushed red.

'Then, just a few days later, another article revealed how he'd given a sizable chunk of his fortune to various charitable organisations, and how he was planning on setting up his own homeless shelter. As far as I could tell, from the few articles I could find on the man, he never revealed what happened to make him change so drastically. Did he ever tell anyone in your family? I mean, I assume he was an ancestor of yours.'

Scrooge just stared blankly for a moment, trying to find something to say, something to justify everything. 'Um, yes… I… Now that you mention it, I do recall something,' he said vaguely. 'I mean I never met him, of course, but it was said of him that he had many regrets about his life. He confided in a family friend: Tim. The old man told Tim about a night, a Christmas eve night, in fact, on which he was visited by four…' Scrooge looked at Dave and tried to gauge whether he was the kind of person who would run for the hills if he started talking about ghosts and visits to the past, present and future.

'Four what?' Dave pushed.

From the look on Dave's face Scrooge decided to play it safe and try to dress up the truth in conservative clothing. 'Four people from different charitable organisations.'

'Oh.' Dave sounded slightly disappointed in the relatively mundane explanation, but he also seemed glad of an answer, so Scrooge continued.

'Yes, they talked to him and made him see the error of his ways. It was a mixture, I think, of scaring him into seeing where he was headed and reminding him of how he used to be when he was a younger man. He used to be kind and honest and he had a girl who loved him. Belle.' His throat went dry at the sound of her name.

Dave looked at him, as if he knew that Scrooge was holding back the truth, but he didn't prod any further. 'It's a shame,' he said. 'I mean, it's nice to know the full story at last, but it's a pity that he only had a few years left in which to spread the joy, as they say.'

'What?' Scrooge said. 'What do you mean?'

'Well,' Dave said in an almost whisper, 'just a few short years after his miraculous transformation, he went missing, Surely you heard about that?'

Scrooge was speechless. Dave's words were like a pair of murderous hands clasped around his throat. 'Um, no,' he managed to say, 'I was never told about that. Another detail he neglected to mention.'

'I'm sorry. What did you say?'

'Nothing.' Scrooge could feel his whole body sinking, losing its fight, and the other type of tears were coming now. 'Tell me, young man, did they ever find his…' He couldn't say the word.

'His body? No, I don't think they ever did, Mister Scrooge. I mean, I don't have every article on it, but there was a lot of speculation. Most of the papers thought that it was probably one of his old enemies, and as you know, your ancestor had many of them.'

'I know,' Scrooge sighed, 'I know.' He was finding it more and more difficult to look at his own grave, as if it were a stranger in the street, staring and pointing and laughing at him. Then, he noticed something. Where were the dates of his birth and death? Surely, they were on there somewhere. And then, he saw it: The top stem of the number one, poking out from some snow still gripped to the stone, daring him to sweep it away. 'I think I'd like to be alone for a while,' he said, not shifting his gaze from the grave.

'Oh, yeah. Of course, of course. So you can pay your respects. I'll be inside if you need me.'

'Thank you,' Scrooge said, 'you've been very kind.'

'My pleasure, sir.'

Scrooge heard him walk off, trudging through the snow. He loved that sound of shoes sinking in the snow. It always reminded him of this time of year. He hoped that it wouldn't now forever remind him of this moment.

He turned around to make sure no one was watching, then bent down on one knee and reluctantly swept away the snow, which was hiding the date of his death from him. He read the dates out loud, as if it would make it easier to take them in, somehow.

'Ebenezer Scrooge. Born May twenty second, seventeen seventy-eight. Died… December twenty fourth, eighteen forty…' As he swept the last bit of snow away to reveal the final digit, he couldn't believe what he was seeing. 'Eighteen forty-one? But that's… that's the day. That's the night I—'

'The night we travelled to the future. To here. Weird, eh?'

Scrooge turned around and pulled himself up, slowly. Jack was stood there, looking a little worse for wear, but not, Scrooge thought, as bad as he would look after he'd finished with him.

11

The freezing cold of the snow-whipped graveyard had been nothing compared to the icy atmosphere that now emanated from Scrooge. He was so angry, he couldn't move. He was like one of the statues scattered around the graveyard, unmoving, yet glaring at Jack, his eyes demanding an explanation. The tables had been turned, because although the spirit of Jack knew that Scrooge could do him no physical harm, Scrooge could see that he felt afraid of him.

Finally, Jack broke the deathly silence. 'Okay, I can see that you're mad at me, and I can't say I blame you. There's an explanation for what you can see on that grave, and I know you've got no reason to believe me. No reason whatsoever, but it's not as grim as it seems.'

Scrooge didn't have anything to say to this. He could see how nervous Jack was, gesticulating each of his fingers with every syllable thrown out of his lying mouth. His stony silence was working.

'I'll get to the grave in a minute, but if I could just explain my actions. I—'

'Oh, I think I can explain your actions,' Scrooge snapped. 'You've lied to me from the very moment we met. I'm here to save Grace, you eventually told me, but that was a lie. You made me think – no – you made me *fear* that if I didn't help you then I'd be doomed for all eternity; that everything I've done since I changed was all for nought. But everything we've done has been for you and your selfish ends, so you don't die. I suppose you're going to deny that as well, aren't you.'

Jack looked like he'd been frozen in time for a moment, gripped by the miniature tornadoes of snow whipping around him. Eventually he spoke, but Scrooge could see that his mind was elsewhere as he stared at nothing.

'You don't know what it's like to be cut down in the prime of your life. You're what? Eighty?

'*Sixty-three.*'

'Really? You've lived a life then. A long life. And you wasted most of it in pursuit of wealth and capital. I was just a young man when I was killed. I still am, technically. I'm not sure how long I've been up there. Sometimes it feels like years, sometimes it's like yesterday. All time is a bunch of yesterdays really, isn't it, and I'm sure even in your time you've heard of the dead watching over the living. Well, of course you have. Your old friend Marley watched over you, didn't he. That's what I've been doing: Watching over Grace, for longer than I can remember. I watched her for her entire life. I watched how sad she was when I died. I watched her move on. I watched her endure loads of really bad relationships until she found the man she chose to marry.'

'You told me I was here to save Grace.'

'And I didn't lie. When I died, her life, well, it was really bleak for her for a long time. By saving me, you'd be saving her as well.'

Scrooge stared at Jack intently for a moment. He knew that his guide's lies had lies sprouting out of them, but this time he seemed genuinely distraught at how Grace's life had turned out.

'I'm sorry I didn't tell you the truth from the start,' Jack said, unable to look at Scrooge for a moment, 'but I thought if I could intimidate you into just doing whatever I wanted, it would be quicker.'

'Quicker?' Scrooge said.

'Well, easier then. It's just that when it comes to Grace, I've never been able to think straight.'

Despite himself, Scrooge could feel himself warming up to the lad again. Yes, he'd lied to him, almost constantly since they'd met, but he was far from perfect himself, and he was starting to see a lot of himself – faults and all – in Jack.

Jack sat himself down on the ground in a gap between two graves and slumped his head into his hands. 'I tried to appear to her all the time, but she couldn't see me. One time, I stupidly shifted her furniture around. I don't know why, maybe just to show her I was there, but it just freaked her out.'

'That's hardly surprising,' Scrooge said.

'I even... I even...' Jack stopped for a moment, as if all the truth telling was becoming too much for him.

It seemed to Scrooge – although it was difficult to tell with Jack's translucent appearance – that he was crying.

'I tried to write notes to her, warning her of all the bad things that would happen in her future. I couldn't do it. Something stopped me. A searing pain. It seemed like another unseen force was watching over her, but not a good one. How could it be? I was trying to *help* her.

'No matter what I did to try to communicate with her – to touch her life – I couldn't. And when she finally arrived in Heaven as an old woman with a lifetime of woe mapped out on her face, she'd ... She'd forgotten me.'

'I'm sorry,' Scrooge said

'When she finally did remember me, she said that what we had was nice, but it was a lifetime ago and we were different people back then.

'She was wrong. Well, maybe she was different, but I was still – am still – the same person I was years ago, because I died all those years ago.'

Scrooge took in a deep cold breath. It was getting so cold now that the air stung his throat. 'I understand now,' he said. He held out his arm but suddenly remembered that he couldn't touch Jack, he couldn't comfort him with a simple pat on the shoulder. 'A part of me died a long time ago. I lied to myself at the time, but I chose all the wrong things over the most important thing in the world, and I spent the longest time of my life alone and miserable and making everyone else miserable. If I could change that turning point in my life, I would. I can't, so the next best thing could be helping you. You didn't have a choice, so yes, Jack, I will help you. But you must promise me – swear to me – that you're done with the lies and deceit.'

The spirit of Jack seemed to Scrooge to have frozen, but he was looking directly at Scrooge. Then, as if time had suddenly restarted, he blinked, and a tear escaped from his eye.

'Thank you,' he said. 'From the bottom of my heart, thank you. And yes, I'm done with lying, I swear.'

Scrooge tried to laugh this off. 'Come on now, son. Let's not get all mushy.' He started to walk, beckoning Jack to follow him. 'Now, I assume you have a plan, cunning young man such as you are.'

'I do. First we have to— AAARGH!'

'What? What's wrong, Jack?' As Scrooge looked on, helplessly, his companion was holding his head, and his mouth was open unnaturally wide, as if the screams were too much for his body to bear.

'Pain. Searing pain. Ripping… me… apart.'

Jack was down on the ground now, with his head in his hands again. He suddenly stood up, his chest puffing in and out, as if he was trying to take control of the monstrous pain coursing through him.

'Are you…? Is it getting better?' Scrooge asked, delicately.

'It's… yeah… it's easing off, yeah. It's never been that bad.' He looked almost normal again.

'Something's changed,' Jack said with a chill.

'What do you mean?'

'Being down here amongst events that play out in order, in the way you perceive them, means that my memories change along the way. I retain everything that did happen and also things that now didn't as a result of me bringing you here. Do you follow me?'

'Um, no,' Scrooge said.

'It's okay. It just means that it takes me a while to sort what did or has happened from what now didn't. Reality from fantasy. Something's changed. Something bad.'

'What is it, Jack? Tell me,' Scrooge demanded.

Jack's face was almost telling the whole story before the words dripped out of his mouth. 'Originally, I died in a couple of days' time, but now, Scrooge, I die… tonight.'

Carl could feel himself shivering. He didn't know whether it was the cold or the fear; he supposed it was a bit of both. The Silent Partner had forced both him and Warren into a van and had driven them to what was presumably his home. It didn't seem like much of one. Perhaps he wasn't as successful at the whole crime thing as he'd led them to believe.

He managed to catch slight glimpses of the rooms as the Silent Partner marched them down the hallway. There was a damp, musty smell, and most of the walls had mould creeping down from every corner. There was no order to anything. Books, magazines, clothes, empty pizza trays and cigarette packets were all just strewn across the floor. He didn't know why this had occurred to him – probably his mind trying to distract itself – but he noticed that there were no Christmas decorations. This didn't really surprise him: their host-slash-kidnapper definitely wasn't a Christmas person, what with the kidnapping and the plans of robbery, and it was pretty much a certainty that he had no family to care for. Family. The fear stood still for a moment, as he pictured Kate and Sara's faces.

He'd escaped. He'd won and they were there with hugs at the ready. He was carving the turkey whilst regaling them with the tale of his brief adventure and how he and Warren had overcome impossible odds and dropped their captor off at the police station on the way home. They were telling him how brave he was, and he was telling them to stop making him blush.

A sudden push from behind snapped him out of it, and before he remembered where he was, Warren was unceremoniously shoved on top of him. The door slammed shut behind them, and that was followed by the inevitable *CLICK* of it being locked behind them.

Carl immediately pushed Warren away, got up and went straight to the light switch. Nothing. No light.

'Great,' he said out loud. As his eyes adjusted to the darkness, he saw Warren sit up.

'This is all my fault, mate. I'm sorry.'

'We can assign blame where it's due later,' Carl said sharply. 'No, actually, let's do that now. You're to blame. There, that was quick and easy, wasn't it. Now, we have to figure a way out of this mess you got us into.'

Warren said nothing.

There was a slight, dim crack of light shining onto the wall next to the door, and from the way the light was cracking through from the outside, he could see that it wasn't curtains keeping them in the dark: it was a wooden panel. In fact, there were several of them. He went over to the window. 'Help me get this panel off, will you.' he said.

'What's the point, mate?' Warren said, flatly. 'We're really high up. We were in that lift for ages.'

'Oh, yeah.' Carl hated to admit it, but his idiot-of-a-mate had a good point. Surely though, some good could come from getting one of the panels off.

Maybe they could tell roughly where they were, if they could just see out of one of the windows. He tried by himself to pull one of the panels loose, and he could feel it starting to give, but it was still a struggle. Then, it suddenly became a little easier, and Carl was surprised to see that, despite his pessimistic words, Warren had decided to give him a hand.

'Can't have you getting yourself injured or pulling something at your age, mate. I'd get the blame for that as well.'

He didn't have the strength to argue, so he just nodded in agreement.

Together, they managed to pull the panel away, and as they did, it snapped clean in two, making a loud cracking, splintering sound which seemed louder than all the traffic in London. Instinctively, they both turned around to the door to see if it had alerted their captor. Carl could hear Warren's and his own panicked breathing, but nothing else. They were in the clear.

'Now, let's see if we can't figure out where we are, shall we,' Carl whispered, as he looked through the small gap.

'What can you see?'

'Nothing. Just... Nothing. Darkness. Maybe we're in the middle of the country,' Carl said, trying not to sound as hopeless as he felt. Then he realised something. 'We weren't in the car that long, were we. Wait a minute.' Just then a part of the darkness shifted. It looked a bit like a figure; a woman. She was like a ghost, floating around in the middle of the night sky. Then suddenly, a blinding light appeared from nowhere and he had to turn away. When he looked back, he felt a bit foolish. 'Of course,' he said.

'What? What is it, mate?'

'It's another building next to this one,' he told Warren, trying not to sound as if he'd not realised the fact straightaway.

'What building is it? Do you recognise it?' Warren came nearer to the window and tried to see for himself.

'No. Look, it's all in darkness apart from that one room. Everyone must be out, apart from her, and she looks like she's getting ready to go out.'

'Ooh. She? Let's have a look then,' Warren said, trying to shove Carl aside.

Carl couldn't help it and gave a snort of disapproval.

'What?' Warren protested.

'It's typical, isn't it. We've been kidnapped and very soon we're going to be forced to rob the place where we work, and all you can think about is copping a look at an innocent woman getting changed.'

His friend looked affronted. 'I can't believe you've got such a low opinion of me. I was going to suggest that we try and get her attention, so she can call the police for us.'

Carl felt terrible, but before he could beat himself up too much, Warren whispered:

'Well, that was the second thought that occurred to me, anyway.'

'I see.' Carl knew exactly what he meant by that.

'Look, does it matter what order it came to me in?' Warren said. 'Let's just try and get her attention if we can.'

'Right. I know it's a long shot, but have you got a mirror on you at all?' Carl asked.

'Um, why?'

'So I can try and reflect the light and get her attention.'

'Oh yeah, good idea,' Warren said, 'but I haven't got one, sorry.'

'Well, there's only one thing we can do then, mate,' Carl said, as he started to pull away another one of the panels. 'We'll get as many of these bloody things off the windows as we can and wave our hands and arms and whatever around, until she sees us.

'Oh,' Warren said, sounding unimpressed.

Between them they managed to prise three more of the panels away from the window of their makeshift prison.

They stopped and looked behind them to see if there was any sign that the Silent Partner had noticed their efforts. There was a white line of light at the bottom of the door and they both watched it for a good few seconds to make sure it remained undisturbed.

'I think we're okay,' Warren whispered.

'Yeah, but don't you think it's a bit odd that he's not heard any of this? I mean, we've not exactly been quiet, have we.'

Warren seemed to consider this for a moment. 'Maybe… Maybe he's gone out. Last minute Christmas shopping.'

'Last minute Christmas shopping? Yeah, that's probably it, mate. He's been so busy organising this little heist that he completely forgot to get his daughter the Elsa dress, and y'know, everyone forgets the crackers until last minute, don't they.'

Warren picked up on the sarcasm. 'Okay, smart alec, what do you think he's doing?'

'I really don't know,' Carl said. 'Maybe he's having a power nap.'

'A power nap? That's even more ridiculous than mine.'

'Oh, so you admit that you were being ridiculous then?'

'You're both ridiculous if you ask me.'

They both froze. The voice had come from behind them, but Carl hadn't seen anyone else enter the room. The only possible explanation was that—

'I've been in here with you the whole time,' the Silent Partner said, confirming what had just dawned on him with frightening clarity. 'Listening to the two of you arguing like an old married couple, I'm starting to question whether I've picked the right crew for this job.'

Suddenly the sound of a slight vibration silenced him. Carl automatically reached into his own pocket, but their captor had already taken both his and Warren's phones.

'Yes?' the Silent Partner said into his mobile. 'What? But you said that_' He stopped and listened to what whoever it was on the other end had to say. Carl strained to hear what that was, but he couldn't hear anything.

'I won't forget this; you know that, don't you. And if I ever see you again, I'll kill you.'

He ended the call and put the phone back in his pocket, and for the first time since Carl had been forced into meeting him, the Silent Partner seemed genuinely shaken.

'Well, boys and girls,' he said dryly, 'it looks like I'll be doing the driving tonight. And there I was thinking my days of working with incompetent staff were over.'

'Just what is it that you want us to do?' Carl said this as forcefully as he could manage. 'I mean, we know what you want us to do, but you haven't told us exactly how we're going to do it.'

The Silent Partner lived up to his name for a moment, stood back and folded his arms.

'Well?' Carl pushed.

'You're right,' he said, as if he was just then realising it himself. 'I haven't told you anything, have I. It's about time I put that right.' He unlocked the door and gestured for the two of them to walk through it.

'Jack?' His voice sounded like it was echoing around the whole world and there was no one else anywhere to hear it. Tears were trickling down the spirit's face, and there was something eerily beautiful and sad about it, like an ice sculpture melting.

'Do you think that it's inevitable?' Jack said. 'Do you think that no matter what I do – what *we* do – I'll always die now. I mean, as young as I am now. Is it impossible for a man to change his fate?'

'No, I don't think it is,' Scrooge said thoughtfully. 'I mean, just the fact of the matter that the day of your death changed; doesn't that prove that nothing is set in stone?'

'I suppose so.'

'Look at me, Jack. Folk always thought I would die the same bitter and twisted Ebenezer Scrooge that they knew and hated, but thanks to good old Jacob's intervention I'm a new man.'

Scrooge expected his words to lift Jack's spirits, but he looked more solemn than ever. 'What's wrong?'

'I've told you so many lies, Scrooge, and for that I'm truly sorry.'

'I know, I know. That's okay, son. We all make mistakes; me more than most.'

Jack turned back to him. He was still crying. 'No, Scrooge, you don't understand. You shouldn't even be here.'

'Well, I certainly know that,' Scrooge said with a laugh. 'I don't even know how I've survived such a wild time and place.'

'I brought you here under false pretences.'

'Yes, so you could save Grace.'

'Well, yes, but—'

'I told you that you were failing at redeeming yourself; that all the good you were doing wasn't enough.'

Scrooge could see where this conversation was going, and as much as he was tempted to string it out and make his companion continue, he could see how bad he felt about his deception. 'Jack, it's alright, son. Be assured that I can see that you're not the all-seeing, all-knowing being I thought you to be on our first encounter. I can see now that you have no idea about my life or my fate. It's not for me to know. I can only do my best to try and make up for, well, everything.'

Jack turned to Scrooge but didn't look him in the eye. His face looked deader than it ever had.

'What? What is it, Jack?' Scrooge said.

'Your best is good enough, Scrooge.'

'What do you mean? I thought you didn't_'

'When Grace arrived in Heaven, she'd all but forgotten me, that was the truth. I was so angry and bitter. Everyone was avoiding me. I was a bad vibe and I don't suppose I can blame them. Then, someone came to me. Well, I say someone; it was… a some*thing*. A blinding mass of pure light. It spoke directly into my mind. It told me about you and how you used to be like me: angry and bitter. It told me that you were a good man now, maybe the best man on Earth. It said you could help me, but it also warned me that it would take a lot to drag you away from all your friends and family. A plan formed in my mind. I thought it was mine at the time, but maybe it was his or its, whatever it was. All I know is that after that I knew exactly what I had to do.'

A warm feeling came over Scrooge, and he no longer felt like he was in a freezing cold graveyard. 'This being? This mass of light? It told you I was a good man?'

'Yeah. I'm sorry I lied to you, Scrooge.'

'That's quite alright, Jack,' Scrooge said. As he said this, he felt a huge weight lift off his shoulders. He felt as light as a feather and he thought he might float off to Heaven right there and then.

'But don't you think it's a bit weird that something or someone up there would give me such a disruptive idea? I lied to you; made you leave your own time. I mean, there must be consequences for that, surely.'

Scrooge was only half listening. He was still giddy with delight but tried to pull himself back down to earth. 'There's an old saying, Jack. I don't know if it's survived into this time. It's that God works in mysterious ways.'

'Yeah, people still say that, but why would He go to all this trouble to help me save myself? I can't be that important, can I? My parents certainly didn't think so.'

'Mysterious ways, Jack my boy,' Scrooge said rubbing his fingers together, 'mysterious ways.'

'You sound like Bono.'

'Who?'

'Never mind,' Jack said dismissively. 'We'd better get a move on, anyway. We haven't got much time.' He looked at his watch, but then realised that it was just as dead as he was.

'So, you believe we can do it?'

'Sure,' Jack said. 'I mean, if God, or whatever it was I saw up there has our backs, we can't fail, can we. And if a crotchety old guy like you can turn things around, then there has to be hope for me, right?'

'That's the spirit, man,' Scrooge said. 'Now, let's get out of this cold and into a taxi. We've got a tragedy to prevent.'

12

Carl and Warren were in the back of the van again. It had an odd smell about it, as if someone had been living in it for a while. The way it was rattling, they felt like forgotten boxes of knickknacks being tossed around, banging against the walls of the metal prison. The driver – who happened to be the Silent Partner – hadn't so much as turned around to make sure they were okay. They were just tools to him. Tools to help him carry out his big masterplan of robbing a supermarket.

Their part in the plan was simple. Well, not as simple as the Silent Partner's part. He and Warren had the task of actually going in there and robbing the place. They had to get the manager to open the safe and hand over the day's takings. That's what the guns and Santa suits were for. The Silent Partner's part in the whole mess was infinitely simpler: he just had to drive. He didn't seem particularly good at that, Carl thought, judging from the amount of horns and swearing he could hear coming from outside. Warren looked relatively calm, considering the insane situation that they'd found themselves in the middle of.

'Is there something you want to share with the group?' Carl asked, covering up his fear with a healthy dose of sarcasm.

Warren looked as though he barely heard him, lost and adrift in his sea of calm. 'I'm sorry, what? What did you say, mate?' he finally said, nonchalantly.

'How are you so… okay?' he asked. 'You are aware that we're about to break the law, holding a gun on one of our managers in the process?'

Warren seemed amused at this. In fact, he looked positively tickled with glee.

'Did I say something funny?'

'Oh, come on, mate. Don't tell me you've never fantasised about doing this. You've never thought "what if?" Now's your chance to see how it feels.'

Carl couldn't think of anything to say to that. He stared at his partner in crime to try and figure out whether he was trying to wind him up or if he had genuinely lost the plot. He couldn't decide. 'Are you insane?' he said finally. 'This isn't a game. This isn't a fantasy. This is illegal. What that guy up front is asking, no – forcing us to do, is illegal, in the worst possible way.'

'Exactly,' Warren said, as if Carl had accidentally made sense of his shockingly blasé attitude to armed robbery.

'I'm sorry? What?'

'We're being forced to do this thing. We have no choice. We might as well try and enjoy it and put it down to one of life's great experiences; a part of life's rich and varied tapestry, as they say.'

'A life experience?' He couldn't believe what he was hearing. No doubt about it: Warren had gone mad. 'No. A life experience is going to New York, visiting the Statue of Liberty or hang-gliding for the first time, and even though I'm terrified of heights, guess what I'd rather be doing right now.'

'You're worried about the guns, aren't you, mate,' Warren said, trying to sound reassuring.

'Well, amongst other things, yes.'

'We'll never have to use them. I mean, yeah, we'll have them there for show, but we'll never have to pull the trigger. The threat of violence is always more effective than violence itself.' He made it sound like he was quoting some great philosopher.

'Oh, I'm so relieved,' Carl said, dryly.

Warren didn't seem to pick up on his tone, because he just carried on as if they were having a perfectly normal conversation over a pint at the pub. 'In my youth – I mean, I'm not that old now – but in my *youth* youth, I tried a similar thing in a newsagent's.'

'I wish I was surprised.'

'I wish I'd had a proper gun and a Santa suit; although that would've looked a bit weird in July.'

He couldn't help himself; he grabbed Warren's chin to force him to look him in the eye. 'We can't do this. This isn't a joke. It's not a fantasy. This is real; and if we do this we'll go to prison for a long time.'

Warren looked at him and pulled himself out of Carl's grasp. 'Okay, Smart Alek. How do you suggest we get out of this then?'

'We run.'

Warren looked shocked, as if he wasn't expecting such a quick response or such a simple plan.

'Once he unlocks those doors and lets us out of here, we run as hard and fast as we can and find the nearest policeman.'

'You mean "cop", don't you? You're so posh.'

'Whatever. Are you with me?'

'That sounds like a terrible plan,' a far too familiar voice chimed in. The van had stopped, and the Silent Partner was looking straight at them through the little cubby hole. 'For one: I have the guns. And two: I have men on the street and in the shop, just waiting for you two to make the mistake which makes their cut of the profits of this job that little bit more substantial, if you get my meaning.'

Carl and Warren looked at each other. Carl with dismay, and Warren with an unbearably smug look of *I told you so* on his face. That was it then. Carl let out a stunted sniff of a laugh and shook his head. How could one problem which seemed so big not that long ago – losing his job – so quickly be overshadowed by a much bigger problem, which never in his wildest imaginings had he thought would ever come up. It seemed that life would do with him what it wanted, and no matter what he thought of it or what he did to try and change it, it would just laugh in his face and carry on regardless.

'Well come on then, girls,' the Silent Partner sneered. 'I'd like this done before Christmas, if that's convenient for you.'

Carl stared at him. He was hoping that he looked more fed up than worried or scared. There was something about the way he spoke to them which seemed very familiar. The spite-tinged words sparked flashes of memory that wouldn't quite make it to the forefront of his mind, but he knew that he'd been made to feel the way those words made him feel before. Did he know this guy? There was really no way of telling. He wore that scarf and hat all the time, and on top of that his voice sounded like the result of a hundred-a-day smoking habit, although he never coughed, so he was probably putting it on. That could be proof that he does know me or Warren, he thought; or both of us, and he's trying to hide it – but before he could finish that thought, the sound of the rear doors of the van opening snapped him out of it. The Silent Partner was stood there, looking at his watch.

'Come on, ladies, we haven't got all night.'

'Oh, so now we're ladies, are we?' Carl challenged, hardly believing his own guts as he and Warren reluctantly got out of the van and found themselves in a very familiar car park. 'What happened to earn us such a promotion?' Carl couldn't see his face, but he could feel the Silent Partner's eyes boring into him, and it gave him a shiver which he knew had nothing to do with the cold winter air.

He completely ignored the question and held up two identical pink and grey backpacks, gesturing for him and Warren to take them.

'Oh, come on, man,' Warren protested, 'you can't expect us to wear them. We really *will* look like ladies.'

'So, these you have a problem with?' Carl said.

'We'll look like a couple on a trip to the lake district,' Warren whinged.

'Just shut up,' the Silent Partner demanded. 'I think you already know what's in them, and you can probably guess what will happen to you if you open them too early.'

They both nodded agreement without a word.

'Well? What are you waiting for? A goodbye kiss? Obviously neither of you can be trusted with your phones, so there's a walkie-talkie in one of the bags, in case things go awry.'

'That's very thoughtful of you,' Carl said under his breath.

'What was that?'

'Nothing.'

'Didn't think it would be,' the Silent Partner said smugly. 'Now get going. I'll be here, waiting.' On that note of comfort, he got back in the van and slammed the door.

The car park was all but empty, maybe five cars at the most.

'No wonder they're getting rid of us,' Warren said glumly. 'The height of Christmas and look at the state of it.'

'Yeah,' Carl said, not really listening.

'Depressing, isn't it. Coming into work on your night off.'

'What?' Carl said. He looked up, and Warren had a big smile plastered on his face. And, despite the situation and the fact that his mouth felt bone dry from stress, he laughed. We should both be miserable, he thought. We're both at a dead-end, with no emergency exit and he's cracking jokes like it's – well, it *is* Christmas. He could feel the tension headache he'd had since the whole affair had started, unravelling, as he gave in to the laughter; to the sheer ludicrousness of the situation. How could he have imagined that this would happen? How could anyone?

'It could've happened to anyone,' he said, between fits of laughter, 'but it happened to us.' Warren was looking at him as if he was the one who was nuts for a change, and he was probably right. He put his hand on his shoulder to stop himself from slipping on the slushy car park surface. 'You were right: We don't have a choice. You think you do, but you really don't. It's a delusion. Oh, there's little things: "Should I clean my teeth? Should I have brown bread or white? A shower or a bath?" Everyday things we're allowed some control over, but the big things? No. Our fates are out of our hands. Out of our reach. You think you have control, but then a creep with a gun turns up and reminds you just how powerless you are. The world is just a big creep with a gun.'

'Right.' For once, Warren seemed lost for words. 'So, what are you saying, mate?'

Carl wiped a freezing tear of laughter from his cheek. 'I'm saying that you were right. We have no choice, no moral obligations. We're free. Free to be told what to do by him. It's no different to working in there, is it.' He pointed to the shop, looming in front of them. 'We moan all the time about being told what to do, but the alternative is much scarier, isn't it? This "job" is no different to stacking shelves.'

'I suppose not.'

'So, what are we waiting for? Let's go!' Carl set off across the car park with Warren at his side. As his feet trudged through the brownie grey sludge, he could feel his resolve teetering already. Did he really believe that they had no choice, or was it just an easy way; an excuse for not fighting back?

I'm right though, aren't I? he thought, as they approached the automatic doors that were forever breaking down. We really don't have any choice. If we don't do as he says, we're basically dead. One of his team will—

Carl's doom-laden train of thought was suddenly cut short by a nudge from Warren.

'Hey, mate,' he said, 'the place is deserted. I think it's all going to go pretty smooth.'

Carl looked around for the first time since they'd entered the place. He had been too lost in his resolve-teetering to notice, but Warren was right. There was an old customer – a regular, who everyone called "Daily Mail Man" – hovering around the newspapers, tutting to himself, a couple of staff stacking shelves, two on the tills, and that was it. In fact, one of the only signs that the place was still open to the public was the seventies-era Christmas soundtrack blasting out of the tannoy, regardless.

'You're right,' he said. 'There's no one here. At least no one will get hurt and—' Something was starting to dawn on him. 'There's no one here,' he said again, this time looking around, slowly, carefully.

'That's right, mate. You just said.' Warren sounded worried, but if his theory was right, then maybe, just maybe...

He headed down to the middle aisle. He could hear his partner in crime protesting, but he had to make sure. There were a few customers hanging around the aisles. One of them was a mum with her two kids, one of which was in a pram and the other seemed to be bemoaning the fact that he didn't get to ride in it with his sister. There were a couple of OAPs hiding in the corner, trying to find the cheapest brandy:

'... but this one's fifteen percent.'

'Yes, I know that, dear, but this one's thirteen percent volume and five pound cheaper.'

There were a couple of staff that he'd known for years, stacking shelves – he made sure to hide the backpack, forgetting that he'd be unrecognisable under the Santa beard – but that was it.

'What're y'doing, man?' Warren had caught up with him. 'He'll—'

'He'll what? Get a couple of OAPs to kneecap us if we don't cooperate? Or maybe you think that mum and her kids are in on it? Don't y'see, mate?'

'See what?'

'I was wrong. I was so bloody wrong.'

'About what?'

'About this not being a fantasy. It is. It *is* someone's fantasy.'

'You mean we're imagining all this? We're going to wake up in Kansas, in olden day black and white times?' As usual, Warren wasn't quite on the same page.

'No. Shut up. No.' Carl immediately regretted his bluntness. 'I'm sorry, mate, but I've just figured this whole thing out. Well, maybe not everything, but a lot of it. It's *his* fantasy. The Silent Partner or whoever he is. That's the bit we've got to figure out. Who—'

Warren held up his hand. 'Wait a sec, mate. What do you mean "his fantasy"?'

Carl tried his best to stay patient and not sound too cocky. 'I mean he's making it all up. He doesn't have anyone.' As he was speaking, he could feel the blessed relief of all the pieces falling into place. His heart was beating faster than ever, but more from excitement now, than fear. 'Think about it: Have you ever seen him with any other members of his so-called crew?'

'Well, no, but—'

'Exactly.' Carl thought he was sounding a bit like a mad scientist and the pointy finger wasn't helping.

'But, mate,' Warren said, looking as though he was about to throw several poorly timed spanners into Carl's big revelation. 'What about when one of his men phoned him to tell him he couldn't do the driving?'

This wasn't enough to stop Carl. He knew he was on to something, and he pulled his itchy beard and Santa hat off as a statement of intent. 'It's all smoke and mirrors, mate. Misdirection. He's controlled us with fear. We were so busy being scared of what might happen if we didn't do exactly what he said, we didn't notice the little things; the crater sized holes in his story. Like why, if he's running such a big operation – if he's such a bigshot – why couldn't he find another member of his "crew" to be the getaway driver? He was making it up. There was no one on the other end of that call.'

Warren looked as though he was joining the side of the true believers, so Carl pressed on.

'It's just him. There's no one here watching us. It's just him waiting in that van. Waiting for us to make the biggest mistake of our lives.'

'Ah, but would it?'

Carl didn't like the look on his face. 'Would it what?'

'Would it really be the biggest mistake of our lives?'

'Let me think now,' Carl started, sarcastically. 'You might have a point – no – hold on, no. No, you really don't.'

'Come on, mate. Like you said, he's on his own. We could do the job, just walk away, and split the proceeds fifty-fifty.'

'Are you—' Carl suddenly stopped and realised his voice was getting a bit too loud. He pulled himself back a notch to a whisper. 'Are you insane? We're not doing this.'

'You're the one who said it was no different to stacking shelves a minute ago.'

'That was when I thought we had no choice.'

'But we're halfway there,' Warren pleaded. 'Aren't you the least bit curious to see how this all turns out?'

'I know how it'll end. With me and you sharing a jail cell, and as much as we get on, I don't think I like you that much, mate.'

Warren looked hurt, and as usual he was completely missing the point.

'You work here, don't you?'

The voice came from behind him, but before he even turned around, Carl recognised its whiney, nasal tone. It was Daily Mail Man. He turned to face him, fake smile plastered in place. 'Yes,' he said, 'we both do, but as you can see—'

'Why, for heaven's sake are there never any Mails left when I come in? Whatever day it is, they're never here. Does someone come in and bulk buy them?'

Carl and Warren looked at each other in frozen disbelief.

'Well?'

Carl made a show of looking at his watch, but before he could tell the almost permanent pain in his neck that it was half nine, and therefore only a couple of hours until the store closed, the pain in his neck spoke first.

'I'm well aware of what time it is, um…' He was looking for his name badge, and he could feel a small smile escaping onto his face along with a pang of triumph, knowing that he had neither his uniform or his name badge on. This wasn't enough to stop Daily Mail Man though, and Carl laughed to himself as he pictured a little name badge on his nemesis with that title on.

'My point is, your store has a moral obligation to provide me – a loyal customer – with whatever I want between the time it opens and the time it closes.'

'Have you ever thought about coming in a bit earlier, like everyone else?' Warren suggested, gesturing towards the empty aisles.

At this, the man tutted and shook his head. It seemed that he had run out of words with which to express his disappointment, for the moment at least, and he wandered off down the tinned fruit aisle.

'I wish he was the manager,' Warren said quietly, 'so we could hold him at gunpoint.'

'What? We're not holding anyone at gunpoint. Haven't you been listening to a word I've been saying?'

'Well, I try not to, to be honest,' Warren said, 'You always put such a downer on things.'

Just then, something occurred to Carl. Again, it was something that should have been obvious, but all the fear had prevented him from seeing it. 'Maybe we could…'

'Maybe we could what?' Warren said, impatiently.

'Maybe if we were quick enough, we *could* hold someone at gunpoint.'

'Now you're talking my language, mate.'

'We could do the right thing,' Carl said. 'We could still come out of this mess unscathed, maybe even better.'

'What? What are we going to do?' Then, Warren finally clicked.

A couple of minutes later they were outside in the freezing cold again. Carl could see that Warren was annoyed that the snow was back, but that would actually help if they were going to pull their – well, *his* – crazy plan off. The automatic doors were repeatedly opening and closing behind them. Warren was stood just to the left of them but still within range of the sensors.

'Mate, do y'want to move a bit?' Carl said, gesturing to the doors.

Warren moved reluctantly nearer towards him and out of the way of the sensor.

'Right, I think if we're going to pull this off, it's best if we go at him from two sides. That way, at least one of us will get the drop on him.'

'Yeah… that… that sounds… that makes sense.'

'What's up?' Carl couldn't help but notice his friend's hesitancy.

'I don't know. I just… Despite all my big talk, I've never really done anything this dangerous before. I mean, yes, I've broken the law and that, but it was for a good reason. I was desperate. I've never held a gun on someone before. I mean, I didn't have a problem holding a gun on one of our weedy managers, cos I knew that they wouldn't know who we were and that we had no intention of shooting them. But the guy in the van knows who we are, and he knows that we don't have a clue what we're doing. Are you sure this is—'

'The right thing to do?' Carl said. 'Yes. Absolutely, mate. I mean, the means with which we're doing it, I'm not in love with, but if we can take him down; get him put away, so he can't do anything like this again, it's worth it.'

'I guess so.'

Carl preferred this more nervous and considered version of Warren. It didn't exactly fill him with confidence for the task ahead, but it was good that he was finally being honest with him. That was the best way to go. 'I'm nervous too, mate. I don't know what's going to happen, but if we don't at least try to stop him then I reckon we're almost as bad as him. I don't think I could look my daughter in the eye if I didn't at least try.'

'I suppose.'

Warren still didn't sound too convinced, but there wasn't any time. Any minute now the Silent Partner would start wondering where they'd got to and come looking for them. Carl closed his eyes for a moment and visualised what it was they had to do. It was simple. Simple but dangerous. Sounds like a good title for a thriller, he thought absently. Focus.

He moved forward slowly, and without looking back, he said to Warren: 'I'll take the driver's side. Meet me at the back of the van.'

'Okay, mate.'

Those next few minutes seemed like the longest of the night so far. The closer Carl got to the van, the slower his progress seemed to be. He wanted to avoid stepping in the snow and to make as little noise as possible, and thankfully when he looked back, Warren had the same idea. It was a long way around because there were only a few sets of tyre tracks – including the van's – which had flattened the snow, turning it to brown mush. They also had to be mindful of the lights around the car park. Fortunately, none of them were in their path.

They finally rendezvoused a few feet from the rear of the van and continued on in silence, crouching down, until they were just inches away from the rear doors.

'Okay, what now?' Warren whispered.

'We made it. We made it, mate.' Carl could feel his relief turning to fear, as he thought about the next part of his crazy plan. He shuffled closer to Warren so he could hear him easier and hopefully wouldn't have to repeat himself.

'Easy there, mate. This is only our first date,' Warren joked.

Carl just glared at him.

'Sorry. I'm just nervous.'

'It's alright. So am I. So, like I said, on the tenth Mississippi we'll both be at the doors on either side, open them, hold the guns on him, force him into the back of the van and take him to the police and explain to them how we got into this mess. Simples. What could possibly go wrong?' Carl felt a bead of sweat dripping down his forehead, betraying how he really felt about the extremely risk-laden plan.

'Um,' Warren started, looking hesitant. 'Once we get there at the station, can I sort of disappear?'

'What? Why?' Carl said, still whispering.

'Why do y'think? My dodgy past.'

'Fine, we'll sort it out later.' Carl got his gun out of the pink backpack and felt a shudder of panic come over him as he lifted it up. It was such a black, evil looking thing, and it brought with it the dark reality of what they were about to do. He made sure not to put his finger in front of the trigger, just in case it went off accidentally.

Could they really pull it off? Then something that Warren had said came back to him with pitch perfect timing: The Silent Partner would know that they didn't know what they were doing. On the other hand, the man in the van seemed to know exactly what he was doing. This was the only time that they'd been ahead of him during the whole sordid episode. What if he made a mistake? What if he *did* shoot someone? What if this was what the psychic old man was trying to warn him about?

'Are we doing this, or what?' Warren said.

Carl could feel the sweat dripping off his hands and onto the gun. 'How do y'get the bullets out of these things?' He cursed the panic he could hear in his own voice.

'Pull the trigger?'

'Funny. You know what I mean.'

'I don't know. As long as the safety's on, you probably won't shoot anyone,' Warren tried to reassure him.

'Well? Is the safety on?'

'I don't know. I've never used one, mate.'

'Okay,' Carl said, trying to calm himself down. 'We'll just have to be extra careful, but act like we know what we're doing, even though he knows that we don't.'

He tried to put all his doubts in the corner and ignore them. They'd got this far. Just the simple, dangerous bit to go. He closed his eyes as if to reset himself into a different, more decisive version of himself: *Carl Phillips: Crimefighter*. He still couldn't believe what he had in his hand, but he wrapped his other hand around the handle to steady himself and turned to Warren.

'Okay, let's do this crazy thing. And keep low until the tenth Mississipi.' He counted down in his head, a million thoughts, doubts and niggles competing for his attention.

With each new Mississippi a fresh doubt and fear crept into his head, setting off alarm bells.

One Mississippi: That scrunch of snow was deafening. Pipe it down, man!

Two Mississippi: How can we possibly pull this off? We have no idea what we're doing.

Three Mississippi: Maybe this is all a nightmare brought on by cheese on toast. Maybe I'll wake up safe and sound next to Kate moaning about my snoring keeping her awake.

By the ninth Mississippi he was shaking almost uncontrollably, but it was too late to turn back now. He took a deep breath and tried to force himself to relax – as if there was any chance of doing that – Okay, he told himself. Let's do this.

He yanked open the door with his right hand, keeping as steady a grip on the gun as he could, and pointed it at… Warren. He was on the other side of the van, but in the middle, where the Silent Partner should've been, there was no one.

'Where is he?' they both said in almost perfect sync.

'Maybe we should just get out of here while the going's good,' Warren said.

'Yeah, you're right.' But then he spotted something. 'Hey, look,' he whispered. 'Our phones. He's just left them there in the middle.'

'Maybe he had to do a runner.'

Carl didn't hesitate and grabbed them. One of them slipped from his grasp, but before he could pick it up again, he felt the full force of what must've been the van door smash into his back. Before he could fully register what had happened, an arm wrapped itself around his neck and the all-too-familiar voice of the Silent Partner whispered gruffly into his ear.

'If you're going to ambush someone, Mister Phillips, you should search the whole area first. It's pretty much ambush rule number one.'

Carl was shaking from the shock of the impact and the fear making its way through his body, and he could see that Warren was feeling the same. Except his friend still had a gun, and it was pointed – very shakily – at him and the Silent Partner.

'So, you're going to shoot me, are you, Mister Connelly? Is the safety off?' The question was loaded with mockery, as if he'd been listening to their every word, which, he probably had been.

'Warren,' Carl said, 'just try and calm down.' He could see his friend's eyelids twitching nervously. 'No one needs to get hurt here. I'm sure we can work something out and—'

But before he could finish, the Silent Partner cut in.

'That's not necessarily true, Mister Phillips.'

The last thing he heard was the bang. It was deafening.

13

'Alright, mate. I've had just about enough of this.'

In his distress, Scrooge had all but forgotten about the taxi driver.

'I don't care if you're crazy, or just pretending to be. I don't need this hassle. Get out now, mate.'

Scrooge started to protest, but he could tell straightaway that there'd be no reasoning with the man, so he braced himself for the cold night air. 'I'm very sorry, my good chap,' Scrooge said as he clambered out of the back of the cab.

'Whatever,' the cabbie said, before driving off into the night, barely giving Scrooge time to reach the safety of the pavement.

He pulled his coat tightly around himself in an attempt to keep the cold out, but it didn't make much difference; his chills weren't just from the seasonable weather, but from his ghostly companion. Before, Jack had been translucent, but with colour in his cheeks, his face, and clothes, but now that colour had faded to white. That was before the cab had arrived, and as it set off, Jack had found it harder and harder to float along at the same speed. He was constantly disappearing and reappearing as the traffic moved and faltered, hence Scrooge's distress. He forgot himself and tried to find out from Jack where they should be going, since history had now changed because of their interference. Understandably, the cabbie mistook his behaviour for that of a madman and chucked him out.

He spotted a bench which looked wet with snow, but he didn't care. He needed to rest and sort everything out in his head. Jack slowly and uncertainly floated over to where he was sat. He appeared to be moving in and out of focus. One moment, Scrooge could see him with crystal clear clarity – like the images on the magical television box in his room at the bed and breakfast – and the next, he was a blurred cloud of smoke with only a hint of the features that Scrooge had come to know.

'What's happening to you?' Scrooge said, as loud as he could without attracting too much attention to himself.

The sound of his voice seemed to snap Jack back into focus, if only momentarily. 'I-I'm not sure. I'm new to this,' he stammered. Every word seemed like it was taking all his effort to break out, and just looking at him was making his head hurt.

'My memories are all mixed up, like in a blender with bad ingredients. They'd make sense on their own… but mixed up, I can't tell what's going on. My whole life… a mess, even the bits before all this.'

Scrooge didn't like the sound of that. 'Is it because we've been changing things, interfering in the natural course of everything?'

'Yes, I think so. I'm sorry. I can't remember your name now.'

'Scrooge. Ebenezer Scrooge.'

'Yes… I remember… Scrooge.' His voice was like a fading echo, as if he were talking from the inside of a bottle. 'A good man.' Then Jack's face changed again. 'I can see them; I can see them all.'

'Who? Who can you see, Jack?' Scrooge didn't care who could hear him now.

'Me. All my deaths. I'm dying at all different ages. I'm an old man in a chair; a young man in a park; a middle-aged man in a hospital bed. They're all true. All possible.'

'I don't understand,' Scrooge said.

'I think… I think I'm seeing all the possibilities, Scrooge. Life is all potential, isn't it. I'm seeing all the potential of my life, all at the same time. Anything is possible now. Everything's in flux.'

The spirit was starting to shift form now, as if to match what he'd just described, but his expression remained constant: he was terrified.

'Just try and focus on something; on someone,' Scrooge said. 'Think about Grace. This has all been about her. Think about her and maybe the path will become clear.'

'I'm trying.' Jack looked older now, much older. He looked down at his own hands and staggered back in shock. 'I'm old. I'm an old man like you!'

'Yes, yes I can see that.' Jack's appearance had changed completely. His clothes, his skin. His hair was grey and thin, barely covering his head. Scrooge guessed that they were now around the same age as each other, the only difference being that one of them was dead.

'Um…' Jack looked puzzled. Puzzled but elated. 'I can't remember—'

'My name's Ebenezer Scrooge,' Scrooge told him, trying not to sound too exasperated.

'Right, right. This is great, isn't it, Scrooge?'

Scrooge didn't quite see his point.

'Don't you see? I'm an old man! An old ghost man, but an old man all the same.'

Scrooge still couldn't see what he was supposed to be excited about.

'I die an old man, in my old age. Old!'

'Oh, I see.' Scrooge finally understood. 'It's worked, hasn't it. That's what you mean. Whatever we've done has worked. We've changed your history. We've changed the age at which you die.'

'That's right, Scroogey baby.'

It was odd to hear an old man speaking in such a way, but his heart lightened because he knew what was coming next.

'And as per our deal, I can now take you home, back to the good ol' nineteenth cent—'

Before he could finish his sentence, the words caught in his throat and it looked as if they were choking him. A deafening scream escaped Jack's mouth and tore through the air. Scrooge could feel it vibrating through his body, and it was so loud it was as if everyone in London was screaming out in raw pain. He covered his ears and shut his eyes, trying to protect himself from the force of the sound, but it was no use; it was as if the sound was just in his head, and there was no escaping it. And then it was gone, just as abruptly as it had arrived, as if someone had just slammed a door on it and scared it away. He gingerly uncovered his ears and opened his eyes and was greeted with a familiar sight: Old Jack. Well, not old old Jack, but old *young* Jack, the bitter young man who died before his time. The despair on his face was so palpable that Scrooge almost felt like it was happening to him, too.

'I don't understand,' Jack said between tears. 'I thought we'd fixed things.'

Scrooge tried to think it through logically; that always seemed to help. 'Didn't you say that everything was happening all at once? All the potential?'

'Yes, yes I did.'

Scrooge could feel the despair in Jack's words flowing into him, but he couldn't give into it. 'So that probably means that you're going to keep changing until everything is settled, like the ripples you spoke of.'

'That's… that's true.'

If his words brought hope to the spirit, it was barely noticeable on his face, but he kept going. What else could he do? 'You need to focus, like I said. Focus on Grace. Whenever I start to feel lost, I think of my long-lost love Belle.' The name sounded strange, almost foreign, coming from his lips. The beauty of it still didn't come close to the beauty of the woman herself. The mere thought of her and the way he'd treated her was enough to tear his heart to pieces.

'If only I'd stayed with her,' he said, 'she would have fixed me, made me a better man, instead of the monster I became. She would've grounded me and kept me true. My damned ambition blinded me, set me on the wrong path, away from her. All those Christmases I could have been with her. Instead, I became so twisted, so black with misery, I couldn't even see. I couldn't—' Tears streaked down Scrooge's face now, and it felt good. For so many years he'd tried to keep his regret hidden, even from himself. He'd filled his life with good deeds, not just for goodness' sake, but as a way of keeping himself from thinking about one of his deepest regrets.

'Where is she now?'

The question snapped Scrooge out of his dark thoughts, and he saw a slightly older man than the Jack he'd been travelling with for the last couple of days.

'She's happy. Lots of family around her and a loving husband. I've not spoken to her for, well, for most of my life; the ghost of Christmas past showed her to me. At the time I thought he was being cruel, but I came to realise that he was showing me what I needed to see. A redeemed man still needs some regret to keep him moving in the right direction. I still remember the last time I spoke to her, and it both hurts and warms me to think of it, if that makes any sense. She was such a wonderful young woman and I was already old and twisted and shaped by what I wanted my life to be. I didn't look it, but I was already the miser that everyone grew to hate.' Scrooge recognised a lost look in Jack's eyes.

'Yeah, Grace was wonderful, too,' he said softly. 'Better than me. I mean, I was no Ebenezer Scrooge; no offense. I could've done more. Even when she wasn't working one of her many double shifts at Saint Luke's she was helping everyone she could. It was a calling for her, like she couldn't help herself. It was as natural to her as breathing, and sometimes…' He stopped for a moment and sighed. 'Sometimes I told her that she went too far. She would tell me that

that was impossible; that when it comes to helping others you can never go too far, and now that I can look back on my life more objectively, I think that maybe she was right, but she did get into some scrapes. There was this one time, in the—' Jack suddenly stopped.

Scrooge thought at first that it was another physical consequence of their misadventures, but then a smile gradually grew on his young friend's face.

'What? What is it, Jack? Are you remembering something?'

'In a word, yes, Scrooge. My memories are coming back into focus. The ripples are settling. I remember where I was tonight. Where me and Grace were. And you.'

Despite the mighty wallop he'd received at the hands of the Silent Partner and the moon-sized bruise he could feel forming at the back of his head, Carl had managed to just about stay conscious. He was so stunned by what had happened, it all felt like an unreal slow-motion blur, happening to someone else, and he struggled to fight off the sweet relief of sleep. The last minute played over and over in his head; the shot of the gun echoing in his head; the van getting smaller and smaller as it left the car park and mixed in with the anonymity of the busy late-night traffic; the faint groaning of… No, the groaning was new.

It was coming from… somewhere, and as it got fainter it seemed like it was trying to lull him to sleep. Sleep: An escape from his troubles. He could see Sara nodding off as he and Kate read her favourite bedtime story. If only he were there with them now. He *was*. He *was* there. He could feel himself nodding off as the words on the page doubled up and became blurry. At that moment, as his cheek touched the snow-covered car park ground, the sudden cold shocked him back to reality.

'Carl! Carl!'

His friend's urgent cries roused him further.

'Carl! What are you doing taking a nap?! I'm the one who's been shot!'

His eyes came back into focus and he saw Warren. A round splash of red lay next to him as he clutched his arm in a failed attempt to stem the flow of blood.

'Get up,' he told himself, as if saying it out loud would make it easier. He managed it with surprising ease, and, aside from an aching back and jaw – probably from the impact of being punched to the ground – he felt fine. He made his way over to Warren, who on the contrary, looked the complete polar opposite of fine. His face was almost as white as the snow around him and his inane everything-will-be-alright smile was taking some much-needed time off. He knelt down and tried not to look at the blood, for both their benefits.

'You okay, man?' he asked, realising how stupid the question was as soon as it left his mouth.

'Well,' Warren said, attempting a laugh, 'apart from a whopping great hole in my arm, I'm absolutely fine and dandy. I think… I think it's gone right through… the bullet.'

'How do you know that?'

'The blood. I read somewhere – or it might've been on telly – that if a bullet gets stuck in your body it stops the blood from getting out, and from the looks of it, nothing's stopping *that.*'

Carl stole a quick glance. There was certainly a lot of blood. He had to stop it somehow.

'Look,' he said as he took off his jacket and started to tighten it around Warren's arm. 'I don't think you should be relying on the wisdom of TV cop shows to self-diagnose, mate. We'll see what the hospital says about it.' He felt a sudden grip on his arm.

'You can't do that.' Warren's face was more serious than he'd ever seen it.

'What are you talking about? We have to—'

'You can't phone for an ambulance.'

Warren's eyes bore into him. He tried to ignore them. 'Why not?'

'Because it'll take me to the hospital.'

'Yeah, that's the general purpose of ambulances.'

They'll have more than a few questions about the gunshot wound, and so will the cops when they arrive.'

Carl hadn't thought of that. His first thought was of saving his friend's life, but now that he thought about it, the police turning up wouldn't necessarily be a bad thing. They could tell them about the Silent Partner and what he'd forced them to do.

'Yeah, they'll be a bit suspicious, mate, but I'm sure once we tell them the whole story, they'll understand.'

'With *my* dodgy past? We don't even know who he is or where he's gone.'

Carl considered this for a moment and panic started to swell his insides again. 'But… but surely if I could vouch for you – I've never done anything illegal before.'

'He's long gone by now, and all we have is our word, and even if they listen to anything we have to say, they'll assume we're lying and trying to cover our tracks. He's been two steps ahead of us the whole way, so who's to say he hasn't planted evidence to make it look like we planned the whole thing? In fact, he could be calling the cops right now, grassing us up.'

Carl could feel his pulse racing. He closed his eyes in an attempt to calm himself. Then, something came to him. 'Wait a minute. Wait one crazy minute.'

'What?' Warren said, sounding weary.

'Nothing's happened. We're at the scene of a crime that didn't happen.'

'Um, aren't you forgetting something?'

'Yeah, but he did that. He shot you. He could tell the police what we were "planning" to do, but how could he know all the ins and outs of it without having been involved himself?'

'You might have a point,' Warren conceded, 'but he'd still find a way—'

A sound coming from just behind suddenly silenced them both. It was Carl's phone, and despite everything that had happened, the familiar ringtone brought with it a rush of joy to his heart. It was Sara. He quickly picked up the phone.

'Sara, sweetie! You won't believe how—'

'It's not Sara, it's me.'

He was still relieved. 'Oh, Kate. Kate!' he said, his whole body almost collapsing to the floor with the weight of burden being removed from his shoulders. He could tell her everything. He *wanted* to tell her everything. 'You wouldn't believe how great it is to hear your voice. You won't believe what's—'

'What are you on about, Carl? We just spoke not twenty minutes ago. You told me to—'

'What?! What are you talking about? We didn't. We couldn't've.'

'Um, yes, we did, Carl. You told me to meet you in the park with Sara because you had some exciting news for us. So, where are you?'

'I-I…' Then it came to him. His heart turned to ice as he realised what had happened; the new low that the Silent Partner had stooped to. 'Kate, you have to get out of there. Take Sara, go home, lock the doors, and don't open them for anyone. No! Forget that. He knows where we live. Go to your parents. Kate? Kate?!'

There was no sound on the other end of the line, and as he took the phone away from his ear, he looked at the screen. It beeped and flashed a couple of times and then died.

A whole new wave of panic swept over him and a million questions shot into his head; the biggest one being: Had Kate heard what he said about getting out of the park? There was no way he could assume she had; he just had to get over there. Presumably it was the park over the road from theirs. She surely would've said the name of it if it was anything different.

'Carl! Carl, can you hear me?'

'What?!' he snapped.

'I'm sorry,' Warren said, 'but that phone call didn't sound good.'

Warren didn't look too good himself. He was losing blood fast. How could things get any worse? 'He's impersonated me. The Silent Partner,' he said. 'He told Kate to meet me – I mean him – at the park over the road from ours.'

The cold night air snapped at them both, but for a moment neither of them could feel it. Time had stopped while they both took in their dire situation.

'I'll go to the hospital,' Warren said.

'What?'

'I'll go to the hospital. I'm not completely selfish, mate. And let's face it: if I don't, I'll probably die.'

Carl couldn't believe how calm Warren sounded about everything. 'But you just said—'

'I know what I said, mate, but your family's in danger and it's down to me getting you involved in this thing, and if the only way I can fix that is by going to the… hospital… If I could help you bring down that dirtball myself, I would, but I'd just slow you down.'

'I don't know what to say,' Carl said. 'Thank you. And I meant what I said; I'll vouch for you. After all, it's the truth and—'

Carl stopped, because he heard the distinctive *scrunch* of someone's foot landing in the snow behind him. He turned around, slowly.

'It's all there, Scrooge,' the spirit of Jack said quietly, almost in a whisper.

They were still sat on the bench and Scrooge probably looked like a madman talking to his invisible friend, but he was beyond caring about such trivial considerations.

'I can see it through my eyes as it happened all those years ago.'

'What can you see?' Scrooge asked.

'It's a bit of a muddle, but if I concentrate, I can make sense of it. Grace is there. She's holding my hand. I can feel the warmth of her, despite the cold all around us. She smiles at me and whispers something into my ear. I can't hear the words; I can't remember them, but the silken tone of her voice is there all the same. I'm about to whisper something back, but then a bang pierces the air and the moment's gone. Grace pulls her hand to her chest and away from me in panic.'

Jack paused and his eyes darted all over the place, as if the different parts of the new memory were scattering, like a flock of panicked pigeons.

'What is it, Jack? What happens?'

'She's running now, down the slope and deeper into the park. She shouts "We have to do something. Someone might be hurt." I think about protesting, but before I open my mouth, I know it'll be pointless, so I run after her, almost slipping on the snow. I had something to ask her, but now the moment's gone. She's getting smaller and smaller as she gets further away, out of my reach; she was always much fitter than me. I had something to ask her, but the moment's gone.

'The sharp, cold night air bites at my skin as I run, like it's trying to stop me. I can't see her now. She's turned a corner. Despite the tiredness, I push on, scared for her.

'I'm around the corner now, but she's not there. My head starts to spin. I collapse to my knees and I can feel the cold seeping through my jeans.

'"Grace! Grace, are you there?!" I shout. No reply. No reply. There's no one around. It's like she's vanished into thin air, but then I hear muffled voices. There's a long hedge with an opening in the middle and a rusty old sign for a boating lake. There's shadows moving and shifting behind the hedge. Without thinking, I get up and push through the gap in the hedge. My heart's pumping like mad. A thought flashes in my mind: Why? Why, if she's only there, did she not shout back to—

'A shot. It devours all the silence in the world. I stop. Why did I stop? If only I'd… I push on, my ears ringing, and then: A frozen lake, a cabin. A body. *Her* body! A shot. I fall. I fall into darkness.'

Jack stopped and the street seemed to follow his cue, out of respect for what he'd just seen unravel in his mind. Scrooge didn't know what to say. After everything, they'd failed.

'We never had a chance, did we, Scrooge.' It wasn't a question, just a final realistic acceptance. 'I guess some fates are written in stone, except yours of course. I was always meant to die in that park. Grace wasn't, but now she does, thanks to my meddling. I've failed in the worst possible way.'

Scrooge had been sat on the bench, going over and over the images that Jack had painted of his final moments. It had all been so vivid, but something Jack had just said had caught his attention.

'What did you say, Jack?'

'I said I failed. I—'

'You said that I was the exception.'

'Yeah, you are. You changed your fate, I mean, with a bit of help.' He sounded ever-so-slightly bitter about that.

'Yes. And how did I do that? I was shown visions of the past, present, and future. I mean, I thought it was all visions, but I suppose the past and the present could have been real enough, now that I see how easy it is to traverse time.'

'Easy?' Jack protested.

'But whether the future vision was a vision or not doesn't matter, because…'

'Because it didn't happen?'

'Exactly, my young friend. Those visions – those memories in your head – did happen to you, but they've not happened to me; not yet. And now that I know what did happen – or what's going to happen – I can change it, so that by the end of all this it will just be another vision of what might've been.'

'Like a deleted scene on a DVD.'

'Um, yes.' Scrooge knew this was yet another modern-day nonsense that would make no sense to him, even if Jack did bother to explain it. 'I'm the exception, as you said, Jack. I, and I alone can change what the fates have in store for both of us.'

'What're you going to do?'

But before Scrooge could answer, Jack started to shift and change again, only this time it was different.

'What?' Jack sounded panicked. 'Why are you looking at me like that?'

'You're – You're fading away, Jack. I can barely see you.'

'What?! No! This isn't fair! What's your plan, Scrooge? Tell me!'

Scrooge could barely hear him now. 'I'm sorry, Jack, there isn't time. You have to tell me where you are. Where are you and Grace tonight?! Which park?!'

But it was too late. Jack had faded into nothingness, and Scrooge was all alone.

14

'Just what exactly is going on here?' Daily Mail man sounded scared, but the pompousness still managed to squeeze itself in there somewhere.

Carl had to admit that it looked bad: Warren lying on the floor, a pool of blood and a firearm for company. He silently cursed himself for not thinking to hide the gun somewhere. 'I know what this looks like,' he started. 'It's a long story, and I'm not just saying that. It really is, but the short version is, my friend's been shot, and we could really do with your help, if you wouldn't mind.'

The man looked at him, eyeballs bulging almost out of their sockets. 'Who – who shot him?'

Daily Mail Man was shaking now, and his bulging eyes were now staring at his waist: His pocket. The gun. It was safely – if guns could ever be safe – stashed in his pocket, but there was a distinctly gun shaped bulge where usually a wallet shaped bulge might be.

'Oh,' Carl said. 'I know what you're thinking, sir.' He made a point of never calling anyone 'sir', but if there was ever a time to start, this was it. 'I didn't shoot my friend here.'

'That's right; he didn't.' Warren just about managed to get the words out, but it was hardly worth it.

'How am I supposed to believe him?' the man asked. 'He's clearly scared of you.'

'No. No, no he's not,' Carl protested. 'He's losing a lot of blood. He just needs—'

'Who shot him then?'

'We don't know. We don't know his name. We don't know what he looks like. We don't know anything about him.' For one hopeful second, it looked like he was getting through to the old man, but then he started to reach for his phone.

'So, a random stranger just came along and shot you in the middle of this car park?'

Warren conserved his energy and just nodded.

'A likely story.' The man still sounded pompous, even when he was scared.

'I'm phoning the police. They can—'

'No, please,' Carl begged. 'I mean, we're planning on contacting the police, but first—'

'Oh, are you planning on getting your story straight first?'

It took every ounce of self-control he had left to not punch the man.

'Why shouldn't I phone them right now?'

He looked at the phone in Daily Mail Man's hand. It was almost as if it was a more deadly weapon than the one in his pocket. In a way, it was, because Carl had no intention of using his.

'It's... It's hard to explain, but we've got mixed up in this thing. Life just takes a turn for the worse sometimes and things get out of your control. I'm sure you can relate to that.' He could see the phone edging closer and closer to Daily Mail Man's ear. It was time to get direct. 'Look. A man – we don't know who – approached us a couple of days ago. He knows us, but we don't know him. He basically kidnapped me and my friend here and forced us to take part in a heist. He wanted us to rob this place.'

'You both work here, don't you?'

At least he seemed to be listening, Carl thought. 'Yes, we do. Well, we're getting made redundant soon, so—'

'Why are you getting— Wait a minute. The shop's not closing, is it? There's been nothing on the news.'

'Thanks for the sympathy,' Carl said, dryly. 'Anyway, this guy who calls himself 'the Silent Partner' forced us to rob this place, but we changed our minds and tried to take back control over the situation. Well, he wasn't too happy about that, obviously, and shot my friend here.' He paused for breath and to let the man take everything in.

'I don't know, it all sounds a bit farfetched to me.'

'What?!' Carl couldn't believe what he was hearing. 'You think I made all that up? Why would I?'

'To shift blame away from yourself. It's all a bit too convenient that you don't know who this mysterious "Whispering Partner" is, or what he looks like. I think you're just covering yourself because I caught you, and you think that I'll believe your little tale because it's *Christmas* and I should be feeling all sentimental and mushy after an overdose of Christmas movies. Well, the jokes on you, young man, because I hate Christmas. I hate everything about it and you've just given me one more reason to add to the list.'

Carl was speechless for a moment, but then he realised, it was really just par for the cause. Out of all the people that could've stumbled upon their predicament, this bitter old man was the worst they could have hoped for. And he'd not even told him about the threat to his family. He'd most likely dismiss it as just another lie. At that moment, he felt something inside him snap. He was still in control, but the thought of Kate and Sara scared in the park scared *him* – no, angered him – and suddenly all his priorities clicked into place.

First, he needed to get Warren to hospital before he bled to death. Then he had to get to the park and stop the Silent Partner from hurting Kate and Sara, and the quickest way – not the easiest way by any means – to achieve these goals was in his pocket.

He could see the old man looking at the screen of his phone. He didn't have much time, so he quickly scanned the carpark. No one else there. Good. Quick as a flash, he pulled the gun out of his pocket and pointed it straight at Daily Mail Man. He couldn't help but feel a surge of what he hesitated to think of as satisfaction swell inside him, as he saw the sheer panic flash across the man's face.

'You wouldn't.'

'You don't know that. You don't know me,' Carl said, trying to look and sound as convincing as possible. 'I'm having a really bad day, and all I need is for you to not make that phone call and for you to hand me your car keys.'

He could feel himself shaking, but he pushed all doubt from his mind and looked Daily Mail Man straight in the eye.

'Give me the keys,' he said, attempting to inject a tone of menace into his voice. Possibly more out of shock than cooperation, the old man dropped his keys onto the ground. He looked speechless; a million miles away from the pompous snob of a moment ago.

Carl moved forward, keeping the gun trained on him – he felt awful about it, but he had to play the part – as he knelt down to pick up the keys. He heard a comment of approval from Warren and suppressed the instinct to shush him. He pressed the button on the fob and a car just to his left clicked open.

'Do you think you can stand up?' he asked Warren.

'Yeah, I think so, mate.' He sounded a bit stronger.

'Okay, get in the back. I'm taking you to the hospital.'

He did and said all this whilst still pointing the gun at Daily Mail Man; he was disgusted with himself. The Silent Partner had done this to him. He had turned him into this. He couldn't help himself and he couldn't let the man – no matter how pompous he was – believe that he was the sort of guy who was capable of doing what he appeared to be doing; what he *was* doing.

Once he was safely in the car, he opened the window and turned to the man, trying to sound as apologetic as possible. 'Look, I didn't want to do this, but everything I told you is the God's honest truth; I swear.'

'Then why are you doing it?'

Carl could hear the pomp returning to his voice, and he lowered his hands, as if to prove that he wasn't scared anymore.

'Why are you doing any of this? If you're so innocent, why not just call the police?'

'I can't. If I do that, it'll be too late. By the time I convince them.' Then an idea came to him; a crazy, stupid idea: 'Why don't you come with us?' he said.

The look on Daily Mail Man's face said it all, but before he could answer, Carl cut him off.

'I don't *want* to steal your car, I really don't. So, if you come with us you could just take the car back when we're done with it.' This sounded like a perfectly reasonable idea to Carl, but Warren had something to say about it.

'Um, mate?'

'What?' Carl hissed.

'With my history, I've had a lot of bad ideas, so trust me when I say I know a bad idea when I hear one.'

'I don't see what's so bad about it. I mean, this way we're not stealing his car, we're just—'

'Stealing *him*. A.K.A, kidnapping, mate.'

'No, no, no. We're not doing that. This is nothing like kidnapping. You get it, don't you?' Carl turned to Daily Mail Man for support for his crazy plan, but he was gone. 'Where did he go?' He turned around, and saw the old man running as fast as an old man can run on a snowy car park surface, toward the shop. Worse still, he had the phone to his ear.

'Well,' Warren said, 'I don't think he's a fan of your plan, mate.'

'Yes, thanks for the commentary there, mate.' Carl pinched the sides of his nose in a hopeless effort to relieve the pain that was threatening to fill up his whole head.

'Come on, mate. Try not to stress about that.' Warren sounded genuinely concerned for the second time since he'd met him. 'The main thing is to get your family safe. Everything else is secondary. Well, it'd be good if you could get me to the hospital at some point, as well. Who knew I had so much blood?'

'You're right,' Carl said. Despite the chaotic state his mind was in, the things that were most important broke through, like headlights cutting through fog: his family and his friend. 'Let's get you to the hospital.'

He sped out of the car park and into the busy city traffic, praying that he wasn't too late.

Scrooge was just on the right side of panic. He wasn't so distraught that he couldn't think straight and focus on what had to be done, but then, he hardly had his rose-tinted spectacles on either.

Jack, his only guide to the twenty-first century, was gone, and God only knew when and whether he was coming back. From the way he left – disappearing into nothingness – Scrooge had to assume and accept the very real possibility that his companion might never return. He would just have to soldier on and hope that saving Jack – the Jack who was still alive – and Grace would get him what he wanted, to return to his friends and family. In order to do this, he needed to find the park in which Jack and Grace were going to be shot so he could prevent it from happening, but where to start? There were signposts all around him in the busy street, and many parks were listed on them, but he didn't have time to search them all.

He knew he'd have to ask someone, but the very thought of that made him shiver. He could feel his old heart pumping faster with the anxiety of it. From what he'd seen of the people of this time – with a couple of exceptions – they were infinitely less patient than anyone from the nineteenth century. They all seemed so withdrawn, and it didn't help one jot that half of them were constantly staring at their phones, even at the risk of their own personal safety. Several times now, Scrooge had witnessed near misses from people walking into the road without bothering to look if a car was heading their way.

Get a grip, he told himself. Lives are at risk, and how hard can it be to ask someone for help? He looked around, and sure enough, most of them were staring down at their little boxes whilst walking along, oblivious to the world around them.

'Excuse me, sir! Excuse me, madam!' No response.

He knew he'd have to take drastic action, so he stepped right in front of a man with salt and pepper hair and a long dark coat on, who seemed like he should be old and wise enough to be looking where he was going.

'Oh, I'm so sorry,' Scrooge said as he collided with his intended target.

'What the hell?' the man shouted. 'You nearly made me drop my phone. You should be looking where you're going.'

He ignored the impulse to point out the hypocrisy of the man's statement. 'I'm sorry, I'll be more careful in the future,' he said. 'I'm afraid I'm rather lost, sir. Would you mind pointing me in the right direction?'

The man sighed and glanced at his phone. He looked even more annoyed than when Scrooge had bumped into him. 'Why? Where are you trying to get to?'

'Well, I'm looking for a park, but I've forgotten the name of it. Old age setting in, I suppose. I'm meant to be meeting a couple of friends there.'

The man raised his eyebrows curiously. 'There's a lot of parks in the area. Could you be more specific?'

'Well,' Scrooge said, 'my friend made it sound like it was rather large and – Oh! It had a boating lake.'

The man's face brightened a little, and Scrooge thought he was going to tell him that the park was just around the corner, over the road, or at least somewhere close by. He didn't. Instead, he lifted his phone up and started tapping at the screen at what Scrooge thought looked like letters. A moment later the man showed him what looked like a map.

'There's a few parks with boating lakes, but most of them are on the other side of the city,' he said, moving the map around with his finger. 'I mean, presumably you're in roughly the right area, I guess, so the nearest one is Victoria Park.'

Could that be the one? Scrooge thought. Either way he didn't have time enough to go too far out of his way. He looked at the screen again, and the man put two fingers on it and moved them apart. From that action the screen magically zoomed in on the park he was talking about.

Scrooge tried to disguise his awe. 'Yes, well, I suppose that must be the place. I – yes, that has to be it. Thank you, sir. Thank you very much.' He went to shake the man's hand, but it was the hand with his phone in, so Scrooge quickly withdrew the gesture.

'That's quite alright.'

He seemed almost genial and proud of what he'd done. 'Oh, one more thing, if you don't mind,' Scrooge said.

'Yes?' The irritation was bubbling to the surface again.

'How do I get there?'

'Well, you're in luck,' the man said, as if he was about to offer to take Scrooge there himself, but then he pointed. 'That goes right past the park.' It was a bus.

To Scrooge, the bus looked like a small red metal building on wheels. The only difference seemed to be that this building had a driver and only two long rooms, one on top of the other. People were moving freely up and down between the seats on the top and bottom floors. He could feel his brain seizing up just thinking about how he would feel once the monstrosity started moving. It was hard enough for him to accept that cabs were no longer pulled by horses, except for romantic purposes, as Jack had explained.

He joined the queue, which was moving forward rather quickly, and he noticed that as people approached the driver's cabin, a lot – not all of them – presented a thin piece of card or paper, or even their phones to the driver without saying a word, and then walked up the aisle to take a seat. They all seemed extremely miserable. Christmas was only a few days away now, and the only people he'd seen over the last few hours who seemed to be in the festive mood were the children, and some of *them* were pretty miserable.

He was at the front of the queue now, and he realised in a panic that he had no phone and no ticket. 'I – um, I need to get to Victoria Park, please, my good man.'

'That'll be six pound twenty, mate.' The driver seemed amused at his cheeriness as he poked the buttons which seemed to cause a piece of paper to jump out of the metal box at the side of the cabin. Scrooge got out a ten-pound note and gave it to the driver.

'Have you not got no less?' he said.

'I'm afraid not.' Scrooge knew he did, but he had no idea which coins constituted which amounts, so he just said: 'You can keep the change, my good man. Think of it as a Christmas tip.'

The man didn't seem particularly grateful, and he took the note off him as if it was a used handkerchief. 'Well?' he said, gruffly.

'Well what, my dear fellow?'

'Are you going to take it? I've got all night to sit here exchanging pleasantries, *my good man*, but I don't think that lot would thank us for it.'

Scrooge looked back at the queue and the people waiting behind him. They were even more miserable than the people already in their seats. 'Of course. Sorry,' he said to the driver, and he tore off the ticket and made his way to the back of the bus.

Most of the seats were occupied by either two people or one person and a pile of Christmas shopping. Scrooge had hoped to find a seat on his own, so he could think about what he was going to do for however long it would take him to get to his destination. He was planning on asking someone when they would get to Victoria Park, but they all looked so miserable that he wasn't sure what the response would be.

Finally, he found a seat with only one other person sat on it, next to the window. The woman was looking at and prodding a phone which looked similar to the one which Scrooge had had and lost. He reckoned that he could probably sit down next to her without saying a word and she'd barely notice, but that wasn't his way, especially not at Christmas time.

'Is it okay if I join you, madam?' he said. She didn't look up, and she didn't even seem to have heard him. 'Madam? May I join—'

'What?' she yelled. 'What do you want?'

He stopped in his tracks, stunned. 'I, um, I was just asking if you wouldn't mind if I join you.'

She seemed confused, but then realised what he was saying. 'Oh, yeah, right. Knock yourself out.'

Two days ago, Scrooge would've been completely flummoxed by a phrase like that. He would've been curious as to why a perfect stranger's response to what he considered to be a perfectly innocent question was to suggest that he do himself harm. He'd asked Jack about phrases like that and at first he tried to fob him off by saying he wouldn't understand, but Scrooge had insisted and his companion explained how a lot of colloquialisms had come from across the water, from America, because of the abundance of American TV shows. Phrases such as "No problem", "Go ahead" and "Knock yourself out", were basically more colourful and enthusiastic ways of saying "Yes". So, Scrooge didn't knock himself out, but he did sit down next to the woman as she continued to poke, prod and stroke her phone.

The bus started moving and he could feel the vibrations from below shaking his old bones, like a horse and carriage moving at a thousand times the speed. He was relieved when the bus got moving properly and the judders smoothed themselves out. He relaxed a bit and looked around at all the different people. There were a couple of people nearer his own age at the front, chatting to each other and sharing a joke, but the rest of the occupants of what he saw as a house on wheels seemed content to remain in their own little worlds, by themselves. Some of them had a device wedged into or over their ears which Jack had mentioned were called "earphones". As far as he could understand, these inventions enabled the listener to block out all other sounds around them and listen to music down a wire connected to their phone. What a world, he mused.

He suddenly realised that he had no idea when he should be getting off the bus. Right in front of him, there was a square red button with the word "STOP" printed on it mounted onto a larger yellow surface, which was in turn mounted onto a bar which went from the floor of the bus to the ceiling above. In fact, there were several of them mounted about. He'd not noticed anyone pressing the button yet, but he assumed that if he were to press it, the driver would stop the enormous vehicle immediately and he could get off. The question was, when should he get off?

He wished that Jack was still with him, so he could tell him exactly what to do. He felt like he wanted all his friends in the world watching over him at that moment, in case he did the wrong thing; in case he made the wrong move.

Ultimately though, he knew that this was a journey he must make alone. He had existed in solus for most of his life, and it felt only right and proper that he should be alone now for what could be the biggest challenge of it.

He tried to look out of the window, to see if there was any sign of the park, but it was no use. It was so bright on the bus (why was it so bright everywhere in this century?) that the light reflected off the glass and made it impossible to see anything except his old, wrinkled face. They could be anywhere. He could've gone past the park. He could've—

Then a miracle happened: The bus stopped. That wasn't the miracle in itself, although Scrooge was relieved that his bones had stopped vibrating in such an unnatural manner, if only momentarily. No, the real miracle was that amongst the ten or so passengers that were now getting on the bus were two familiar faces: Grace and Jack.

Grace looked the same, but Jack, well, he looked more solid than the Jack that Scrooge knew; a given considering he was still alive. His skin was redder; more vital; and he carried himself along with more purpose. I suppose that's what being young and alive does for you, Scrooge thought, but it wasn't just that. There was hope there; not just in the way he moved or even in his eyes and expression. Hope seemed to be emanating from him, much like the eerie glow that surrounded the ghost of him, except it wasn't something that Scrooge could see: It was a feeling, brighter than anything his eyes could register.

This hope affected Scrooge – infected him – blessing him with the feeling that now that he could follow Jack and Grace off the bus and to the park, everything on that cold December night would work out just fine.

'Are you sure you don't want me to wait with you? Just until you're signed in at least?'

'Nah, I'll be fine, mate. You've got more… important place to be,' Warren said, trying but failing miserably to sound like he hadn't lost a couple of pints of blood in the car on the way to the hospital.

'I know, but I feel bad just leaving you here on your own.'

'Believe me… mate. You'll feel a whole lot worse answering the kind of questions the police are going to want to ask you when they notice that the blood coming out of my shoulder or elbow, or wherever it is, looks suspiciously similar to the blood on your coat.'

Carl looked down at his coat and in an instinctual panic tried to cover up the stain with his arm, but there was blood on that as well.

'And besides,' Warren said, trying to look conspiratorial but only managing to sound and look drunk, 'I won't be alone. There'll be lots of hot nurses climbing over themselves to be the first to look at my war wound.'

'Ever the optimist, eh?'

'You better believe it, good buddy.'

He looked around the A & E. It was so busy, and he and Warren had to pretty much shout to each other. All the seats in the middle of the large room were full, and so were most of the seats around the edge. If they'd been any later there was no way they would've got a seat.

'Looks like I picked the wrong night to get shot,' Warren commented, as casually as if he were discussing a disappointing footie result.

He knew that if his friend survived the night, he'd be dining out on this story for months and years to come, that's if they didn't both spend those months and years in prison somewhere. He looked around the worried, panicked and mostly drunk faces to see if Sara and Kate were amongst them. They weren't there as far as he could tell. That would've been too easy, wouldn't it; for them to have escaped the madman. It would take a while for them to forgive him, but at least they'd be safe, and he could explain things in his own time. No, they were still in the park; the sick feeling in his gut told him as much. It was a shame it couldn't tell him exactly what he'd find waiting for him.

'Oh, what do we have here?'

This new voice startled him. It had a tone of concern with some tiredness thrown in. He looked up, and there was a nurse examining Warren's arm.

His friend was very pale now, but he still managed to get across a smug expression which said to Carl: *I told you they'd be crawling over each other to check out my war wound.* He couldn't figure out whether Warren's complete lack of self-concern was something to be admired or not.

'Well?' the nurse said, looking back and forth between the two of them for an explanation.

Warren went to put his hands on Carl's shoulders, but the sudden movement made him yelp with pain. 'Well,' he said, struggling, and with an expression that looked as though he was trying to wink at Carl but couldn't manage it just then, 'you've been very kind, sir.'

Carl looked at him uncomprehendingly.

'What do you mean?'

'A complete stranger.' Warren addressed the nurse now. 'This complete stranger was just passing by when he saw me struggling in the road out there. Everyone else was just passing by. They didn't want to know. Why would they? It's only Christmas. What's another bleeding man in the street when you've got shopping to do?'

Carl could see what he was trying to do: Absolve him of any involvement so he could leave without being questioned. He tried to join in.

'Yeah, I had a bit of shopping, but y'know, I just left it out there. I mean, who could leave a guy looking like he did in the street? Not me.'

The nurse looked dubiously at them both, or was it just tiredness? Whatever it was, they had to wrap it up fast. An awkward moment of silence hovered between the three of them, threatening to give the nurse a chance at some questions, but Warren jumped in.

'Anyway, thank you so much for your help—' He suddenly stopped, realising that he very nearly said Carl's name. 'I'm sorry, I didn't catch your name.'

Carl could feel his eyes widening as he struggled to think of a fake name. He felt like a contestant on a gameshow whose mind had gone blank for the simplest answer. Then a name popped in there.

'Jeff.' That's too deliberate, he thought. Too forceful. It's just your name. You don't have to convince anyone. Be more natural. 'Jeff Carlson,' he said. He said this far too softly and slowly. I might as well have a sign on my head with the word "LIAR" printed on it, he thought. That look on the nurses face definitely wasn't tiredness.

She eyed them both, sceptically, and without saying a word, walked over to the desk with the obvious intention of calling for help.

'Time for you to leave I think, mate.'

Carl started to move, but then turned back. 'What about you?'

'I've got a bullet wound. I won't get far.'

Carl couldn't help but agree, and he needed to get to his family, but he couldn't just leave his friend to the wolves either.

Warren could see he was about to say something. 'Look, I need to get this stitched up and you have to get to the park. Either way, those two things need to happen. Nothing's changed. They'll have questions, yeah; and I'll answer them, but it's a hospital. They'll fix me up before any of that. Just go, mate; I'll be fine.'

Carl couldn't help but feel bad that his friend would bear the initial brunt of all the questions, but he was right. He had to go, or who knew how much worse the night would turn out. He wanted to say something to show how grateful he was for Warren's uncharacteristic selflessness, but he couldn't think of anything.

'Just go,' Warren said, pushing him with his good arm. And without another word, he went.

He moved slowly at first. He didn't want to draw attention to himself, but he couldn't move so quickly anyway with the crowds of people surrounding him on both sides of the corridor. He looked back every few seconds to see if he was being followed. No one official seemed to be on his path, so he allowed himself to push forward towards the exit, not looking back.

As he got nearer the exit, the density of people lessened. If he'd chosen to, he could have broken into a run, but considering the fact that the nurse had most likely alerted a warden or whatever by now, he thought it best to stick to the brisk but non-running, non-suspicious pace he was currently keeping. Then, as quick as a flash, that line of thought changed. Two men dressed suspiciously like hospital wardens came marching around the corner, about fifty yards in front of him. They were stopping every few seconds to look at faces, and he could feel the panic rising in his veins.

What could he do? He had to get out of there. He looked to his left as a man with his arm in a sling came out of a door and nearly walked right through him, as if he wasn't there. He looked at the sign on the door, and without a second thought, ducked in there.

Finally, a bit of luck. After checking all four cubicles, he knew there was no one else in the toilet with him. He couldn't help but notice his reflection in the wall of mirrors facing him. There were no actual injuries, scratches or anything; a minor miracle, considering the day and night he'd had. No, the roughness was in his overall complexion. He looked gaunt and haggard, and his eyes looked as though they were ready to melt halfway down his face.

He shook his head to shake himself back into the hell that was his current predicament, and quickly ducked into the cubicle farthest from the door, locking it behind him. A second later, he heard the main door of the toilet open.

There were a few brief seconds of muffled, busy sounds from the corridor outside, and then the relative silence of the gents with a few odd drops of water in the pipes returned. Two sets of footsteps moved purposefully across the floor.

'Hello? Anyone in here?' The first voice was deep and serious and brought to Carl's mind's eye the stubbly, overweight warden he'd seen moments before in the corridor.

'Anyone here?' A higher voice this time. The one who looked like puberty was still shadowing him? This is perfect, Carl thought. If I just sit here and say nothing, then eventually they'll go away. Give up. But then, if they keep searching and find me and I say nothing now, they'll definitely know it's me that they're looking for. There was only one thing to do: Put on his best old person voice.

'Hello? Is – Is someone there?' That sounded pretty old and dithery, he thought.

'Oh,' the stubbly, fat one said. 'We didn't mean to disturb you, sir. We're just, um, checking the cleanliness of the toilets. There's been some complaints.'

He would've punched the air with triumph if he hadn't been in such a confined space. They fell for it. But then:

'Wait a minute, Doug,' the younger one said in an almost whisper which he probably thought he couldn't hear. 'How do we know that's not him. He could be putting on a voice or something.'

'Putting on a voice?' Doug threw back at the rookie. 'So, what do you suggest we do? Force him to come out in the middle of what he's doing in there, to prove that he is who he seems to be? Why would some crim hide in the toilet? He's more likely to sneak into a closet and dress up as a doctor and sneak out of here.'

Why didn't *I* think of that? Carl thought.

'It's not beyond the realms of possibility that he's in there.'

'Yeah, mate. And it's also not beyond the realms of possibility that you're out to impress some pretty nurse who flashed her overdone eyelashes in your direction at the Christmas do.'

'Well, that's where you're wrong,' the younger one said. 'It was her birthday do. I didn't go to the Christmas one.'

'Yeah, 'cos you struck out at the birthday do.'

There was an awkward silence between them, and Carl could imagine them glaring at each other. Then, the younger one said something.

'I'm just trying to do my job properly. Just think how bad we're going to look if it does turn out to be him and you just dismissed it.'

He didn't like the way this tide was turning. He tensed up, ready for a confrontation, or maybe just to make a run for it. The room went silent again. Even the dripping water in the pipes seemed to be weighing up the possibility that he wasn't what he'd tried to sound like. The footsteps started up again, and just as they stopped outside his cubicle, a loud crackle of one of their radios made him jump and nearly fall off the seat.

'We've spotted a likely suspect outside Ward H,' the muffled voice on the radio said. 'Fits the description. All teams to H Ward.'

That's lucky, Carl thought. What are the odds? He listened carefully to see if this new development had settled the argument as to whether he was who he said he was, but he couldn't hear anything. The room had a veil of silence over it that made him feel like if he made one false move, he'd be trapped. Had they gone? Then, something occurred to him: He hadn't said anything for a while either. The innocent old man, who he was claiming to be, surely would've said something else by now, if he was who he was claiming to be.

'H-hello?' he said, trying to remember the voice he'd put on moments earlier. 'Anyone there?' A few delicate seconds of silence passed. He found himself counting them and thinking that if he made it to ten, he was safe. He made it to four.

'Yeah, we're here, sir.' It was the stubbly, overweight one. 'You okay in there? You're very quiet. You shouldn't let us distract you from, y'know… whatever.'

There was something in his tone. Something a bit too courteous and deliberate. I suppose maybe it's because he thinks I'm deaf or something, because I'm old. Maybe—

But before he could finish that thought, the stubbly, overweight one spoke again. 'Alright, well everything seems to be in order here, sir. I'm not sure what all the complaints were about, but then people are so fussy these days. OCD and all that.'

Again, the overly friendly tone.

'We'll leave you in peace now, sir.'

Too many "sirs". They were on to him. But then he heard two sets of footsteps head toward the door; the door opening; the brief hustle-bustle sound of the corridor; and then nothing. Silence dictated its terms again, and the only sounds it was letting pass were the *drip drip* of the pipes and his own heartbeat, which was thumping away like a train running two hours late. He tried to tell himself to breathe, to relax, at least for the moment. The time to panic was when he got to the park, although he knew that wasn't exactly a viable plan. After a few seconds (it felt a lot longer) he stood up and let out a heavy sigh. He'd just been paranoid. Understandable really, but there was no reason for them to have doubted him. It'd been relatively easy. He unlocked the cubicle and opened the door… and his heart fell to his feet. In the mirror in front of him was the younger security guard, with his arms folded, looking as smug as a Cheshire Cat who'd just come first in a smugness competition.

Now, all the pieces were falling into place, Scrooge thought. All he had to do was convince Jack and Grace not to go into the park.

He thought about getting up from his seat and walking over to them, but the moving metal building was so crowded, and people were already stood up, holding on to odd looking harnesses which were suspended from the ceiling. Also, the mere thought of walking along whilst moving at speed through the London streets made him feel queasy, as did most of the experiences he'd had over the last couple of days. No, he decided. I'll wait until they get off this contraption and I can think straight again.

It had occurred to him that he had no idea what he was going to say to either of them. He knew that he couldn't tell them the truth; they'd surely run off, screaming. Although, as long as they ran off screaming in the opposite direction to the park, that would be just fine. Of course, there was no guarantee of that, and who knew; in doing so, they might make things much worse. There were no set rules here, he knew that. His guide was gone. He only had himself and his best judgement for company, and his faith in that was not as unwavering as it once was.

He looked over to them. They were about five rows in front. They seemed so happy. Whereas most of the other passengers were glued to their phones, Grace and Jack were talking and laughing with each other. Although, in between the laughter and the conversations Jack seemed distant. He kept turning away from Grace towards the aisle and putting his hand in his pocket, as if to check that something was still there.

Something suddenly clicked in Scrooge's mind. That was it! That was how he would convince them. He felt awful and elated at having discovered Jack's little secret. He would ruin a sacred moment, but it was entirely necessary, in order to prevent a tragic one.

A myriad of thoughts raced around Carl's head as he turned slowly to face the security guard. He thought of all the ways he could possibly get away. He thought about all the circumstances that had led up to this moment and how unfair it had been.

The voice of his mum's uncle suddenly chimed in:

'There is no such thing as fair and unfair. There's only what you do and don't do. Don't waste time blaming the universe for your problems.'

He was pretty sure that his mum's uncle Roy had been spectacularly sozzled at the time of his philosophical statement, but it actually made a lot of sense.

He needed to do something, and quickly. A public toilet didn't usually stay this quiet for long. Focussing on the end he had to get to: his family, he found it simpler to look at the means. The guy in front of him – who was in the midst of slowly reaching for his walkie-talkie – didn't look that tough; not tough at all, in fact. He'd probably never been in a situation like this before. Probably. Maybe they'd covered it in his training when he'd first got the job, but he'd been reassured – probably by his stubbly, overweight colleague – that stuff like this would rarely happen, and as the weeks and months went by, "rarely" morphed in his mind to "never" and he became comfortable, just seeing the job as something that had to be there for the sake of everyone's peace of mind, but actually had no danger attached to it whatsoever.

Of course, Carl had never been in this situation before either, but the guy seemed younger than him by at least ten years, and he probably thought he was in more danger than he actually was. Surely, the blood on his shirt contributed to the fear factor as well. He decided there and then that if he had to punch him, he would, but words might do the job just as well. What was it that Warren had said? Something about the threat of violence being more effective than actual violence itself?

They were both still staring at each other. The warden was trying his best to look like he was in command of the situation, but his eyes gave the game away: he was terrified. He hated what he saw, but at the same time he was glad of it. It meant that half his work was done before he'd even opened his mouth. 'You're scared of me, aren't you.' He gave himself goose bumps. His voice sounded alien to him, like someone else was in control.

The warden shook his head in an unconvincing gesture of defiance. 'No. No, I'm not,' he said, too quickly.

The words had the opposite effect when said so fast. I'd love to play a round of poker with this guy, Carl thought. I'd clean him out.

The warden's eyes were flickering and moving back and forth between him and the door. He was obviously hoping for the cavalry.

Well, they're not going to come. Not before I – *Before I what? What am I going to do?* He felt a cold chill flow through him, and as he looked again at the young warden's eyes, he saw himself: Scared, alone, and losing hope with every passing second.

He couldn't go down this road. He couldn't pretend. He couldn't act like someone he wasn't. The truth was the weapon he needed here. He'd have to relay what had happened to him – to him and Warren – at some point, and he might as well start now, with the least intimidating hospital warden in the world.

He looked him square in the eye and took a deep breath, hoping that the right words would come. 'I'm not who you think I am.' Not the best opening line in the world.

'Oh yeah? Well, that blood on your shirt tells a different story, pal.'

"Pal"? He was trying to sound tougher. He had to get through to him before he started believing his own act. 'I have a story,' he said softly, loosening his shoulders, attempting to look as relaxed as possible, 'but it's not the one I'm guessing you're thinking up in your head.'

The warden's face looked even tenser and focussed than before, but maybe that was proof that he was listening. Carl carried on, encouraged that maybe he could confide in the guy.

'My family are in danger.' He had hoped that last sentence would garner some kind of sympathetic response, but the warden was either unmoved or just too scared to show any reaction. He tried not to let this put him off and told the guard the whole story from the beginning.

'Well?' Carl said, five seconds after the end of his story had left the room silent once more.

The warden screwed his eyes up as he thought about what Carl had told him. At least he didn't look scared anymore.

'It seems a bit over the top…'

Carl's heart sank.

'But why would anyone bother making up a story like that?'

'I'm not making it up. I swear, it's the Gods' honest truth, and once I've sorted this mess out, my mate can back me up,' Carl said. 'God, I hope he's okay. He lost a lot of blood before we got here.'

'We have a great staff here. If they can help him, they will.'

'So, you believe me?' Carl could hear the desperation in his own voice, but he didn't care. He needed to wrap this up quickly and get away.

'Yeah, I think so,' the warden said, looking away. 'It sounds kind of insane, so it's probably true, I suppose, and you don't seem as dangerous as I thought you were.'

'I'm not,' Carl said, 'I just need to get to my family.'

They were suddenly interrupted by the rustle of the warden's radio and the voice of his chubby companion.

'Hey, Kev. You there? Seems like you might've been right about that old fella in the toilet. This lead was a dead-end. Over.'

Kev, as Carl now knew him to be, looked at him. He couldn't tell what he was thinking. Was he having second thoughts?

'Kev, are you there? Over.'

Kev shook his head and had that confused look on his face that people who've just woken up on the bus have. 'Yeah, I'm here.'

'You had me worried then, mate. Over.' Then the voice on the radio said something very odd: 'So, do you wish it could be Christmas every day? Over.'

Staying silent, Carl looked at the warden. What was the other guy on about?

Kev was unmoving and his eyes were focussed on nothing in particular. He was weighing things up, Carl thought.

He spoke into the radio at last, but their conversation wasn't getting any less surreal. 'No. I unwrapped the present and it wasn't what I was hoping for. Over.' He took his thumb off the button and said to Carl, almost apologetically: 'It's code. It means you weren't who I thought you were. His idea.'

The voice on the other end sounded almost disappointed. 'Oh. Well, he must've got away by now. He's someone else's problem. Over.'

'Yeah, I suppose so. Over.'

'Anyway, after all that excitement I need a pee, so I'm on my way back up. See you in a sec, mate. Over and out.'

Carl's heart dropped to his feet. The warden could see it.

'It's okay, if you leave now and go left down the corridor and down the stairs on the… er… first left, you won't bump into him.'

'That's great, thanks,' Carl said.

'I'm pretty sure, anyway,' Kev said, looking doubtful.

'You're *pretty* sure?'

'Well, yeah. As long as he doesn't come back up the long way, and he probably won't 'cause like you heard, he needs a pee. I suppose he's not seen you anyway, so as long as you don't look too suspicious and you cover up all that blood, you can just—'

Suddenly the door burst open. It wasn't the other warden; just a random man, and he headed straight for one of the cubicles without looking at either of them.

'That was a close one,' Kev whispered. 'Are you going to be okay? Do you want me to call the police or something? I mean, they're probably on their way already I suppose, on account of you nicking that old guy's car.'

'They probably are, aren't they,' Carl said, mostly to himself. He had been feeling slightly less panic-stricken for having told his story to someone, but now the reality of it and the pressure was rising in his veins again.

'I – I'm not sure what to do.'

He looked at the warden. His mouth was opening and closing, as if he wanted to say something, but didn't know what. Finally, he spoke. 'I could come with you; be your backup.' Again, Kev's eyes told a different story to the one his mouth was telling.

He had no doubt that the guy wanted to help, but he could see that chasing after the bad guys wasn't really his thing. He could still help though. 'I can't ask you to put yourself in the firing line for me, but you could still help me here, in the hospital.'

Kev's face brightened. He knew what he was asking of him. 'Your friend. You want me to make sure he's okay.'

'Yeah. If you wouldn't mind. And if you could, back him up. Back up our story when he tells it to the police. He's had trouble with them in the past.'

Kev backed away, suddenly doubtful.

'Nothing serious, don't worry. It's just that he's made a few bad choices, that's all.'

'Right.' Kev didn't look as sold on the idea as he would've liked, but he didn't have any more time to convince him.

'Can I trust you to help him?' he said, as he backed towards the door.

'Yeah, sure. I'll do that for you. I hope… I hope it all works out okay, for you and your family.'

Carl stopped in his tracks at this. Maybe it was the pressure getting to him, or the fact that a complete stranger was willing to listen to him and believe him and help him, but he could feel tears welling up in his eyes.

He managed to get out two words before leaving the room, escaping down the corridor and heading toward his uncertain fate:

'Thank you.'

Scrooge was fighting a losing battle with sleep. Fortunately, the journey was so bumpy and noisy that as soon as he realised his eyes were shut, the bus knocked him back into reluctant consciousness. Every time this happened, he panicked that he'd been out too long, and his eyes automatically flipped towards Jack and Grace.

They were still there, but not talking as much as they had been. They were both looking out of the window, Jack more anxiously than Grace. Then, the now familiar ring sounded at the front of the bus and they both got up. It was lucky that he saw this when he did, because at the same time almost everyone else on the bus got up and formed a long line, even before it had stopped moving.

Before he had a chance to think about his next move, the young lady sat next to him got up, wanting to join the line. Instinctively, he got up and gestured for her to go ahead of him, but all he got for his trouble was a contemptuous look.

'It's alright. You go ahead,' she said, looking for all the world as if he'd just slapped her in the face.

The bus came to a sudden stop, and everyone who was stood up along the aisle in the middle, shunted forward as one. He was grateful that there were so many of them, otherwise he would've fallen flat on his face. On the other hand, there were so many people that he was finding it next to impossible to keep track of Grace and Jack. He knew that they must be at the front of the line by now, but he would feel so much better if he could at least see the backs of their heads. All he could see at the moment were several different and bizarre hairstyles that made him feel more like a man out of his time and comfort zone than ever. *Pink hair?* The world's become a circus, he thought.

The line was moving at an agonizingly slow pace, and he tried his best to look out of the windows on either side to see if he could spot Jack or Grace. He couldn't see anything. There were so many people on board the metal miracle that the condensation was steaming up the windows of the whole carriage. He could feel himself getting more and more impatient, but by contrast, no one else seemed to be bothered by the slow-moving queue. They were probably used to it, he supposed. He hated the feeling of being hemmed in, but he tried his best to relax and go with the flow of the line; he wouldn't get off any faster by panicking. Slowly, ever so slowly, he could see the exit of the bus looming nearer, and then finally he was there. He thanked the driver who proceeded to laugh at him, and then looked around for any sign of the couple.

His eyesight wasn't what it was, but he could see a sign, just across the way. There were several different ones bunched together pointing in all directions, but the one he wanted was right at the top of the pole: Victoria Park. He looked towards where it was pointing, and there it was, just across the road. And there *they* were, underneath an electric streetlamp.

This was it. This was the end of his journey. He was certainly ready for it, but the thing about endings is, a lot of the time they're just new beginnings in thinly veiled disguises. Scrooge stepped forward and into the road.

Carl had been running. He felt like he'd been running all night; all week, but he'd only actually been running in a literal sense for the past ten minutes. When he'd got outside the hospital, after much ducking and diving, he finally thought he was home free.

He was wrong. Just as he approached the car which he'd borrowed from Daily Mail Man – without his permission, of course – a policewoman stood up from behind it. He had no choice. He had to keep on walking, and when he got to the car park entrance – after looking discreetly over his shoulder several times – he started running, and he didn't plan on stopping until he reached his family and knocked the Silent Partner into next Christmas. But the thing about plans is, they don't always work out.

The park looked beautiful, Scrooge thought. The snow-covered treetops gave it an almost heavenly appeal. It was a nice change from the tall, cold, lifeless buildings of the city; a place frozen in time; an escape from the constant noise and hustle and bustle. Not a place where a murder would happen. Well, not if he could help it, anyway.

There they were, still walking, approaching the entrance. He followed at a discreet distance. And then, they stopped. Jack was about to do something, and he knew he had to intervene. In order to save them both; in order to make Jack believe he could see the future, he had to stop him from proposing to Grace.

He stepped forward, ready to destroy a man's dreams. He'd done plenty of that in the past, he thought, but this was for a good cause. If Scrooge could really see the future, he might've managed to avoid what happened next.

'OUT OF THE WAY!'

The warning came too late, and before he knew what was happening, Scrooge was on the floor with a fresh bang to the head, shell shocked old bones, and a familiar face just inches away from his own.

15

'You?!' Carl screamed at Scrooge, whilst still on top of him.

Scrooge's vision was going in and out of focus from the shock of the collision, but as he looked up, he recognised the man who seemed destined to bring about tragedy for Jack and Grace.

'You,' he said, with no less shock than Carl had said it, seconds before. 'What are you doing here? I didn't think you'd still be the person to—'

'Be the person to what?' Carl said, not even attempting to disguise his anger and anguish. He was tired and confused, and why did he keep bumping into this old man? Then it came back to him. 'Oh yeah, I remember now. You think I'm going to kill someone in an armed robbery.' He almost forgot to keep his voice down, in case anyone heard. 'Well, you were right about that.'

'What?' Scrooge could feel the blood rushing away from his head in shock.

'Eh? Oh, you think – No, no, no. I managed to get out of it. I didn't rob anything, and I certainly didn't kill anyone. Alright?'

Scrooge felt relieved. History had changed, but now fate had brought Carl Phillips and Jack and Grace together again. 'Of course,' Scrooge said to himself, forgetting Carl hovering over him for a second. 'The robbery still happened, but on a different night. Jack and Grace went to the shop tomorrow night, but now—'

'What are you on about? Who are Jack and Grace?'

'It's a very long story, young man, and I'm not sure you'd believe me if I told you the whole tale, but I don't have time, I just need to ask you to turn around and walk away from here. Please.'

'What? Walk away?' Carl could feel the anger swelling up in him, and even though the old man looked so frail lying there in the snow, he thought that it would make him feel so much better just to – No. That wasn't him. Then something occurred to him that made him reconsider. 'Wait a minute. Did you – Did you know this was going to happen? You – You're involved in this somehow. You know where they are, don't you! You know where my family are.'

'Your family? You've lost your family?'

'You know I have. You know where he's keeping them!'

Scrooge could feel fear getting a grip on him, but he needed to calm Carl down. 'Listen, I… I have nothing to do with your family going missing. Is that why you were going to rob the shop? Because someone had your family? I can help. I—'

'I don't need your help; I need my family.' Carl could hear his voice cracking. He didn't know how much time he had left. 'Tell me something. If you're not involved in all this – and the jury's still out on that – then how did you know about the robbery? Tell me the truth!'

'Very well, I'll tell you,' Scrooge said, gesturing for Carl to help him get to his feet. 'You may think me mad, but I'll tell you.'

Carl thought about when he'd told *his* mad story to Kev, the warden at the hospital, and he seemed to believe him, so maybe there was a chance that he'd believe the old man. Then, something suddenly came back to him: the old man had been talking to an invisible friend down in the tube station. Maybe he was just mad.

'Alright, young man,' Scrooge said, taking in a deep breath of cold London air. He tried to order events in his head, to try and make the whole ordeal sound as plausible as possible.

'Oh, I don't have time for this,' Carl moaned. 'I've got to—'

'I'm from the past.'

Carl had been turning to leave, but this got his attention. 'You're from the past? You mean you're old. No offense, but I can see that. That doesn't explain—'

'No, I mean I'm literally from the past; from the nineteenth century,' Scrooge said with a touch of gravitas. 'The year of our Lord, eighteen forty-one, to be precise.' He paused to allow Carl to take this in. The slack jaw and glazed expression didn't look too promising, but he carried on.

'One Christmas, many years ago now, four spirits came to me and helped me change my ways. Recently – well, recently for me – another spirit came to me. He said I wasn't doing enough to improve my life, and so I agreed to come here to the twenty-first century to fix something. It turned out that he'd lied to me. It was him I had to fix. He originally died in that robbery you see, but now, as far as I know, he's going to die in this park tonight, unless I stop it.' There was more to it than that, he knew, but he was quite proud of how succinctly he'd summed up recent events, no matter how unbelievable they might sound.

Carl still didn't seem convinced. His face gradually moved again, as if it was coming unstuck or defrosting from the cold. 'You're joking me, right? And I suppose that invisible friend of yours down in the station was this "spirit"?'

It took Scrooge a moment to recall that last encounter. 'Oh… yes. Yes! So, you believe me?' Before Carl opened his mouth again, Scrooge could see what the answer was going to be.

'You are sick. Either you're sick and you need help, or you're deliberately stalling me, keeping me from finding my family.' He turned to leave. 'And if I find out that it's the latter, I'll – I don't know what I'll do.'

'No, Carl,' Scrooge protested, 'why would I do that? I want to help you. I know my story's a bit…' It was too late. Carl had already broken into a run. A run of a desperate man who had no idea where he was going. Scrooge knew he had to follow: The ripples he and Jack had caused hadn't just affected Jack's life, other lives were shifting in the current too, and whether he chose his mission or not, he knew that he had to follow it through and fix it, or he could never live with himself.

'It *is* him! I told you, Jack.'

The new voice belonged to Grace.

'Well, I don't know. I've only seen him once before.' This was the living and breathing Jack.

It was still odd for Scrooge, seeing his guide for the twenty first century in the flesh, so to speak. It was like seeing a painting come to life, which, until a few days ago, he would've considered completely out of the question.

'Grace! Jack!' he said, with his arms outstretched. 'It's so good to see you. You weren't thinking of going in there tonight, were you?'

'The park?' Grace said. 'Yeah, we were about to, and then we saw you were having a bit of trouble and—'

'Oh, him?' Scrooge said, gesturing towards where Carl had been moments before. 'He's my… nephew. He's just got himself into a bit of bother and I need to help him out, but you should definitely stay out of there tonight.'

'Oh,' Grace said, looking dubious. 'Why? What kind of trouble is he in?'

'Nothing that you need worry about. I need you to both promise that you won't go in there tonight. Swear on your lives to me,' he snapped.

'Okay, fine,' Grace said. 'We won't go in there, we promise, don't we, Jack.'

Jack wasn't happy. 'No. I'm promising nothing of the kind. We don't even know you, old man, and I've got – I've got something I need to do in the park tonight, and I'm not going to let you ruin my plans, okay? Why are you even listening to him, Grace? He's just a random nutter.'

'I don't know,' Grace started. 'Maybe you've got a point.'

'Damn straight I have,' Jack said victoriously.

Grace suddenly turned back to Scrooge. Her eyes were sharp and piercing, even in the darkness, and they seemed to be poking and prodding Scrooge for the truth. 'Tell me something,' she said, her eyes still focussed on him. 'Why do we – Why do *I* keep bumping into you? This is the third time it's happened in less days. Are you stalking me or something?'

'*Stalking* you?' There was no time for this. He had one last trick; one last hope up his sleeve. Then, whether Jack and Grace chose to believe him or not, he would have to go and help Carl and pray that he wasn't too late. 'Jack,' he said, 'could I just have a quick private word with you?'

He opened his mouth and started to protest.

'It won't take a minute,' Scrooge assured him, 'and then you can go in the park or not. It's up to you.'

Grace didn't look too happy about it, but Jack whispered something to her and let go of her hand and joined Scrooge, who had backed off, nearer to the road.

'Okay, old man, what have you—'

'You're planning on proposing to Grace tonight, aren't you.'

Jack turned as white as a sheet and shifted his head quickly to see where Grace was.

'It's okay, she can't hear us,' Scrooge assured him. 'Now, do you believe my story?'

'I – I'm not sure. I… You could've guessed that. You could've—'

'But I didn't. And if you're not sure, don't you think the best thing to do would be to avoid the park, anyway? You could propose somewhere else.' He closed his eyes and prayed that he'd convinced him.

'Okay,' Jack said finally, 'I'm still not sure I believe you, but I'll take Grace away from here. I've always dreamt of proposing to her here, but I'll just have to…' His voice trailed off, and he seemed at a loss, and Scrooge felt terrible for him, but relieved at the same time.

'Thank you,' Scrooge said softly. He could feel his time in this time was almost up. He just had one more thing to do, and as he headed into the park, bidding Grace and Jack a final farewell, Ebenezer Scrooge realised he had no idea what he was heading into.

Carl had no idea what he was heading into. It didn't help that every emotion in the world was filling up his head and heart, all at the same time. They seemed to be pushing him forward with no real direction. It had occurred to him to look for the Silent Partner's and Sara and Kate's footprints in the snow, but he immediately dismissed the idea when he saw just how thick and fast the snow was coming down, covering any prints that might have been there. How would he ever find them? There was no time for despair. He needed to be cold – colder – clinical. He needed to find them. He *had* to find them. He tried to look through the wall of ever-falling snow for any signs of struggle, already knowing that he wouldn't know what that looked like anyway. There was nothing.

At any other time, or in any other circumstances, the scene before him would've been quite beautiful: The snow-covered trees and the glow of the light pollution from the city would've reminded him of a Christmas card, but right now it looked and felt like a huge faceless monster, mocking him. It knew what he wanted to know, and it was taking great pleasure in keeping its secrets from him.

There was only one more thing to try. It was probably pointless, but he had to give it a go.

'KATE! SARA!!!'

Nothing. He'd never felt more alone. There was no one else in the park. No dog walkers, no couples. Nobody. What if it was a trick? What if he'd taken them somewhere else? The old man *had* been trying to slow him down. He claimed that he wasn't, but the story he told him about his invisible friend; how could he possibly expect him to believe that? It was a distraction to help his partner. No. He was working alone, wasn't he? Maybe he wasn't. Maybe—

A strange sound snapped him out of his endless questions. A phone. Not the phone in his pocket; that was dead. No, it was somewhere in the park. The tune: it was 'Lonely This Christmas'. It sounded like it was close, but something was muffling it. If the park hadn't been so completely deserted, he probably wouldn't have been able to hear it. It doesn't matter anyway, he told himself. All that matters now is—

And then something occurred to him: What if…

He followed the sound, and there, just to the right of where he'd been standing was a small bush covered in undisturbed snow; and next to it, in the shape of an arrow pointing towards where the phone was, were boot prints. 'Lonely This Christmas' was for him: The Silent Partner's sick sense of humour. As he went to reach down for the phone – which was in a small jiffy bag – he laughed cynically to himself: How things had changed since his first phone call from the man who called himself the Silent Partner. He'd thought that he could avoid the whole situation by simply refusing to speak to him. How many times had he and Kate shouted at the TV screen to the dumb but pretty characters: *Don't pick it up! Don't pick it up!* After all, if they can't threaten you; if they can't tell you what they have of yours that you want back, then they're in no position to control you. So much for that. He could feel the anger and fear welling up in him again. His heart was pumping with it. One beat: anger, the next beat: fear. He didn't know which one would come out when he answered the call, but he knew which one he hoped for.

As he picked it up, an idea came to him. A tiny, petty idea, perhaps, but at least it might give him a slither of satisfaction: He wouldn't be the one to speak first. He would make the man on the other end start whatever conversation they were going to have. He would at least have some control, rather than the feeling of being a snowflake in the wild winter wind, being blown around at the whim of a criminal.

Silence. Two seconds, then three, then four seconds passed. He felt satisfied, but a feeling of guilt started floating to the surface. Was he risking Sara and Kate's lives with this stupid behaviour? He was too tired to know what to do for the best anymore. All he could do was react to what came at him; what had been coming at him from all sides over the past couple of days. He was about to buckle, but then the familiar voice spoke up.

'Mister Phillips?'

He couldn't help but enjoy the slight uncertainty clearly audible in the cracks of the criminal's voice. He held on for another second. Despite his better judgement, the feeling was addictive, toxic.

'Mister—'

'Yeah?' It felt even better to interrupt him. There was a sudden silence again, followed by the sound of a throat being cleared.

'Mister Phillips, I do hope you're taking this situation with the seriousness that it merits.' The voice was cold and clinical. The voice of a man who knew he had the upper hand. 'Now, are you going to stop messing around, or shall I tell your family that you're not taking their safety seriously? Actually, that might not tally with what I've already told them.'

'Why? What have you told them, you psycho?!' he screamed.

'Now, now, now, there's no need for name calling, Mister Phillips.'

He wanted to call him something else, he wanted to let out a barrage of threats that probably sounded more convincing in his head, but what would be the point? He just had to accept that he had no control over the situation and listen to what the man had to say. 'What do you want me to do?' He said the words as coolly as he could.

'That's better, Mister Phillips. Why can't you be like this all the time? It would save so much, well, *time*.'

He could almost hear the laughter in his voice, but he tried not to rise to it. 'Where's my family?' he said, as calmly as he could manage.

'They're safe. They're with me, and I'll tell you where we are. There's just some terms and conditions I need to run by you first. Well, just one really.'

'Haven't I done enough for you already?'

'Well, if you look at the facts, Mister Phillips, you've done precisely diddily squat for me.'

He was about to argue the point, but then he thought for a second, and yes, the Silent Partner was right: He hadn't done anything for him. At least there was that to comfort him. 'Okay, what are your terms?'

'No police. This is just between you, me, and your family. It's another one of those things that should go without saying, but someone in your… uniqueish situation might be stupid and panicked enough to call them. You haven't called them, have you?'

'No, I haven't,' he said without hesitation. He couldn't promise that Daily Mail Man hasn't though.

'Good,' said the Silent Partner, 'at least you're doing *something* right.'

Carl knew he was still trying to get a rise out of him, but he wouldn't give him the satisfaction. 'Where are they then? My family.' He could hear the fear coming through in his voice, he couldn't help it. He thought about how he would feel when he saw the Silent Partner, when he saw Kate and Sara again, and he realised something: He wasn't scared of the Silent Partner. Everything he'd done to him, to hurt him, he'd done, and he'd survived. He'd come out the other side, relatively unscathed. He was worried about how he was going to explain everything to Kate and Sara, but how much harder could it be than everything else that had happened to him recently? Surely, they'd have some sympathy for him, after he'd told them everything he'd done to rescue them. He was scared though, and now he understood what it was he was scared of. He was scared of what he would do when he saw the Silent Partner next to his family. He was scared of what he might be capable of. Maybe he'd be able to hold himself back for the sake of his family and what they might think of him. He didn't want them to think he was a monster, but he didn't want them to think that he didn't care either. He was so tired he didn't know what to do for the best; he didn't know if he could trust his own judgement.

'Do you know where the boating lake is?' the Silent Partner said.

'Um, yeah. I think so, yeah.'

'We're in the cabin. Don't dawdle.'

There was a click, and then he was gone. The boating lake? He hadn't been there in years. A series of unexpected but welcome images flashed into his head: Kate and him in a boat on the lake.

You're going round in circles.

No, I'm not.

Well, sweetie, I think the ducks beg to differ.

It was one of their first dates, and he remembered how happy Kate had been when they found the house so close to it. That was it. That was the memory he needed to kick him up the backside. He wouldn't let the Silent Partner destroy one of his most important shared memories; a root memory for him and Kate.

There it was: The boating lake. Just two patches of snow covered grass and two paths of sludge away. He started running. He was focussed on one image: His hands wrapped around the Silent Partner's neck. They would come back to this park again, the three of them. Him, Kate and Sara. And they would remember this day proudly as the day that he saved all their lives. He would be a hero. He would be *their* hero. Books would be written about him. Those books would be turned into blockbuster movies. They would divide opinion, but he would always be—

'That's quite far enough, Mister Phillips.'

The voice came from somewhere ahead, but he couldn't pinpoint exactly where. The Silent Partner said his name very slowly, emphasising the *s*'s, like a snake, if a snake could talk. This wasn't quite enough to burst the bubble of his adrenalin rush though. 'No. *You've* gone quite far enough, whoever you are. Now, give me back my family.'

There was a slow and deliberate pause, as if the man calling himself 'The Silent Partner' was actually considering doing what he asked. But then, a new voice spoke out. The same owner, but a different attitude and tone.

'You really don't recognise me, do you. I made so little impact on you.'

Carl couldn't believe what he was hearing. 'You've kidnapped my family; tried to ruin my life. Oh, you've made an impact on me, believe me.'

'But not so much that you've tried to figure out who I am.'

'I don't care who you are! You're the man who's terrorised me and my family.' He stepped forward without even really thinking about it and immediately regretted it. A couple of inches from his feet the snow exploded with a bang.

'That's what's known as a warning shot, Mister Phillips.' The voice sounded more composed now, as if he'd remembered the situation and how he should be acting. 'Take one step closer and I'll be firing another type of shot.'

It was so deathly quiet in the park. Scrooge found it hard to believe that there was another soul in there with him. The sounds of the city seemed muffled now, as if an invisible dome was covering the park, keeping it separate from the constant buzz.

He felt completely alone; an old man, trying to save the day. It was such a big park. How was he supposed to know where to start looking? He felt like an author or an artist with a blank sheet of paper sitting in front of him, daring him to action: *Come on, do something, old man*. He made a decision. He was about to turn right, but then, the first gunshot shattered the silence.

Carl stood frozen to the spot, not knowing what to do next, every possibility racing through his mind, like highspeed trains on ever-changing tracks. He'd finally spotted where the Silent Partner was, in the window of the old boating lake cabin: Little flashes of movement gave him away. He'd not said anything for a minute. Maybe he was losing his nerve. Or maybe he was just drinking a coffee, casual as anything, as if kidnapping a man's family was an everyday occurrence for him. No, Carl told himself. With the little he knew about his nemesis; he knew that he wasn't experienced with all that was going down. He was a con artist. He wanted him and Warren to think that he was the boss of a big criminal gang, but in actual fact, he was all alone and desperate. The old man had nothing to do with anything; he was just some random craziness thrown into the mix. Yes! The Silent Partner's actions were those of a desperate, lonely man, backed into a corner. He hadn't planned all this: He was improvising. Desperate men improvise. Desperate men make mistakes.

'Okay, so what's the plan here?' he shouted. 'You summoned me here to what? Shoot me? Doesn't sound like much of a plan to me.' He said it so loud in the double hope that it would unnerve the man and Kate and Sara would hear him and know that he was there to save them. The next voice he heard sounded infinitely less confident, less rehearsed.

'No, no. That's not – I, I… You wrecked my plan!' He sounded like a spoilt child who'd been given the wrong Christmas present.

'Oh! How inconsiderate of me!' This was usually the kind of thing that Carl would just say in his head, but he'd turned a corner and wasn't looking back.

The Silent Partner didn't seem to be picking up on his sarcasm, and shouted back: 'Yes! It was! I'm glad you've acknowledged that. We'd all be better off if you'd just stuck to the plan!'

Carl almost felt sorry for how pathetically delusional the man had become; maybe he'd always been that way. 'Look!' he shouted. 'Why don't you just give yourself up? There's nowhere for you to run, and I don't think you're—'

'You don't know anything about me!' he shouted back. 'You don't know what I'm capable of!'

Carl felt an anger rising in him, as if he was being lowered into boiling water. The feeling of control was starting to slip away, and somehow, he was glad of it. 'I don't know what you're capable of? You're capable of kidnapping my family, I know that much. You should be worried about what *I'm* capable of; about what you've turned me into: A man on the edge! A man willing to do anything to protect his family!'

Without another word; without thinking, he ran forward, towards the cabin. There was no visible door, but there was a gap in the hedge right next to the cabin, and the door couldn't be far past that, surely. No shots came as he got nearer. Maybe he's put the gun down, was a thought that flashed through his mind, but he didn't have time to dwell on it. He was through the gap in the hedge now, and just to the right was the cabin door. He burst through it. Kate and Sara were in the corner, bound and gagged in the shadows. The click of a gun pierced the silence. Before he had time to think about how scared he was, he jumped on the Silent Partner with a surge of energy he didn't know he had left in him, but the man pushed him back with even more force and he broke the frame of the door with his shoulder. The next second the impact of the icy ground rocked his whole body. The pain shook him, but he ignored it and tried to move to get up, but he stopped, because the Silent Partner now had the gun aimed squarely at his head.

'You see? You see what you've forced me to do?'

Carl looked into his eyes. There was something missing behind them: The cold and calculating man was gone. There was nothing left but a scared and desperate one. His eyes were shifting, as if he was trying to keep track of a fly buzzing around Carl's head. 'I've not forced you to do anything.' He tried to say this as calmly as he was capable of with a gun pointed at his head. 'I tell you what, even though you've done all this to me and my family, I'm going to let you just go.' No, I'm not, he thought. As soon as your back's turned, I'll have you. 'No real harm's been done yet, and we can all just walk away. It's Christmas, after all, and I don't even know who you are. I haven't even seen your—' Carl stopped, because as he said that, the Silent Partner took off his hat and unwrapped the scarf from around his face. 'Oh, no, no, no. You don't need to do that. I—' He knew the face. He knew the face! 'You're… You're…'

The man stood above – still with the gun pointed at him – looked comically disappointed, as if he'd just met him in the street for the first time in years. Then his expression suddenly changed, as if the shadow which the brim of his hat had cast over his face for so long was back.

'What's the matter, Mister Phillips?', he said, 'Should I have worn a name badge?'

'Calvin? Calvin Fairweather?'

'Oh, so you *do* remember me?' He said this as if it was the most important part of the whole affair.

'Of course I do. You were a manager at the store,' Carl said, failing to contain his disbelief.

'A *team* manager. I was a *team* manager, until they decided to reshuffle things and lay a load of us off. I was on my way up the ladder, and they just pulled it out from under me, just like that.'

Calvin Fairweather was the last person Carl expected to be behind everything. No one had particularly liked him when he was there at the store, and even fewer missed him when he was gone. He was one of those people who Carl assumed had nothing else to do, no other skill set to fall back on, so he got into management. He wasn't even particularly good at that, and it didn't help that none of the other managers liked him. He might have almost felt sorry for the man if he hadn't kidnapped his family, shot Warren, and had a gun held on him.

'You're not the only one who lost their job, you know. What gives you the right to—'

'Yes, but I am the only one who had the nouse to use his redundancy package and savings to set up a criminal network.'

'A *criminal network*?' Carl laughed. Most of his fear was gone, now that he knew who he was up against. He was just waiting for the right moment. 'It's just you on your own.'

'Ah, but that's where you're wrong. Mister Phillips. It's me, you, and that loser Warren. We're all in it together, aren't we.' He was swinging the gun around now, as if it was a pen or a laser pointer aiding him with his twisted lecture. 'If the police ever catch up with us, that's what I'll tell them. I've told *them* as well.'

'Who?'

'Who d'you think? Your family. They were pretty convinced I have to say. Seems you've been acting rather suspiciously of late. I wonder why that is – Ha!'

He'd heard just about enough. He needed to put an end to it now. Surely Kate and Sara wouldn't believe the rantings of a mad man. Maybe they could hear him now, and— There was a rustling behind him, and suddenly Fairweather turned to the gap in the hedge where Carl had come in. There was a man clambering through. It was him! It was—

BANG!!!

Scrooge stumbled forward clutching his chest. It had gone from ice cold seconds before, to a burning, white hot sensation he could feel spreading to every part of his body, faster than his old frame could fathom. Everything was a blur as he struggled to keep his eyes open. Carl was in front of him with a man he didn't recognise, and as these images faded away, he could hear his name: Someone was screaming his name. It could have been behind him, but his sense of direction was gone. It sounded like Grace, but that couldn't be right; Jack had promised to keep her out of the park. He tried to open his eyes, but he couldn't, and even his ears were failing as he realised what was happening.

BANG!!

BANG!!

The two gunshots echoed in his head and then suddenly stopped, leaving a deathly silence. It had happened again. He'd failed. He'd failed…

16

He was surrounded by pure beautiful white light. It reminded him of something, but he couldn't recall what. In fact, the more he tried to remember, the faster he felt it slipping away. What had been before; what he feared was to come. It was as if he was becoming one with the light, and everything that made him who he was was being forgotten, like words on a page fading over time. His story was done. But it wasn't. There was unfinished business to attend to. He had to… There was the… He couldn't remember. The feeling remained of something undone, but the facts were gone. Then, just as he could feel a glimmer, a smidgen of a memory returning to him, the pure, beautiful, brilliant white light was gone, and the sense of loss was almost palpable, but then, he saw where he was.

'I'm home,' he said. His own voice seemed alien to him, as if he'd not heard it in a thousand years. 'How can this be?' I was— I was somewhere else. No! It was the same place, but different. Why can't I remember?'

He lifted up his nightgown, expecting to see something, although he had no notion as to what it might be. It was like the sensation of walking into a room and then forgetting why you went in there in the first place. Brief flashes of images came into his head but immediately vanished, as his brain failed to make any sense of them.

He looked around the room and found comfort in the familiar surroundings, but it seemed as if there was something missing here as well, and he couldn't for the life of him tell what it was. It was like he was looking at it from the wrong angle and the answer was just around the corner. From the light coming in from the window he could see that it was morning, and that simple fact made his heart leap for joy.

Then he heard them: The bells, singing to each other in celebration. He jumped up in the air as he realised what day it was, but how could he be sure? He went over to the window and opened it. A waft of fine winter air flooded in, reassuring him that he was indeed in the land of the living. Then he saw a boy; a very familiar boy, somehow. Where did he know him from? He was curious and tempted to ask the boy if he did indeed know him, but somehow, the words refused to come. Instead, something more familiar came to his quivering lips:

'What's today?' he shouted. Those words. This situation.

'Eh?' the boy shouted up.

Without thinking, he came out with the next line: 'What's today, my fine fellow?' And before the boy could answer, Scrooge knew what he was going to say.

'Today! Why, Christmas day!'

Those words usually filled his old heart with almost more joy than he could express, and they still gave him some elation, but his sense that all of this had played out before in exactly the same pattern was growing, as if he was part of a story with an ending that had already been written. He so wanted to say the next lines and just pretend that nothing odd was occurring, but he needed to know something.

'Boy!' he shouted back down. 'Do you – Do you –' It was a struggle, and it was almost as if some invisible force was trying to shape his mouth and thoughts into forming words that he'd already spoken, but he finally managed to break free. 'Do you know what year it is? The year?'

The boy at first looked confused, and why shouldn't he? After all, it couldn't be every day that a mad old man asked him questions like that. Then, to his surprise, the boy's face took on a whole new expression. He couldn't quite put his finger on it, and then it came to him: The boy looked exactly the way Scrooge was feeling; not just mimicking him. It was as if he was looking in a mirror at himself as a young boy. Then, everything changed.

The boy was first to go. His features, his eyes, nose, mouth, and ears disappeared in an instant, and yet the boy was still looking up at him, like a shop store mannequin. Scrooge shuddered and backed away, and the next moment, the street and the boy outside shimmered away into millions of tiny bubbles, popping before his eyes.

'What's happening?!' Scrooge bellowed. He grabbed the curtain for support, but just as soon as he did, the same thing happened: It was gone, but to his surprise, he didn't fall to the floor. As the tiny bubbles – which, until then had been his curtains – floated into the air with the mesmeric grace of a ballerina, he realised he couldn't feel the weight of his own body. He held his hand up to look at it, to prove to himself that his body was still there, and it was as if he was looking upon a mere memory. He had the strangest feeling that it wasn't really there, and yet, he felt almost overwhelmed by the beauty of it, as if he'd not seen anything like it for the longest time. He started jiggling his fingers, and the creases and wrinkles in the skin – the way they moved and shifted – made him giggle to himself; he didn't know why. Again, it was as if he'd never seen such a thing in his life for a very long time. It felt like a novelty to him, like a child with a new toy.

Then, just as he was getting used to it, bits of his fingers started floating away. Yes, they were turning into the tiny bubbles, the same way the boy, the street, and the curtains had. He looked around and was not greatly surprised to see that the whole room had transformed into bubbles which were now floating around him like snow in a snow globe. He had a vague sense that he should be more alarmed. After all, everything he knew and held dear – including his own body – was evaporating into nothingness, but he wasn't the slightest bit worried. In fact, he felt an overwhelming sense of relief washing over him. As his body followed the lead of his hands, he could feel himself breaking apart and floating off in all directions at once.

Carl couldn't believe what was happening. Events were bearing down on him like a fifty-foot tidal wave that couldn't be stopped. The old man with the odd name was lying motionless on the floor, most likely dead. And behind him, two others – one of which seemed familiar to him – dead. Shot by the Silent Partner, Calvin Fairweather.

He could feel himself shaking, but he knew he couldn't allow himself to be taken over by it. You can collapse in a nervous wreck later, he promised himself. He looked over at the Silent Partner. Even though he now knew his real name, he couldn't bring himself to think of the twisted individual who'd just shot three innocent people as the same person he'd known as Calvin Fairweather, an annoying, but non-murderous ex-team leader. The guy was just staring at the bodies, and even though he was barely moving, the panic in his eyes was evidence enough of how much he wanted to move, to be anywhere but there. Carl knew exactly how he felt, because he wanted the same thing: To be as far away and as far removed as possible from the all-engulfing nightmare that his life had become. Except for one thing: His family. Kate and Sara. He needed to get them away. No matter what they might have believed about his involvement, it didn't matter, as long as they were safe.

He took another look at the murderer. He didn't look as though he'd notice if Carl spontaneously combusted, let alone went into the cabin to rescue his family. He backed up and slowly inched towards the cabin. He could feel the frame of the partially broken door, and he looked over to see Kate and Sara, their mouths gagged, and their hands tied behind their backs. Their legs were tied too, so there was no chance of them running away and finding help. It was breaking his heart to see how truly terrified they looked, but were they scared of him now, or just the situation?

He approached them, slowly, non-threateningly; the way you would approach a wild animal, scared that it could turn at any moment. As he got closer, he attempted a smile, but after everything that had happened over the last few days – the cracked mess that his life had become – he couldn't do it. The best he could do was to move slowly and try to show them through that, that he was the same old husband and father that he'd always been: a bit of a screw up, but still mostly reliable and loving. He knelt down in front of them in the cold, dark cabin and tried to judge how they felt about him being there from the look in their eyes.

If anything, Sara looked more pleased to see him than Kate, terrified and shaking, but at least there was a warmness there. Kate was a different case entirely. She was justifiably terrified, and her eyes were red with tears, but there was something else there. She was looking at him as if… as if she didn't know him. He wasn't the hero come to save them. She was looking at him as if he was the one who kidnapped them in the first place. He decided then – maybe it was the wrong decision – that even though he wanted to hear their voices more than anything in the world, he couldn't untie them; not straightaway. He had to explain himself. He had to explain the nightmare he'd been put through by the lying scumbag outside who seemed determined to wreck his life.

He looked them both in the eyes. Then he looked behind him to the door, and he could just see the Silent Partner's shadow on the snowy path, unmoving. Still, he didn't know how much time he would have: the police couldn't be too far away. Surely someone must have heard those gunshots.

'I don't know where to start,' he said. 'All this started with a phone call that I didn't answer, but it turns out that that didn't make a jot of difference.'

He looked at them to see if they were listening. Sara still looked terrified whilst Kate looked more angry than anything else. 'None of this is my fault.' He didn't want to sound so angry, but he couldn't help some of his frustration letting loose. 'And I don't know what lies he's told you or how deep they go, but he is the one behind all of this. He—'

But before Carl could say another word, he heard voices outside. For a split second he foolishly thought that maybe, yes, maybe it had all been some mistake; that the Silent Partner hadn't shot anyone; that maybe they'd just been playing dead all the time. The notion of this disappeared almost as soon as it occurred to him, because suddenly the voices became harsher and shouted:

'POLICE! Don't move!'

Then, to Carl's shock, he heard another more familiar voice. It was higher pitched and panic-ridden, but it was unmistakably the voice of Calvin Fairweather. That wasn't so much the shocking part of it. It was the words themselves:

'It wasn't me, officers. It was him! He's in there! I was forced to kidnap his family, so he'd leave me alone!'

17

Scrooge looked around and decided that, until now, he'd never really known what true beauty was. He was stood on a patch of perfectly green grass (he couldn't quite recall how he got there), and in the distance he could see buildings rising up into the clouds. It reminded him very much of London, except in other ways, it was very different indeed. Whereas the buildings in London were all cramped into a limited space, these buildings had room to breathe; their own space. And the way they moved and shimmered; it was almost as if they *were* breathing.

And there was snow. SNOW! The odd thing was, he could see it falling, but it didn't seem to land anywhere, as if when it reached the ground it simply disappeared. It was as if it was there for its aesthetic quality alone. He thought to himself how much he would like to touch it; to feel it between his fingers, the way it had felt that day when he'd rolled some up in his hands and thrown it at Tiny Tim. And then, just as the idea was passing, he noticed a part of the grass that was growing whiter and whiter, seemingly the more he looked at it. It was snow, piling up on the ground; snow that he could touch and feel! It glistened like crystal, and it was the most perfect, unspoilt snow he'd seen in his life. Before he knew what he was doing, he was dancing around in it like a giddy schoolboy, tossing it up in the air and letting it land on his cheeks and tongue.

Even on his best days his life had never felt like this: So complete, like a perfect circle. He'd never felt such tangible joy. And it wasn't just in what he could see: The perfect blue sky; the spacious city in the distance. No. Joy was there all around him, comforting him like a gigantic blanket. It was a friend holding his hand, and promising never to let go, leading him forever onward. He'd never felt so connected in all his life. He'd been closed off from this wonderful feeling, but now he could feel everything. He could feel people. He couldn't exactly hear their thoughts, but he could feel what they felt: Their emotions, and it was overwhelming joy. The feeling was so powerful that it had a physical effect on him. It was like countless little rays of sunshine of differing intensity, yet all blissfully delightful, warming his skin. And speaking of his skin, he couldn't remember the last time it felt so fresh; so new. He looked at his hands, and all the wrinkles that had grown longer and more pronounced over the years were all but gone. A gasp of joy escaped his lips. 'Truly, this is Heaven,' he cried, 'where a man looks as young as he feels himself to be.' To his surprise, he felt only a vague regret at the realisation that he was no longer alive, as if it was just a touch of toothache which would pass in time.

Tears trickled down his cheeks. The sudden coldness shocked him, and then… then there was something different. Something bad. It felt like a spike piercing through the joy in his head. It was panic, but it wasn't his. A young man suddenly appeared in his mind's eye. He was getting closer; running closer. He was on top of him now, and Scrooge turned around to face him. He was a blur at first, but as he looked, the young man came into focus, and the panic on his face was no less piercing than when he'd seen him in his mind's eye.

'What are you doing here? You shouldn't be here! What are you doing here?'

Even though he knew it to be the truth and he'd accepted it so quickly and without question, the words sounded peculiar coming out of his mouth: 'I died.'

This didn't assuage the man from his panic. 'I know you died. We *all* died! But you shouldn't be here.'

Again, Scrooge was stumped. Surely, if he was dead then he was supposed to be there, in Heaven. Then, a dreadful all-consuming and poisonous notion came to him. Maybe he wasn't supposed to be there; maybe there'd been a huge celestial mix up. Maybe he was supposed to be… in the other place. No! That couldn't be right. It was time for Scrooge to question his interrogator. 'What do you mean I'm not supposed to be here? If I'm dead, then surely—'

'Yes,' the man said, obviously attempting to sound a bit calmer now, 'but there are different stages of death. The first stage – the stage that you were in – is denial. It's quite a shock to the system, death is, and the normal reaction is to completely ignore the fact that it's happened and wrap yourself up in a memory of your life.'

'That Christmas morning, with the boy in the street.'

'Yeah, now you're getting it. Anyway, that's usually the simple bit. He or she just relives that memory a few million times whilst we tweak it ever so subtly and gradually, until he or she comes to realise the truth of their situation.'

'A few *million* times?' He couldn't believe what he was hearing.

'Well, it varies from person to person, but you, Ebenezer Scrooge; you ripped up the rule book, you did. You didn't even relive your memory once. It's as if you couldn't wait to get here, even though you shouldn't have even been aware that here was here.'

'I couldn't wait to get here…'

'I know! And now you've probably got me in trouble with *Them*.'

The man looked even more panicked than before; almost fearful. Even so, Scrooge wasn't sure whether he should be apologising. Surely if it was his time to move on to a "different stage" as he'd put it, then no one could have prevented it from happening. Then he realised that another question had presented itself. 'Who are "Them"?'

The man looked around, thinking that they were behind him. When he realised they weren't, he looked slightly less fearful. 'The ones in charge. They tell us what to do. Who to watch over.'

'I thought there was only one person in charge up here.'

'There *is* only one person in charge, although to call Him a person seems very odd. I've never met Him. I don't even know if I can; if I ever will. No one here that you can feel has ever met Him, except maybe—'

'Them,' Scrooge said.

'Yes… Them.'

There was too much fear in his voice, Scrooge thought. It seemed unnatural in a place of such purity. 'Why are you so scared, my friend?' He said this as calmly as possible. 'We are where we are. No harm will come to you, surely, for something that was beyond your control.'

'Beyond my control? I've done it countless times before. I was supposed to keep you in your perfect moment.'

'Yes, and that tells me that maybe this time you weren't supposed to. Maybe I'm—'

'Maybe you're what? The exception to the rule? Special?'

Scrooge was taken aback by the man's outburst. 'Well, no, no. I'd never think of myself as that. It's just that—' Suddenly, a feeling out of nowhere hit him like a tidal wave. The feeling coming from his new acquaintance felt like a tiny pinprick by comparison. 'Do you feel that?'

The man nodded and said nothing.

He looked behind him, and Scrooge noticed something in the far distance. Curiously, the grass he'd seen when he'd first arrived had gone now, and in its wake was a white fog. Beyond that was something that looked like the manifestation of what he could feel: A surge of panic. As it got closer, it got higher and higher, and he saw a face emerge and then another one and another, until he realised that the whole wave was made up of hundreds, maybe thousands of people. As it got nearer, Scrooge could hear an odd humming sound emanating from it. The more he listened, the stranger it sounded, until he started to hear individual words emerging from it. It was a crowd of people, all talking at the same time and saying different things. Scrooge realised that the only words he could hear clearly were the ones that some of them were saying more or less at the same time. The delay between them made it sound like an everlasting echo, but he could clearly hear the words: "They're here."

Scrooge looked to his new acquaintance to see what he made of it. He looked just as stunned as Scrooge felt, and yet, he wasn't actually looking at the wave of people which was getting closer by the second. He was remembering something; Scrooge could feel it.

'Years ago, there was talk of such a scene, before I even got here.'

'What?' Scrooge said. 'What is it, man?'

'They are here. The ones that He gives his commands through.'

'Oh…'

'They never come down here… We just hear their instructions in our heads.' His face changed, as did the feelings emanating from him. It was as if his body and his mind were one and the same and every subtle change of expression on his face betrayed what he was feeling. 'It's you,' he said. You've caused this. Coming through early; breaking the rules.'

The man's conviction was so solid that Scrooge could feel himself shaking. 'Me? You think *I've* brought them here? I am but one man, sir. How can I possibly be—'

Before Scrooge could finish what he was saying, the tidal wave of souls immersed them both. He could feel himself getting lost amongst the vastness of feelings and voices, and then everything went white…

18

Scrooge suspected that he would never fully comprehend, much less, be capable of describing the place where he was now. The closest he could get to a comparison was the biggest theatre or auditorium he had ever seen. No, he decided, it wasn't big: it was endless, and the more he looked at it, the bigger it got. This wasn't just a feeling; it was actually growing before his eyes. The whole place defied any sense of logic. Yes, it was like a theatre, but there was no stage, just balconies; ever-expanding balconies.

He looked down, and there again, balconies as far as he could see. He looked up and felt crushed and tiny by the balconies forever expanding above him. And the people: Countless people of all shapes, sizes, colours and creeds, and they were appearing in their seats almost as quickly as the balconies appeared. He could feel their confusion and fear, and it came as some relief to know that he wasn't alone.

The place glowed with a preternatural light that made the last place look dull by comparison, but the light which reached the furthest recesses of the theatre (Scrooge had decided to think of the place as that, to prevent himself from being overwhelmed by the vastness of it all) was, incredibly, becoming even brighter. He couldn't help but gaze into it, along with everyone else. It was hypnotic, and then, right in the middle of it, a dark shape began to emerge.

It started as a tiny spec, but as it expanded, arms and legs emerged from it. It was becoming almost as bright as the light now, as if it were a part of it.

The light had consumed almost everything, but now it was beginning to fade, as if that were the end of the matter; the performance over. It wasn't. A voice so loud – as loud as the light had been bright – filled the theatre. The words were almost an afterthought, as if the booming volume of the voice was the only point, but everyone heard the words none-the-less. Scrooge could feel the fear all around him.

'SOMEONE HAS DONE WRONG.'

He could see the faces of men and women all around him, searching memories of their lives to see if, in fact, they had done something that would deem them unworthy of being where they now were. He thought about his own life, but then realised in a panic that there was nothing there: He couldn't remember any of it.

'YOUR THOUGHTS BETRAY YOU,' the voice boomed out.

Scrooge could feel panic all around him, like a million screams; a million guilty consciences. There was something else as well; something that had been there all along. It was almost drowned out by all the panic, but it was very clear all the same, as if it was trying to hide, but couldn't. It was doubt; a huge feeling of doubt, and it was growing. Scrooge could feel it filling up the gaps between everyone else's fears. It was almost as if—

'AND YOU ARE REVEALED, EBENEZER SCROOGE.'

He froze at the pronouncement. He tried to stop his thoughts from flowing out of him, but he couldn't. All he could feel was fear and doubt, now. Why couldn't he remember anything about his life? Was it denial? Had his life been so bad that somehow he'd chosen to forget it? But there was the boy; the boy on Christmas morning. How did he remember that, but nothing else?

He could see the people all around him getting further away, fading into the light. They were safe. The feeling of relief coming from all around was a crushing blow to his heart. He felt numb and barely noticed that he was being pulled closer and closer to the figure in the centre of the light. He tried to clear his mind of all questions and doubts, and as he did, the doubt which had filled the theatre came back; it had probably never left. This time, he knew exactly where it was coming from: The figure before him. As he got nearer to it, he knew for sure that whoever it was in that ring of light had questions of their own; millions of them, all being asked at once.

Just as he realised this, he felt the very real pain of being slammed forward. A face appeared, and then, in a flash, it was gone. He thought he recognised it but had no notion as to where or when he might have seen it before.

'Do not presume to know what I am thinking, Ebenezer Scrooge.'

It was the same voice from moments ago. It echoed, but it was nowhere near as all-encompassing as it had been in the theatre. A question started to form in Scrooge's mind, but before he could express it, even before he knew what it was properly, the figure before him answered it.

'It is a memory of pain that you are feeling. You have a lifetime of them, which we can pluck from your past at any time.'

'Isn't that a great comfort,' Scrooge said.

The figure in front of him, whose features were only now coming into focus, didn't look too pleased at this comment. She had long, flowing blonde hair which was constantly moving in a wind which only affected her. Her face was soft and youthful, and it seemed like it should've been kindly, but the harsh expression she wore – glaring eyes, tight, spiteful lips – sharpened the features.

The contradiction was unsettling to say the least. Her eyes were widening and lay fixedly on him, as if there were no words to express her anger at his words.

Wait a minute, Scrooge thought. She said, "we can pluck memories from your past." As soon as he realised this, other figures came into focus in the impossible bright whiteness of wherever he was, and suddenly the enormous feeling of doubt, the millions of questions made perfect sense. It wasn't all coming from one person, it was coming from *all* of them.

There were so many of them. Nowhere near as many as in the theatre, but the feeling of panic seemed intensified here, as if the place where he was now was the starting point of it all. There were men and women rushing about, stopping abruptly and almost crashing into one another. Scrooge didn't think he'd been a witness to such a chaotic scene in his life. He noticed something else. The more he focussed, the more detail came out, like looking up at the night sky and the stars gradually appearing one by one. The people rushing around were carrying things. They looked like – yes, they were carrying books. And behind them, gradually fading into existence, there was a bookcase, then another and another, all in a row, in and amongst where everyone was almost falling over each other in panic. As Scrooge looked upon the bookcases, he saw that they stretched back as far as he could see, and he knew that they would most likely stretch beyond that.

'Yes. This is The Library.'

The woman before him said this with no small amount of gravitas, but the doubt and questions were still there. She glared at him again, hearing what he was thinking before he was even sure of it himself. All the confusion was infectious, and he suddenly felt an overwhelming need for answers and, again, before the question could properly focus in his mind, an answer came.

'Yes, there are countless books, Ebenezer Scrooge. There are as many books as there are or have been or will be lives.'

An explanation for that confusing sentence came almost instantaneously.

'Each book is the story of someone's life. We read them to garner knowledge, to find answers to questions that the people below us have never even considered.'

There was a touch of snobbery about that statement.

'We have earned our place here,' the woman bellowed. 'You couldn't possibly understand.'

He could feel frustration coming from her now. There was something she didn't understand, and it was clear now that she wanted him to explain it. The woman stretched out her hand. It seemed bigger than it should have been, somehow, but Scrooge instinctively moved his hand to grab it, and she pulled it away with a slight smirk on her face.

'You don't need my help to get up.'

Scrooge looked and saw that the spirit or angel or whatever she was, was right: He was already standing. It was going to take some time to get used to this place.

'Until recently, this was a peaceful, idyllic place.' The angel said this as if she were providing an answer, but if she was, he had no idea what the question was. 'We would sit in circles,' she continued, 'surrounded by books. We read in silence, learning the simple truths of life. Truths that seem so obvious now but were hidden by all the clutter of our former existences.'

Scrooge could only suppose that she was talking about life before death. All the distractions were everything that made up that life: Jobs, hobbies, other people. She was making it sound like all these things were inconveniences that she was glad to be rid of.

'It does no good to dwell on the beforelife. Material possessions, material existence. It will be hard for you to adjust. It will be hard for you to understand.'

'That's why I was reliving that memory of Christmas morning with the boy at the window, wasn't it,' Scrooge said.

'Yes, it's a way of helping you to adjust to what you knew as death.'

'Then why did I get out so quickly? That young man said that I got out too soon and—' Scrooge stopped in his tracks, but it was too late. He'd said too much, but then, the angel probably knew about what had happened anyway.

'He should have watched you more carefully,' the angel said as they moved closer to the bookcases. Scrooge had only just realised that they were moving at all. 'But I don't believe it was his fault.'

'Oh,' Scrooge said, pleased that he hadn't gotten the young man in trouble, but still confused all the same.

'I believe that you were meant to come here, Ebenezer Scrooge.'

The angel stopped and looked ahead of them at a bookcase which was impossibly – a word which Scrooge was gradually accepting to be redundant at this point – tall. However, this was not what was so remarkable about it. Before Scrooge's eyes, the books contained in the shelves were changing. Some got thicker as he stared at them, and some got thinner, whilst others disappeared completely; the space they left quickly filled by the ones that had gotten thicker. Scrooge had to look away, the sight was just too much for him. He looked to the angel for some kind of explanation.

'They're not supposed to do that,' the angel said. 'Each book represents a life, and each life has a fixed length. All lives affect other lives, but it was all laid out in the beginning, a delicate tapestry, not to be changed.'

'So why are they—?'

'I believe you hold the answer to that, Ebenezer Scrooge.'

'Me?' Scrooge said. 'How could I possibly know anything about this? I've only just arrived here, madam. I don't know anything.'

'Perhaps not, but you hold the answer none-the-less.'

'What makes you think that?'

'Because the books started changing right before you died.'

Scrooge couldn't believe what he was hearing. How could he be responsible for what was happening? All those lives changed. Gone.

He looked at the bookcase. The angel had said that the books held the truth. One of them caught his eye. It wasn't shrinking or changing like all the others around it. It just sat there, silently beckoning him, willing him to reach out and take it.

'You must have a deep connection to the life contained within that book,' the angel said. 'Your life and theirs must have crossed at an important time for both of you.'

The book was in his hand now, before Scrooge even realised he'd taken it off the shelf. Everything here was like a dream. One only had to think of doing something and it happened. He was looking at the cover of the book now. It read like a gravestone, with the birthdate and death date written below the name; a name which for some reason seemed familiar to him, and which brought with it brief moments of blissful clarity.

CARL JOSEPH PHILLIPS

MARCH 2ND 1975 – DECEMBER 24TH 2045

'Hi, Dad.'

Her voice sounded flat but patient. But it was as if the patience was draining out of it as she spoke, even in those two little words which meant the most to him; the words which seemed to be the only proof of his former life.

'Hi, honey. How are you?' he said, trying but failing not to sound too enthusiastic. These phone conversations were one of the only things that kept him going. The only thing worth waking up for since the events of almost exactly three years ago.

'I'm okay, I guess. I've a lot of homework to get through—'

'Oh, I'm sorry, I didn't—'

'No, no. I didn't mean it like that,' Sara said, the impatient tone gone now, thankfully. 'It's just that they dole out so much of it, it's like they think we don't have lives outside of there. And it's Christmas as well.'

Carl wanted to agree with her. He wanted to say something funny and blasé, but apart from the fact that he was too stressed out to think of anything funny to say, he wanted to say something fatherly. He needed to pass on some fatherly wisdom, after all, he *was* still her father. 'Well, your teachers know best, and there'll be plenty of Christmases after this one when you can enjoy yourself without the worry of homework.'

'You sound just like mum,' Sara said.

'Well, I must be right then.' He immediately regretted sounding so bitter. 'Honey, I'm sorry. I didn't mean that how it sounded.'

'It's okay, Dad. I understand.'

There was an awkward silence. There always was, nowadays, and it was almost always an indicator of the halfway point; an interval; the end of act one or two. Carl had never been to the theatre. A flash of a memory of Sara as Mary in her school nativity when she was seven came to him, but he pushed it away. 'How *is* your mum?'

'She's… okay.'

Another awkward silence. He knew what was coming.

'She's got a new boyfriend.'

'I know.' Carl sighed. 'She told me when I bumped into her at the supermarket.' Had she mentioned it to Sara?

'Oh. She didn't tell me about that.'

'It's okay.' It wasn't. He could feel his heart sinking and he didn't have the energy to reach for it. That little smile that Kate had tried to conceal when she saw him hadn't been for him.

'Dad? Are you alright? Are you still there?'

'Yeah yeah, I'm here, hon'.' He tried his best to sound reassuring, but he had to know something before the conversation descended into a mess of awkward "goodbyes". 'What's he like?'

'He's an idiot.' She said this without hesitation.

That's my girl, he thought, triumphantly.

'He thinks he's funny but he's not, and he's got this really annoying laugh he uses for his own lame jokes.'

Carl couldn't help but feel a little better. At least Sara was on his side. He knew at the back of his mind that the feeling would be temporary, but he would cling to it for dear life.

'I miss you, Daddy.'

She only ever called him that by accident these days: She was upset. He could hear the tears in her voice. Here was his chance to step up and be the father he was supposed to be, but he could feel the moment getting to him, too. He needed to say something before it overcame him completely. 'I know. I miss you too. But you have to be strong. Be strong for both of us. When you're older we'll be able to see much more of each other. Your old dad will be the one annoying—'

'Mum misses you, too. She won't admit it, but I know she does. I catch her looking at old photographs of you; of all of us together; the way we're meant to be.'

'Sara, I—' The words caught in his throat. What was he supposed to say to that, anyway? He had tried everything. Every possible way of explaining his side of what had happened that night. Sara had helped him, even going so far as to suggest starting a vlog in which he'd describe every detail: *Come on, Dad, it's a great idea. You could end up getting millions of subscribers, and then Mum would* have *to listen to you.*

He'd ultimately shot the idea down, based on the grounds that he didn't much fancy humiliating himself in front of, potentially, millions of teenagers.

Maybe Kate did still love him, but she didn't trust him. Eventually, a jury had decided that he was telling the truth about his involvement – or lack of – with Fairweather's crimes, but that didn't seem to be enough for Kate. If only he'd told her everything as and when it happened. Sometimes he could console himself with the fact that he had no choice at the time. He'd been scared and in a very unique situation, and most people would've done the same to protect their family, but it didn't change what had happened and what was still happening. He was alone, working a dead-end job which was a little bit worse than the job he'd had at Locomart, and the only thing he had to look forward to was the little time he was allowed to spend with his only daughter.

If only things had been different, if only he'd managed to get them away from the situation before the police had gotten involved. All his errant thoughts were possessed by those two small words, and he was so tired of trying to silence them on his own in his pokey three-room flat.

He realised he'd not said anything for a while. He needed to say something reassuring; something that he believed to be a lie: 'It'll be okay, hon.'

He could hear her trying to say something, but her tears were stopping her.

'I've got to go now,' he said softly, 'but I'll see you next weekend. Remember, I love you very much.'

All he could hear were her tears as he ended the call, and he felt a pain in his chest, like someone was trying to squeeze the life out of him. He slumped in his chair until it passed, and a thought came to him. It was something that had been at the back of his mind for a while, and he'd prided himself on being able to keep it at bay for so long. He couldn't hold it back any longer; it took a grip and wrapped itself around him like a warm blanket: He needed a drink.

19

Scrooge stared at the book. It was an odd feeling, quite literally holding a man's life in his hands. The book itself felt like it was alive. It was almost as if it was talking to him, telling him things. The images in his head were getting clearer now. He could see himself outside a large park, arguing with someone. Someone he somehow knew to be Carl Phillips. I wonder, he thought.

'You're right,' the angel said. 'It will all become clear once you read it.'

Scrooge still found it extremely odd how she could read his thoughts, how she knew exactly what he was thinking, even before he knew it himself.

'That's not how it works. It's hard to explain to a newcomer, but we can sense emotions rather than thoughts, like colours instead of words, and we can make a good guess as to what you're thinking from that. We have, after all, had a lot of experience in this matter.'

'Oh,' Scrooge said, 'so now I'm supposing that you're sensing more confusion.'

'You'll get there in the end. Truth be told, you're not really supposed to be here. We brought you here because we need your help to figure out what's gone wrong.'

'I don't understand,' he said. 'Why do you need my help? You're angels, and I'm just, well, me. I—' He stopped, because as he shifted the book in his hand, his fingers touched the edges of the pages, and a burst of pure clarity hit him, almost knocking him off his feet. He was back there in the moment, reliving the whole event as if he were alive again.

'What can you see?' The angel sounded concerned.

'He… Carl Phillips. I *did* meet him. There was something wrong. His family! He told me they were in danger. Yes! That was it! And I was trying to help him. There was a park… I was shot! That's how I died. There was a couple. What were their names? Jack and Grace! I knew him, but I didn't know him. He was different. Why can't I remember properly? I heard other shots, just as I was fading away. They must have been shot too!'

Scrooge tried to grab the angel, but she backed away. 'I must go back! I have to save them. All of them!'

For the first time the angel looked truly confused. 'You want to go back? Down there?' she made "down there" sound like the least desirable place possible.

'Yes!' he exclaimed. 'Send me back! I have to save them. It was what I was supposed to do.'

'I'm sorry.' The angel sounded more sympathetic now. 'There's no going back. You're dead. There's no going back from this.'

'I… I… I…' But he didn't have the words. The damning finality of the angel's words hit him like a force he'd never felt before. He'd had so much more to do; so many more people to help. That was clear to him now.

'You *can* help,' the angel said, reading his emotions again. 'You can help us find out why all this – this terrible disaster – is happening. History is changing. People who should be alive are dead, and people who should be dead are alive. Each life touches other lives in positive and negative ways, and somehow your death is behind it all.'

He could feel black despair swallowing him up. Not only was he dead, but his death had triggered a catastrophic chain of events which he didn't fully understand. As his mind slowly accepted his fate, he could feel memories of his life trying to push through the fog. He wanted to reach out and grab them, even though they felt wrong somehow, but they fell away before he had a chance.

Even the memories of Carl were starting to blur and fade away. These are my memories, he thought, frustrated. Why can't I—?' Then something occurred to him; something for which he mentally kicked himself for not thinking of before, but surely the angel or one of the others rushing around with arms full of books had thought of it. If they wanted to know anything about Mister Ebenezer Scrooge and his life, all they had to do was read his story.

'We already thought of that, of course,' the angel said. 'Let me show you why you are such a mystery, Ebenezer Scrooge.'

The angel led Scrooge down one of many corridors of bookcases. The whole time, other angels were moving up and down, some of them with literal towers of books in their hands, and some of those books were changing as they were being carried. This would have been slightly disconcerting if he'd not already had his fill of unreal experiences. As they moved along, Scrooge realised that the white foggy atmosphere which seemed to cling to every edge and surface was fading away. The angel explained to him – without him asking, naturally – that it was because he was getting used to his new surroundings; his eyes were settling to the new quality of light.

As they came to the end of the bookcase corridor – which Scrooge thought was going to go on forever – a staircase came into view. There weren't many steps to it – perhaps twenty at most – and there didn't seem to be much at the top; just a table.

'That's where we keep your book, Ebenezer.'

'Oh,' Scrooge said, 'can I ask why you keep it up there, away from all the others?'

The angel looked evasive and almost afraid to answer, but she did, eventually. 'We've found that it's best kept away from the other books, in case anyone accidentally comes across it.'

'Why?' Scrooge asked. 'What's wrong with my book?'

'The fact is, Ebenezer Scrooge, that out of all the mysteries of life and death; all the questions that just create more questions on these shelves around us; your book, your story is the biggest mystery of them all. It's a closed book.'

Scrooge looked to the top of the stairs. He could just make out a faint glow, the source of which he couldn't see, but he supposed it must be his book. 'Did you mean that quite literally?' Scrooge asked. 'That no one has been able to open my book and read it?'

The angel looked ashamed and embarrassed, somehow. 'Yes, that's right. It has been a long-held belief that you and only you will be able to open it and see what is contained within.'

'Oh, I see,' he said. He wasn't sure that he was ready to read about his life. He had a bad feeling about it. Those brief glimpses of Carl Phillips' life clashing with his had left him with a bad taste in his mouth, and he needed more time to think on it. He looked to the angel, expecting sympathy, but there was none in her demeanour. In fact, she seemed angry.

'I *am* angry,' the angel said, answering Scrooge's unspoken question. '*We* are angry. All of us are. We have accounted for everything. Everything! And the only mystery left is you. This means that you're the only one who can possibly be responsible for all the chaos up here and the mess down there.'

'Me?' Scrooge said, trying with all his might to sound as innocent as possible.

'Yes, you! All the war, famine, suffering. Somehow it all came about as a result of something you did. It wasn't there before, and there must be a reason we can't read your book.'

'But all the books are changing,' Scrooge protested. 'How do you know it wasn't someone else?'

This seemed to throw the angel off temporarily, but she soon regained her ground. 'That is true, Scrooge, and it would take a long time to find the culprit if that were the case. Therefore, I'm giving you a chance to prove that everything that has happened is not your fault.

The way that the angel was acting reminded Scrooge of someone else; another situation which he felt he had been in recently, but he couldn't quite recall it.

'If you cannot prove it, then we will have no choice but to banish you from here and you'll be doomed to the other place, which we do not speak of here.'

Horror filled Scrooge's head; desperate horror. And then, a name. A name came to him: Jacob.

'Jacob?' the angel said. 'Who is that?'

'I – I'm not sure, spirit. Someone I knew in life and death. What you said, about the other place, brought back a memory – no, just a feeling of him, and not a pleasant one.

The angel was glaring at him, and he couldn't decide whether it was fear or anger on her face. She suddenly spoke, making him jump, and every word was pronounced and presented with the sharpness of a dagger piercing his heart. 'Maybe I should have done with it and send you to the other place right now. If the way you feel about your life is accurate, then that's most likely the best place for you.'

'No, please! I've done nothing wrong. I mean, I don't think something I did could have caused what you're claiming it has. I'll open the book. I'll read it!' He could feel the fear touching every part of his soul, burning from the inside out. He'd forgotten what it felt like, and he was almost paralysed at its sudden resurgence.

'Very well.' The angel's demeanour was a sea of calm once more. 'Shall we?' She swept her arm upwards, as if strumming a harp, indicating that she wanted him to lead the way up the stairs.

But before either of them had taken a single step, they were there at the top of the stairs. It was as if that just by thinking about where he wanted to be, he was transported there.

'That takes a while to get used to, if you get the chance.' The angel said, with an air of menace.

Before he could bring himself to look at his own book, Scrooge looked around from his vantage point. The library was seemingly endless. The rows and rows of bookcases went on forever, fading into the distance, and the flashes of light zooming through them – which he supposed were all the angels rushing around in panic – were none-the-less, beautiful. As much as he found it hard to fathom, it must have been true: Each and every book on those shelves contained the lives of everyone who had ever lived, or ever would.

'It really is beautiful, isn't it.' The angel sounded desperately sad. She was looking upwards, away from all the books.

He wasn't sure what she was looking at, at first, but then he saw them: Grey storm clouds, floating ominously above. If they were anywhere else, they'd be nothing to worry about – just a sign of a shower to come – but they were where they were, and they felt wrong; unnatural. Just looking at them filled Scrooge with dread, and he could see why the angels were so worried.

'That will be the least of it,' she said, 'unless we can get to the source of what's causing all this. Now, open your book,' she demanded.

Scrooge could feel the fear coming from the angel, almost as if there was another person there with just as much emotional energy. He had to do it, he had to open the book of his life, despite how he felt about it. Now that he was so close to it, he could feel an immense sense of clarity sweep through him, as if everything was finally making sense. Until then, he hadn't realised he was missing so much, but it was his life, and the good and bad of it were his to own, and just knowing that he'd had a life – no matter what he'd done with it – felt right, somehow.

The book was right in front of him now, on a wooden table, and he could see that it was different to the others. In most aspects it was very much the same as the others. It was leather-bound with a red cover and gold framing around the edges, but there were two major differences: It did indeed look as though it had never been opened, but the most surprising thing was that it only had his name on the front. No birthdate. No death date.

He instinctively looked to the angel for answers, even though he knew she had none; only questions. All she said was: 'That is why you are here, Ebenezer Scrooge.'

He looked back to the book. The temptation was overwhelming now. It was as if the book itself was alive and wanted to be opened. He had to know what kind of life he had lived, and yet, he was torn. Somehow, he knew that he shouldn't read his own book, not yet. But it was there, right in front of him. Why shouldn't he take a peek? And then he realised that he'd already opened the cover, and the words were there in big, bold type.

THE LIFE OF EBENEZER SCROOGE

The pages glowed with a pure whiteness which surpassed even the brightness of his heavenly surroundings, and they seemed to be singing to him, inviting him to turn over the next page; to read the story of his life. He didn't want to be rude, so he turned over the next page.

Nothing. There was nothing on the next page, just blank, bright whiteness. He tried again. Nothing. And again, nothing. Was every page blank? What did this mean? He turned to the angel, but she looked just as shocked as him.

'I – I don't understand,' she said, '… you were supposed to bring the answers; clarity. You were supposed to open the book and—'

She stopped, and a look of pure dread came over her face. Scrooge could see she was looking at the book, and when he turned around, he could see why. The pages were still blank, but now they had started to turn by themselves and they were pulsating, getting darker, then lighter, then darker again.

The darkness held for a moment, as if it was waiting, and then suddenly, a blast of white energy threw them both off their feet. It seemed to consume everything, because Scrooge could see nothing but the white. It was as if he was drifting in it. He didn't know how much time had passed, but as it did, familiar images, familiar faces came to him. Familiar voices. Memories! Memories from before were coming back to him. A mixture of good and bad, but each one led to others, like a spiderweb weaving out across time. He had had a bad life. He had wasted it, but there was hope at the end. Goodness. He'd changed. And the change in him saved others. It was bewildering, his whole life coming back to him in a matter of seconds, but he felt like himself again, and he could feel a smile growing across his face as he realised something.

'What? What is it?'

He could hear the angel, and she was coming back into view as the brightness faded. 'I remember! I remember my life. All of it!' he said, as a deep joy threatened to overwhelm him, 'and I know what I have to do next.'

20

I was taken,' Scrooge said. 'I was taken out of my own time, to the future, to help a young man.'

'You broke the laws of time?' the angel screamed furiously.

'I had no choice,' Scrooge protested. 'I was told that the good I was doing wasn't good enough, and that if I helped this young man, I could be assured redemption for my past sins.'

'Who did this? Who?!'

'I – I can't remember.'

'Don't lie to me, Scrooge. You said you remembered everything.'

The angel looked desperate now. There was a burning in her eyes that Scrooge could feel piercing through him, but still, he wanted to protect his young friend if he could. It seemed like the noble thing to do; the sort of thing a father would do for his son. And then he realised something: The angel couldn't see what he was thinking, much less who he was thinking about. Her face was a perfect picture of frustration. 'You can't, can you.'

'Up here, we have near limitless power.' The angel spoke calmly, but Scrooge could still feel her frustration. 'We can see things that the people down there couldn't possibly imagine in their limited corporeal existence. We can think on higher levels and, yes, we can see and visit other times. But we are taught the rules. We are given these gifts in order to watch over the living, to understand life and its limitations, and we're taught not to interfere. And yet you, Ebenezer Scrooge are a puzzle to me, to everyone up here. I can interpret your current thoughts, but I expected – as is the case with everyone – to be able to see your memories once you had read your book.'

The angel's admission, rather than please him, worried Scrooge somewhat. Why was he different? Unless… Maybe the angel was tricking him.

'It's no trick, Ebenezer,' she said. 'What would be the point?'

He had to agree with her, and he could sense no deception in her words; only fear and doubt. This made him feel a little bit more confident, even though he had no more notion of what was going on than she did. 'I have to say, Spirit, for a people who claim not to interfere with the affairs of the living, you've certainly done more of your fair share of interference with this old man's life.'

'What do you mean by that?' the angel asked, suspiciously.

He was tempted to tell her about the first time his life had been changed by the spirits. The memory of it had come back to him along with all the other memories of his chequered past, but he had no wish to get Jacob in any more trouble.

'What are you hiding from me, Scrooge?'

'Nothing. It's nothing,' he insisted.

The angel's face suddenly shifted. No, it was as if the light hitting her face had shifted: He got a cold chill just looking at it.

'You think that you're in control here, do you, Scrooge? You think that because I can't see your memories that you're special in some way?'

Scrooge backed off and then stopped as he realised he was right at the top of the steps. 'No, no,' he said. 'I'm as much in the dark as you about—'

'I am not in the dark, Ebenezer Scrooge!'

Her voice was coming from everywhere and despite what she said, the grey clouds seemed to be getting darker and increasing in number, gathering in one spot above her head.

'I am in charge up here, and if I so choose, I could make death very difficult for you.'

A sudden flurry of images appeared around Scrooge and he shuddered as a face, which he recognised as his own, screamed at a pitch that he didn't think was possible for him. A ring of fire ignited around him. He had assumed that it was just an image, but he could feel the heat intensifying with every passing second.

'Do you really want to test me further?' The angel's voice had a sharp edge to it, as if every word had the potential to do him harm. 'This is bigger than you! If we don't fix this, it could spell the end of everything. Tell me what you know!'

Scrooge couldn't move; the fire had him cornered. Was this a sign of things to come if he didn't cooperate? Was she telling the truth? Were he and Jack truly responsible for what was happening? As the questions flew through his mind, he could already feel the words coming to his lips, and as the flames got closer and closer, he knew that he didn't really have a choice. *I'm sorry, Jack.* 'It was Jack! His name was Jack Thornhill,' Scrooge shouted above the sound of the crackling flames. 'He wanted me to help him prevent his own death!'

The flames were gone in a flash, and although Scrooge was shaken, he didn't feel anywhere near as bad as the angel looked.

'Why would anyone do that?' She looked as if she might faint. 'Why would anyone want to go back to life?'

Despite what she'd just put him through, he felt like he should comfort her or at least offer an explanation. 'He was too young. He felt that he died too young. There's more to it, but I can fix this,' he told her. 'I can go back down there and prevent it from—'

'What?! Fix one problem by patching over it with another?'

'You can do anything, can't you? Just send me back to life!' Scrooge pleaded. 'I can do it differently! I can save all of them!'

'As I told you before, Scrooge, there is no going back from death. The memory alone of this place would drive you mad, and you can see for yourself all around us the consequences of someone trying to hold back the inevitable.'

'So, what are we supposed to do. Can't we at least try to fix it?' He felt sick at the despair he heard in his own voice.

'First, I need to see Jack. And then maybe… maybe we can stop all this ending. Just picture him in your head and I can take us to him, wherever he is up here.'

Scrooge gasped, for as the angel instructed him, the image of Jack popped into his head, and just as suddenly – instantaneously – they were somewhere else. Scrooge could tell from the look on the angel's face that it wasn't a good somewhere else. He couldn't hear anything but the howling wind and lightning cracks, but he could see the angel, and she was pointing toward something in the distance. The sheets and sparks of lightning were cracking the sky open, and as he looked into the distance, he could see a clear difference in the clouds. The ones on the left were white with light shining through them. It looked odd because there was still lightning splitting the clouds open, cracking them into a million separate segments. They were trying to pull themselves back together, but almost as soon as they did the lightning ripped them apart again, as if Heaven itself was falling apart.

The same was true of the other side on the right, although it was getting harder and harder to tell the two sides apart. The dark clouds were being ripped apart by even brighter lightning, but maybe it just seemed brighter and sharper by contrast with the black clouds.

'This is very bad!' the angel shouted. 'We're at the crossing point between Heaven and Hell, and the storm is tearing them both apart!'

Scrooge could feel the wind knocking him about, threatening to whip him away from the angel, but he still managed to stay close enough to her to hear her shouts. 'I don't understand!' he shouted. 'I thought we were supposed to go to Jack!'

At this, the angel pointed again, and Scrooge could just make out a round shape in the distance. It looked like a large star, and it was the only thing that wasn't being affected by the maelstrom. In fact, it looked as if the lightning and winds and everything else were exuding from it, as if it was the source of it all.

'I think Jack is in there!' the angel shouted.

'You think? You mean you're not sure?'

Without saying anything else, the angel floated forwards through the unpredictable storm, beckoning him to follow.

The space around him was crackling, as if it were alive and threatening to harm him every second he moved further through it. He felt hot and cold at the same time, as if the two elements were fighting over him for dominance. As they got nearer to the round shape, he could now see some of the surface detail, although, detail wasn't really the appropriate word for it. The surface of it was murky, and he could see now that there was as much darkness emanating from it as there was light, and rather than being made up of light like the star he thought it to be, now that they were getting ever closer to it, it seemed to be made up of clouds. As a final touch, there were minor bolts of lightning going off all around the clouds, as if warning them to stay away.

'This isn't good,' the angel said, 'this is not good at all.'

Scrooge wasn't sure what to make of it. 'I thought you were taking me to Jack,' he said, and then something clicked. 'Wait a minute. Is this Jack? Has he been turned into whatever that is?'

The angel just looked at him, and the expression on her face gave him his answer.

'Well, I don't know, do I.'

'This 'thing' as you so eloquently put it, well, it doesn't really have a name. It appears to be Jack's perfect moment, except, I can't see through it, so it's difficult to know for certain. Everything is falling apart, and I need to fix it.'

A thought started to form in Scrooge's head. *They watch over the recently dead until they become accustomed to the idea. If that's the case, then why was Jack so upset about it? Did they not watch him properl*ARRRRRRRGH! A blinding pain filled his head. It was like he was being crushed and stretched at the same time. And then, it was gone, and he looked up to find the angel's eyes fixed on him, like a silent warning.

'That's it, isn't it,' he said. 'You were supposed to be watching over us – over Jack – but he slipped through, somehow. You're the one ultimately to blame for not doing your job properly. Now that I think on it, the poor soul I met when I first got here said that *They* hadn't been down to check on him and the others in years. Yes, it's all starting to make sense now.' He tried not to sound so satisfied with his deduction, but he couldn't help it.

The angel was still looking at him like she wanted him to die all over again. 'Listen to me, little man,' she said. 'We will all suffer if you don't help me fix this. Don't you see? Look around. Everything will fall apart. Literally everything, if we can't fix this.'

Scrooge could see that the storm was getting worse. There was an unnatural change in the air. The universe was tearing itself apart, and yet, he still found it hard to believe that something he and Jack did could have caused all this devastation.

'Now,' the angel said, holding her hand out, 'will you help me?'

Scrooge nodded in silent agreement and took her hand as she took them into the clouds of Jack's perfect moment.

As soon as they broke into the outer wall, the darkness and deafening lightning of where they had been disappeared and was replaced by near-silence and bright white clouds speeding past them. He felt an overwhelming feeling of goodness touching every part of him. It reminded him of that Christmas morning; the one he was supposed to have relived again and again. He wanted to feel bitter about having that taken away from him so quickly, but as soon as the feeling surfaced, it was knocked back down again by the potent and pure happiness in the very air around him. Suddenly the angel's voice was there in his head. It was like a whisper, but he could hear it as clearly as if the words were his own thoughts.

'*Scrooge, I'm not sure what we'll find in here*,' she said.

He turned to her, remembering that he was still holding her hand. Her mouth wasn't moving as she spoke.

'I'm talking directly into your mind, Ebenezer. You must do the same. If this is what I think it is, we must not do anything to shatter the illusion of Jack's perfect moment. Not until I know what to do.'

'How do I do that?' he said, before realising that he was already speaking directly into the angel's mind. *'But... how?'* he said again, *'I didn't think it worked that way. I thought it was about reading emotions and—'*

'The rules work differently in here.'

'What do you mean?'

'Calm your mind, Ebenezer. We are at our destination.'

She was right. The clouds were thinning out now, but as they moved, they altered. Clouds that reminded him of trees and bushes gradually became those very things. All the clouds changed and swirled around together to form a very familiar place. Two clouds in the distance were the last to change. They reminded Scrooge of a couple: One standing, and one kneeling down in front of the other, and suddenly, that's what they were. It was Jack and Grace. They were in the park in London, but somehow it was different. For a start, there were no giant buildings reaching up into the clouds, and the park seemed to stretch off in every direction for miles. He looked behind him and, yes, there was nothing but snow-covered trees, bushes and paths in that direction, too. Before he could ask, he heard the angel's voice in his mind.

'It's an idealised version of the place in his head; how he wants it to be.'

'Oh…'

'We need to get closer, so we can hear what they're saying.'

'But won't they see us? Didn't you say that—'

'They won't see us, Scrooge. As long as you keep hold of my hand.

The angel pulled him forward, and as they got nearer to the couple, it became clearer what was going on: Jack was proposing to Grace. He was down on one knee and proposing. Grace, however, did not look like a girl who was being propositioned. In fact, she wasn't even looking at Jack. She seemed to be looking off into the distance, confused at her surroundings.

'Well? Will you marry me?' Jack asked her, hope burning in his eyes. There was an odd resonance to his voice, as if they were in a large hall or cavern, and it made his words sound all the more distant, explaining why Grace was finding it so easy to ignore them.

A recently recovered memory came screaming back to Scrooge. Jack *had* been planning to propose to his lady friend. He'd seen him fumbling with the ring in his pocket on the bus, and later on in the park he'd used that knowledge to convince Jack that he was telling the truth; that he should heed his warning and leave that place before something terrible happened. He hadn't listened to him. They were here. Dead.

Grace turned back to Jack as if she'd just noticed he was there, and she responded to his question like he'd just mentioned the weather. 'Marry you? We've only been seeing each other for a couple of months. Don't you think it's odd?'

Jack looked devastated. 'No. I – I know how I feel, and… and I thought you—'

'Not your proposal. This place. It doesn't feel right.'

At this, the angel let out a gasp so loud that Scrooge was surprised that neither Jack nor Grace heard it. He was so shocked at the angel's response he almost spoke out loud.

'What? What's wrong?'

She seemed inconsolable and was staring at the couple, as if searching desperately for answers. The angel finally turned to him and let out her thoughts. *'These two... They're two* people. *Two actual people. Spirits of the two people you knew back on Earth.'*

'Yes, I can see that. What's wrong with that?'

'Don't you see? This is only supposed to be Jack's perfect moment. Grace should be somewhere else, in her own moment. She can see right through this moment because it's not hers.'

'But I saw through mine. What does that—?'

'That's why everything's wrong out there. These two are not meant to be in one perfect moment together. No one is.'

They both watched helplessly as the drama played out in front of them.

'Wait! Don't go!' Jack shouted as Grace walked away.

Without turning back, she shouted: 'I'm sorry. I have to go. I don't belong here.' And with that, she disappeared off into the distant realms of the impossibly beautiful park.

The moment seemed to take forever to pass, but as soon as she was gone, the scene shifted back into that which the angel and Scrooge had first come across with the couple back in their original positions, as if what they'd just witnessed was a mere rehearsal for what was to come. He looked to the angel for an explanation.

'I wasn't sure what was going to happen then. But it seems as if Grace is incapable of leaving, at least for the moment. I don't know how much time we have, but we can't have long if she's already begun to see through the illusion.'

A recovered memory suddenly flashed back into Scrooge's mind. *'Angel,'* he said, *'I might have an inkling of what is happening here. I could be wrong—'*

'You probably are,' the angel interrupted. Scrooge ignored her.

'But something Jack told me about when he finally saw her again after waiting years for her up here—'

'What do you mean "after waiting—"'

'I'll get to that,' Scrooge said, *'but what I was going to say is that when they finally met again, Grace didn't want to know him. She'd lived a long life with other people, and he'd been holding on to her memory for all those years they'd been apart.'*

'You mean, before your meddling, she died years after him?'

He couldn't help but hang his head in shame; even though none of it had been his idea, he felt responsible none-the-less. *'Yes. Yes, I'm afraid so.'*

'DO YOU REALISE WHAT YOUR IRRESPONSIBLE ACTIONS HAVE DONE?' the angel screamed in his head. *'Everything that girl could have done with her life has no longer happened. It's all gone. All the good and bad. Oh my... That's why all the books in the library are changing. All the people she affected in her life. It's all been irrevocably changed because of this. That's why the universe is tearing itself apart. She must've been so important. Maybe one of the most important people that ever lived.'*

Scrooge didn't think that now would be the best point at which to mention the fact that he himself had died over a hundred years after he'd lived, and that that might be having an adverse effect on top of everything, but he did have an idea of how he might help matters. *'Angel, I think I have an idea of how I can fix this thing.'*

She just glared at him.

'If you could just trust me on this, I think I can put everything back the way it was supposed to be.'

'Trust you?' the angel scoffed. *'I don't know anything about you, and that's one of the most disturbing things about all this.'*

'Maybe it's not such a bad thing that you don't know anything about me.'

She didn't say anything. She just shook her head in disbelief.

'Listen, Spirit. Maybe there's a reason my book couldn't be opened by anyone except me. Perhaps there's a more profound reason why Jack picked me out of everyone else. Maybe I'm the only one who can help him now. Maybe it's a test of some sort.'

'That's impossible.'

'Um, why?'

'Because I'm in charge up here. If anyone was being tested, I would be told.'

He wasn't sure how to put what he had to say to that, so he just came straight out with it. *'But what if* you *were the one being tested? Surely then... you wouldn't.'*

The angel looked shocked. She clearly hadn't considered the possibility. Then she shook her head as if to convince herself that this couldn't be the case, and looked back to him, more determined than ever. *'I have done this job for longer than you could possibly imagine, little man. Who are you to question my authority?!'* However, her resolve was not as absolute as it sounded, because then she asked: *'How do you think that you can help fix the entire universe as we know it? What do you know that I don't? What do you propose on doing that I haven't already thought of?'*

The fact that the angel had become so defensive made him believe that maybe, just maybe, his idea had some merit. *'You just have to trust me, angel.'* And with that, he let go of her hand and walked over to where Jack and Grace were standing.

21

As he got closer to Jack and Grace, who were once again repeating the cycle they were trapped in, Scrooge could hear the angel's voice echoing around his head. It was getting fainter, but he could still make out the words.

'Please, Scrooge, don't do this… I know you think you're helping, but things can still get a lot worse for us… for everybody.'

With the words fading, he found them easier to ignore, but he could still feel the angel's fear. She was paralysed with it; the indecision tearing her apart. On the one hand she wanted to intervene, to stop him from making things worse, and on the other, she wanted to see if his gut feeling was true; that he could help fix everything; that he was the only one who could. The fact that she felt this way served to make Scrooge believe even more so that it could be the truth. He took one last look back and said to her: *'I believe that this is what is meant to be. Please, have faith in me.'*

He felt an immense sense of satisfaction wash over him, as if the true end of the story of his life was just on the horizon. For what greater purpose could there be than to restore the world – the universe – to what it had been; to its former glory?

Jack was the first to see him, and along with a look of confusion, Scrooge could physically feel a change in the air. It made him stumble, but he quickly recovered and corrected his footing. He'd been thinking of Jack as two different people: the one who visited him back in his own time, and the one who didn't know him; the one who lived in the corporeal world of the twenty-first century. This one was really a bit of both, but at the same time, neither of them.

'Hello there,' he said nervously. Grace looked shocked to see him, and again, he could feel it physically in the air, as if someone had just shoved past him. 'You both remember me, don't you?' There was a moment of silence which hung in the air, longer than Scrooge was comfortable with.

'Of course we remember you,' Jack said, clearly annoyed, 'we were just talking to you.'

'Whatever do you mean?' For a moment, Scrooge felt just as lost as Jack and Grace were, and then he remembered: It felt like a lifetime since he'd spoken to them, but he had done, just before he went running after Carl. 'Ah, of course,' he said, 'we did just see each other moments ago, when I told you to stay out of the park, and yet, here you are.'

'Why are you here, Mister Scrooge?' Grace asked, looking as confused as she had done moments earlier when she'd sensed that there was something wrong.

'Yes, why are you here, old man? Other than to ruin my perfect moment.'

Scrooge fell silent for a moment. He looked at both of them and was at a loss for words. He looked back toward where the angel was, but he could barely see her. It was almost as if she were a mere trick of the light, a mixture of light and shadow and mist conjured up in just the right places to give the appearance of a figure, miles away. He looked down at his feet. He couldn't stand to look at Jack's face when he said to them both:

'I wish I could say otherwise, but that is exactly why I am here; to stop this.' He looked up, and as expected, Jack looked mortified, but Grace's expression was an odd mixture of confusion and enlightenment, as if what she had been puzzled by sort of made sense to her now. He knew he had to be careful. He had to reveal the truth about where they were, but they had to realise it for themselves without too much prodding. He wished for a moment that the angel was with him to help, but ultimately, he knew that only he could do this.

'Grace,' he said, a deliberate and purposeful smile growing on his face. 'I think you suspect what's going on here.'

'I – I'm not sure,' she said.

'This place doesn't feel quite right to you, does it? But you can't figure out why.'

'What are you on about, old man? Why are you talking like that?' This was most definitely a different Jack to the one Scrooge knew or had known. He looked as though he wanted to throttle him, but he knew that Jack couldn't possibly do that in his current state, so he continued his gentle prodding.

'Look at this place.' He swept his arm around, encouraging both of them to take in their surroundings properly. 'Does it look the same place as before?'

'Before when?' Both Grace and Jack said this together. Scrooge didn't answer them, he just watched as they looked around properly for the first time. Grace was the first to realise.

'It is different, Jack. Don't you think it seems different?'

Jack looked around, but something in his expression told Scrooge that he didn't want to see what was different about his perfect vision of the park. Then something clicked in his mind. Of course. He and the angel had witnessed Grace's questioning of the reality of the place. She didn't belong there. This was Jack's perfect moment; not Grace's. Her own moment was somewhere else entirely, but then, she wasn't even supposed to be dead yet. His and Jack's interference had changed everything. They had changed the natural flow of events. Maybe Grace's perfect moment hadn't even occurred yet. She hadn't lived long enough to see it. Maybe that was why she had ended up in Jack's: His love had somehow called her there.

He looked at both Grace and Jack. The look on Grace's face: she knew or was on the verge of knowing where she was. What would that do to her, finding out that she was dead before her time? Jack still looked as though he didn't want to know the truth. He was quite happy to keep believing the park was real, that he and Grace should stay there repeating the same loop over and over. It was preferable to what happened the first time. All that time waiting on his own only for her to break his heart at the end of it. How does one move on from that? That's it! Scrooge almost punched the air in triumph. He could save him. Not in the way he intended, but beggars couldn't be choosers.

'Could I have a moment to speak to you alone please, Grace?' Scrooge said. Jack wasn't happy about it – Scrooge could tell from the tremor in the air – but Grace silently agreed and followed Scrooge to a tree which was just far enough away so they could talk without Jack listening in.

'Okay, Mister Scrooge,' Grace said, 'what's going on? I've bumped into you, like, three times now in the last couple of days, and you seem to know more about what's going on than me. Are you my guardian angel or something?'

Scrooge laughed at that. 'I suppose I am in a way, except, I've not been a very good one. In fact, one could argue the fact that—' He could see that she was getting impatient for him to get to the point. 'Never mind. The point is, I'm here to help. To help you and Jack.'

'Jack? We've only been going out for like two months. I mean, we've known each other a bit longer from his time in the hospital, but why would you need to help us both?'

Scrooge tried to think of the best way of saying it, but there was no best way. 'Because… he cares for you – he loves you, more than you do him.'

'He loves me? But like I said, we've only really just started going out.'

'I knew a girl, a very long time ago now, when I was young and far too foolish. She loved me, and I think if I had been a different, wiser person back then, I would have loved her back, the way she deserved. My point is, love isn't always fair, isn't always balanced. We see things in others that aren't necessarily there.'

'So, what are you saying? That I should love him back?'

'No, no,' Scrooge said, surprised at her response. 'If you don't love him, you don't love him. You can't make your heart do something it doesn't want to.'

'What do you want me to do then?'

'He was about to propose, before you both—' He almost said: "before you both died," but stopped himself just in time. 'Before you were both so rudely interrupted by this old man.'

'Propose? But we've—'

'I know, you've only just started going out.' Scrooge felt bad for sounding so impatient and blunt, but she was starting to sound like she was still trapped in the continuous loop. 'I need you to give him the chance to say goodbye.'

Grace looked confused by his words.

'It's hard to explain, and I'm not sure I can without giving too much away about this place.'

'What do you mean?' she shouted. 'The more you tell me about how much you can't tell me, the more I want to know. What is this place?'

'I know, I know,' Scrooge said, 'but it's just something you need to figure out for yourself and accept.'

'Accept?'

He turned away from her. He could feel an unsettled shaking in the air, as if it was solid and trying to cut him loose. She was starting to figure it out.

'Why would I need to accept where I am?'

Cracks were beginning to appear in the sky now. Grace didn't seem to notice them, but Scrooge looked on in dread as they spread and split off in all directions. It was a very disturbing sight, as now, the cracks weren't just in the heavens at a relatively safe distance. They were right in front of and around them, and the way they were spreading, they had the appearance of odd, bright white exotic flowers growing with unnatural speed and twisted elegance. Grace was squinting now. Could she see them?

'The only reason I would need to accept where I am,' she said, 'would be if—'

He knew he'd made a mistake. He shouldn't have said what he'd said, and now everything was falling apart. He grabbed her by the shoulders, as if to stop her from flying off into the abyss. 'Forget about that now, Grace. You have to let Jack say—'

'Let me say what?'

Scrooge and Grace turned to face Jack who looked paler somehow, and more like the ghost Scrooge had known. The cracks in the sky were all around them now, and they looked like snowflakes frozen in time. They would have been beautiful if Scrooge hadn't have known what they really were: Jack's perfect moment breaking down. Jack tried to touch one of them, but his finger passed right through it. He looked confused at this, but not as much as he should have been. He seemed to just dismiss it as an optical illusion.

'Well?' Jack said. His voice was gentle, wispy, and yet full of accusation. 'What does she have to let me say?'

'Goodbye,' Grace said. 'We have to say goodbye, Jack.'

Jack was stunned, his face frozen in confusion, staring at Grace. And then his head shifted, and his gaze fell upon Scrooge. The rest of his body remained still, as if the shock had frozen everything but his neck. His face shifted, figuring something out. 'Are you? You can't be. Are you?'

'Am I what?' Scrooge let out.

Jack looked disgusted with him and then turned back to Grace. 'You're not dumping me, for *him*?'

'What?!' Grace said, looking shocked and almost equally as disgusted.

Scrooge wasn't sure what to make of it all.

'Well? Are you?' Jack demanded.

'Of course not, you idiot.'

Jack looked hurt, but then started to smile. Before the smile could settle though, Grace spoke again.

'But we do need to say goodbye, Jack. I'm sorry.'

'What?'

'Don't you see? Don't you see what's going on here? These odd shapes in the sky?'

'What? You mean the snowflakes?' Jack said, looking bemused.

'Snowflakes that grow in the sky without falling?'

He looked again at the cracks in the air and seemed to be considering what his lady friend was trying to tell him, but then dismissed it with a shake of his head. 'What's so strange about that?' But his words were hesitant, false. He knew there was something wrong, but Scrooge and Grace could see that he wasn't ready to admit it. He needed more time for it to sink in and—

'We're dead, Jack. All three of us.'

Grace's words were sharp, and even though Scrooge had come to accept his situation, they cut deep. He looked at Jack, and his expression didn't make him feel any better. Betrayal, bitterness, loss; they were all there in his quivering lip, dark eyes and heavy tears, and Scrooge could feel it in the air, shaking, rumbling, like the world was threatening to pull itself apart forever.

'No.'

His word was defiant and powerful, as if that word alone could stop the truth from being so, but Scrooge could see and feel that Jack's resolve was breaking down.

'You know it's true,' Grace said, pleading with him. 'Mister Scrooge,' she said, turning to him,' you told me I have to accept this situation, so what else could it be?'

'No, no, no.' Jack's head was in his hands now, and his fingers were covering his ears, as if to keep the truth from penetrating his skull. The cracks in the air were growing all around him, but not touching him, as if there was an invisible bubble protecting him from the effects.

Grace looked sad, as if she was just realising what being dead meant. All the people she'd miss, all those she'd never see again.

Scrooge knew how she felt, and he suddenly felt very cold and alone. It was hard to tell how much of that feeling was coming from himself and how much was coming from Grace and Jack, but as before, he felt physically moved by it all, and it was getting worse. He could hear thunder, deafening him and filling his head. He looked at Jack and his face was a bizarre mix of anger and sadness, as if he couldn't decide which one to settle on. And still, the cracks in the air didn't touch him, but now they were everywhere, as if he and Grace were caught up in a web made up of Jack's fears. Despite how scared he felt, he knew he had to try and get through to him. He had to calm Jack down and ease him into the idea of being dead.

Deafening winds swirled around them now, knocking him and Grace from side to side, and yet, Jack was unaffected. It was all coming from *him*, so why should it? He had to stop this before there was nothing left. The trees in the facsimile of the park were being ripped in two, and the snow was swirling around in miniature tornadoes. It was like some kind of nightmarish snow globe.

'It's true,' Scrooge shouted, trying to make himself heard over everything, 'we are dead. All three of us; but you know what, my friend? That's okay. It's just a natural part of life; of existence.' Before he could say anything else, Jack shouted something back.

'But it's not fair! I wasn't ready! I'm too young! Me and Grace are both too young!'

He couldn't argue with that. 'You're right, Jack! Life is not fair. An old man like me got to live a long and miserable life, infecting others with my misery, whilst you and Grace were only just beginning, but there's nothing we can do about that now. What's done is done.'

The winds and the thunder were fading now. Not gone by any means, but fading, and Jack's face had a glint of hope in it. Maybe his words were getting through to him.

A smile formed on Jack's face, but it wasn't a good smile full of happy thoughts and memories. No, it was a smile with a plan behind it, and Scrooge should have seen it coming.

'Look at this place. It's a perfect recreation of Victoria Park.'

'Well, not perfect,' Scrooge said. 'The buildings aren't there, and—'

'But it's close enough. And how is it here? How are me and Grace here, in the past?'

'It's not really the past, Jack. It's a memory.'

'Yeah, but it's like I've actually travelled into the past. It's… it's a miracle.' Jack's eyes were shining now, lighting up with ideas. 'And if this is possible, then other things must be. *Anything* could be possible; boundless possibilities. This place isn't bound by the rules of time, is it. I could escape at any point and go back. Back to before I was killed.'

'No, Jack! Not again, you mustn't' He regretted the words as soon as they escaped his mouth.

'Maybe all those ghost sightings aren't fake. Maybe it's just people – Wait! What did you say?'

'Nothing,' Scrooge said, but he knew it was already too late.

'No. You said "not again", didn't you.' His face was contorting, and an idea was being reborn.

'I - I didn't mean anything by it.' He knew it was hopeless to try and convince him otherwise, but he had to try. 'It was just a slip of the tongue.'

'Yes, it was, wasn't it. I've done it before, haven't I.'

Scrooge could feel something or someone prodding around in his head, but he somehow managed to ward it off. He looked over at Grace; concern etched all over her face.

'Wait a minute, that must be how I know you. But I don't know you, do I. You know *me*.'

Scrooge felt like his head was in a vice, and it was taking every ounce of his energy just to stay steady.

'How is it possible for you to know me without me knowing you? Unless I did do what I think I did.'

'I can't tell you, Jack. You can do your worst, but I can't tell you. All I know is that we shouldn't interfere with the natural order of things; the way things are meant to be.'

'The natural order of things?! The natural order of things is that we're born, we live, we fall in love and have a family, grow old and die. I wouldn't say that what happened to me and Grace was natural at all, Would you?!'

'What happened to you wasn't fair, I can't deny that,' Scrooge said weakly, 'but people young and old die every day. We can't save them all. You just have to accept what happened and somehow get over it, otherwise it will tear you apart, my young friend.' As he spoke, he had to raise his voice higher and higher as the winds rose up again, as if they were trying to shut him up.

'Why do you keep calling me that?' Jack boomed. 'I don't know you. I never met you before today. Tell me how I can change what happened to us or I'll let these winds tear you apart!'

Scrooge could feel himself shaking. Somehow, he knew it was a combination of his fear and Jack's anger directed upon him. 'You're never going to listen, are you,' he said to himself. 'This is all just going to repeat on a cycle until the world just flies apart.'

'What?! What are you saying, old man?!'

It was time for the truth. He didn't know what would happen, but Jack wouldn't leave him alone until he'd said it. 'You've tried it before. I don't know how, but you've tried changing things before, and it made things much worse.'

An explosion of rage came straight out of Jack in the form of a highly focussed burst of wind which knocked Scrooge clean off his feet. His body spun around and around until he finally caught up with the ground beneath him. Grace rushed over to him to see if he was alright, but he just shooed her away. He couldn't stand to look at her, knowing what Jack was forcing him to reveal.

'What do you mean, old man? How could things possibly be worse?'

'Because that's how I know you, Jack! You came to me back in my time and told me I had to save Grace.' He wants the truth, Scrooge thought, well, he's going to get it – All of it. 'You told me that Grace was in danger, and that if I didn't stop a man called Carl Phillips, he would kill her. That wasn't it though, Jack.'

'What do you mean?' Jack bellowed. His voice sounded as though it was directly linked to the storm now, as if each syllable brought with it a fluctuation of wind and razor-sharp spitting rain.

'I mean, Jack, that it wasn't Grace who was supposed to die that day. It was supposed to be you! We changed things, and now all the good that this young lady did with her life; all the lives she touched and all the lives that those lives touched as a result, are gone.' He braced himself for the storm to get worse, closing his eyes tight and wrapping his hands around his head. On quite the contrary, it seemed to be subsiding; the many flecks of snow which had been swirling around everywhere were following steadier paths now, and even the air itself seemed warmer. He looked at Grace through the gaps in his fingers; she looked purely dumbstruck.

'Is – is that true?' she said.

Scrooge moved his hands from his face, so he could see her properly. She was staring into space in disbelief.

All the rage and anger was gone from Jack now, and he looked just as lost as Grace did. 'I could never do that. I could never see you come to harm,' he said, weeping.

'But you did,' Grace said; not angry, but her sadness was just as potent. 'You tried to save yourself and got us both killed in the process. I remember now. It's coming back to me. We were both shot in the park, but, Mister Scrooge, you say that that was never supposed to happen. That he changed things.'

He didn't know what to say. He knew that nothing he said would change the result of what happened, and maybe nothing would help her forgive Jack, but something occurred to him that might lessen the pain for both of them, if only a tiny bit. 'Grace, the Jack standing here is not the same one that I knew; the Jack that changed things.'

She looked confused. So did Jack for that matter.

'I know that sounds like absolute claptrap, and I'm not sure I completely understand it myself, but you, Jack, are the result of your former self's actions. The Jack I knew was alone here in Heaven for – I don't know how long – but a very long time indeed, waiting for you, Grace. When you finally died as an old lady you barely remembered him, and this changed him. He became bitter and twisted. So, you could argue that this Jack is a completely different person as a result of his past self's actions. He's changed, like I did.'

He looked at them and could see that they were both lost in his words. Finally, Jack spoke up.

'I don't understand anything of what you just said, but I know that I could never let Grace come to any harm.'

'But you did,' Grace said, softly. There was still anger in there somewhere, but maybe something of what he'd said had got through to her. Maybe, just maybe, things would work out for the best.

He looked over to where Jack stood. There was no sign of the storm that had been raging and threatening to tear everything asunder moments ago. All that was left was a sad looking young man. Sad, but accepting of what had happened to him.

'I'm sorry, Scrooge.' The voice didn't belong to Grace or Jack: It was the angel. She sounded different, somehow. He turned to her and jumped as he saw her expression. Gone was the kindly countenance and glow of before. She looked more determined, somehow; her eyes boring into his.

'Who's this?' Grace asked.

'I'm truly sorry.' The angel's words did not reflect her voice. 'But I've waited too long to get to my position to let a couple of mistakes ruin it all for me.'

'I–I don't understand,' Scrooge stammered.

'You're right. I was supposed to be watching over the Earth. We were all supposed to be – I was in charge – but we were too absorbed in the books. I have to take you and Jack somewhere where He'll never see you, and never find out what happened.'

'He? You mean—?'

'Yes. You know who I mean,' she said in an almost whisper, as if she'd be able to hide what she was saying.

'Where are you taking us? Who are you, anyway?' This was Jack. He and Grace were stood either side of Scrooge now.

The angel stared at Jack for what seemed like a lifetime, and she almost looked sympathetic. 'Nowhere. I'm taking you nowhere,' she said, finally.

'What do you mean?' Scrooge said. 'You just said that—'

'I'm removing you from existence. I'm sure the world won't miss a young man who died before he ever achieved anything, and an old man who only ever did anything good with his life towards the end of it. You see, with you gone, the problem out there disappears, too, and no one will ever have known about it.'

22

A chill came over Scrooge. To never have existed? How was that even possible? Everything he'd ever done – good and bad – gone. Surely, this was the cruellest fate of all. Jack looked like he was thinking the same thing, his eyes glazed over, as if he was half gone already.

He looked over to the angel, ready to beg for his and Jack's lives, but now there was something else going on with her. Her head was moving jerkily from side to side, as if she was having an internal argument with herself, and losing.

'Spirit, what's wrong with you? Can you not see that—?'

She ignored him and addressed Grace directly. 'I'm sorry, Grace.'

'Why? What are you—?'

'Because you're going to have to disappear with them. I can't leave any evidence of my misdemeanours behind.'

'What?' Grace gasped. 'How can you do this?'

'Because I have more power here than you could possibly realise. He is not here all the time. That's why He left me in charge, and mostly I've done a perfect job.' She wasn't looking directly at anyone now, as if she was trying to justify herself to, well, herself. 'Why should I be held to account for a couple of small mistakes?' Her voice was shaky, manic. She as clearly not in her right mind.

'Please, don't do this.' This was Jack, and Scrooge could feel the despair all around him. This was, after all, still Jack's moment, albeit no longer perfect; far from it.

'You don't need to do this. I'm sorry, okay? I'm sorry I tried to cheat fate, but that's not Grace's fault. Why should she suffer for something I did? Why should the world suffer? Why should all that good be wiped out because of me? It doesn't make sense. If I never existed then she'll never meet me, and she won't die when she did, so she and no one else will ever know what I tried to do.'

For a moment the angel looked like she may have been considering Jack's heartfelt and logical pleas. Maybe there was a chance.

'He's right,' Scrooge said. He quickly looked over at Grace who hadn't said anything in her own defence yet. She looked too stunned to say anything; the idea of never having existed looked as though it was pulling her apart in so many directions that she couldn't move. He could barely comprehend it himself, but the idea of saving Grace – a young lady with so much potential – helped him to ignore his own stake in matters. 'He's right. Why do you have to take away the good that she's done? Surely there's another way.'

The angel looked torn; split down the middle by what she felt she had to do. It was driving her mad, and she was visibly shaking, as if a power much greater than her body could contain was trying to break out. Just as Jack, Grace, and Scrooge were backing away in the vain hope of avoiding whatever was about to happen, the shaking stopped, and the angel's head dropped to her chest like a wind-up toy soldier that had run out of power. A moment passed, and they all looked at each other with one silent question between them: Were they off the hook?

Grace started to speak. 'Do you think that—?'

Then suddenly, the angel raised her head again, and the look on her face told them that the answer to Grace's question, whatever it was going to be, was a definite "no". The angel's eyes slowly faded to a dull grey, and Scrooge had never seen anything quite so unsettling in all his years. She slowly raised her arms, as if they were out of her control now, like a puppet. Between her fingers, sparks were dancing and bouncing off of each other.

'THERE IS NO OTHER WAY. ONLY MY WAY, NOW.'

The words which blasted forth were enough to turn even the boldest bones to ice. The voice was devoid of all compassion, humanity, and sympathy, and there was an unnatural resonance to it; every word was throbbing with fury. The vibrations penetrated the air, and all that he could see of Grace and Jack were blurred colours moving back and forth at impossible speed. Then, a deafening sound which held the same power as the angel's new voice shook him to his core, and he could feel every one of his bones and organs tremble. This was it. This was the end. But it wasn't the end, because there wouldn't ever have been a beginning.

He used all his will power to look up at the angel. She was aiming at Grace. Why her? Why get rid of her first? Why get rid of her at all? Scrooge could hear his thoughts deep in the back of what was left of his mind. It was full of shadowy regret, all coming back to wave him goodbye in his final moments, but a few instances of light and goodness remained. An image of Bella formed in his mind. Such a good woman. Too good for him, but she loved him, and he let her go. What goodness did she give to the world? By leaving him the way he was back then, she did the right, the good thing. He would have corrupted her if she'd stayed. He would have been responsible for denying the world a spark of hope. This one thought drew him in like a fisherman's line. He could not let Grace's goodness be snuffed out. He had to save her somehow, even if he could only save the goodness that she'd done in the past, and not the goodness that she was supposed to have done in the future. With his last act he had to make Bella proud, or at least do something that *would* have made her proud. He would stop the angel.

Every step felt like a lifetime's struggle; every movement an unbearably slow eternity, but he could feel himself breaking through. There was a simple truth that kept him moving: No matter what, he couldn't let his and Jack's mistakes cause any more pain to the world. And Jack was feeling the same thing. He could hear him in his head. Jack was moving towards the angel, and from the look on his face he was struggling just as much to get through the immense force emanating all around them.

We can do it, Scrooge could hear in his head. This wasn't his voice, it was Jack's, and he could feel himself speeding up slightly. His foot suddenly jerked forward and landed, and his goal – their goal – no longer felt as far away as it had done. Scrooge sent the very same thought back to his young companion, and the next step was even less of a struggle. He felt the same thought come from Jack again, and immediately he sent his own back to Jack. They were in perfect synch now, like two legs on the same body. Moving onward at a steady pace.

Scrooge looked over to where Grace was standing and realised how little distance they'd covered. That wasn't the worst of it: She looked horrified. Her hands were almost covering her face entirely, but through her fingers Scrooge could see her eyes, and they were practically bulging with panic. The poor girl had only just realised that she was dead, and now she was due to never have existed at all, thanks to some power-crazed fallen angel.

Nearly there now. Jack was trying to spur him on.

You're right, Scrooge said. *You know, Jack, you're a good man. I know you made some bad decisions,* (he could feel their progress quickening as he spoke the encouraging words) *but when you were with me in London, I had a real sense of a kindred spirit; someone with regrets, like me.*

Neither of them spoke for a moment, and then Jack said: *I wish I could remember you. You seem like a good man, too, and I'm glad that if I have to be erased from existence to save the girl I love, that you're at my side, helping.*

Thank you, Jack. That means a lot.

They were approaching the angel now, and the grey in her eyes had now turned to red fire, as had the sparks emitting from her fingers.

Um, Ebenezer?

Yes, Jack?

How are *we going to stop her?*

He faltered for a moment. The angel could probably hear their thoughts as well – if not better – than they could hear each other's. And then something happened that forced their hand. The angel turned to them and raised both her hands, which were full of the red fire reflected in her eyes. Without a second thought, Scrooge said to Jack in his head:

Grab Grace and get as far away from me as possible.

A question started to form in Jack's head; something about where they could go, but Scrooge cut him off:

Just go!

This time, Jack did as he said and moved with the grace and speed of a man whose thoughts were as pure and as free from constraint as he was from his physical form.

He couldn't see where they'd gone, but now he had bigger worries. The angel loomed large over him. Before she could say anything, he spoke. The words came out of his mouth this time, not his mind, making them seem all the more real. He felt braver, even though he was still petrified.

'Forget about them, Spirit. You don't need them.'

The angel looked off into the distance, and almost seemed sad for a moment, as if she could see all her hopes walking off into the sunset. Then the anger came back: 'Don't presume to tell me what to do, Scrooge. Just because I couldn't open your book, doesn't mean you hold any special power over me.'

He could feel doubt in the angel's words, as if she felt the complete opposite of the words' intended meaning. He stared at her, and something incredible happened: She flinched.

'Now you listen to me, Spirit,' he said with renewed confidence 'Mistakes happen. In my business, when I was alive, I made mistakes, yes.'

'I hardly think you can compare—'

'And, yes, I covered them up. I let people whom I thought at the time to be beneath me take the blame, and I would increase their debt to cover myself, but that was wrong. And what you are trying to do is wrong.'

'Do not presume to—'

'Yes, yes, yes, you've said that already.' He was on a roll now. He felt like an actor at the theatre, riled on by his own momentum. 'What I'm trying to say is, that no matter how many mistakes you cover up, they'll always come back to haunt you in the end. I should know.' Even Scrooge himself was shocked by what came out of his mouth next. 'Just kill me. Destroy me. Wipe me from existence. Lord knows I deserve it. And if I'm gone, then my mistakes are gone. A great many people will be much happier, and my actions of the last few days on Earth will be gone as well; just a memory – well, not even that – and Jack will never meet me, and Grace will live to do all the good she was supposed to do in the world.'

He felt an immense sense of relief. Oh, he didn't really want to be erased from history, but it felt good to know that all the bad he'd done with most of his life would be gone forever; it would never happen. He realised at that moment that he had closed his eyes, ready for the killer blow.

'You're right.'

These words made him open his eyes.

'If I just erase *you* from existence, then everything else will fall back into place.'

He braced himself for what was coming. He didn't close his eyes this time; he wanted to face his fate with bravery, the opposite of the way he'd faced most of his life. All the bad in his life would be gone, but all the good would be gone too, forever. He felt a tear trickle down his nose – or was it a mere memory of one? But still, he kept his eyes open, and looked at the angel as the fire in her hands got larger, more intense. He thought of Bella. They'd been happy once. Now that would never happen. He knew that she had found someone else; someone that deserved her, but he still felt sad at the loss, of course he did.

'I'm sorry, Scrooge,' the angel said, not really sorry at all, 'but your right. This is the only way of fixing everything.'

The fire in her hands throbbed and pulsated. Would it hurt? he asked himself.

'Only for a moment,' she said in answer to his final, unspoken question. The angel raised her hands, building up for the killer blow, and at the last, Scrooge closed his eyes for the final time, bracing himself. All went silent, and he could feel it coming.

But nothing happened. Was this what it was supposed to feel like? Surely not, Scrooge thought. He could think! He could feel! Slowly, ever so slowly, he opened his still-existent eyes, and he was greeted with the same scene which he thought would be his final one. The angel was still lurching above him, and a fireball was emitting from her hands, but it wasn't moving; nothing was. Time had apparently frozen, and yet, he could move. Then, a voice thundered through his head. A familiar voice, somehow. A voice that shook him to his core, and yet, filled him with joy and oh-so-glorious hope.

'THAT'S QUITE ENOUGH OF THAT!'

He blinked, and then a second later when he opened his eyes again, he found that he was somewhere very familiar indeed.

23

The street. The snow. The cold feeling on his cheeks. The people rushing past with arms full of presents. Except no one was rushing anywhere, because although it seemed to Scrooge that he was back in his own time, "time" was an altogether inappropriate word for his new situation. For a moment he'd been so overwhelmed with joy to be back, that he hadn't realised that everything was still frozen, even the snow in the air.

As was the case mere moments ago, Scrooge found that he wasn't frozen, although something had changed. He looked down at himself and realised that he had his old familiar clothes on; the very ones that he was wearing on the night oh-so-many years ago when Tiny Tim hit him with a sneaky snowball. The memory of this brought a smile to his face, the stress of moments before all but forgotten. He hadn't forgotten though. He was supposed to be dead. No, not just dead: Gone. Forgotten. Never there for anyone to remember in the first place. Was this a consequence of that? Was he fated to be trapped in this moment forever? Then he remembered that there had been a voice. Perhaps the owner of that voice had brought him here.

'You are right, Ebenezer.'

Scrooge spun around to see who had spoken and was immediately faced with the very snowball that Tim had thrown at him on that Christmas Eve. It was frozen in time like everything else, but from behind it, he could see movement. Surely, it couldn't be.

'Tiny Tim?!' He thought for a moment that he'd imagined what he'd seen. Then, the oh-so-familiar voice said:

'I thought I told you to call me Timothy, Ebenezer.'

He didn't know what to say. He opened his mouth to speak, but no words were forthcoming. He never thought he'd see Tiny Tim – sorry – Timothy again, and he could barely contain the joy that swept over him. 'I – I,' the words started to stagger through, but Scrooge knew that no words in his sixty-three-year-old vocabulary would be enough. Only a hug would do it. But before he'd even started to spread his arms, Timothy put up his hand with an air of authority unbefitting of one so young.

'I'm sorry, Ebenezer, but you can't hug me. You can't touch me.' His face was suddenly stern and morose, and Scrooge's bubble of joy burst.

'Why? Why not, Timothy? Why can't I—?' And then something clicked: Timothy was here in Heaven. He didn't look a day older than the last time they'd seen each other. No! It couldn't be! 'Timothy, are you—?'

'Everyone dies, Ebenezer.'

'Yes, but you're so young, and I thought that what I was doing was—'

'But Timothy, in your time at least, is not dead.'

Again, Scrooge had no words.

'He went on to live a good, long, and happy life, thanks to you.'

'I – I don't understand.'

'I am like the rest of this place: A memory. I have chosen this way to communicate because I thought it would be the most pleasant for you, Ebenezer.'

Timothy – or whoever was inhabiting Scrooge's memory of Timothy – suddenly looked floored. And now, when Scrooge looked at him, he could see quite clearly that he definitely wasn't the Tiny Tim who he knew and loved so much. All the mannerisms were wrong, and indeed, why should he, she – or could it be *Him*? - even try to imitate Timothy, since they'd already admitted that they weren't him.

'Exactly,' "Timothy" said.

'So, who are you?' Scrooge could hear the exasperation in his own voice, but he didn't care anymore. He'd had enough, and he wanted answers. 'Is this my punishment? Are you —?'

'Just think of me as Tim. Afterall, this memory of yours is from just before he asked you to start addressing him by the more grown up or formal name of "Timothy".' An old smile appeared on the borrowed face. 'And in answer to your other question; no, I'm not here to punish you. Not at all. You did nothing wrong.'

'Then why?'

'I'm here to tell you that you passed the test.' His eyes widened, and his arms spread as if he was going to hug him, but Scrooge knew that wasn't his intention. 'Each person up here – each soul – is at one point or another tested, to see if they are good enough to go on to the next phase of existence.'

Scrooge suddenly remembered something. 'What about Jack? And Grace? Did they pass the test? Where are they?'

'They are safe for now, but the test wasn't for them. It was for you, Ebenezer, and – as you speculated – the other one. The one you thought of as an angel.' The memory of Tim looked sad now; the real Tim had never looked so sad.

'The one I thought of as an angel? She tried to kill us. No; to stop us from ever existing.'

'Yes.' Tim looked slightly pained by what Scrooge said, like he had an itch on his leg. 'Her test was a test of power. She failed her test. I have much to explain; shall we sit?'

He gestured to a bench which Scrooge remembered as always having been there. He'd often rested on it when his old legs had gotten tired. 'We don't need to, do we?' he said.

'No, but I thought you might like to, for old time's sake.'

Scrooge sat down and found great comfort in it.

'Now, the nature of the first tests are always different. They are uniquely tailored to suit the soul they are for.'

'So, she was a powerful woman then?' Scrooge said.

'No. Quite the contrary. In life she was weak and powerless. She always felt that she was hard done by, and to an extent, she was. She had no control over her life, and so, up here—'

'You gave her power to test her.'

'Yes,' Tim sighed, 'and as well you know, it was too much for her and drove her mad. Perhaps it was the wrong test. Perhaps it was too much too soon.'

'Perhaps?' Scrooge bellowed. 'Perhaps?! She tried to wipe my friends and I from existence, and you say *perhaps* she had too much power?'

Tim looked dumbstruck at his outburst, and for a moment he regretted it and froze, preparing for some kind of retribution.

'It's alright, Ebenezer,' he said, 'I understand why you're upset, but let me assure you that I never would've allowed her to inflict any real harm on you. You've done too much good. Your life has changed other lives, and their lives others. The world is a better place because of your presence in it.'

He felt a great pang of joy at hearing this, especially from Tim's lips. Of course, Jack had already told him that someone or something had told him the same thing, but with all the lies the young man had told him it was difficult to know what to believe.

'Your young companion told many lies to aid his self-preservation, but he spoke the truth of what I told him about you. Jack has changed now. He's better because of you, but when I allowed him to leave here to test him, he abused his power and tried to change his own fate, and, well, you know what happened.'

'That was all a test?'

'Yes, Ebenezer.' Tim said plaintively, and then looked Scrooge right in the eye and said: 'And in answer to your next question; yes, Jacob Marley was tested too.'

Scrooge could feel his eyes widen and his heart leaping with joy at the sound of his old friend's name. 'Jacob? Is he—?'

'He was part of something different. He was a test of a test, is the plainest way to put it.'

That's the plainest way? Scrooge thought.

'Well, maybe not the plainest. I suppose the plainest way is to tell you the whole story from the start. We appear to have time, for now, and perhaps the telling of it will provide me with the answer I've been looking for.' As he said this, Tim looked all around at the people and the snow frozen in time.

Scrooge could feel a slight rumble in the air. It was a stark reminder that although the apocalyptic atmosphere of Jack's less-than-perfect moment hadn't followed him to wherever he was, it was still out there somewhere, waiting to break through.

'If you are ready,' Tim said, 'I'll tell you everything. Ever since the beginning of, well, everything, the dead – as you would call them – have always watched over the living.'

To Scrooge's surprise, moving pictures appeared all around him. He saw three people glowing so brilliantly that he couldn't make out whether they were men or women. They were looking down from the clouds at a world which Scrooge didn't recognise, although he knew it to be Earth.

Tim could obviously sense his confusion. 'Do not threat, Ebenezer. These visions are perfectly natural. This story is so old and has been told so many countless times that the images have become a natural part of the telling of it.

We have seen all the good in the world, and all the bad. We can see far into the past if we choose to do so, and far into the future.'

All of a sudden Scrooge was surrounded by images of great fire exploding in the sky and screams of men, women and children. It was a great blur of chaos, and there was no escaping it.

'That is the future that I observed, and I thought I was helpless to prevent it. Maybe I am. I found that the recently dead could be made to drift through the world, to not be a part of it. I used this as a form of torture for those souls who had caused the most harm in their time down there. You could argue that this was cruel and that the very notion is just as evil as the acts and deeds of the men and women that have been subjected to it; to be a witness to all the joy the world had to offer and to all the harshness and cruelty; never to be able to be part of it.'

With these words came images of thousands of men and women drifting slowly, yet unrelentingly, through the Earth. As they witnessed innocent children playing; families enjoying each other's company, he could feel all their hearts breaking over and over, on a seemingly endless cycle. He could feel his own heart breaking out of pure sympathy, and a scream started to form at the bottom of his throat. Before it could surface, he spoke. 'Stop! Stop it! I can't take any more of these pictures. You speak of torture, but I am the one being tortured.'

'I am sorry, Ebenezer.' The voice sounded softer now, more like Tim's than it had been. 'But I needed to tell the whole story. After all, hope on its own is indeed a good thing, but to see where that hope came from, through the oppressive shadows of despair and out the other side, is so much better.

'There was one man whose life had been particularly torturous, and all through his own doing: His greed, his lust for power over those he deemed less worthy than himself. When he died I sent him straight back down to Earth, never to return; to be left drifting without aim or purpose; to witness all the happiness he'd never even tried to be a part of, and to lie in the torture of all the evil he'd had a hand in.'

'I think I know of whom you speak,' Scrooge said.

'Yes. Jacob Marley.' The being who looked like Tim seemed to grow paler as the name left his mouth.

'Despite never being capable of staying anywhere for too long, a pattern of movement began to make itself apparent. Somehow or other, he always managed to pass through the English city of London; your area of London to be precise, Ebenezer. He was watching you.'

'All that time?'

'Not all the time, of course, but somehow he managed to slow his movements whenever he was near you. His regret and sorrow at seeing you repeat the same mistakes as he did somehow steadied him until eventually—'

'He stopped and appeared to me through my doorknocker.'

'Yes, Ebenezer. That was unexpected to everyone, including Jacob. I pulled him right back here in the hopes of an explanation. A spirit such as he should never have been able to appear to a mortal in that way.'

'But he did,' Scrooge said triumphantly. 'Good old Jacob.'

Tim didn't seem too happy at Scrooge's words, but carried on. 'Yes, well, as I tried to figure out what had happened, your friend made a strange request. He wanted to save you; to show you the error of your ways, but he knew he couldn't do it alone. He wanted to show you your life; your entire life from start to finish, and how you were wasting it. Well, needless to say, I was reluctant at first, but eventually I thought it might make an interesting test: Could the dead influence the living? Change the course of their mortal lives? Well, you know what happened next, of course.'

'Yes,' said Scrooge, 'my life *was* changed.' He thought to himself, maybe now. Maybe now is the right time to ask what happened to my old friend.

'I will get to that later, Ebenezer. The test was indeed a success, and your life became an example to others; to people that you would never even meet. So, I tried it again with other lost souls. These tests were… less successful. A lot of the time it was down to the fact that the chosen subjects down on Earth couldn't see the ghosts I sent to them. Maybe they were too close-minded; only believing in science. Other times the ghosts were at fault. They just ended up haunting their old homes and doing nothing of importance. Stories were written about them, but they were just seen as an unexplained phenomenon. The people who reported sightings were mocked and ridiculed, and no good came of it. The sightings were random, and the spirits were incapable of communicating properly with their earthly witnesses.

'I came to the conclusion that you were special, Ebenezer; a one off. Maybe I was never meant to change anything, but you had it in you to change your fate.'

'With help from Mister Jacob Marley, of course.'

Again, Tim looked none-too-happy.

'Yes, well, I suppose that's true,' the spirit admitted. 'Whatever the case may be, I had to see if it could be done again, partly to test you, to see if you could still see spirits; to see if you were the only one in all of time who could successfully converse with them.'

'You were testing Jack as well?' Scrooge said.

'As part of the test I took Jack out of his perfect moment early, and as a result he was left upset about dying so soon. So, I gave him the ability to move through time, so he could possibly change things. I was hoping that he wouldn't give in to that temptation, but he did.'

'You were hoping—? Tell me this, "Tim": Once you saw that he had changed things, or even that he'd travelled in time with me, why did you not pull him back here? Stop him from doing any damage? A girl who shouldn't have died is dead because of your little test.' Scrooge couldn't stop the anger bursting out of him, but Tim seemed completely unphased.

'That is regrettable, Ebenezer, but all tests have their drawbacks.'

'Drawbacks? Drawbacks?! You sound like I did once; not caring about the little people; thinking they were beneath me.'

'That's simply not true, Ebenezer. I—'

'Then how can you justify Grace's death? All that good she was going to do with her life is gone. It will never happen now. All because of your precious tests.'

'All of life is a test, Ebenezer. Everyone is constantly being tested. The men and women in the library you saw were supposed to be watching over the Earth, to make sure nothing out of place was happening. That was their test, but they were seduced by the books. They thought they could learn more from reading about life than actually witnessing it.'

'You put those books there then?'

'Yes.'

'And all those books; they actually tell the stories of everyone who's ever existed?'

'Yes, Ebenezer. That is why they are shifting on the shelves, readjusting to a world without Grace. They will settle down eventually, and the universe will move on, and in answer to your next question: yes, Jacob Marley's book is amongst them.'

That *was* his next question.

'I can show you Jacob's book. That will tell you the story of his life, but that's only half the story.'

'Then tell me; tell me what I want to know. Tell me what has become of Jacob Marley.'

Tim fell silent and disappeared, and for a moment Scrooge thought that he had gone, leaving him stuck in his memory. Then, in the manner a piece of paper burns and crumbles to ash, the street changed and shifted, and suddenly Scrooge was in an old-fashioned room like something from his and Jacob's time. The only light was coming from a large fireplace on the far wall. The fire looked as though it was about to go out, and from the dying light he could just make out a figure sat in a crooked and dilapidated old chair.

'Jacob?' The name came out in a raspy whisper, so he said it again. 'Jacob? Is that you, old friend?' He stepped forward, half expecting him not to be able to see or hear him, but at the sound of his voice the figure in the chair looked up in Scrooge's direction. His eyes were odd, unfocussed. Then he spoke.

'Ebenezer? Is that you? Are you there?'

'Yes, yes, I'm here, my dear friend. Can you see me?'

Then Jacob said something else, but his lips didn't move. Scrooge realised that he was hearing his thoughts.

No, no, no. It's a trick; another one of their blasted tricks, like the voice and the light.

Scrooge looked around to see if there was any sign of Tim, but there was only himself and Jacob in the room.

'What do you mean, Jacob? I'm here. It's not a trick.'

Jacob just shook his head, his face and mouth tightening as he did so. 'No!' he shouted, then his thoughts took over again. *I'm not hearing anything; it's just my mind playing tricks. Just my mind.*

He looked on, helpless, as he watched his friend fall apart before his eyes. Then, on the far side of the room a tiny pinprick of light appeared on the wall. At first, he dismissed it as a trick of the light or a reflection of flames from the dying fire, but as it grew larger and broader it became clear that it was neither of those things: It was the light that Jacob had spoken of mere moments ago. It seemed to be blinding him, but it had no such effect on Scrooge. Then, a big booming voice full of authority filled the room.

'WALK TOWARDS THE LIGHT, JACOB! IT IS TIME FOR YOU TO MOVE ON.'

For the first time since seeing him again, Scrooge had real hope for his friend, so he was shocked by his answer.

'No! I will not fall for any more of your tricks!'

'THOSE WERE NOT TRICKS, JACOB,' the voice said. 'THEY WERE TESTS, AND YOU HAVE PASSED THEM ALL. IT IS TIME FOR YOU TO MOVE ON.'

'I'd rather stay here, thank you very much.'

Scrooge could hear Jacob's words, but his face told a different story. He was seriously tempted by the light, and he had already gotten up out of his chair by the fire, which was now barely visible with all the light consuming the room. Scrooge didn't know what to think; what Jacob should do.

'Do you promise this time? Do you promise this isn't a trick?'

'OF COURSE,' the voice boomed out.

Scrooge couldn't help but notice a hint of malice in there, as if the voice might erupt with laughter at any time. Jacob moved further into the light, and in a flash, all was dark again.

As his eyes adjusted, the very same room became visible again, and the same chair with Jacob sat in it. The only thing that was different was the fire. Instead of a dwindling single flame threatening to go out at any moment, there was a virtual furnace. Then he noticed something else and stepped forward to get a closer look. His friend was shedding tears of complete and utter despair. The voice *had* lied to him, and it obviously wasn't the first time.

Despite the heat from the fire Scrooge felt cold to the bone. How could someone be doing this to his friend? He stood up straight, making sure his resolve was clear in his every limb. 'Spirit! Whoever you are; I've seen enough!'

And with that, the scene changed again, back into Scrooge's memory of the street and Tiny Tim.

'How could you do that?' he shouted. 'How could you do that to the man who saved me? The man who changed me and made me a better person?'

Tim was still sat on the bench next to him. He looked unsure of himself, but finally he spoke. 'True. After he died, he did do a very good deed, which in turn led to other good deeds, but during his life he committed such acts of evil – such atrocities – that it has put me in an awkward position. Therefore, I have put him in an awkward position.'

'What do you mean?' Suddenly from out of nowhere there was a rumbling in the air. It caused Scrooge to lose the focus of everything around him, but then a moment later it was gone.

Tim looked worried but answered Scrooge's question. 'He's neither here nor there. He's somewhere in between. He doesn't deserve it, and yet it can be argued that he doesn't deserve the other place either. He's repeating the same path over and over, until, until… until…'

'Until what?!' Scrooge yelled, just about resisting the urge to grab him by the shoulders and shake him.

'Until someone tells me what to do with him!' Tim blurted out.

'But – But I thought you were in charge up here. I thought that you were…'

He looked at Scrooge as if for the first time with Tim's eyes. It was an honest look; a look of resignation. It was a look that told Scrooge everything he needed to know.

'"Everyone is constantly being tested", you said. Even *you* are being tested, aren't you.'

He looked solemn now. Not like Tim, but not like whoever it was Scrooge had been talking to. 'Yes, Ebenezer, and I'm failing the test. The world – the universe, is falling apart.'

All his authority was gone, if he ever really had any. Scrooge found himself asking why this person had been left to watch over *anything*.

'Because I was told that I would know what to do when the time came.'

'You were told?'

'Yes.'

The rumbling which Scrooge had felt earlier suddenly became more intense, threatening to knock him sideways. He could feel it deep in his heart this time. Something was very wrong. An end was coming; an end which there would be no coming back from. He looked around, and the memory of the street was rippling away. There were gaps in between now, like millions of tiny lamp posts all lined up, but moving like vertical waves on the ocean. Even the image of Tim was failing now.

'So, you were told that this might happen? That the universe might fall apart?' He had to shout, as great spasms of thunder and lightning accompanied the vibrations.

'I was told that it *would* happen. I was told everything, except how to fix it. I was even told that I would meet you!'

'It was all planned from the start. It must have been,' Scrooge shouted. 'He must have known that you would make all the mistakes you did. That was the test! To see if you could still learn from the people down on Earth.'

'I don't understand.' Tim said this with some sense of relief, as if the burden of understanding had been lifted.

'I was recently there. I'm the closest you'll get to speaking to someone from down there, and maybe you've become so far removed from where you were that you can't see the answer to all this, even though he's staring you right in the face.'

Everywhere was fading now. Even the waves were disappearing into nothingness, and Scrooge could no longer see the spirit who'd borrowed his friend's face, but he could feel his presence all the same.

'What do you mean?' The voice sounded desperate, echoing in Scrooge's head.

'All the mistakes; they can all be fixed.'

The spirit said nothing as darkness engulfed the light around them.

'You can send me back. You can send me back to Earth; back to life. To save Grace.'

24

Silence hung still in the air as if it were a living and breathing beast, waiting for the right moment to pounce. Scrooge was surrounded by darkness. No, darkness would've been a relative comfort. He knew what it was: It was nothingness. He had no form now; he was just thoughts and ideas, drifting, and there couldn't be long left before even he became one with the void. The other voice suddenly started talking in his head again.

'Why would you want to do that? Go back?'

'Ah, so you *can* send me back then?' Scrooge said.

'I didn't say that. Why would you want to?'

'For the same reason you need me to. To stop all this from ending.' He could feel doubt in the air, coming from the other spirit.

'All this might not be what we think it is, Ebenezer. It could be a new beginning, a new form of existence.'

'You don't really believe that, do you,' Scrooge said plainly. The spirit's silence gave him his answer.

'But how do I know that sending you back will fix everything? What if it makes things worse?'

'You said that I was special. That I was the only one who had it in me to change my fate. Maybe, just maybe, I can change all this. Besides, all I'd be doing would be changing things back to the way they were meant to be in the first place. And how exactly could things get any worse?'

Scrooge could feel the spirit leave; he could feel the change deep in his soul, and he felt truly alone for the first time in a long while. Had he pushed him too far? He knew he had to be right, but maybe he should've said it differently, less forcefully. Then, without any warning, the spirit who had disguised himself as Tim was back, along with such a euphoric feeling that Scrooge thought he'd explode with it.

'You're right,' he said.

'I am?'

'You're the one part of this puzzle that doesn't sit neatly with the rest. This is my test. I've become so used to knowing what's going to happen that I've forgotten what it is to have faith in other people. You were the answer all along, Ebenezer Scrooge, and it's about time I started listening to you.'

Scrooge was taken aback – honoured even – for such a high being to be speaking to him in such a way.

'Yes! Yes! That's it! That's the answer!' the spirit said without explanation. 'How did I miss that? So obvious, yet I've been so far removed, so detached that I couldn't see it.'

'What? What can you see, Spirit?'

'The idea. Your idea. The idea you're about to have. You can probably feel the germ of it forming as we speak.'

'My idea about what?' he asked, feeling increasingly frustrated.

'About Jacob Marley, of course. About what we should do with him. Ha haaa! So beautiful. So poetic.'

Scrooge suddenly panicked. 'Why? What are you going to do with him?'

'Oh, nothing bad; how could it be? It's your idea, after all. It's a shame you didn't die earlier, if you don't mind me saying. It could have saved your old friend a lot of grief, but then, that will serve him well for the task ahead.'

Scrooge was starting to feel jealous of the spirit, knowing about his idea before he did, but then a small part of it shone into his mind.

'It's coming to you now, isn't it.' Joy permeating from the spirit's every word.

'I – I think so, yes.'

'You should be very proud.'

'So, what happens now?' Scrooge said.

'You go back, like you said. You go back and save the universe. You save the universe by saving Grace. But be aware, Ebenezer, you can't save everyone who died that night, because not everyone who died that night needs saving. That's not to say that the people who didn't die don't need saving in other ways. There are worse things than death: A life half lived is much worse, as well you know. Before you go back, there's a book you need to read.'

'I think I understand, but how do I—?' Before Scrooge could finish his question, he was back in the street where he had last seen Tim – Timothy – the real Tim. He was just getting used to his physical surroundings again and finding how much he missed what had been his own time, when from out of nowhere, a cold solid snowball hit him clean in the back of the head. It struck him how odd the physical sensation was. He was about to react in the way that he remembered reacting at the time – a mimicry of his former miserly self – when everything went white; as white as the snow-covered street.

Everything was white. Every tree, bush and building covered in the same awful, freezing snow. Carl suddenly slipped on a bit of ice which had been lying in wait for him. He just about managed to keep his balance, but he could feel his old bones creaking under the strain of the sudden and unexpected movement.

Stopping for a moment, he let out a long drawn out sigh which caught the attention of a *thoughtful* passer-by: one half of a seemingly happy couple.

'Cheer up, old fella. It's Christmas, it might never happen.'

He hated it when people said that. What did some random stranger know about his life and what had and hadn't happened in it. He was going to shout some abuse, but his fifty-nine-year-old body just didn't have the energy. And then, to top it off; to make the moment just perfect – a perfect Christmas moment – a snowball hit him clean in the back of the head. He fell forward from the impact and slipped on the same bit of ice from a moment ago. This time he fell. He couldn't save himself. He'd been falling for a long time, and the worst of it was that as he caught the impact of the fall on his old butt cheeks, he knew that he still had farther to fall.

The giggles of the kids that had thrown the offending object chilled his heart even more. Sara. He thought of Sara. He'd not seen her in years. She used to giggle like that at his stupid jokes. He used to love that giggle. It was usually followed up with *Daddy, that's terrible*, but she still laughed.

There was a stabbing pain in his back: The whisky! His only friend for the evening had smashed as he fell on the pavement. He remembered hearing the sound now, and he could feel the cold seeping through his jeans.

He wanted to move, to get up and away from the cold. The flat was only metres away, but he was just as alone out here as he would be in there. Well, that wasn't quite true. The photos were there; ancient photos of a time long gone. A relatively happy time. Before the phone call; the phone call he avoided, but still got dragged down by. There was no getting away from it: no matter what he'd done, no matter what decisions he made that Christmas all those years ago, he'd been fated to end up there on his back on the pavement, cold and alone. He'd been destined to lose his family. To save them and lose them on that same night. It was destiny that Kate would lose all trust in him and stop loving him. It was destiny that Sara would do the same as her mother.

He knew it was the end. He could feel his chest tightening and the sweat from his forehead stinging his eyes. And yet, somehow, he didn't care. At least he'd have control over this. Life could no longer torture him and laugh in his face. Maybe the next life would treat him better. And yet, if he was given another chance to start over, he'd still give it his best shot. Why should everyone but him be happy? He closed his eyes and waited. Waited to fade away.

All was black, and then, just as he could feel himself drifting away, the darkness did the same. Clouds of white flew towards him, and at the end of a tunnel made up of the same clouds he saw someone looking down on him: Someone he knew. Someone he hadn't seen in such a long time. He wanted to be angry. He was from a time in his life that was the turning point where everything went wrong. And yet, he felt no anger. He was at peace with everything.

Ebenezer Scrooge. That was his name. Such an odd name; hard to forget. The old man was looking down on him with pity. He'd claimed that he wasn't a part of the events from all that time ago; that he was trying to help. Carl could see so clearly now that this was the truth, and that somehow the old man was still trying to help.

His last conscious thought was a sadly cynical one: *Bit late now. Time's up, old man.*

The pure beautiful white faded into black, and before Scrooge opened his eyes, he felt the strangest sensation. It took a moment for him to comprehend it, but as soon as he did, panic set in. He couldn't breathe! He was drowning! He opened his eyes. He was back in the park. In the future! He was surrounded by snow, but how was he drowning? His head was swimming, and he could see someone stood there. His whole body was shaking. His body. All the aches and pains from all the years were back with a vengeance, and so was he, because Scrooge realised: 'I'm not drowning! I'm living! I'm breathing!'

The realisation made his lungs fill up faster with joyous, life-giving air. He could feel the cold even more than before, but it had the opposite effect of warming every fibre of his being and giving him the strength he needed for what he had to do next. His eyes suddenly focussed, as the man in front of him started to step back, his face as white as the snow around him.

'I – You can't be – I just shot you – You were dead! I don't understand.'

The man seemed more shocked than Scrooge was to find him alive and kicking again. His memory was still a little foggy, but the shock of being killed was in there somewhere, and it suddenly all came back to him like a tendon snapping back into place. 'I was shot. I died. The blood's still wet on my coat and shirt. There was something else though. Just after I was shot the first time—'

'The – The first time?'

'Don't interrupt, man,' Scrooge snapped. 'I'm trying to remember. Ah! There were two other shots!' His eyes were still struggling to focus, but the sudden realisation seemed to sharpen his surroundings, along with his senses. He'd just been born all over again, and it felt incredible. The blood was pumping around his body like a finely tuned machine, and he cursed himself for almost forgetting why he was there; why he'd been sent back from paradise.

He looked up at the man before him who was still stone white from the shock of seeing a dead man walking. 'Listen,' Scrooge said, 'you're about to do something really bad that there is no coming back from.'

Fairweather's eyes widened and were completely focussed on him. Scrooge imagined it was what he himself looked like when faced with all the spirits he'd met in recent years. 'You're going to—'

But before Scrooge could finish, he heard a rustling behind him, which could only be one thing. Or two.

'What's that?' Fairweather shouted, his voice unnaturally high.

Scrooge whipped back around to face the man. He looked so unhinged, and his eyes were darting everywhere now, as if he thought danger could strike from anywhere around him at any second. This was it.

The next few seconds seemed to Scrooge like he was walking under water. Another voice emerged through the gap in the hedge: Jack's voice.

'What's going on here? What was that—?'

Before he could finish, the shot came, and Scrooge watched helplessly as the bullet sped through the air towards Jack. He knew he couldn't reach him in time, but still, he had to get over there. Moving with seemingly impossible speed, he saw Jack fall, out of the corner of his eye, even as he saw Grace – still very much alive – in front of him.

Another shot. Not much time now. No time at all, and yet, time was moving slower than usual, or perhaps he was moving faster? Grace had seen him speeding towards her, and she was instinctively moving to avoid him. Maybe that would be enough for her to dodge the bullet, but he couldn't take that chance. He grabbed her, and with all his strength pulled her to the floor. He could hear the bullet flying past with a high-pitched squeal, as if lamenting the fact that it had missed its intended target.

Time seemed to have returned to its normal pace. Had the spirit done that? Or maybe the universe itself had lent a hand, out of a sense of self-preservation. It doesn't matter, Scrooge told himself. The main thing is that Grace is safe, and Jack is… Jack is… He couldn't even bear to think of it, but Jack had to die. He was always supposed to have died. It was all part of the plan; the plan that the Spirit who'd borrowed Tim's form had sensed growing in his mind, before Scrooge knew what it was himself. Maybe Jack would thank him when he joined him up there again.

Grace was looking at him. He still had her pinned to the ground. 'I'm sorry,' he said, and let her go.

'What do you mean?' she said. 'You just saved us. How did you move so fast? How did you know—?' And then she saw him: Jack lying there, half dead on the floor.

He was still breathing – Scrooge could feel every living and breathing being around him, as if coming back to life had connected him to it all – but he didn't have long. He looked over to where Fairweather was, down on his knees in the snow. He didn't seem like he was really there at all. The look on his face had a thousand questions emanating from it; questions he would never have the answers to. He was no danger to anyone anymore, at least for the time being.

Scrooge joined Grace over where Jack was lying. She was trying to talk to him through her tears, and Jack was trying his best to stay with her. His voice was raspy, and every word was a struggle for him.

'I was… I was going to…'

'Please,' Grace said, 'save your strength, hon'. I need to phone for an ambulance.' A look of panic flashed across her face, as she looked around.

'What? What's wrong?' Scrooge said.

'My bag! Where is it? My phone's in my bag!' She looked around, but there was no sign of it. Then she saw the wreck of a man on his knees in the snow, the gun next to him on the ground. 'You! You did this!'

He didn't respond, he just stared into space, lost.

'Give me your phone!' Grace shouted.

'Grace…' Jack's voice was weak and strained. He was trying to hold on to his final moment. 'Grace,' he called again. 'Please stay with me.'

'But I need to…' She couldn't finish her sentence and she could see that he wouldn't make it, even if they could phone an ambulance in time. Despite this, she took her scarf off and pushed it down on the wound to pressurise it.

Jack managed a smile of appreciation and was about to say something, when he saw Scrooge standing next to her.

There was a look in his eyes Scrooge couldn't quite put his finger on. Was it recognition?

'I… I remember you. I don't know how, but I remember you, Scrooge. I came to find you in your own time. I had a plan.'

Grace looked to Scrooge for an explanation, but he had none. How did he remember? He wasn't really the same person.

Jack sounded stronger now, as if each word he spoke was spurring him on. 'How do I remember all this? Why do I feel guilty when I look at you, Scrooge? How do I know you?'

Grace looked at both of them alternately, more confused now than upset, although her eyes were glistening with tears.

Scrooge felt terrible for her. She would never know the full truth and depth of Jack's love for her. 'I can't—' he started, 'I can't explain the whole affair now, Jack. You need to spend your last moments with Grace, but I *can* tell you that everything you remember – even though it makes no sense that you should remember it – is the truth. Someone will explain it to you soon. Someone who is waiting up there with a new plan; a plan which will benefit everyone.'

Jack looked peaceful and content, a look that Scrooge had never seen on his face before. Everything would work out fine, but there was still more to do. 'Now,' he said, 'I have another task to perform before the police arrive. Goodbye, Jack. You're a good man, and you were a good friend, eventually. And goodbye, Grace. You're a good woman; maybe the best that ever lived.' With that, he turned and headed towards the cabin, where he knew Carl and his family were.

'Wait,' Grace said, still on the floor next to Jack. 'How do you know us? How do you know *me*?'

Scrooge could tell she had more questions, but she was too upset to get them all out. The streams of tears rolling down her cheeks made it look like her face was melting. He could see that she was scared to take her eyes off Jack, in case he slipped away, but he could also see she needed answers, and he had the perfect one: The truth. 'It's like you said, Grace, back before all this, before we all came into the park. I'm your guardian angel.'

She looked confused and comforted in equal measure, but he could see that she believed his words. It was the truth after all. He was the guardian angel of the most important woman – the most important person – the universe had known for a long time. He was the guardian angel's guardian angel. 'It's been an honour,' he said. And before she could say anything else, he headed over to the cabin.

Carl was in the doorway of the cabin trying to figure out what to do next. He'd been watching as the old man with the strange name talked to the girl who seemed vaguely familiar. Her boyfriend had been shot by his old supervisor, Calvin Fairweather, the man who was now almost catatonic, kneeling in the snow just a few feet away. How was he going to explain all this to Kate and Sara? How could he possibly explain any of it, especially since that evil man had been feeding them God only knew what kind of lies about his involvement in the whole mess. Maybe if he had enough time he could explain. Maybe if he wasn't so spent he could think of something, but surely the police would be arriving any minute, and if the Silent Partner repeated his lies to them he wouldn't stand a chance; and he had to assume that someone as conniving as him would have planted some kind of apparent evidence – online and otherwise – that he was fully involved in everything that had happened.

The old man was approaching the cabin now, and what was that look on his face? Carl looked over to Kate and Sara, but as he did they turned away. At that moment his heart broke – no – it shattered. How could he ever come back from this? How could his family ever trust him again? He turned away from them, and just as he was about to turn back, hoping against hope that they would listen to what he had to say, the old man was right there in front of him, uncomfortably close. That look again. What was it? And then, he leant forward and whispered: 'I have all the answers,' and pushed right past him and into the cabin.

Before Carl could stop him, he was standing right over Kate and Sara. He spoke in a hushed tone, but the cabin was so small that he could still hear what he was saying.

'I'll remove your gags, but only if you both promise not to scream.' His voice was cold, calculated. The warmth Carl had heard in the couple of times he'd heard him speak was gone. They both nodded their heads in agreement, and he removed their gags. Carl was about to protest at the way the old man was talking to his family, but Kate had something to say to him first.

'How could you do this, Carl? Why couldn't you just—'

'Madam,' Scrooge said, with a bite in his tone, 'am I right in assuming that you think that your husband had something to do with all this?'

'You mean he's not?' Kate said. Sara said nothing; she looked terrified of the old man.

'Wait a minute,' Carl said. But before he could continue, Scrooge spoke again, with an authority that demanded everyone's hushed attention.

'This poor young man had nothing to do with our original plans. I'm afraid that my partner out there has a bad habit of taking matters too far.'

Carl couldn't believe what he was hearing. The old man *was* in on it all along?

'He kidnapped you and your daughter here – without consulting me, may I add – in order to blackmail Carl here into helping, using his inside knowledge of the shop, in order for the whole affair to run smoothly. I suppose it won't be much comfort for you to know that I didn't agree with this.'

Kate didn't say anything, but to Carl's surprise both her and Sara were looking at him less harshly now. There was sympathy in there somewhere.

'So, you see, Carl didn't have much choice but to go along with us. He only had your safety in mind. Isn't that right, Carl?'

'Yes, that's – that's right,' Carl said, stunned at Scrooge's confession. 'But—'

'So you see, Carl – your father,' Scrooge said, turning to speak directly to Sara, 'is not responsible for any of this.'

The old man seemed genuinely regretful at how badly things had turned out, but Carl couldn't help but feel angry that he'd lied to him. 'When I asked you how you knew who I was, you claimed to be psychic.'

The old man looked flawed. He obviously thought that his little speech would be the end of it. Carl could feel a rage building inside him. The man didn't have a gun, he noticed.

'It was all part of the plan,' he said, looking unsure of himself. 'All apart from the kidnapping of course.'

Carl could feel his control slipping away, giving him permission to do what he wanted to. Before the old man could say anything else, Carl grabbed his coat by the collar and forced him up against the wall. His adrenalin was calling the shots now, his control well and truly gone. Kate and Sara were shouting something, but he couldn't make out the words. His rage was clouding everything, and almost without thinking he punched the old man and he fell down and out of the door. Carl picked him up by the collars of his coat again and was about to strike another blow, when the old man whispered to him. He couldn't quite make out what he was saying.

'What? What did you say?!'

'I said,' Scrooge whispered again, 'that this isn't you.'

The man's expression was soft and compassionate; not the face of a man who'd just been punched – apart from the blood trickling out of his nose. Despite this, Carl couldn't help his rage surfacing. 'How do you know what is and isn't me, old man? You don't even know me.'

'I know enough about you to know that you're not about to hurt an innocent man.'

'An innocent—? You just said that you were behind everything.'

'Shh!' Scrooge said, putting his finger to his lips. 'I said that for your benefit. Yours and theirs.'

Suddenly, another, younger voice shouted out from the cabin. 'Dad? What's going on? I want to go home.'

Scrooge nodded to Carl, as if he was granting permission for him to speak to his own daughter.

'It's okay, pumpkin, I'm just sorting something out.' *Sorting something out*, he thought. What a ridiculously mundane way of describing what he was doing. He turned back to the old man. 'What are you playing at?' he said.

'Listen,' Scrooge whispered, 'there's not much time before the police get here. You just need to trust me and—'

'Trust you? You must be joking.'

'No, I'm not, Carl Phillips. I'm here to save you, and I plan to confess to everything that's happened to you, including your family's kidnapping.'

'Which I take it you're claiming to have had nothing to do with.'

'That's right.'

'Then why?' Carl said, on the verge of tears now. 'Why are you doing this?'

Scrooge wanted to tell him everything. That he'd been shown Carl's miserable life from beginning to end. Every detail. There were highlights, of course: meeting and marrying Kate; the birth of Sara; but if he didn't let him take the blame – let him help – his family would be torn apart by mistrust and he'd end up dying alone on the pavement outside a dingy London flat.

'My whole life, well, most of it, I spent – wasted – making other people's lives miserable, and I was never really punished for that. I may not have committed this crime, but if I do whatever it takes to convince that man over there to tell the truth about your involvement in this, then I'll be happy to live with the consequences, no matter where I end up.'

'What do you mean? Carl asked. 'What are you going to do? And what about those people out there? The couple. Are they—?'

'I'll deal with that. I'll help them. You need to go, Carl, with my blessing, before the police arrive. Take Kate and Sara home and give them the best Christmas you can afford.' He suddenly remembered something and put his hand in his pocket. Yes. The money that was left from selling his watch – it was still there.

'Take this,' he said, thrusting it into Carl's hand before he could protest. 'I don't know how much is left, but I hope it helps.'

Carl didn't know what to say. There must have been at least five hundred pounds there, if not more. 'What did you say your name was again?' he asked.

'Scrooge. Ebenezer Scrooge. Why?'

'I don't know why you've taken it upon yourself to help me and my family, but I will be forever grateful, and—'

'Never mind that, man. I can hear those odd sounds in the air, and I believe that—'

'Sirens, yeah, you're right,' Carl said. 'Are you sure this is the only way?'

'Yes, I'm sure,' Scrooge said.

'Okay, okay, I'll go. *We'll* go.'

Scrooge got up and headed over to where Fairweather was, still kneeling in the snow and staring into space. He knew his plan wasn't without its flaws, but hopefully Carl's part in it was now concluded.

Carl untied Kate and Sara. They were both shaking – probably a mix of fear and cold, Carl told himself, but they were both looking at him now with much more trust.

'Is it true?' Kate said. 'What the old guy said? That you had nothing to do with this? With any of it?'

He couldn't find the words. He was so glad to see them both; so glad that they didn't hate him and blame him for what they'd been through. There were no words that existed that could possibly describe how happy he was at that moment in time. So, he put his arms around them, and showered them with more kisses than he'd ever given them. Sara giggled nervously, and Carl found it hard to let go, but he knew they had to get out of there: the sirens were getting louder by the second.

Kate, the voice of reason spoke up. 'Are you going to tell us what *did* happen?'

'Yes,' he said. There were never going to be any secrets between them ever again. 'But I need to get you both safely home first. I will tell you everything, but my brain is fried after the last couple of days, and we need to get out of here now.'

Kate didn't argue, so he took them both by the hand and led them out of the cabin and as far away from the park as possible. Everything was going to be alright. He knew that he had a lot of explaining to do, but he also knew that his family were safe again, and in the end that was all that mattered.

'Calvin,' Scrooge said softly. No response. The man who had called himself the Silent Partner was staring into nothingness and didn't seem to be aware of any of his surroundings. 'Calvin Fairweather,' Scrooge said, louder this time.

The man blinked slowly and looked lost, as if waking from a dream. He looked over at Grace kneeling next to Jack's body. 'Oh my God. I shot him. He's dead.'

'Calvin, I know you're in over your head, and—'

'How do you know my name?' he demanded.

'It's a bit of a story. I—'

'I shot you, too,' he said, finally standing up and facing Scrooge. 'But you're not dead.'

'I did die,' Scrooge said, 'but I'm back now.'

'What? What are you talking about?'

Scrooge saw no reason to hold back like he had done with Carl. 'I died, and I woke up in a wonderful place. There was light everywhere, and a library. It had countless books with everyone's lives contained within them. So much goodness, it was overwhelming, but there was also darkness. I saw an old friend. He was trapped because he'd done so much wrong in his life, but now, hopefully I've changed that. I'm special you see. They were waiting for me to show them what to do next.'

Fairweather was staring at him doubtfully now. He seemed more composed than moments ago. 'Are you… Are you feeling alright? Have you escaped from somewhere?'

'Escaped? Escaped?! No. I volunteered to come back to stop you. To stop you from killing the most important person on Earth.'

'What? Him?' Fairweather said, dumbly, looking over at Jack. 'Well, you didn't do a very good—'

'No. Her. The young lady.'

'What?! But she's fine.'

'Exactly,' Scrooge said.

The man was looking even more sceptical now, and Scrooge knew he didn't have much time; the sirens were getting louder. He had to cut to the end. 'I've seen your life, Calvin Joseph Fairweather. You used to be a good man, but even before you lost your job and Stephanie left you, you had greedy aspirations.'

'What? How do you know about Stephanie? How do you know me? You don't know me.'

'I told you,' he said, 'everyone's life is in a book up there, beginning to end.'

'What? You're mad. You're insane! You could have found out that stuff anywhere.'

'But I didn't.' Scrooge was starting to scare himself, the way he was talking reminded him of the ghosts that helped him all those years ago. 'I think you know that I speak the truth.'

'No, I don't. And I don't have to listen to this. I'm getting out of here. You're just distracting me until the cops get here, aren't you. I bet I didn't even shoot you.'

Scrooge suddenly saw his opportunity. He could do something that would convince Mister Fairweather without a shadow of a doubt that he had died and come back. He pulled up the garment underneath his coat. 'If I didn't die, then how do you explain this?'

Fairweather's face turned white as he looked upon Scrooge's wound. There were still blood stains around it, but where the bullet had gone in there was a clearly visible and ugly scar. 'But – But how?'

'I told you. I volunteered to come back and stop you. I wouldn't be much good with blood pouring out of me, would I. They,' he said as he pointed upward, 'must have speeded up the healing process for me.'

The Silent Partner was truly living up to his name now: He just stood there gaping at Scrooge, not saying a word, his eyes practically escaping from their sockets. And then, just as Scrooge thought he was going to say something, he did something that he should have seen coming: He ran. He ran, but he didn't get far, because unbeknownst to him, Grace had been listening in on the conversation. And, as the pathetic little man broke into a run, she intercepted him and tripped him up. He went flying, and just as he was about to land, a tree broke his fall and he was knocked unconscious. Grace stood there, frozen, as if she wanted to do something to him – as if she wanted to do lots of things to him – but couldn't decide which one to do first.

Scrooge put his hand on her shoulder slowly, as a calming gesture, but she jumped. 'It's okay,' he said, 'he'll face justice now. He'll get what he deserves; we all will.'

'He's gone,' she said. 'Jack's gone.'

'I'm so sorry, Grace.' He was expecting to stand there for a moment with her in quiet mourning; in silence, but he could tell she needed to know something, and she hastily came out with it.

'Is everything you told him true?'

'What? You mean you heard all that?' He wanted to deny it. His first instinct was that she would think him mad, as Fairweather had done, but the poor young lady had been through enough losing her boyfriend in such a horrific manner. She deserved the truth. 'Yes, Grace, it's all true. I died and came back. *You* died and came back.'

'What?! No, I didn't. I—'

'It's a very, very long story, but trust me. You weren't supposed to, so I came back to stop it from happening, and it worked.' He could see that he was starting to lose her. 'I'm sorry, Grace,' he said, 'but there's not enough time to tell you everything; the police will be here any second.'

'You said – You *told* him I was the most important person on Earth. What did you mean? How can I be the most important person on Earth? I'm just—'

'You're not *just* anything. You're special, Grace. What you do – what you're going to do will ensure that—' He was putting too much pressure on her. If she knew too much it might affect what she did in the future. 'You need to just keep doing what you do, and everything will be fine.' He looked over at Jack. He was far too young to die. No one should die like that. But then he consoled himself, thinking of the bigger plan that was waiting for his young friend.

'Eventually, everything will be fine,' he told her. 'I'm sorry I can't be more specific, but I can't risk changing anything.' He expected her to push him further, but she suddenly got upset again and looked over to Jack, lying motionless on the floor.

'What am I going to do? What am I supposed to tell his family? I've never even met them.'

'Tell them the truth,' Scrooge said. 'Tell them that he was a brave young man who was in the wrong place at the wrong time. I'm truly sorry, Grace; I really am. Tell them that an old man called Ebenezer Scrooge and his partner Calvin Fairweather shot him because he surprised them.'

'What?' Grace said. 'What do you mean? That's not the truth. You said that—'

'I need to keep an eye on him, and the best place to do that is in prison. I need to make sure that he tells the police what I want him to; to make sure he doesn't drag anyone else into the mess he's made of his life.'

'That's not fair!' Grace shouted. 'Why should you be blamed? You're a hero.'

'Ha!' Scrooge laughed. 'I'm many things. Maybe I am a hero. Maybe heroes are just people trying to make up for the wrong doings in their past. That's what I'm doing you see. I know I've not done this terrible thing, and I've never shot anyone, but who knows how my past actions have affected this time. Maybe I'm even indirectly responsible for the way that his life turned out.'

'That's crazy.'

'Is it?' Scrooge said. 'I've done many terrible things that I was never punished for. Maybe this way things will finally balance out, and, who knows, maybe while I'm in there I'll do some real good. I can help all the lost souls.'

'But—'

'Grace, you need to let me do this. When the police get here, don't contradict what I—'

'Police!' The voices came from all over in unison. 'Everyone on the ground, now!' As the last part was spoken figures emerged from the gap in the hedge and from the other side of the cabin. 'You have the right to remain silent, but anything you say—'

'Officer!' he interrupted. 'My name is Ebenezer Scrooge and I have a confession to make. My partner and I are responsible for this,' he said as he pointed to Fairweather, who was just coming to. 'The young lady has nothing to do with this. The young man on the ground is her boyfriend.' He looked over at Grace and gave her a subtle nod to make sure she was going to play along. She just looked away. Good enough, he thought.

25

As Scrooge was led into the back of a police van which had arrived moments after the officers had slapped the handcuffs on him and Fairweather, he saw Grace one last time. She was looking right at him, sad and confused, and how could he blame her? For one, her boyfriend had just died – after the medics had done everything they could to save him – and his body was being wheeled into the back of an ambulance. And two, the one person she could talk to about the truth of the whole thing had just falsely incriminated himself, and she'd probably never see him again. One day she would understand.

She took one last longing look at him, and then one of the officers let her into the back of one of the police cars. Scrooge felt sad and almost bitter that he'd probably never see her again, but he also felt a surge of gladness wash through him knowing that his plan had worked, the world – the universe – was safe again.

They were in the van now, and he and Fairweather were both unceremoniously pushed down by the officers onto opposite benches on either side. They were then chained onto the legs of the benches so there was no earthly possibility of escape.

'What are you smiling about?' This was Fairweather.

Scrooge hadn't realised that he'd been smiling and immediately stopped, in case the police officers saw him. 'Um, nothing. Just nerves I suppose.'

'Why did you do that?'

'Why did I do what?' Scrooge said.

'You know what. I don't even know you, and suddenly I'm your partner?'

Scrooge looked over to where the officers were, standing just outside the back of the open doors of the van. They didn't seem to be listening. 'It's part of my plan,' he said softly. 'I need to keep an eye on you. Make sure you don't ruin Carl Phillip's life.'

'That's going to be a bit difficult from behind bars, isn't it?'

'You could still name him.'

'I suppose. But why sacrifice your own freedom?' Fairweather said. 'Why – and I'm not saying I believe you – but why go to all the trouble of coming back from the dead, just to get yourself trapped in a prison with a bunch of scumbags? It makes no sense.'

'I once had a partner,' Scrooge said, 'and after a lifetime of sin he ended up floating around the Earth aimlessly. His punishment was watching other people's happiness, but he managed to save me by showing me where I would end up if I didn't change my ways.'

Fairweather still looked dubious, even after all he had seen, but Scrooge carried on.

'Until recently, I had no idea where he ended up after helping me. It was a horrific place – a place that you may well end up if you don't change – but I helped him in return for him helping me, and now, if they do what I asked, he'll be alright. Knowing that has given me some peace, but it's also made me realise that I can't ever stop striving to better myself; to make the world as good as it can be. When I'm in prison, I'll be able to help all sorts of—'

Scrooge stopped, because the armoured officers were getting into the back of the van, and the engine had started up. They both sat at the front, to the left of them, with their backs to the driver's cabin, and didn't say a word to Scrooge or Fairweather. He could feel the van moving forward, and although Scrooge knew that he could do so much good where he was going, he was nervous. How long would he last in there on prison rations? Would anyone listen to him? Fairweather had seen his fresh scar and he still seemed doubtful.

Just then, he noticed that his “partner” was staring at him, as if he was trying to figure out whether he was telling the truth or not. Maybe there was hope for him. And, if he could convince him, then he’d be able to bring out the good in others. Maybe he’d even assist him, eventually.

Fairweather looked away, shaking his head.

Maybe not, but he had to try. He owed it to Jacob.

He suddenly realised that the engine had stopped. Surely, they couldn’t have arrived at their destination already.

‘EBENEZER, YOU HAVE DONE WELL.’

Scrooge instinctively looked over to the officers to see if they’d heard the voice, but they were still just sat there as if nothing had happened. No, not just sat there—

‘THEY CANNOT HEAR US. I HAVE FROZEN TIME, FOR NOW.’

‘How are you doing that? That – That’s impossible!’ Fairweather’s face was white with fear, and his eyes were darting around the van looking for the source of the voice.

‘You heard that?’ Scrooge said. He looked upward for some kind of explanation from the spirit.

‘IT SUITS MY PURPOSE FOR HIM TO BE A WITNESS TO THIS.’

‘There it is again,’ Fairweather yelped. ‘How are you doing that, old man? Is this all part of your plan?’

Scrooge almost denied it, but then he said: ‘Yes, I suppose it is.’ Then, addressing the voice this time, he said: ‘Spirit, why are you here? Do you have more to tell me?’

‘YOU DIED, EBENEZER. YOU DIED AND CAME BACK IN THIS TIME. IF THE UNIVERSE IS TO BE RESTORED, THEN YOU CANNOT STAY HERE.’

Scrooge was torn. He had a warm feeling in his heart at returning to Heaven, but he was absolutely determined to do more good down on Earth. He felt grateful and cheated at the same time. 'But why? You know how much good I could do in that prison; how much hope I could spread.' He looked over to Fairweather who was still looking everywhere for where the voice was coming from. 'And what about him? He's my responsibility now, and what if he just carries on the way he has been?'

The voice had an almost jovial tone to it now. 'AFTER WHAT HE WITNESSES TONIGHT, CALVIN FAIRWEATHER WON'T BE CAUSING ANYONE ANY MORE TROUBLE.'

'What?! What does that mean?' Fairweather said. 'How *are* you doing this? How have you set this up?'

Scrooge didn't answer. He just watched as the inside of the van started to get brighter and brighter. Fairweather's face said it all. The spirit was right: After this, the man's life would never be the same again. The feelings of fear and hope coming from him were almost tangible. He would gladly pay for his crime and do everything he could to one day be deserving of reaching the light.

The light was all-consuming now, and Scrooge had the by-now-familiar feeling of being separated from his body. Almost as soon as the details of the van and the faces had faded away into the white, Heaven started to fade into view. And then, just as he was accepting his new reality and circumstances, the voice spoke to Scrooge again, more softly this time, like a whisper in his ear.

'Oh. Ebenezer, did you think that was where you were headed?'

Scrooge's heart sank.

'I showed it to Calvin Fairweather to set him on a better path, so you wouldn't need to stay with him.'

'But I thought—'

'It's not time for you to return here; not yet,' the voice said.

'Oh…'

'Like you said, you have so much more good to do on Earth. But you must do that in your own time, surrounded by friends and family.'

'Spirit,' Scrooge said, 'I – I don't know what to say. I will be forever grateful for what I have seen; this wonderful and strange future, my time in Heaven—'

'Your memories of it will fade in time, Ebenezer. If you did remember anything, it would drive you mad and set the universe off balance once again.'

Before Scrooge could say anything else, the pure white of Heaven receded into darkness. The last thought he remembered having was: *You're wrong. I will remember. How could I forget all those incredible things?* And then he opened his eyes.

His first sight was a familiar one: The roof of his four-poster bed. It filled him with joy. Why did such a common sight fill him with such elation?

'It's so quiet,' he said out loud. 'Why does it seem so quiet?' He sat up quickly like a coiled spring and immediately regretted it. The sudden pain in his back made him scream in agony, but he was shocked at how glad of it he was; glad of the reminder that he was alive and kicking. More cautiously now, he swung his legs around to the side of the bed and dropped to the floor. He could hear his bones clicking into place, and he was glad of even that. And then he saw it: the Christmas tree. That was why everything seemed so wonderful.

'It's Christmas time,' he said quietly to himself. No, it was wrong to say it like that. 'It's Christmas time!' he shouted at the top of his voice. 'That's much better,' he said 'Much better. Well better. Well better? That doesn't sound right. Scrooge, old man, you must be going mad in your dotage.' He did a little dance on the spot, and he realised that he had a tune going over and over in his head to accompany it, although he had no clue as to which song the tune belonged to. 'Perhaps I *am* mad. Ha haaa! What of it?! Ha!'

The window suddenly caught his eye. He went over to it and struggled to open it with the ice freezing it shut. He half expected that same boy to be there who told him the best news ever: that it was Christmas day, and he hadn't missed it. Of course, he wasn't there. In fact, no one was there; it was so quiet. The snow was undisturbed on the ground and it was as if no other living soul was awake in London. This wasn't right. Surely, there should be more people up and about on Christmas morning, but then, he didn't know for certain that it *was* Christmas morning. Maybe he'd missed it. He tried to recall the previous evening. He remembered getting home, but after that it was all a hopeless blur.

'How very odd,' he said. And then suddenly, out of the corner of his eye, he saw two people – a couple – walking in the same spot where the boy had been all those years ago. They were looking into each other's eyes, obviously besotted. He was a little jealous but pushed it aside.

'Excuse me! Sir! Madam!'

They were about to pass behind the next building when the young lady spotted him waving.

'Yes! Hello!' Scrooge shouted.

The young man turned around so that both of them were looking in his direction. 'Good morning, sir!' he shouted.

'And a good morning to you, sir, and your lovely lady friend. And I'm hoping that I'm not too late in wishing you both a happy Christmas?'

'Too late?' the young lady said. 'Why would it be too late, sir? The day is still in its infancy.'

'You mean… it's Christmas day? It's Christmas morning?'

'Of course. What other day would it be?'

'Then I haven't missed it,' Scrooge boomed out. 'It all happened in one night.' Then he stopped as he realised he had no idea what he was talking about.

'I say!' the young man shouted. 'Are you not Ebenezer Scrooge, sir? The man whom they say keeps Christmas so well? If anyone should know what today is, it should be you.'

He recognises me, Scrooge thought. Maybe he'll ask for a selfie. Scrooge stopped in mid-thought. What am I thinking? What on earth is a selfie? Where are these peculiar thoughts coming from?

'Excuse me, sir. Not wanting to be rude or anything, but me and my lady really must be going.'

Scrooge snapped out of his trance. 'Yes, yes, of course, my good fellow. And a merry Christmas to both of you!'

'And a merry Christmas to you too, sir!' they both shouted.

He was about to ask them one more thing, but they were gone. All these odd thoughts and phrases swirling around in my head, he thought. Where have they come from? A dream? I don't usually remember my dreams, but these things are so fantastical they couldn't possibly be from anything real. Perhaps I am losing my marbles as they say.

There was a knock at the door and a shout from a familiar and very welcome voice.

'Mister Scrooge? Are you decent?'

It was Wilkins. Wilkins! 'I'm here, Wilkins!' Scrooge bellowed, and I am—' He suddenly stopped, because he realised that he was decent. In fact, he was wearing his most decent suit. Although, couldn't recall putting it on. And then he saw that although it had been his most decent suit, it was scuffed and dishevelled. Not only that, but—

'Are you alright, Mister Scrooge?' said Wilkins, who had poked his head around the door. Then, his warm expression turned to alarm, and the breakfast tray he was holding crashed to the floor.

Scrooge knew what he'd seen, and he knew exactly what to say. 'It's alright, Wilkins, it's alright.'

'But, sir, the blood on your shirt.'

'I neglected to mention last night that I had a somewhat violent encounter with, well, someone I had wronged in the past. I know that doesn't narrow it down, but it's all good now.'

'It's all good?' Wilkins sputtered. 'There is nothing good about this. You should have told me. The man should be arrested and charged.'

'No,' Scrooge said firmly, 'As I said, Wilkins – Bertie; it's all been sorted out.'

'Then why on earth did you put the suit back on this morning? In fact, this isn't—'

Scrooge knew that Wilkins was about to point out the very real fact that he had not, in fact, been wearing that suit when he had come home last night, but Scrooge, having no explanation for the phenomenon, (he couldn't even remember shedding any blood at the time of the encounter) decided that a change of subject would be preferable. 'Mister Wilkins! I'm very disappointed in you,' he snapped.

Wilkins looked up at his master, a mixture of worry and confusion plastered on his face. He looked regretfully at the fallen breakfast tray and its contents, as if that was the problem.

'We have been standing here for a good two minutes now on this day of all days, and not once have you wished me a happy, or indeed, a merry Christmas. What do you have to say for yourself?' He couldn't help himself, he burst out laughing, grabbed Wilkins and gave him a big hug.

'But, sir, your clothes. I—'

'I don't know, Wilkins,' Scrooge said, pulling back with tears of laughter in his eyes. 'I really don't know how it happened.'

'But you said—'

'I know, I know, I know. Let's just leave it between us, shall we, Wilkins? It's Christmas!'

'Yes, indeed it is, Mister Scrooge. And I still haven't wished you a happy one yet, have I. A happy and merry Christmas to you, Mister Scrooge!'

Scrooge found this hilarious, and he couldn't control his laughter now. He found himself laughing at everything around the room; from the smallest vase, to the largest painting hanging on the wall. 'A happy and merry Christmas to you, Bertie! Ha!' He looked down at himself again. He really had no idea what had happened, but then, it wasn't his first confusing Christmas. What did it matter? It was Christmas.

'I'll change out of this *bloody* suit,' he joked, 'and then we'll see about me helping you fix another breakfast for all of us.'

'But, sir—'

'Surely you don't expect me to eat off the floor, do you, Bertie?'

And Scrooge did just that (he helped make the breakfast. He didn't eat off the floor). Although he didn't make the entire meal on his own, Mrs Wilkins couldn't stop complimenting him on what a sterling job he'd made of it. Scrooge made sure that Bertie got his due credit, and the whole meal was such a roaring success that all three of them agreed that it would be criminal indeed if the whole thing did not become a Christmas tradition.

As promised, he arrived early at the Cratchit's to help with the preparations of the meal. He especially enjoyed peeling the potatoes; he didn't know why. Maybe it was because of the way that when he cut away their outer skins they looked all shiny and new. He still couldn't shake the feeling that he was forgetting something about the previous evening, and different members of the Cratchit family commented on his more-subdued-than-normal manner, but just as soon as they did, he snapped out of it and became his old self again.

Tiny Tim's – sorry – Timothy's enthusiasm for the day egged him on even more, and as they were tucking into the prize goose, he said something that jogged Scrooge's memory. 'This has been the best day of the year,' he said. 'I wish it could be Christmas *every* day.'

'That's it! That's the song!' Scrooge yelled, banging his fist on the table, making everyone jump. 'I'm sorry,' he said, 'but I've had a song stuck in my head all day – an earworm I think they call it – and that's the name of it, Timothy: "I Wish It Could Be Christmas Every Day."'

Everyone including Bob was staring at Scrooge, looking for some kind of explanation.

Timothy was the first one to speak up. 'Eee, what's an earworm? Sounds rotten.'

'It's just a term for a song that pops into a person's head, seemingly from out of nowhere. I would've expected you to have heard of that, Timothy.' Although he was addressing one of his dearest friends, Scrooge looked around the table appealing to the young lad's siblings, as well. Perhaps understandably they all had uncomprehending expressions on their faces, and each of them were poking their ears to make sure there were no "earworms" poking around in there.

'"I Wish It Could Be Christmas Every Day"?' said Mrs Cratchit. 'I've never heard of that carol.

'I don't know how you've managed to avoid it,' said Scrooge, laughing. 'They play it in all the shops this time of year. Sometimes they start playing it as far back as November or even September.'

'November? September?' Martha said. 'Why would anyone be singing Christmas carols so early?'

Scrooge had to admit that the notion did seem rather peculiar, and he couldn't recall where and when he had come across it.

'Are you feeling alright, Mister Scrooge?' said Bob from the head of the table. 'Maybe you need a lie down.'

'What, Bob?' he said. 'Oh, no no no, I'm fine.' The way he said it, everyone could tell that he was far from it. 'And how many times have I told you? When we're not in that dusty old office you are to call me "Ebenezer", Bob. Even Timothy here calls me that, so why shouldn't you?'

'Is this true?' said Mrs Cratchit, reproaching her youngest son.

'Yes, Mother. It is, but only because—'

'Mister Scrooge,' Mrs Cratchit said, ignoring Tim's pleas.

'Please, call me "Ebenezer".'

'Very well, Ebenezer. We try to instil it in Tim and all our children—'

'Actually, Mother, I call myself Timothy now. Ebenezer calls me Timothy.'

'Tim!' Bob shouted. 'Don't interrupt your mother.'

'I'm sorry,' Scrooge said. 'It wasn't my intention to cause an argument. Timothy, maybe it would be best, for the sake of social normality, that until you're a bit older you call me "Mister Scrooge".'

Tim was about to argue his point, but "Mister Scrooge" had more to say.

'I'm truly sorry for ruining an otherwise extremely pleasant meal and gathering. This is always the highlight of my year, but I can't deny I have felt rather confused since awaking this morning. I'm having trouble recalling the events of last night. Perhaps you're right, Bob; maybe I do just need a lie down. Whatever the case, I think a nice dose of fresh air will do me the world of good.'

'But Mister Scrooge, you can't go. We've still got the party games to play.'

It saddened Scrooge to see how quickly young Tim had reverted to using his former title, and Mrs Cratchit must have seen this because the next thing she said was:

'Perhaps "Mister Scrooge" is a tad too formal a name for such a dear friend. Perhaps "Uncle Ebenezer" would be more appropriate and pleasing to the ear.'

A wide smile spread across Scrooge's face. 'I like that very much,' he said.

A great cheer erupted from all of the Cratchit children. 'To Uncle Ebenezer, the keeper of Christmas!'

A tear trickled down Scrooge's cheek, and all thoughts of confusion – temporarily at least – washed away with it, and he felt a huge joy fill his heart at being so lucky to know and to be a part of such a loving and understanding family. In the end he decided to stay for dessert and for the party games of which Tim was oh-so-fond. He resolved to keep anything that seemed even slightly unusual to himself, and not share it with anyone. Perhaps it was all a part of growing old; his brain reverting to its more imaginative, youthful state. This self-awareness comforted him, at least for the moment, and it was with great joy and merriment that he parted ways with the Cratchits in the early evening. In fact, he'd had so much fun that he found himself running late for his traditional appointment with his nephew and his other extended family.

He was so happy as he rushed through the streets. "Merry Christmas" uttered from the lips of everyone he met on the way, and he was more than happy to engage with each and every one of them, although it was making him later and later. He even bumped into – in quite the literal sense – the young couple whom he'd seen that morning, and joked with them: 'It's still Christmas, isn't it? I've not missed it?' All three of them laughed as Scrooge reached for his watch.

It wasn't there! Where could it be? He always wore it, especially today. Another thought popped into his head, but he immediately dismissed it out of hand. 'No. I couldn't have sold it,' he said out loud, 'I wouldn't have sold it.'

'Are you alright, sir?' the young man asked.

Not wishing to seem mad, Scrooge quickly recovered. 'Yes, yes, I'm quite alright, young sir, although I seem to have mislaid my watch. I wonder, would you be so good as to tell me what time it is?'

'Of course. It's—'

But before the young man could finish, the chimes in the church tower answered Scrooge's question.

'Eight 'o' clock?' he uttered. 'How did it get so late? I really must be going.' And before another merry or happy Christmas could be uttered, Scrooge broke into a run and headed to his nephew's for an evening of festivities.

After a few near misses and slips and slides on the snow he found himself standing outside the house. The warmth and joy within was more than evident in the laughter and the dancing shadows cast upon the curtains, and Scrooge was about to lift the knocker when something peculiar caught his eye: A snowflake. Peculiar, because for the most part there was no snow falling, although there was plenty underfoot; but the oddest thing by far was that it didn't appear to be going anywhere. It was dancing to-and-fro, as if a puppeteer had attached invisible strings to it and couldn't decide which way he wanted it to go. Before he could do anything, he found himself caught in its spell. Anything could've been happening around him and he would've been none the wiser.

The puppeteer seemed to have finally made up his mind, because the snowflake – which was all Scrooge could think about – started dancing off to the left, and he had a vague sensation of movement as he obeyed its silent summons. His vision was blurry, and the snowflake was all he could see, but now, even that was fading away, and a profound sense of loss consumed him. But then, from out of the nothingness a figure emerged, getting closer and closer. And just as he thought it was going to pass straight through him, it stopped, and a face which he knew he recognised was smiling at him. Silence hung in the air, as he gradually came to realise who it was.

'Jacob? Jacob Marley? Is that really you?'

The man said nothing, but he nodded, still smiling as if his life depended on it.

'But – But you look so… so… so well! You look… You look alive! Are you? Are you—?

'No,' Jacob said finally, 'I'm not alive. But I'm *so* much better off than the last time we spoke.'

'The chains; that horrific bandage you had around your jaw…'

'Gone, my old friend. All thanks to you.'

'I don't understand. You helped *me*, remember? I never got the chance to thank you. Thank you, Jacob!' he bellowed. 'Thank you so very much for my second chance!'

'You are more than welcome,' Jacob said. 'But I can see that you do not remember what you did for me. I was told this would be so.' He looked for a moment to be mulling something over in his mind. 'I think you deserve a temporary reprieve from that gap in your memory, Ebenezer. Consider it my first gift to you.'

'Now that you mention it, my friend, I have had the strangest day. I've been having thoughts and notions that can't possibly be true, and—'

Scrooge stopped talking as his oldest friend swept his hand through the air, like a magician casting a spell.

'Open your mind, Ebenezer. Those thoughts and notions are echoes of the memories and experiences they took from you. If you let the rest of it in, it will all make sense.'

And suddenly, as if someone had lit a candle in his head, he remembered. He remembered everything: Meeting Jack; the trip to the future; dying and going to Heaven and coming back. Jacob was right: as it all seeped back into his head, it all made sense again.

'How did I forget all that, Jacob? It was all so fantastical and beautiful and scary.'

'It was a necessity. It still is. If you remembered everything, it would drive you mad. The longing that would grow in you would send you back on the wrong path again.'

'I understand this time,' Scrooge said, 'but I can't believe I forgot about helping you.'

'*Saving* me,' Jacob said. 'Saving me and Jack. Your plan to have us work together, to watch over the Earth and to help each other is perfect. This way we will never lose our way again, and we can help people in small ways and set them on more righteous paths.

'Like a couple of guardian angels…' His own words sparked a renewed memory of someone else calling him that very thing. 'Is Grace well now? How about Carl Phillips and his family, and Jack?'

Jacob laughed at Scrooge's sudden outburst of questions. He reminded Scrooge more now of the ghost of Christmas present.

'Yes, yes, my dear chap. Grace went on to live a very good life – the very one she was supposed to – and influenced and helped others to do the same. She was very happy. Carl and his family thrived and loved each other very much. And Jack? Well, you can ask him yourself.'

Another figure slowly emerged from the bubble of blurriness that surrounded both Scrooge and Jacob. 'Hi, Scrooge. How's it hanging?'

Having never heard that phrase before, even in his many frustrating conversations with Jack in the twenty-first century, Scrooge wasn't sure how to respond, so he just said: 'It's hanging fine, Jack. It's good to see you. You're looking much healthier than the last time I saw you.'

Jack's eyes widened, and his jaw seemed to go slack at Scrooge's words. 'It's good to see me? After what I put you through? Where I took you? You truly are one of the most benevolent men in history. My selfish actions almost destroyed – well – everything.'

'Yes,' Scrooge said, 'but if not for those actions, Jacob would still be trapped in that living hell, and you would still be the tortured soul who I first met all that time ago. Or, just last night, depending on how one chooses to look at it.' He chuckled to himself at how queer and complicated his life had become.

'I guess so,' said Jack.

'And everything has changed up there, not just me and Jack, because of what you did,' Jacob said.

'What do you mean?'

'Can't you feel it, Ebenezer?' Jacob seemed to be glowing brighter now with each word he uttered.

Scrooge *could* feel something. He didn't know what it was. He had assumed that it was his joy at seeing Jacob again, but he knew now that it must be more than that.

'Between the two of you – the three of us really – we've changed things up there. Your idea to partner me and Jack up has grown and grown, Ebenezer. *Everyone* wants to do it. Do you remember the library?'

'Yes,' Scrooge said. 'It was in quite a state the last time I was there.'

'Of course. Now it's back to normal because you saved Grace, except for one thing. It's quieter now. People are reading less and doing more. They want to be involved in the living world as much as they can be; as much as Jack and I are. They want to make the world a better place, instead of just observing all the time.

'That warm glow you're feeling now, Ebenezer? That's all the goodness that has come from that; all the goodness that has ultimately come from you.'

'I – I don't know what to say, Jacob.' He could feel tears escaping the corners of his eyes.

'You don't have to say anything, my dearest friend.'

'We just thought you deserved to know.' Jack looked as though he wanted to hug him, and Scrooge could see that this, again, was a different Jack to any of the other versions he had met. When he looked at him now, he felt like a father who had guided his son and helped him to become a good and honourable man, and this gave him the warmest feeling of all.

'We have to be going now, Ebenezer,' Jacob said.

'So soon? But there's so much more I have to ask you.'

'Anything we tell you will be forgotten, anyway. I'm sorry, Scrooge,' Jack said.

He felt torn in two. He wanted to go with them; to be with his friends, but he knew he couldn't.

'Don't fret, old friend,' Jacob said softly. 'You will not remember how, but you will know that I and Jack are at peace, and the warm glowing feeling that is shared by everyone – yet felt in different measure – will never leave you, and you will feel reassured that everyone you love will be watched over and cared for, for all of time.'

'Thank you, Jacob,' Scrooge said, 'And thank you, Jack. I'm so very proud of both of you.'

'You're most welcome. As soon as we leave here the memory of this meeting and all your recent experiences will leave with us, but Jack and I have one last gift for you. Goodbye Ebenezer, and a merry Christmas to you.'

Jack clenched his fist, stuck his thumb up, and said: 'Merry Christmas, Scrooge.'

'And a merry Christmas to you…' Scrooge said, but he was talking to thin air.

How peculiar, he thought. How did I find myself out here? Then, all his confusion washed away, as a warm feeling and knowledge came over him. 'What does it matter?' he said out loud. 'It's Christmas, and anything can happen. Jacob's at peace and my old friend Jack, and all is right with the world.'

'Ebenezer?' The voice was soft like silk and far away, but Scrooge recognised it as if not a day had gone by since he last heard it.

He looked up and saw a silhouette lit up underneath a lamp post. The face was unclear, but he moved towards it because he already knew who it was.

'Ebenezer? It *is* you!'

Scrooge was almost afraid to say the name for fear of it breaking the spell and making her disappear like a ghost in the wind. He was there in front of her now, and he slowly stepped into the protective light of the lamp post. He was so afraid to say her name that it came out as a raspy whisper. 'Belle? Is it really you?'

She said nothing for a moment, as if she was afraid of something as well, but then that wonderful voice escaped from her lips. 'It's really me, Ebenezer.'

'I thought I'd never see you again.'

'Well, looks like you were wrong,' she laughed. She had the same laugh. The same smile!

'I was wrong about a lot of things, I know,' he said.

'It sounds like you've been more than making up for that.'

'I don't know about "more than", but I do what I can.'

'My Ebenezer is humble now. It sounds like what they say about you is true.'

Scrooge was touched by her name for him, although he knew she had a family of her own, including a husband. He still remembered how happy they looked when the ghost of Christmas past showed him. 'I'll always be your

Ebenezer, my Belle, and I know you've had a good life. I hear you have a fine family.'

'That I do.'

Her words were joyous, but her face was tinged with sadness. Scrooge knew why. 'I can never make up for the foolish young man I was, and all the regret I have for the way I treated you could never come close to filling all the books in the world, but if there's ever anything I can do for you and your family, you must let me help you.'

'I appreciate that very much, Ebenezer.' It seemed as if she was about to say something else, but the words caught in her throat. Then something new occurred to her. 'I don't know why I came here tonight. I think of you a lot at this time of year, because they say you keep the season so well, but I've always put off seeing it for myself. Something – I don't know – it's an odd notion, but something drew me here, to this spot. It's very peculiar, but I'm glad you're here.'

'As am I,' Scrooge said. 'I'm so happy to see you, Belle. I'm on my way to my nephew's home for our traditional festivities. In fact, it seems late. They must be wondering where I've got to. Would you care to join me?' As he was saying this, he fumbled in his jacket to see if, somehow, he'd been mistaken about his watch not being there earlier.

'Oh, I'm not sure,' Belle said. 'My family will be wondering where I am. I just sort of left without telling them. I suppose I could join you for a short while.'

'You could always just text them to—' He stopped, as he found something in his pocket which wasn't his watch.

'"Text them?" Whatever do you mean, Ebenezer?' And then she saw the look on his face. 'What's that? Are you quite alright? You look like you've seen a ghost.'

It's a reminder, my dear sweet Belle. A reminder that I still have so much to make up for.' He showed her the picture of Charles' son. 'Last night I made a promise to find this boy. To find him and reunite him with his father. How can I possibly continue with these celebrations knowing that he's out there alone and afraid?'

'You shouldn't be so hard on yourself, Ebenezer,' Belle said, touching his shoulder softly. 'After all, it's not your fault that he's missing. You're not responsible for all the—'

'Ah, but that's the thing of it, Belle. It *is* my fault, and I need to fix it.' His heart was abuzz with energy for his new quest, but he couldn't fail to notice the look on Belle's face. She looked like she'd made a decision of her own, and yet, he was still taken aback when she said:

'Let me help you, Ebenezer. I hear of many children going missing on the streets and, well, I'd just like to help.'

Scrooge couldn't believe it. Moments ago, he hadn't spoken to his long-lost love for going on forty years, and now, not only was she talking to him again, but she wanted to help him in a possibly extremely dangerous task. Despite how much he wanted her to join him, he couldn't allow it. 'The streets of London are a dangerous place, Belle. I can't in good conscience allow you to—'

Before he could finish his sentence, Belle answered him. 'You're a couple of years older than I am. How do you think you'll fair on your own?'

Scrooge couldn't help but be reminded of his encounter with the boy's father the previous night. 'I know, but this is my responsibility, Belle, and I can't have you getting hurt; I'd never forgive myself. And besides, what would your husband say?'

'Mister Ebenezer Scrooge, I can do what I like; I don't need my husband's permission. Between the two of us we'll find this boy in no time. You said you'd help me if ever I needed it, so why can I not do the same for you?'

Scrooge still didn't like the idea, but he could see that the argument was only going to end one way. 'Very well,' he said, 'I would be most glad of your company and assistance, Belle.'

EPILOGUE

And the very next day, Scrooge and Belle started their quest to find the toymaker's son; but that's a story for another time and place, and perhaps another author. So, for now, let's be content with this tale of how Scrooge kept Christmas, and the entire world – the entire universe – from falling apart.

Scrooge never did remember the events of those few days which he spent in our time. The only things that stuck with him were the occasional phrase and the fifth visitor's name. He never knew why, but whenever he thought of that name, he felt a great sense of pride and love – the way he would have felt about a son. So, when Martha Cratchit – or Martha Fielding, as she became by marriage – asked her Uncle Ebenezer to suggest a name for her second son, you need only guess once to come to the name which he presented her with. Martha thought it to be a fine name, too, and it survived several generations up to and including a young man born in the city of London in the year of our Lord nineteen-eighty-nine, who tragically died in an incident in a park in that same city. You may also be glad to know that the name "Ebenezer" lived on, as well. When Carl and Kate Phillips had a son, Carl thought it would be fitting tribute to the stranger who saved him to pass on his name. Although, Kate and Sara managed to convince him to relegate it to middle name status – to avoid any bullying – and so, he became Stephen Ebenezer Phillips.

As for Scrooge himself; he never forgot the lessons of that Christmas night when Jacob Marley came to him swathed in chains, and he used the story as a cautionary tale for all the young boys and girls who might otherwise have forgotten the true meaning of Christmas; that it was a time of joy to all men and women, not a time of greed and getting. He went on to live a long, vital life; much longer than he would have if he'd carried on the way he was, and near the end of it he called for Tiny Tim – as he once knew him – and all the Cratchits, young and old. Timothy was in his thirties now, and married, but Scrooge always saw him as the helpless but hopeful young boy of years gone by. He recounted their many happy times together, and at the end when he knew his time was finally up, Scrooge whispered something into Timothy's ear. He confessed that the tale of Jacob Marley and the Three Spirits of Christmas was true, and Timothy told him that he knew it to be so, because his Uncle Ebenezer – as he still called him – would never lie to him, because he had the best heart of anyone he knew. At these kind words Scrooge's eyes filled with tears and then closed for the final time.

'God bless you, Uncle Ebenezer,' Timothy said. 'And God bless us, everyone, whose lives have been touched by your love and kindness.'

Acknowledgements

Thank you to everyone I know for your support. To Mum and Dad, Rob, Geoff, Alan and Lynne, Mike, Matt, Jim and Mags, Ian, Sylvia, Dan (the man with cucumbers in his eyes), Tom, Joe and Mike H, Keith, Carol Fenlon for being the first to hear the first version of this story, and, of course, to Denise for your love.

If you enjoyed my book, please review it online in all the usual places. Even if you didn't, and you still managed to get to the end, please review it. Afterall, a bad review is better than no review (maybe).

If you want to follow me for any reason, you can find me on

Facebook @JohnDPaynesWriting

Instagram @john.d.payne.author

Twitter @JohnPay12854799

Check out my website for updates on my latest releases and random bits of writing and musings at johndpayneiswriting.com

Printed in Great Britain
by Amazon